No

Ordinary

Thursday

NO ORDINARY THURSDAY

a novel

ANOOP JUDGE

Text copyright © 2022 by Anoop Judge
All rights reserved.

Published by Lake Union Publishing, Seattle

www.apub.com

Amazon, the Amazon logo, and Lake Union Publishing are trademarks of Amazon.com, Inc., or its affiliates.

ISBN-13: 9781542037754
ISBN-10: 1542037751

Cover design by Shasti O'Leary Soudant

Printed in the United States of America

For Tony: my best friend and partner.
For Amaraj and Ghena: my heart, my soul,
my lifelines.

Chapter 1

Sameer's laugh sounded like a trapped wasp—like he was always just a moment away from breaking. An offhand comment by one of his drinking buddies, an unintentional truth that hit too close to home could do it. And yet, in this bar just around the corner from his low-paying job, the beers came, and the beers went, and aside from a nagging feeling that there was somewhere else he should be, Sameer Sharma was having a great night.

Then he saw her.

Sameer was still in his blue-pinstripe suit and tie, now crumpled from the day, while she was in a short red dress. They had shared dozens of lunches and hours of idle chitchat on quiet afternoons, during which he had learned that she drank a cup of bone broth every day for healthy skin and was a spelling-bee winner—made it to state finals, then choked on the word *obituary*. Yet he had never seen her in anything other than her trademark pearl blouse and light-gray office slacks. The moment had an element of wish fulfillment.

"Ruchi!" he called out, sobering as his coworker's gaze found him.

She came over, halting as her wide brown eyes and lashes swept disapprovingly over his drinking pals. The men became alert, looking up from their drinks. All of them were from other departments in the towering office block where Sameer and Ruchi both worked selling roadside-assistance policies. They were older men in more responsible positions where policies were made, rather than merely sold, men who should be home with wives and children instead of joining Sameer on his regular binge. Sameer's fists formed tight balls, and his mouth set in a thin line. *Wipe the drool from your faces, fellas.*

"Are you meeting someone?" he asked, trying to keep his tone even in the noisy bar.

"I was meeting some girlfriends," she replied, her mouth pursing. Sameer tipped his head toward her in what he hoped was a sympathetic, engaging manner, while trying to keep the glee from his eyes. "But they've all let me down. What a waste of a night, eh?"

"You could—" Sameer gestured to an empty seat, but the politely remote look on Ruchi's face stopped him from finishing the suggestion.

"I'll head home. Cut my losses, I think."

Sameer got to his feet, almost tripping over the legs of one of his companions. "Let me give you a ride," he said.

Ruchi pinned him with a narrow stare. "But you've been—"

"Just a couple," Sameer lied easily. They had worked together for months; when would this opportunity come again, if ever?

Behind Sameer, one of his drinking buddies snickered. Either Ruchi didn't hear or assumed it was one of those private jokes that people share. "Okay." Her voice wavered with hesitation.

Once outside in the cold night air, Ruchi seemed to relax a little. "How do you know those men?" she asked.

"Oh, I don't, really." Sameer kicked at the loose concrete on the sidewalk. "They're just, you know . . . guys from work."

"Upstairs?" Ruchi asked with a raised eyebrow, using the blanket term for anyone above gofer level—their level, where they spent their days in a tiny cubicle with a headset on. It was one of those companies where the floor on which you worked denoted your career progression.

"Yeah."

"You looking for a promotion?" Ruchi joked. "I'd miss you, you know."

"Ha," Sameer laughed. "Me? A promotion? You must know by now I'm the least likely person to get a promotion."

"Brownnoser," she teased. "Your drinking buddies there are so old, you could be the son one of them never had or something."

As soon as she had said the words, Sameer could see that Ruchi regretted them. If there was one thing she seemed to have quickly understood when getting to know Sameer, it was that discussions about family led rapidly to an awkward silence.

It almost did again, but Sameer jumped in before the awkwardness could settle. "I'm sorry your friends let you down."

"We planned it at the end of yesterday," Ruchi said. "That's why I brought a change of clothes with me."

"You look nice." He sucked in his breath, regretting speaking.

"It happens, I guess," Ruchi continued as if he hadn't given the compliment. "I just hate wasting an evening, you know? Especially a Thursday night. It's the perfect evening to go out because you deserve to let off a little steam after working four whole days in a row."

They came to his car.

"Wow," Ruchi said, seeing the Nissan for the first time. "I knew you liked your cars, but . . ."

Sameer beamed. He had known she would love it, but it still sent tingles through his body as he watched her eyes light up. "Well, when you speak about vehicles all day . . . ," he said.

"Doesn't get to me in the same way," Ruchi countered, but she smiled at him like he was a cute puppy in the window begging for a home. He got the door for her, then raced around to the other side, eager to start it up, for her to hear the throaty roar softened by the upholstery of the plush interior.

"Straight home or you want to go anywhere else first?" Sameer asked.

Ruchi laughed, giving him a look that might even have been affectionate. "Home, if you don't mind," she said, as she gave him her address.

"Yes, ma'am," Sameer said, mimicking what he thought of as cabbie lingo. "Straight home."

Ruchi leaned back against the headrest and closed her eyes as they cleared the tight city streets and found the freeway. Sameer sneaked a glance at her profile. Her brown hair shone, and she smelled of lavender moisturizer. There was a tiredness about her eyes as she sat, legs pressed neatly together, her handbag firmly anchored on her lap—the result of the week's work, perhaps. Ruchi was a conscientious worker, a hard worker who was going to escape gofer level and do something with her life, whether at the insurance company or elsewhere.

So very unlike him. He was twenty-nine years old and going nowhere. He knew his looks were unremarkable. A pale, slender man of average height, he had a long face and dark eyes, with small, tight-set lips. He drank so much some nights he wondered if he would live to see his fortieth birthday. On the worst nights, alone and out of his tiny fucking mind in his one-room apartment, he thought it might be best if he did not.

In the months they had worked together, Ruchi had probably come to realize that Sameer Sharma liked to party. But she had no idea of the truth of things, and somehow that made her pure to him.

A lump came to his throat. Just watching her made him want to be a bet—

~

He was hot, and something was dripping into his eyes. There was a pressure on the base of his skull. By instinct more than thought process, he undid his seat belt—and fell.

4

It was only a short fall, an inch or two, but landing on his head caused Sameer's neck to bend and sent a bolt of pain through him. It brought him to his senses a little more, though. At least there was that.

The sound of the crash, like a horrible metal thunder. That last shard of memory brought the rest of it flooding back, and adjusting himself, Sameer looked across at Ruchi. She was cut and bloodied, her beautiful red dress torn raggedly around the knees, her hair hanging down to pool on the roof of the car below her, strands of it matted with blood.

Sameer realized through his haze that they were upside down. The Nissan had flipped over. The car's roof had held, and there was enough space for Sameer to rotate so that his head was toward Ruchi, his backside and his feet against the driver's window.

"Ruchi?" he tried, with no response. He could feel heat streaming through from the front of the car. In the confined space, it was making him sweat. Sameer went to wipe the sweat from his face and eyes, but his hand came away covered in blood.

"Ruchi," he said again. "Come on. Wake up. The car might . . ."

Sameer did not finish the thought. He could see the flames now, somewhere beyond the dash. "Ruchi, please," he pleaded, "we have to go." Then, more quietly: "Don't be dead."

What a stupid thing to say, a voice in his head observed. His father's self-righteous tone. *Are you a child or a man?*

What a *man* should do—even an idiot of a man—was get them both out. He reached up to unclasp her seat belt, preparing as best he could in the confined space to cushion her fall. The belt would not release.

Sameer pushed it again. Once, twice, six times in rapid succession as panic took over.

"Fuck, fuck, fuuuuck!" he bellowed. The flames were getting bigger. Already the heat was almost unbearable.

Other side, stupid boy, said the voice in his head.

Sameer thought about booting through the glass of the driver's-side window but was clearheaded enough to spin around and just open the door instead. As he crawled out and got to his feet, he did not recognize the road they were on as a freeway, and then he realized that they had somehow ended up on a small side street next to an exit ramp. A section of barrier was twisted and crumpled, but there was little else to indicate what had happened aside from the burning car on its roof. Cars were still coming down the exit ramp, reaching the bottom, and driving away, perhaps not even noticing the accident as they carried on with their journeys.

The whole thing had a surreal air to it. His life was screwed, while theirs just carried on.

As Sameer ran around the vehicle, the flames at the front of the car leaped, becoming monstrous orange tongues that danced wildly, reaching several feet into the night's darkness and pushing it farther back with each passing moment. Thick, oily smoke rose from the tips of the flames like evil spirits being set free.

Sameer reached the passenger's-side door, knowing in every ounce of his body the importance of trying to get Ruchi out of the burning wreck. But he was scared now. What if it exploded? He didn't want to die, he realized, after all. Not like this.

The voice of his father, the one and only Goldie Sharma, sounded in Sameer's head again. He expected the voice of his father—both the devil on his shoulder and the monkey on his back—to call him a coward.

Instead, it said, *Run, boy, run!*

Chapter 2

A moment ago, Maya Sharma had been wondering where her brother was, but now she was wondering what the hell Veer was doing. Her boyfriend of more than a year had lowered himself to one knee in the middle of Saison restaurant.

It was kind of obvious what Veer was doing, although her brain was making at least a half-hearted attempt at denial.

Now Veer was struggling to pull something out of his jacket pocket. *The jacket!* That should have been a clue; he never kept his jacket on at dinner. Come to think of it, he rarely wore a jacket for dinner—only in the presence of his parents, who were not there tonight.

Veer finally managed to pry out a small black box. He took a deep breath and pulled his shoulders back, now looking less like a guilty little boy caught doing something disgusting. The slightly defensive way he was holding himself, the look of embarrassment and fear lingering on his still-youthful features, made her want to cry and laugh at the same time.

Saison may have been one of the more expensive San Francisco restaurants, but the atmosphere wasn't exactly intimate. A three-star Michelin restaurant, its kitchen and dining room shared the same open space so that the guests could appreciate the action on the exposed wood-burning stove—but now its culinary delights were being upstaged by the drama unfolding at the large table at the back. Veer had told her only that they were going out to dinner with their friends, but she hadn't expected all twelve of them to be there; now the proverbial penny dropped like a cartoon anvil. Veer and Maya's friends were witnessing the entire show with complete bug-eyed enjoyment, as were plenty of people Veer and Maya had never met before. Not exactly what Maya would have thought of as romantic.

"Maya Sharma," Veer Kapoor began, opening the small square box, in which glittered a solitaire engagement ring. She could see the name of a well-known jeweler engraved on the box's side—he was, after all, the son of one of the wealthiest men in the Bay Area. "It's always been you, long before you had any idea that it might be. Marry me, and I'll spend my life making you happy."

Although she kept her gaze trained on her boyfriend, Maya could see some of the crowd's reactions from the corners of her eyes. Amusement, shock, joy . . . their audience excluded only those suffering from a surfeit of good manners. *Why does he have to do it here, in front of everyone?* She felt a flush of irritation.

Because he is Veer, came the answer, *forever the performer, and that's why you love him.* Tender love flooded divinely through her body as she remembered he was waiting for an answer.

"Yes," Maya said, though her answer brought about a frown that wrinkled Veer's perfect face. Veer Kapoor, thank the gods, had the looks of his mother, Pinky Kapoor—a prominent wide nose, a square jaw, high cheekbones, and deep-set brown eyes—rather than his father's receding chin and fleshy nose. All the young Kapoor had inherited from his lanky father in the looks department was the little gap between his front teeth in an otherwise Tom Cruise–white smile.

Maya realized that her reply had come out as a hoarse whisper and must have gotten lost among the hum of restaurant chatter and noise.

"Yes!" she said louder this time, reveling in the look that her one simple word brought to Veer's face. A face so expressive, it could always tell you so much, and right now, it was flooded with a mixture of relief, joy, and desire. "Now get off your knees and kiss me, you idiot!"

He stood, and she did as well, the short and figure-hugging black dress that Maya was now even gladder she had bought especially for this evening adjusting perfectly around her hourglass figure. As they kissed, cheers and applause erupted throughout the restaurant. But Maya shut it out, along with the rest of the world. It had become a habit.

~

"Don't get me wrong, I love them both, but it was all I could do out there not to burst out laughing."

The sentence was followed by a giggle barely six feet away, just beyond the stall door. Maya tried to hold her pee in as she listened. "Esther, you're so bad. It was cliché, sure, but . . ."

"I don't mean the proposal. *Come on*, Veer Kapoor could propose to me naked in the street—it's all good if you're getting that big diamond ring on your finger, am I right?"

Esther "Beanstalk" Vora—whom Maya knew as the very tall girl born of a German mother and an Indian father—didn't wait to find out if she was, indeed, right before speaking again. "I mean, the two of them together was weird enough. She's twelve years his senior, you know? Twelve years! That sort of age difference would be funny on a night out, a one-night stand, or a holiday fling. But anything beyond that . . . ?" Esther made a disgusted noise. "And now they're getting *married*."

Bitch. Maya wanted to pull up her underwear and march out of the stall, just to see the look on Esther's face, just to hear what groveling excuse or apology would drop out of that spiteful mouth. But since that second glass of wine, Maya really needed to pee, and she could not very well let them hear her do so for thirty seconds before making her dramatic entrance.

"Twelve years?" the other woman mused. "I mean, it happens. My uncle's eight years older than my aunt."

Maya could not see her, but this other woman was likely Moira-something, Esther's fawning assistant, whom she had brought to the dinner as her plus-one because her fiancé, Faisal, was on a business trip. Moira was a short, dark-haired young woman in high heels and a too-tight red pencil skirt whose earnest gray eyes—Maya had noticed earlier—followed Esther's lips, drinking in every word.

"It's different," Esther said in a tone that suggested she was not enjoying the other woman's disagreement. "She's a woman. A few more years' difference, and she could have given birth to him."

The other woman giggled again. "Well, there's a picture."

"Uh-huh," Esther agreed.

"Still, it's not so rare nowadays, not really. It just, you know, puts a limit on that biological clock."

"Wow, I hadn't even thought of that," Esther said, sounding far too gleeful. "You think it's because she's pregnant?"

No, it's not, bitch face! Maya could barely stop herself from storming out of the stall to cause Esther some kind of pain.

"I thought she looked surprised when he got down on one knee, though."

"Hmm," Esther grunted. "I guess you're right."

There was a silent moment outside the stall, broken by a slight smacking sound of someone reapplying their lipstick. Maya remained frozen and continued to clench. It was becoming painful, and if she was gone for much longer, surely Veer would start wondering where she was.

"Still, I don't think you get it," Esther said, clearly trying a different tack. "She might have been born in America, but she's Indian."

"So are you," the other woman said in a way that sounded almost like an accusation.

"And you're not." For the first time, Esther's tone became uncharacteristically earnest. "There are some things that Indian people just don't do. I'm so thrilled that Faisal is at least the right age for me," she finished. Maya could picture her now—preening first one way and then the other as she surveyed her reflection in the three mirrors.

Something closed with a loud clack, making Maya jump slightly. A compact, perhaps.

"Still, what can you do?" Esther said with a sigh, the spiteful tone returning and sliding across the words like honey. "Go out there, smile, and pretend it's all normal, I guess."

Maya relieved herself once they were gone, then hastily pulled everything into place, the beautiful black dress clinging to her body unhelpfully. Then she turned around and almost vomited. She knew this, what Esther was saying—she knew all of it.

And sure, she also knew that she and Esther Vora had been on-and-off-again girlfriends for many years, but they had known each other for most of their lives. Maya had gone to school with her and lived in the same neighborhood. She still remembered when Esther had become four inches taller than the rest of the eleven-year-old girls in their class and everyone started referring to her as Beanstalk. They had never been the closest of friends, but she had not expected something as toxic as what she had just heard.

Maya was sweating as she came out of the stall. That woman in the mirror looked ill. She wanted to splash some water on her face, but the makeup malfunction that would follow would not be worth it.

The worst part of this was that everything Esther said had already flashed through her own mind when Veer had knelt and rooted around in his jacket pocket. *Damn,* those thoughts had been with her for almost every day of their one-and-half-year-long relationship.

None of them knew Veer as she did. Last year, the company where Maya worked had run a beauty campaign around age being just a number. It had been her idea to take the concept even further by numbering the various ranges of products, and she was still proud of that one. In fact, she was wearing "Forever 25" lipstick and "Fabulous at 50" nail varnish this evening. Numbers were just numbers, and with twelve years between her and Veer, the cliché about age being only a number was true.

"Veer, I'm twelve years older than you. Twelve frigging years!" she had protested when he first tried to woo her.

Veer had laid a warm hand over her cold fingers. "Well, I'm an old soul. Plus, I've been secretly in love with you for years. So there's that."

She had never relished the role of "cougar" that she had been cast in, but after he knelt in the restaurant, Veer, her sensitive, hot boyfriend— who always wore the same yellow-banana costume on Halloween and had never voted for a political candidate—had spoken and washed all those doubts away. She had entered the restroom a happy person, or, at the very least, thinking she could dream of an uncomplicated life for the one night.

What a fool.

She ran her hands up and down her dress, smoothing it into place as she thought back to what her mom's reaction had been to the news of Maya dating her best friend's much younger son. "Don't think for a moment the traditional Indian community is going to accept it," she had warned like a harbinger of doom.

No kidding. Maya shoved away from the sink, biting back a groan.

When Maya came back into the restaurant, Veer stood in the middle of it, surrounded by his friends. One of them clapped him on the back, and another ruffled his hair. She didn't resent him for being a man, but she could imagine how they would be congratulating him for "landing" an older woman. The hypocrisy of the whole thing could be sickening at times.

Her gaze slid across to the gathered women. Perhaps she was imagining it, but it seemed that every pair of eyes was either avoiding her or judging her. Except for Beanstalk Esther Vora, who was happily chatting to her eager work friend like a person with a clean conscience. And not including Anita Aunty's daughter—Selena—who had just turned twenty-one and was out with them for the first time. A sweet-faced girl in a short yellow dress with big gold buttons down the middle, she was walking toward Maya, a mobile phone in her hand, her face stricken.

"It's-your-brother-Sameer," she said in a breathless whisper almost too quick to catch. "There's been an accident."

Chapter 3

Lena was standing right next to the phone when it rang. She was in the hallway of her single-story house in Walnut Creek, squinting at a note tacked on their cork-and-pin bulletin board that her husband, Manuel, had made. He rarely bought something if he could make it, and most of the time, he made things better than the factories that supplied the stores did.

The recipe on the note had been jotted down maybe six months ago, maybe more, and Lena was trying to decipher what it said, and whether she had already tried her hand at the tikka masala mac 'n' cheese so that she could decide what to make for lunch tomorrow—which was a Fresh Friday at the restaurant, so she had to come up with something new. She would have to go and get the glasses that she never wore, which always felt a little like a defeat, because she had gotten them only about a year ago—or it could be two; Lena was the wrong side of fifty now, and the years seemed to slip by like streetlamps in the night—and wearing them made her feel old. Like a grandmother.

Of course, she would not mind being an actual grandmother at all. She might even wear the glasses more often if doing so would miraculously conjure up a grandchild. Maya would soon be too old and always insisted on messing around with the wrong men—or boys, as the current case happened to be—and Sameer . . . well, Sam—

Ring!

Although their landline phone was a modernish push-button instrument—a 2018 model, bought at the beginning of this year—its tone sounded like an authentic ringer from thirty years ago or more, and it made Lena jump a little as it went off right next to her.

"Lena?" It was the ever-nervous voice of one of her best friends, Anita, on the other end of the line. Lena had known Anita since they were teenagers, yet the woman always began a telephone conversation with her—and just about everyone else, she assumed—in the same way, like she thought she was upsetting them by calling.

"Anita," Lena answered, a little surprised. It was late in the evening for a call from Anita, who had long been an early-to-bed, early-to-rise sort. "Everything okay?" She hadn't meant to say that, as it risked opening the proverbial door—a little like telling a hypochondriac that they sounded "a bit chesty."

"Oh, yes. Yes, fine." Phew. "Sort of." Here we go. "It's just that my mother's coming to stay."

Lena brightened straightaway. Anita's mother, Kookie, was a delight. Everyone loved it when Kookie came to stay. Well . . . except Anita. For Lena and their other best friend, Pinky, she was a fun aunty, but mothers were usually more complex when they were your own. Anita would spend most of the time blushing as Kookie regaled everyone with her daughter's most humiliating childhood stories.

"Why is it she is being so embarrassing, I am telling you?" Anita had privately mocked her mother's very Indian-English way of speaking—"You know how Mummy always mixes her tenses maddeningly"—during the older woman's last visit in a rare and highly amusing act of rebellion. "I will be shoving her out of the backside entrance soon, just you watch."

Lena and Pinky had still been laughing about that one in the car on the way home—Lena had dropped off her friend at her big Piedmont mansion, even though it was out of her way. She smiled a little sadly as she remembered Pinky giggling like a schoolgirl as she got out of the car. "I am coming home so late," Pinky had managed to splutter between tears of laughter. "I will have to be sneaking in through the backside entrance."

"Mom's flying in tonight," Anita now continued on the other end of the line. "Chintu's on the way to pick her up right now. She should be landing any minute."

"Oh." That was a bit out of the blue.

"Yes, I know, I can't believe I hadn't mentioned it. But it was all a bit sudden, you see. Only arranged a few days ago." Something in Anita's tone was even graver than usual.

In Lena's hand, her cell phone started to ring and vibrate as a call came in.

"I've, um . . . made an appointment for her with a top-notch neurologist," Anita said, although Lena only half heard her.

"Huh?"

"I was saying . . ."

"Sorry, Anita, my cell phone is ringing. It's . . . Your daughter is calling me. Isn't Selena supposed to be at the dinner with Maya and Veer? Why is your Selena calling me?"

Chapter 4

"You all right, dude?" the cab driver asked.

Even in his state of full shock, Sameer did not mistake the man's question for genuine concern. The tone was somewhere between "Are you a criminal?" and "Don't bleed on my seats."

"You've got quite a bit of blood on your face there—a nasty cut on the head by the look of it. You sure you don't need the hospital? I could drop you at Zuckerberg, it's just a few blocks. No fee for that."

The guy was clearly desperate to get rid of him; he must look a mess. The hospital was probably a good idea, even if all he wanted to do was get back to his dirty little flat and curl up in bed. Deal with the rest of his ruined life tomorrow.

"Yeah, you're right," Sameer said after a few moments. "The hospital would be good. Thanks."

As they slid through the semidarkness, passing tired-looking buildings cast in various shades of orange under the glow of the streetlamps, the driver looked at him in the mirror again, caution and curiosity warring in his eyes.

"So, what happened?" the driver finally asked, the three words bursting out as if they had been held in there, pressure building behind them.

Just in time, Sameer pulled his cell phone free from his pocket. It was a flip-top, not even a smartphone of any sort. He liked his gadgets and his tech almost as much as he liked his cars, but after the third expensive phone in as many months had gone missing during a drinking binge, it had come down to drinking less or getting a cheaper model. And that had been no contest.

Sameer held up the phone instead of answering the question. "Do you mind?" he asked, and the cab driver shrugged.

The phone had survived the crash in working order and Sameer pulled up his contacts list. For several seconds, he flicked between entries.

"Mom" was the first he stopped on, but it took Sameer all of half a second to realize that he wasn't ready for her yet.

He flicked back up, surprising himself when he paused briefly on the entry that read "Manuel da Mouse" a couple of places above. He had not even realized his supposed stepdad was in the list. Sameer kept scrolling up and stopped on "Dad," thumb hovering over the call button. He didn't want to call Goldie, either, but he was probably the best of a bad set of choices.

The cab had stopped at an intersection, and Sameer looked out the window as the phone dialed his father. The Mission Bay neighborhood appeared to be a downtown on the confused side of gentrification—housing projects on one block, towering renovated Victorians on the other, boarded-up liquor stores on the next.

Sameer slumped down in the passenger seat, poking his finger into a hole near the cuff of his ripped and bloodied white shirt.

"Sameer?" came Goldie Sharma's thickly accented voice on the other end of the line.

"Dad," he answered, a feeling of unexpected relief flooding through him, although he did not know what he was going to say next. "Look, I—"

"This isn't a good time, son. I'll call you in the morning, eh?"

Sameer fell silent, struggling to find the words he was looking for.

"You all right, yeah?" A statement, not a question. Goldie Sharma's idea of fatherly concern.

"Yeah," Sameer found himself saying, swept along as always by his father's force of will. "I'll . . . I'll catch you some other time."

He cut the call.

Sameer zoned out as he focused on the voices in his head. The cab driver's eyes in the mirror; the black-and-orange night sliding past again. Slightly nicer-looking buildings: a barber, a pharmacy. Just a block or so to the hospital, Sameer thought blearily. He continued to flick upward through his contact list, and then, at last, he felt himself starting to break, his grief overdue, growing and swelling inside him.

"Maya."

He should have been at the dinner—that was the vague sense of somewhere else he needed to be that had been penetrating through his drunken haze all evening.

Both Maya and Veer had called separately to invite him, and Veer had said it would be important for him to be there. The way he said that had annoyed Sameer, as if it were necessary to say it to make him come. Veer had even told him not to worry about the bill—the night was going to be his treat. Bastard. *We're not all trust-fund kids.*

He probably had not felt the need to mention that to anyone else. Only Sameer, who would not have the money for Saison; only Sameer, who could not be trusted to turn up unless both of you called him, unless you told him how important it was. All right if you were a Kapoor, all right if you were Maya, Mother's darling daughter, even when you fucked a man twelve years younger than you.

He should have been there. If he had been there . . .

Sameer put his knuckle to his mouth and breathed in deeply.

They hit another intersection, and the hospital loomed ahead of them to the right. The driver turned, skirting the site to one side, heading toward the emergency-room entrance.

Sameer found himself looping back up the contact list, as if his thumb had a will of its own, although he knew where it would stop as the cab driver pulled the car to a halt.

"There you go, dude." His voice was a call to action: *Hope you're okay, but get the hell out of my cab.* "No charge, just get yourself seen to, you hear me?"

"Thanks," Sameer replied, stumbling as he climbed out. His legs were weaker than he had realized. They felt cramped, tingling like someone had sat on them. The car pulled away, and he looked at his phone, and the name his thumb had stopped on: Ruchi.

Tears were falling now as he walked up to the entrance. He selected the entry, brought up the options, and moved to "Delete."

Sameer's weak legs were not improving, and there was a rushing sound in his ears now. Everything was . . . too much. Then he saw her, standing by the entrance of the hospital.

He could make it there, he could make it there at least. He looked at Ruchi's name on his phone; if he just pressed that button, she would be gone forever.

The woman tensed as she saw him, hand moving instinctively to her belt. Sameer held up a placating hand, or at least he thought that was what he was doing. Parts of the world were going black now, his perception narrowing.

"Officer," he said to her, holding his phone up with his thumb carefully away from the delete key, as if the thing were a weapon and he was ready to place it on the floor, all digits clear of the trigger. "I need to turn myself in."

~

"Sorry, ma'am," Sameer heard from somewhere beyond the curtain. "It's immediate-family members only."

He had been drifting. The hangover was already kicking in, making him sleepy. Then again, perhaps it was the fact he had been in a car accident.

"Jaitly is my maiden name; I am divorced from his father," a woman's voice explained slowly and deliberately as if speaking to an idiot. His mother had arrived, then. Of every reality that Sameer had known was coming, this was the one he had been dreading the most. "Let me through. He's my son."

"We were about to move him; the doctors have said he's fine to go."

"That's nice," came a dry reply, "but I still want to see him."

There were a few moments of silence, broken by an audible sigh. "You'll need to be quick."

The cop guarding Sameer pulled back the curtain surrounding his bed and revealed Lena Jaitly in the familiar midaction of jabbing at the screen of her mobile phone with a fat index finger as if the harder she jabbed, the better the thing would work.

"Ahem"—the cop cleared his throat—"when you're ready, ma'am. And you're really not supposed to be using that in here," he added.

"Just trying to contact his father," Lena said as she clumsily jammed the phone back into her purse and pushed her way past the cop.

Lena was an ample middle-aged Indian woman—although Sameer's father tended to refer to her mostly as a "fat bitch." Her graying hair was tied back in a loose bun and straggled around her large square forehead like a fringed awning. She wore one of her trademark loose-fitting cotton *kurtis* over stained blue jeans. His mother's look of concern almost warmed Sameer for a moment, then her eyes found the handcuffs that chained him to the hospital bed, and the stunned expression that crossed her face shamed him more than any slap could have.

"What?" Lena mouthed as much as said, before pulling back the curtain about ten inches to glare at the police officer beyond it. Six feet and robust with a pronounced paunch and a mop of salt-and-pepper hair, the man had the look of someone counting down the minutes until the end of their night shift.

"Two minutes," the officer said. "That's all you've got. I'm just waiting for someone to come so we can move him."

"Why?" Lena demanded, and Sameer almost loved her for her pretense that the moment hadn't finally arrived. The moment they had all known was coming. That was well overdue, even. "My son has been in a car accident," she said. "Why is he in handcuffs?"

The cop looked from Lena to Sameer, his eyes hardening, the tired look receding for just a moment, replaced with a narrow stare. "Your son is under arrest for driving under the influence, ma'am," he said, pinning Sameer with a narrow stare. What the cop couldn't know was that the dumpy Indian woman was far scarier for Sameer than he was. Just the look that he knew would be coming at any moment . . . "And there was a passenger," the officer continued, "dead at the scene. The scene that your son *fled* from."

Even with Lena present, the man's words hit home harder than expected and made Sameer's skin crawl, bringing with them a reality that somehow hadn't quite sunk in before that moment: Ruchi was dead; it was his fault. Almost subconsciously, he reached across with his free hand—the right hand—and pinched the skin on his left forearm. He did it until it hurt.

The curtain fell back again as Lena turned to her son, the look on her face familiar. He had seen reproach cross that face more than once before. "Is it true?"

He rattled the handcuffs that were attached to the bed rail. "What do you think, Lena?"

She flinched, although he almost never called her "Mother," anyway, not since she had married Manuel. "Who was in the car with you?" she asked, looking like she was going to be sick. Her mouth quivered a moment, and Sameer saw by the wrinkles beside her eyes she was trying to hold in tears.

"No one you'd care about," Sameer answered. "Not the number-one child." He clenched his jaw and tried to hide years of heartbreak in that mocking reference, but he could feel his shoulders contract into his body like a pangolin curling into an armored knot.

"Sameer . . . this is serious."

He looked away from her. "Get out," he said quietly.

"Son," Lena began, moving to the side of the bed, reaching for him, "we've got to get you a lawyer."

"Don't touch me!" Sameer hissed, shrinking back from her touch and causing the handcuffs to make a loud clink. Lena snatched her hand back as if burned. Behind her, the curtain opened.

"It's time," the officer said.

Sameer, however, was not finished. "This is your fault," he exploded. "You fucking left me. Broke up our family! I hate you, I fucking hate you!" His face was red; hate drifted from his skin like a stink.

The officer pushed past Lena, giving her the most sympathetic look he could muster. "You'd best go now, ma'am," he said. "Get some sleep. Start again tomorrow."

Lena backed out, looking over one last time as she left the cubicle to see so much hatred still seething in her son's eyes.

Chapter 5

"It's just like him, Veer. It really is."

"You think your brother crashed his car to, what, steal your thunder?" Veer asked, no hint of irony—or even accusation—in his voice as he watched his new fiancée pace up and down a very small portion of the hospital floor.

Maya paused for a beat, a wry smile touching her soft features. "No," she answered, "but . . . it would have been nice if he could have not been a deadbeat just for one night. You know? It would have just been . . . nice."

The trauma center seemed quiet, given that it was late on a Thursday night, and Maya could have ranged farther with her pacing if she had wished to. As hospital waiting areas went, it was cheerful enough. Veer sat in a sea of mostly empty chairs, while Maya's Anita Aunty and her daughter, Selena, had ventured off to find coffee.

Maya stopped and sat down next to Veer, whose smart clothes were working even better for him the further the night wore on. The jacket—which, miracle of miracles, he was still wearing—had become crumpled, and the collar of his shirt seemed looser. Looking at Veer's clothes was making her want to get him out of them.

Sameer had long shown a talent for ruining things, but it was a true talent indeed to ruin things without even turning up. Veer and Maya should be in bed together—that was how a proposal night should end, not in a hospital waiting area. They would both be far too tired for anything interesting by the time they got back to her apartment now. And, even worse, her mother was present, occasionally favoring Maya with a look that made it feel like she was to blame for everything, even Sameer's accident.

Or perhaps that was her own paranoia, although when Maya had asked her mother when Pinky Aunty was going to arrive, Lena's raised eyebrows—which coupled together looked like a caterpillar bunching up its back—had delivered all the daughter-blaming subtext that went along with her actual spoken words. "I didn't call her," Lena had answered sharply, eyeing Veer, who had at the time been safely out of earshot. "We had . . . words earlier this evening."

"Words?" Maya had been unable to stop herself from parroting it back as a question.

"Apparently the fact that her son will not listen to her is all my fault."

Maya had nodded and backed away from the conversation. So, Pinky had tried, earlier in the day perhaps, to dissuade her son from proposing to Maya. She had been attempting to sabotage Maya and Veer's relationship for some time now, but now it was coming between the two mothers, who had been friends since they were teenagers.

In another time in her life, Pinky—and by extension, it always seemed, Anita Aunty—had felt like a daily presence in their lives, especially back when Maya's mom and dad were going through their messy divorce. The other two women were a constant source of support, Anita Aunty bringing tiffins of warm home-cooked dinners, and Pinky Aunty delivering happy-hour specials and the gift of an in-home masseuse for Lena's sore, aching muscles.

Around that time, Maya had belatedly discovered the TV series *Sex and the City*, and in an odd way and with very little sex involved as far as Maya knew or wanted to imagine, her mom and her two friends sometimes seemed like an older Indian version of those women as they had hung around the Danville house that was then still the family home, lunching together, sometimes drinking wine dangerously early in the afternoon, and throwing around a multitude of detrimental observations about men.

Or was it more like *Desperate Housewives*? Maya had watched that one, too. Ha! Maybe the Aunty Army, as Maya sometimes referred to them, should have been called *No Sex and the Suburbs*?

Either way, Pinky had always been the last to leave and the one that Lena had confided most closely in. The shoulder to cry on, especially when Sameer had chosen to live with his father—even if it was a shoulder attached to a straight back and a chin held high, as if she were always about to walk into a ballroom. That was Maya's future mother-in-law, and the two families' closeness should have only been a positive thing for the relationship, since it was oft repeated among the community that when Indians marry, "we marry the family—not just one person." Yet somehow, in their case, it made everything more complicated. Veer was Pinky Kapoor's precious only son, and with Lena's much older and already-divorced daughter apparently sinking her claws into the billionaire trust-fund kid, the cracks in the mothers' almost lifelong friendship were beginning to show.

"Everyone's going to be too worried about your brother tonight," Veer said, taking a deep breath and stretching his arms over his head. "At least that might spare us the inquisitions for now." It was as if he had been following her train of thought, able to reassure her even about those private fears that she kept locked in her brain. He did that a lot.

Maya had not been looking forward to the conversation she would have to have with her mother about the engagement, but at least a scathing, in-depth discussion would be shelved for now, especially as Veer and Anita Aunty were present, too. They had all been far too worried about Sameer—at least until they had found out that the fool was just fine aside from cuts and bruises, and was being checked over by doctors.

He must have been drunk. Sameer was always drunk by about seven or eight in the evening, so Maya was expecting a DUI to follow. It would serve him right, and might even give him the sort of scare he needed, although she seriously doubted that. It would take something far worse for Sameer to change his ways, if a change was even possible.

Lena appeared again, on the other side of the waiting area, coming from the direction in which the doctor had taken her just a few minutes before. The yellow embroidered *kurti* she was wearing was rumpled and grimy. She was moving slowly, although Maya's mother only ever moved quickly when partaking in her true vocation, cooking. Maya stood as she got closer and felt a little sick when she registered her mother's eyes, which were red and swollen, as if she had been crying.

"What is it?" she asked in a squeak. "He's all right, yeah? They said he was okay."

Lena did not say anything; all that came out was a brief choking noise. Then Maya caught sight of more movement from the corridor behind her mother. It was Sameer, a large dressing taped in place on one side of his head. Two policemen flanked him, each with a hand on one of his arms, which were behind his back.

"Are they taking him in now?" Maya asked. It seemed a bit harsh because, for one thing, he looked like crap. Then again, Sameer almost always looked like crap when she saw him these days, which was not so much, even though they both worked in the city, only a matter of blocks from each other. There was something heartbreakingly sad in that, and sometimes it was hard to imagine an in-between—from the sweet, bright boy she had secretly been proud to call her baby brother to this sallow stranger who had quietly excused himself from every contact until, eventually, she started to fall into the same habit.

Lena clutched Maya's arm and said something, but Maya did not hear her, transfixed as she was by the sight of her brother being taken away. Sameer and the two officers moved at a slight angle to them, and as they passed, she caught sight of the cuffs around his wrists.

Beyond Sameer, farther along the corridor, she could see Selena and Anita Aunty on their way back, successful in their hunt for coffee. They stopped in their tracks. Their eyes and mouths were little ovals of surprise. Despite the inevitability of it all, the scene was shocking. In her mind's eye, all Maya could see was the pint-size brother he had once been, and a part of her was remembering, with a catch in her throat, that she had been there when he was born and had heard the first words he had ever spoken. *"How can they be taking little Sameer away?"*

"What?" Maya said absently to her mother, realizing she had spoken.

Lena repeated herself hoarsely, though more audibly. "He killed someone in the accident. Someone's dead."

An invisible fist punched the air from Maya's lungs. She couldn't have heard that right. It must have been the number of drinks she'd consumed at that goddamn restaurant. The room was getting warmer. She could smell her own metallic sweat, the shock of what Sameer had done seeping from her armpits, darkening her blouse. Maya fiddled with the slightly loose ring on her third finger, looking at Sameer with glassy eyes as she watched him being led away. *I knew my brother was a screwup, but not,* she thought bleakly, *that he was capable of killing someone.*

Chapter 6

The main hall of the police station was possibly the most terrifying place Sameer had ever found himself in, a cavernous space of concrete and tile, lit well enough by windows on both sides from the dawn that had been beginning to break as they drove him over, if only for the light to show the grime to its best advantage. The terrazzo floor was cracked and yellow brown around the edges. The walls were institutional green up to shoulder level; the higher portion had been cream originally but was now mottled gray with years of cigarette smoke. The paper clippings, apple and nut relics, and dirt on the unwashed floors mixed in with the general air of hopelessness and despair.

Sameer had thought at the age of about ten that he might want to be a policeman. The idea had hung there vaguely for a year or two in his adolescent mind, but if someone had brought him to this place when the thought first popped into his head, it would not have lasted a day. He closed his eyes tiredly as a shudder racked his whole body, his thoughts and feelings twisting into impenetrable knots.

Ruchi is dead and you are to blame. That did not sound right. It did not sound like it could possibly be true.

A big-bellied cop with broad shoulders and a grim face booked him, then marched him over to the lockup. The cell door slammed shut behind him, and the lock cranked like a grinding shaft without grease.

Sameer's cell was a bare, unlit room with iron bars, rough walls, and a damp floor smelling of urine. It was small—only four-by-two, with a single metal chair by the wall, but it had the advantage of belonging only to him. Most of those brought in had been thrown into a larger holding cell that Sameer could just about make out if he stood up and pressed his face close to the bars. Maybe he was in the "killer" cell.

Minutes before, they had brought in a tall, skinny white man dressed in too-tight ripped blue jeans that looked like they should be worn by someone in a late-eighties rock band. Attired in a crop top that fit the same image, the man had short, slicked-down hair and was wearing makeup. Sameer had found himself smiling at the getup. He had not meant to smile, he had not felt like smiling at all, but nonetheless, his lips quirked for the briefest moment and for just long enough that the man had seen it.

Sameer had averted his eyes—turning away from the metal bars of the cell and dropping down to one knee to fasten a shoelace that had come undone, but he was not quick enough. The wannabe punk rocker lunged for Sameer, even though the bars separated them, straining against the grip of the two policemen who held him. "Something funny, you brown-Paki piece of shit?" the man had seethed at him, foamy spittle coming from his mouth. "I'll fucking pull your balls off, you laugh at me again." The two cops restraining the man had glared at Sameer like they thought the whole thing was his fault, too.

Fuck, Sameer's hangover was really starting to kick in. He scratched irritably at his forearm. Every now and then, Sameer shifted a little left or a little right on the metal seat, trying to get away from the persistent reek of the urine. After a while, he started to wonder if the smell was coming from him. Had he perhaps pissed himself in the crash and not even realized it?

Pissing your pants, eh, boy? came the voice of his father in his head. The one and only Goldie Sharma.

"No," he whimpered to the empty room, which, although small, threw the sound back at him like an accusation.

You're a killer now, boy, a real man. The voice continued, relentless. *Don't wanna go pissing your pants, not where you'll be going.*

~

Fifteen-year-old Sameer sat in his father's Mercedes-Benz 230 SL while Goldie put the last of his suitcases and boxes in the back. His mother stood in the doorway, face full of harsh accusation every time she fell into Sameer's sight. They had argued before Goldie arrived when Sameer had finally lost patience with her telling him it was okay to go with his father while also interspersing those snide, nasty little comments that she tried to pretend were innocent.

"Remember, it's okay to be your own man."

"If you ever need to come home, any time of day or night . . ."

"Don't let your father bully you."

She spoke as if none of this were her fault. His mother could have done things to make his father stay. She could have forgiven him his unfaithfulness, could have lost a few pounds—quite a few pounds—made herself more appealing in the first place.

Sameer had told her so, all that and more. And he did not regret it, no matter how many times she turned those reproachful eyes toward him.

Sameer looked around the interior of the car. He had always loved the Mercedes, even if his father was a bit overprotective of it. He remembered the time he had spilled sauce on the faux-leather upholstery while eating drive-through in it. Man, his father had been pissed. Understandable, though, and it was still a fond memory, that day. The Sharma boys out together, taking in a game. There would be way more days like that now.

"All set, boy?" Goldie said, flashing his son one of those charming grins.

Yeah, Sameer loved this car. It was slick and expensive, just like his dad. That was why all of Sameer's school friends thought Goldie was cool—because he was so different from their dads.

He knew he wasn't going to miss his mom, although some weekend visits were, apparently, nonnegotiable. He would miss Maya, he supposed, but she wasn't at home so much anymore, and he might still catch her on the weekends. She wasn't seeing their dad, and as a full-fledged grown-up, she didn't have to. Goldie didn't seem so bothered.

"You ready to move into chez Sharma?"

Sameer laughed. His dad was cool, even when he said stupid shit like that. "Sure am, Dad."

Of course, chez Sharma turned out to be a dump, a two-bedroom apartment with peeling wallpaper, a mold problem in the bathroom, and a seventies kitchen that came complete with damaged flowery linoleum. There was also a cooker with one of those top-mounted grills. Fortunately, for "cooking" Goldie used only the microwave and a list of local food places that promised the delivery of homestyle goodness. The fallout, he would explain to guests, of having lived with a "kitchen dictator" who had never let him cook. It was a statement he would often contradict just moments after making it, leaning toward his son conspiratorially, and blowing boozy breath as he whispered, "Cooking's not a man's job anyway, though, is it, son? We know that."

Sameer decided he had always thought that, too.

On that first day, walking into his dad's decrepit little apartment—which happened to be not all that far from the little one-bedroom dive Sameer would graduate to about fourteen years later—Sameer found himself wondering why his mother got to stay in the big house in Danville, especially as Maya was now away at college. He didn't understand any of it. It was all her fault for being so unattractive—that was what his dad said anyway—so why should he and his father be the ones to suffer? Men had needs; his dad had been telling him that one for a while. Why hadn't she understood that? Why hadn't she taken his looking elsewhere as an incentive to get on a treadmill, use a bit more makeup?

"Settle in, son," Goldie said as they brought the last of the boxes in. "I know it's not much, but we'll make something of it, eh?"

The doorbell rang about twenty minutes later. It made a sort of wet jangling sound, but unlike most of the power sockets in Sameer's bedroom, it at least worked. Goldie answered it and returned with a woman who had permed, bleached-blonde hair and wore a short skirt that revealed blotchy white legs.

"This is Janice," Goldie said in a way that made it clear he didn't expect them to swap pleasantries. "I thought it would be best if I just got out of your hair tonight, yeah? Let you settle in without me in the way. Dinner's ready to go in the microwave, like I showed you."

Janice had barely even glanced at Sameer, let alone acknowledged him, as the pair backed out of the room.

"Don't wait up, eh? Might be late."

In any event, they hadn't been that late.

Lying in bed on that musty-smelling mattress when Goldie and Janice had returned that night—tucked up tight in a sleeping bag because he had been unable to find any sheets or a duvet cover—Sameer took a sip of water, wishing he could wash away his queasiness. It was Sameer's first encounter with sex, and he heard the whole thing.

Sure, he had seen those rehearsed, sterile performances in R-rated movies but, contrary to what he had always told friends at school, had never seen a porn movie and had most definitely never been anywhere near the act itself. He guessed that it must have gone on between his mother and father at their own house when they were together, although, thankfully, he had never heard it.

But he heard it then, all right, and had been unable to stop his mind from imagining the scene in response to every creak of the bedsprings, every moan and giggle and, eventually, scream. When they stopped, and he realized what had happened between his own legs, Sameer had felt sick with shame.

∾

Now, in his jail cell—which, as it had occurred to him earlier with a manic giggle, rhymed with *hell*—Sameer scrambled to his feet and finally emptied the contents of his stomach down and around the gleaming steel toilet bowl.

Behind him, the door clicked open. Sameer turned around, wiping away strands of bile-laden drool from the corner of his mouth. The same police sergeant who had brought him to the cell—he didn't know how long ago, he realized; could have been minutes, could have been hours—came in. The cop showed no caution in his movements, made no shout to "stand back." Apparently they weren't too afraid of this particular felon. A mean grin played across the man's face, as if this, right here, were where his job satisfaction lay.

"Court-appointed attorney," the sergeant announced as a suited woman walked in. She looked younger than Sameer did, and he—even when he looked like shit, as he must now—didn't look his age. She had dark hair and almost translucent skin, her eyes dark pools. The slightly horrified look in them was understandable, although he might have thought that an attorney would be better at hiding their true feelings. Glancing between the woman and the mess around the toilet, the sergeant appeared to take pity on her.

"You want to do this somewhere else?" he offered. "I think we could set up an interview room, but you might not have long there."

"No," Sameer said.

"Mr. . . . ."—she looked at her notes—"Sharma, I think it would be better if we did so."

"No," he said again, looking at the police sergeant. "I don't want her, I want someone else."

That's right, son. She's a woman, what's she going to know about the law?

The other man looked incredulous. "You don't get a choice, dumbass."

"I said I don't want her," Sameer hissed, vomit and spittle spraying across the cell, causing the attorney to take an involuntary step back. *It's not that, Dad.*

The cop looked at the attorney and shrugged. She appeared unsure whether to be upset or relieved. Eventually, the police sergeant turned back to him. "All right, can't make you, I guess. Can't say when you'll get to see another one, though. You sure?"

Sameer nodded, and they backed out of the room. *You wait 'til I get there, son. I'll sort things out, get you a man who knows what he's doing.*

It's not that, Dad, Sameer thought again, then found himself saying the last part to the room.

"It's those eyes. They were just like Ruchi's."

Chapter 7

"Lena, *beti*," Kookie said as Lena punched at her phone screen like it had upset her, "have I ever told you the story about how Anita transferred from Lady Irwin College?"

The restaurant business had Lena almost permanently attached to her mobile phone, and she sometimes wondered how anyone had run a business and had a life before smartphones were invented. Things had been even more hectic in this last week, since Sameer's arrest, as Lena had been distracted and had spent much of her spare time ringing up solicitors and learning far more about the law than she had ever wanted to know.

All the same, sitting across from Kookie Aunty in the south-facing lounge in Anita's beautifully decorated family home, Lena suddenly felt very rude and placed the thing down with an apologetic smile and a motion that made it seem like the phone might contain an angry hornet. Hmm . . . that was why it vibrated the way it did.

"Mummy," Anita said, frowning heavily, "I'm sure Lena hasn't come to hear stories about me." She cringed noticeably, the fingers of her free hand unconsciously rising to fiddle with her diamond nose pin.

Lena smiled encouragingly at Kookie. *Oh yes, I have.* She had come to see Anita's mother, who always cheered her up, whose fun, irrelevant, and often irreverent ways could be like a salve on life's open wounds and could, at least for a couple of hours, make her forget everything else.

Kookie sipped at her tea noisily. She had a way of slurping her drink that appeared to extract the minimum amount of tea with the maximum amount of noise. "You wouldn't have guessed it," Kookie began, "but my daughter was once a topper at Delhi University. She stood first in her class, but the problem was that Lady Irwin College, where she studied, was an all-girls school, and you know what a terrible tomboy she was being."

Lena laughed, and the action felt like a release. She couldn't remember the last time she had laughed, and inside her chest she could feel the pressure dissipate just a little.

"And I think she was bored of looking at all those upper-class women, almost forgetting what a boy is looking like. In fact, when a woman is looking at Chintu, one might be thinking she has still forgotten, eh?"

Lena laughed again at the mention of Anita's husband, Chintu— this time almost choking on her tea. She looked guiltily over at Anita, who was twitching noticeably.

"Mummy!" Anita protested, but Kookie, in full flow, waved her daughter's protest away like she was swatting a fly.

"So, what does my Anita do, I am asking you? She calls the principal's office at St. Stephen's College, which was a coed school, and asks for a meeting. Brave girl, although she was shaking with nerves when I dropped her off. But the principal was so impressed with her, he offered her a place straightaway. I am hearing later that he was telling it was a mind-blowing moment: 'Who would say no to the top-graded student of Delhi University?' This is what he was saying!"

Lena nodded her approval and wore her most impressed face, although it was hard to picture the usually nervous and always obliging Anita ever having been so . . . forthright.

Anita was chewing her cheek nervously and eyed her mother like she was waiting for more embarrassing things to be said. Lena made circles around the top of her teacup with her finger. She knew the anecdote was a colorful story of Kookie's making. Anita had never topped Delhi University, and it was the old boys' network that had enabled the transfer—the principal having been a childhood friend of Anita's father from a provincial town in India.

"The thing with my mother," Anita had said to Lena during a previous visit, "is that she has never been good at separating the world she wants and the world that is. Sooner or later, they always end up becoming the same thing."

"Takes after her mother, this one," Kookie continued. "Did you know that I was the first woman in my village to graduate from high school? Still, that is another story . . ."

As Kookie finished talking, her attention appeared to wander. There was a faraway look in her eyes, and her mouth continued to move, although nothing audible came out. Lena looked on, time seeming to freeze for her as the older woman's cup of tea—held in a delicate and exquisite traditional fine china cup—began to tilt forward ominously in her hand.

"Mummy!" Anita called out, and Kookie's attention snapped back, although she jumped a little, and some of the tea splashed out of the cup and onto her clothes.

"Oh, look," Kookie said with notable irritation in her voice, "you've made me spill my tea, daughter, shouting at me like that." She looked over at Lena. "Excuse me, dear, I will have to clean myself up as we are due another visitor later."

Kookie levered herself out of the chair, slapping away her daughter's attempts to help her up. "I'm not helpless yet, daughter," she snapped, before stomping off in a huff.

"Is she okay?" Lena asked Anita as the other woman sat back down, not quite knowing how to frame the question any more clearly. Behind the hostess hung heavy bespoke blinds that ran the full length of their wide french doors. They kept the sun from blinding those sitting in the house's south-facing lounge and, Lena knew, were still a source of pride and joy for the house-proud Anita well over a year after their fitting.

"The neurologist said there's nothing we can do," Anita replied testily. It was easy to spot that there was something going on—Kookie was having too many senior moments. Lena's affection for Kookie Aunty—who, in some ways, felt like half a mother for Lena herself—almost led her to push the point, to ask Anita to seek a second medical opinion or try a different test. In the end, however, she decided to pursue something else that was suddenly bugging her.

"So," she began, unable to completely keep the edge from her tone, "you've got more company coming later, huh? Busy day."

Anita straightened, tucked her hair behind her ear. "Yes," she admitted. "Pinky is due to stop by a little later on."

"Hah. I would have kept us at least a day apart," Lena said, trying to make a joke of it, although her voice sounded too brittle in her own head. She shot out a square hand and picked up a sticky-sweet *gulab jamun* from the silver tray that had been placed temptingly in front of her with the tea. Definitely not a coping mechanism, she thought wryly, as she pushed it too eagerly into her mouth.

Anita looked uneasy, her mouth opening and closing a couple of times like a goldfish in a bowl. However, as the silence lengthened and Lena continued to chew on the bite of *gulab jamun*, Anita's discomfort eventually got the better of her.

"It's not that bad, is it?" Anita asked carefully. "The two of you?"

"I'm not sure what it is," Lena answered with a shrug as she swallowed the bite of her sickly sweet treat, "but I feel that Pinky somehow holds me responsible for our children's engagement. Like I have some control over Maya's decisions. Anyway, it takes two people to get engaged. I think Pinky seems to forget that." Still, Lena went on, a little of the force leaking out of her voice, "I can't remember the last time we went so long without one of us calling the other."

"But how can she be angry with you?" Anita said, a rare hint of exasperation creeping into her voice. "You haven't done anything wrong. Nothing to feel guilty about."

Lena just looked back at her friend for a moment, a sad smile playing on her lips, while the nicely laid-out spread of Brooke Bond Taj Mahal tea and Indian sweets on a silver platter sat between them. When she finally spoke, her voice was a pained croak. "Then why haven't I called her, either?"

"Is there any more news about Sameer?" Anita asked.

Lena raised her shining eyes to Anita, and Anita flushed with guilt. "Oh, Lena. I'm sorry . . . I didn't think," she stuttered, evidently shocked by her own drastic change of subject to the other most painful thing in Lena's life.

"Court hearing tomorrow afternoon," Lena replied distantly, the mention of her son's situation bringing down her mood even more quickly than thoughts of Pinky had. She placed the half-finished *gulab jamun* back down on the silver tray and wiped the back of her hand across her mouth, her appetite suddenly gone. "We can apply for bail then."

The doorbell rang, breaking the substantial tension that had built in the room. Anita leaped to her feet as Lena attempted to quickly move the conversation so that they wouldn't come back to the same subject when her friend returned. "Oh, is it a delivery? I have to admit to having become quite the Amazon addict; it's like having a birthday every week." She knew that the words sounded forced, but she did not care too much.

Anita didn't reply, although the look on her face suggested that she wasn't expecting any deliveries right then. Moments later, Lena heard a familiar voice carry from out in the hallway, just before Anita's own voice called out an unusually loud greeting that Lena knew was for her benefit. "Oh, Pinky! You're early!"

Another time, perhaps it might even have been funny.

Pinky was a tall, slender woman with porcelain skin and a signature streak of white in her shoulder-length black hair, carefully groomed to give her a touch of distinction. She always smelled like one of those overpriced boutique shops in seaside towns: sandalwood and roses.

There had always been something different about Pinky, well before she ever gained an advantageous match to a billionaire. Odd as it may seem, marrying Harry Kapoor was the lowest point in her life—her father dead and in disgrace, her family ruined.

Pinky had been born into a measure of wealth and success, into privilege. And, Lena had to admit, this was initially a part of the thrill of being her friend. There was never a point that Lena could remember when Pinky walking into a room had not changed its atmosphere. She had beauty, but she also had something far harder to define: presence. Lena and Pinky first met as teenagers at a Himalayan hill-town boarding school—Jesus and Mary Girls' High School—and, for young, frumpy Lena, feeling close to someone who exhibited such an aura had made her feel special by mere association.

It was the start of a lifelong friendship. Once you knew her, then you knew that Pinky's charisma was like an infectious energy—especially as a young, precocious girl—that made life more exciting, and bursting with possibility. When you were Pinky's friend, sometimes those bullshit stories that teenage kids told to make their lives sound more exciting were actually true, and Pinky was always the instigator. Pinky took chances in everything: boys, driving recklessly, sneaking out in the middle of the night. The most unforgettable escapade was an infamous nighttime raid on the nearby all-boys school, an adventure that couldn't possibly be true with the all-black outfits, balaclavas, and a climbing rope with a grappling hook. It had remained a legendary story well after the girls had left the school, and it was almost all true. Lena had been there, for a part of it—although, of course, Pinky had been the first over the wall.

Decades later, drinking prosecco in the garden of Lena's Danville house as she tried to put her life back together post-Goldie, it was still Pinky who was the instigator. The twinkle in her eye now dimmed to become like the pulse of a distant lighthouse, but hanging in there, saving Lena's life when it was needed, steering her clear of the rocks, and even encouraging her to stick two fingers at said rocks as she did so.

Back in Anita's fussily neat and orderly lounge, Lena shifted, trying to make herself comfortable on the Victorian love seat with the heart-shaped back. "Oh, am I early?" Pinky said.

Although Lena couldn't see them, she guessed that Pinky must have—in true Pinky fashion, walking in a virtual strut that had earned her the nickname Peacock with her peers—pushed straight past Anita, as if an invitation were never a thing that she needed.

"That's so typical of my husband," she continued as she drew nearer. "I asked him to check the time for me this morning, and he told me it was midday." She walked into the lounge, still talking half over her shoulder. "Honestly, I don't know how that man ever ran a multibillion-dollar company. Oh—"

Today, Pinky was sporting one of her many classic looks—so Lena's inner catwalk commentator droned on—with slim-fit denim jeans and a green cashmere sweater, a cream trench coat slung lightly across her shoulders in acknowledgment of a slight chill in the air. And, of course, those huge sunglasses that no one else would ever risk—or get away with. Seeing Lena, she had stopped in her tracks. If she hadn't been the cause of it, Lena could almost have found it funny. "Hello . . . ," Pinky said with forced brightness. "I didn't expect . . ." She put her hand over her mouth as if trying to stuff her words back in, but it was far too late. With Pinky, Lena ruminated, one never knew whether such an action was quite as accidental as it seemed. "Nice to see you."

Was it? The thought came unbidden, and Lena hated it the moment it forced itself into the front of her consciousness.

Behind Pinky, Anita rushed into the lounge, looking about as worried as she ever had. A moment later, Kookie appeared through the lounge's other door, and noticing Pinky, she said, "Oh, Pinky dear, I did not hear you come in. My daughter isn't making you use the backside entrance, is she? I cannot believe it is that time already. Did I fall asleep?" And then, noticing the larger of the three younger women still sitting there, even greater confusion further creased her wrinkly features. "Lena, you are still here."

Yes, I am, Lena thought wryly.

They were in danger of descending into farce, like in those TV sitcoms that always used to make Goldie laugh hilariously and Lena could never stand—the ones that had characters coming in one door while others left through another, the timings of accidental meetings and "missings" providing the comedy through ever-higher levels of improbability.

In Anita's lounge, however, nobody laughed, although Pinky broke into a broad and genuine smile as she removed her sunglasses and swept across the room to greet Kookie. "Aunty, you look so well!"

"Ah," Kookie said, beaming at the compliment as Pinky stepped back again. "It is because I am still in my prime. How is Harry?" she asked, as she always asked within the first minute of seeing Pinky. Anita had once complained to Lena about her mother's fixation with Pinky's billionaire husband, taking it as an affront against Chintu, Anita's own much-less-wealthy spouse.

"He is well, thank you," Pinky replied, before giving a big theatrical shrug. "He keeps himself busy with his charitable work, yet he is still a trouble around the house." Around the mansion, Lena thought bitterly, then mentally slapped her snippy brain on the hand.

"Ah, yes," Kookie agreed, and nodded knowledgeably while taking her seat again, as if she knew exactly what Pinky meant. "This is the curse of the successful businessman; they are born with a drive they never know how to switch off. There are worse things."

Oh yes, she most definitely eyed Anita pointedly with that last comment. Lena loved Kookie, but despite the half-a-mother thing, she sometimes didn't envy Anita. Mothers were always hardest on their daughters. Lena knew that intimately, had been on the receiving end of it with her own mother. But, when the time came that Kookie was no longer around—an almost impossible thing to imagine, it seemed— Lena wondered if Anita would know that it was mostly only the good memories that remained. At least, that was the way it had been for her—her own mother, her *ammi ji*, teaching her to cook in the soot-stained kitchen—the sharp tang of mint leaves filling a corner of the room, blending with garlic from a hanging basket in which green stalks snaked through the weave. *Ammi ji's* deep, significant, but enthusiastic tones as she had given instruction, let her daughter know that cooking was a serious thing, but also to be enjoyed and experienced. In so many areas of her life, her mother had judged her, but in the kitchen, things had always been more easygoing, not so much "right and wrong."

Oh, how Lena wished *Ammi ji* could have been there when the restaurant had opened, and her mother had not missed it by much. Of course, she was there, if only as the critical eye—an imagined presence on her shoulder giving judgment along with Lena on every element of the preparations, the menu, the design.

Pinky looked for somewhere to sit. There was Kookie's chair, which clashed with the room like a Volkswagen Beetle in a showroom of Ferraris and Lamborghinis. Then there was the cream three-piece set, which featured a curved, tufted sofa, an armless love seat, and an ottoman. Anita sat on the sofa, while Lena sat on the love seat. It looked like Pinky threw a long hard look at the love seat on which Lena was perched before electing to join Anita on the sofa.

Lena watched the other woman settling in, appearing to adjust herself, her clothes, and her sitting position for at least twice as long as could have possibly been necessary—all the while managing not to meet Lena's eyes even once.

Damn you, Pinky, look at me, Lena thought to herself. *Our children are engaged to be married. Am I not even worthy of your gaze now?*

And my son is about to go to prison for causing the death of a beautiful young woman, her subconscious added unhelpfully. In fact, perhaps that was the ghost of her mother popping up to observe things and offer her opinion from atop her daughter's shoulder like an annoying cartoon devil. Or angel. Yes, she meant *angel.*

"I think we'll need another pot of tea," Anita said hurriedly as she got straight back up to her feet and collected the teapot. Anita looked a little relieved to quickly exit the room.

They sat silently—Pinky, slightly flushed, and Lena with her arms folded aggressively—while Kookie fussed with the pleats on her silk sari as she looked with narrowed eyes back and forth between the two of them. Pinky leaned toward Kookie and clasped her hands gently.

"I'm sorry for turning up early, Aunty," Pinky said, still not having looked at Lena since sitting down.

Kookie broke into a huge gracious smile and batted Pinky's apology away with her hand.

"Nonsense, Pinky," the old woman answered. "You are a breath of fresh air at any time. Now, I'm not sure if I have told you this before, Pinky, or you, Lena, but I was just thinking of a funny story about Anita when she was—and you won't be believing this—a topper at Delhi University."

Geez, Lena thought to herself, with an exaggerated inner eye roll.

As Kookie carried on with the story that Lena had already heard, she found herself looking at Pinky, feeling invisible as the other woman gave her full attention to the storyteller. *Are you looking down at me?* she thought. Then again, hadn't she always looked down upon Lena and Anita to some extent or another? She was *the* Pinky Kapoor, and they had always been her less privileged, less influential friends, the ones she was close to because "they went way back," rather than that they actually belonged in her social set.

45

This wasn't the first scandal that Lena had faced with the Bay Area's censorious Indian community. Divorce was always a mark against you, even as warranted as Lena had been in finally sending Goldie packing. To lose a son to the absent, canoodling father was another mark against her, though, and even that was nothing compared to when she had then begun a relationship with, and eventually married, a Mexican man.

Lena blinked, and her mind wandered to a women's-only rummy card night at the Kapoor mansion not long after Lena and Manuel had become engaged. Pinky's rich Silicon Valley friends had been there—the ones who wore their success in designer shoes, and brand-name handbags—and then, there had been Lena and Anita.

"Lena, I hear you're going native . . . well, Mexican at least," had come a voice booming across a long cherrywood table around which all the women were gathered. Lena hadn't even been talking to the woman—her name was either Dimple or Twinkle Vora, and she had full red lips and jet-black hair swept back in a severe coif. Lena couldn't stand her, even though her daughter, Esther, and Maya were in the same class, and often hung out together. "How's that working out for you?"

"He's a good man," Lena had managed, caught off guard as polite but slightly uncertain laughter murmured its way around the kitchen table, which was as big as a bed within the pristine white kitchen. Pinky's kitchen—in which Pinky herself almost never cooked—was impressive, but not the snug kitchen with its usual disarray that Lena would always prefer.

"Oh, what does he do again?" Red Lips had asked.

"He's a farmer," Lena replied, unable to stop from gulping halfway through her own sentence.

"Oh. Oh." Red Lips said, rolling her eyes downward and pulling her mouth out to one side. "That's nice," she managed finally.

Lena could feel the embarrassment whistling around her icy shoulders, and looked directly at Pinky, her eyes bright. Guilt rippled across Pinky's face as she squinted hard at her cards. A deathly pin-drop silence hung in the air. Pinky's thin lips almost vanished, but she had said nothing as the game and the loud chatter of the women resumed.

Lena closed her eyes at the memory and winced. "I've, um . . . got to go," Lena said, getting hurriedly to her feet in Anita's lounge and unintentionally interrupting Kookie's story.

"You don't want to hear—?" Kookie began.

"Sorry . . . uh, work emergency."

She half waved at Pinky—who was finally looking at her, a slight bemusement pulling at her sharp, still-attractive features—and the returning Anita, laden with a tray of fresh samosas. "Thank-you-so-much. Lovely-to-see-you-Kookie. Sure I'll see you soon."

Lena fled her miserable memories. She snatched the front door open, lumbering awkwardly in her gray shabby *kurti*, then hoisted herself behind the steering wheel of her car and shoved the Camry into first gear before tearing down the Gupta driveway.

Chapter 8

While the sound of an ascending and descending guitar riff drifted in from the main bedroom, Maya made coffee in the kitchen and thought about how much her mother, Lena, hated this room.

Maya lived in a luxury three-bedroom apartment overlooking the San Francisco–Oakland Bay Bridge in the Rincon Hill area of the city. She could have saved plenty on the mortgage if she had gone for the more modest two-bedroom option a dozen floors down, but it just didn't have the same view. She knew it was an extravagant expense. Several months after moving in, she still felt guilty every time she came back to it, yet there was an odd sort of thrill in that. Something almost addictive. It had been an impulsive decision, though not the most impulsive thing Maya was being accused of these days.

The lounge was the real centerpiece of the place—a large quarter circle with windows set along most of the curved side and affording a breathtaking view of the bridge and the ocean. An enormous L-shaped sofa dominated the middle of the space, and there was a television built into one wall. It was a great room.

The kitchen that lay behind the lounge, on the other hand, was a galley kitchen. Nice enough, but small considering the size of the apartment. That was a choice that Lena Jaitly was never going to understand—not as a woman who, in her late thirties, had begun a food business that had seen her become something akin to San Francisco

Bay's curry mogul. Okay, that was overstating it, but her food stalls, restaurant, and subsequent franchise operations had been so successful because she was, quite literally, a legend in the kitchen.

If Lena Jaitly knew how little her daughter cooked in her own kitchen, she would turn in her . . . tandoor? But again, there were bigger chickens to roast lately when it came to Lena's general disappointment in her daughter. Speaking of which, the guitar playing had stopped . . .

"Morning, beautiful," Veer Kapoor said as he emerged from the direction of the main bedroom, his favorite Takamine guitar held casually in his right hand. He wore sweatpants but nothing else.

"Nowhere to be too soon?" Maya teased as she offered him a cup of coffee.

Veer gave her a lazy petulant grin as he took the coffee and laid the guitar down on an ottoman in front of the sofa. Behind and below him, the tiny dots of cars and trucks drove along the freeway bridge as they came into the city from Yerba Buena Island.

"Got a rehearsal with the band," he replied, settling back into the sofa. Maya moved around to join him, tucking her knees up against her face. She was already showered and dressed. "Then I might see Mom and Dad."

Maya looked up at that, unable to hide her concern—not so much about Veer's father, Harry, but rather about what his mother, Pinky, might have to say during that visit. "Have you seen your mom this week?"

"No, not since before . . ." Veer began, using Maya's knee as a lever to help him reach over for the sugar.

"The night at the hospital," Maya said, finishing his thought for him. That's what it had become for them and for almost everyone else. Not the night that Veer proposed—the night that should have been all about them—but the night that her brother had been involved in a fatal DUI. She had been so angry with Sameer for stealing her thunder until she realized that a woman had lost her life. Perhaps she should have been even more angry with him after finding that out, yet she hadn't been. All her anger had melted into sorrow—for the woman, Ruchi, and for Sameer.

She had thought of him a thousand times in the last few days, her mind always drifting back and questing for what could have been done to avoid getting to where they were now, as if there was a magical answer, some key that could have sent her little brother's life in a different direction. Even at twenty-nine, that was what he still was—her baby brother, who, when he started to walk, walked from their mother straight to Maya. She caught him just before he fell when he took the first steps he ever took in this world.

Maya had been awake some of the previous night, just thinking through so many little moments—like how she could pinpoint the exact day, fourteen years ago, when their family had begun to fall apart.

"I've left your father," Lena had said in a muffled voice.

Maya couldn't remember the last time she had seen her little brother cry. He was fifteen—a man in many respects—but, almost as far back as she could recall, Sameer had never been a crier. She, on the other hand, even though she was seven years his senior and had already graduated from college, was still known to cry at charity ads that asked for money for sick children.

His lips went first, quivering in a way that seemed almost cliché, like it should happen in a cartoon and not on the lips of a real person. There was a lump in her own throat, a feeling like when a piece of food has scratched the back of it. And there was a sense of dread, of foreboding. But, for her, no tears were coming yet.

"He left last night after I told him to," Lena went on, "and, if I have anything to do with it, he won't be back." There were spots of color high on her mother's cheeks, and Maya could see tears welling in Lena's eyes as she spoke. That lump in her throat grew a touch larger. But no tears still, not for Maya. Sameer was blinking, and she could not tell if he was trying to force the tears out or back in.

The three of them sat in the cozy kitchen, the room that Maya had always thought of as the most comfortable room in the house—more so than the lounge and even her own bedroom. Lena was sitting in a tan leather armchair to one side of the room. The two children had quickly grabbed chairs from around the kitchen table, worried by her ominous tone and the words *I need to speak to you both*.

"Why?" Sameer asked, his increasingly manly voice reverting to a prepubescent squeak, the first tear starting to trace a meandering path down his right cheek.

Maya saw her mother's brow crease for a moment and realized that she was wrestling with telling them the truth. "He has been . . . unfaithful."

Sameer shook his head; the flood was about to be unleashed. While he was still in high school, Maya was twenty-two and had been out of the house for four and a half years—firstly, being away at university, and then working at her first job and sharing an apartment with two coworkers. An unexpected side effect of moving out, right from those first few weeks of being at college, was that she had started to miss her pain-in-the-ass little brother. There was enough of an age gap between them that their sibling relationship had always been a distant one. Yet, over the past couple of years, perhaps as he started to grow up, they had grown closer.

Indeed, as little brothers went, Maya figured he had never really been that much of a pain, just more of a daddy's boy. Which was fine, as she was definitely a mommy's girl. She felt deeply sorry for Sameer as she watched him begin to crumble before her.

To her, Goldie Sharma was, well . . . just her dad. She loved him, although she didn't always like him. Sameer, however, idolized his father, and she was waiting for the shouted denials to come. They didn't, however, and Maya was not sure whether she was impressed with him or whether that made her more worried about him. Instead, Sameer just sat there, tears streaming silently down his suddenly pasty-white face, against which his pimples stood out like a splatter of red dots. It was her mother who broke first, erupting into loud, mournful sobs.

That was what finally set Maya off, diving from the chair into her mother's arms, cradling her mother's head, almost as if she were the parent. Although Sameer did join them eventually, for several minutes he just sat there, quietly weeping and staring past them with unfocused eyes.

Later, Maya would often wonder if he was deciding, even then, that he would be going to live with his father—and that it was all his mother's fault.

Her mind jumped to that first year Sameer lived with Goldie and seemed so sullen during a weekend visit to the Danville house when she, too, had been home. Their mother had tried to pry, to see what was wrong, and Maya had tried more subtly to join him in watching TV and starting up conversations. An effort that had proved fruitless, and last night, so many years later, she had lain in bed and wished into the darkness that she could have jumped on Sameer and pinned him to the ground, tickling or otherwise torturing the troubles out of her teenage brother, who looked at her from the depths of his private life like an animal waiting to be coaxed into the light. Because maybe, just maybe, that would have been the answer to all of it.

Stupid, of course.

Either way, the whole terrible affair of Sameer's accident and subsequent arrest had produced the side effect of putting the biggest thing in Maya and Veer's life on hold. They were engaged; it was a fact. And yet, somehow it would never quite be real until it was approved by their respective mothers and the families came together.

As every Indian aunty she knew was fond of saying: marriage is bigger than a mere union of two people. It is not personal; it is communal. She had a strong memory of being young and sitting on a kitchen stool overhearing Kookie narrating the Romeo-Juliet love story of a boy and girl from two warring Indian families who cruelly separated them, causing them to commit suicide. Maya chewed her bottom lip thoughtfully, remembering how the story made her cry.

"I'm going to see my mom and Manuel today," she said, sitting up quite properly and modeling her very Indian attire—she was wearing a *salwar* in the blue shades of ocean water with a saffron-colored *kameez*—the sort of thing she wore only to Indian events and, on occasion, a family gathering. The rest of the time it was either suits, jeans, or short, clingy dresses on a night out—something that no good Indian girl's mother would ever want to see her daughter in.

"Are you sure the outfit will help?" Veer laughed.

"Thanks!" Maya snapped, jumping up from the couch, but Veer caught her arm and pulled her down onto his lap.

"Sorry," he said, although Maya didn't think he looked all that sorry. Long, dark eyelashes that were wasted on a man, framed eyes the color of melting chocolate in a face that was grinning down at her cheekily. "I was just wondering if a traditional outfit doesn't look like . . . capitulation. Maybe you should be reminding your mother that you're an independent and highly successful thirty"—he caught a look—". . . ish woman who has grown up in America and can do what she damn well pleases."

Yeah right, Maya mused, giving a contemptuous bark of laughter, quickly suppressed. *And, while I'm at it, let me shoot all the Aunties who have no blood relationship with you but are allowed to have opinions about your life and all your shortcomings.* Sometimes Maya fucking hated being Indian. More specifically, she hated being an Indian in America. Was that a fair thing to think? She remembered how her mother had cooed over Kookie's arrival the other week, about hearing "news from home"—a sentiment equally shared by their network of friends who had one foot in each country—a home Lena hadn't lived in for nearly forty years. But Maya was already running late, and she'd have to pass up the opportunity to bore Veer with a teaching moment about the challenges of straddling two cultures.

Instead, Maya leaned in and kissed Veer on the cheek, just about resisting the urge to continue on to all the other delicious bits of exposed skin, then stood up again. "You know something, fiancé," she said, enjoying the word, "you should think about stand-up comedy with material like that. I'm Indian; I'm supposed to do what I'm told."

∼

In direct opposition to the many-storied monster where Maya owned a corner apartment, her mother lived on a quiet horseshoe-shaped street near downtown Walnut Creek, named Ramsay Circuit. The fresh smell of warm country air complemented the views of sun-dried deer grass and short deciduous trees that lined the licorice-black streets, one of which Maya now turned onto.

Maya's favorite thing about her mother and Manuel's little two-bed-room house was the front garden. There was no gate. In fact, there seemed no transition between being on the sidewalk and their property, although a slightly leaning section of cream-colored metal fencing over to one side did make at least a half-hearted attempt at demarcation.

The path to the front door zigzagged around a sizable vegeta-ble-and-herb patch that was Manuel's domain. Rosemary and lavender were strategically placed next to the path to offer up their scents to any visitors. It was the most nonsensical layout for the entrance to a house that Maya could possibly imagine, and she would never have been able to deal with having to use it every day herself. But then that was what made it so wonderful: what it said about the people inside the house.

Off to one side, surrounded by an enormous variety of potted plants and vegetables, was a simple white plastic garden table with four chairs. In one of them sat Manuel, chewing on a cocktail stick. He had smoked cigarillos when he met Maya's mother a decade before, and it had taken several years of Lena's nagging to get him to stop smoking them. Since then, he had taken to chewing on cocktail sticks in their place, and to picking his teeth clean with them after meals. It was a habit Lena hated almost as much as the cigarillos, so Manuel took himself outside to do it.

In some ways, he might as well still have the cigarillo habit. Sometimes Maya would see him absentmindedly fiddle in the breast pocket of his shirt and pull out a cocktail stick before taking himself outside. Just like a smoker.

Manuel smiled and stood up to greet Maya. Although time was inexorably turning his sun-aged skin leathery and more wrinkled, he was still as handsome as when Maya's mother had met him. More so, perhaps, as age became Manuel: the oft-broken nose—a short stint as an amateur boxer, apparently—the ridiculously square jaw, the stubbly salt-and-pepper beard, those silver streaks only recently beginning to invade his sideburns and moving up toward his hairline.

"Good to see you, Maya," he said, leaning in to kiss her cheek. Maya welcomed the itchy irritation of his stubble, the familiar smell of the musk he used. Even after so many years of being away, the smell of him was as comforting to her as the aroma of her mother's cooking.

There was an undigested lump of yearning lodged in her throat, making it difficult to breathe.

"Is she—"

"—in the kitchen?" Manuel finished for her. "Of course," he said, with a gentle look in his eyes. "Where else?"

"And how's she been?"

"Let's just say that I've been putting on weight lately." Manuel gave a wry chuckle, his eyes crinkling at the corners.

Lena Jaitly cooked all the time, but when she was upset she cooked obsessively. Running amok in the kitchen after her divorce was what had led to her business success.

"I'll give you both a few minutes," Manuel said as Maya headed toward the front door.

Although it didn't quite have the majesty of the kitchen in the old house in Danville, or its old-world charm, Lena's kitchen was nonetheless a large one, particularly in relation to the size of their little two-bedroom dwelling. A central island provided extra cupboard space on one side and a two-seat breakfast bar on the other. The cupboard doors were made of the same light-maple wood throughout the kitchen, and the oven and cooktop were the largest that Lena could fit in there, with a plate warmer at the bottom. Several pots bubbled away on the stove, but Maya's nose had known that back in the hallway. It smelled of mint chutney and cumin—a smell Maya loved.

Homelife when they were younger had revolved around the kitchen. "This is the Indian way," her mother would say sagely, radiant and flushed with life and purpose, as she always was when she was cooking. "Life is food, huh? We must eat, so why not make it joyous? The kitchen is the heart of the home."

There was a time, Maya remembered, when Lena had taken it upon herself to teach both her children to cook at the same time. Mustard seeds popped and crackled in sizzling oil in the frying pan, and the stove-top kettle whistled. Well, she might have altered that memory slightly. Maya had been the intended target of the lessons, but little Sameer—he would have been about nine or ten at the time—had insisted on joining in, too. The teenaged Maya had been relieved Sameer joined them as, even back then, she had already realized that cooking was never going to be her thing. Of course, there was no way she could possibly have explained that to her mother. It would have been like saying "I'm not so sure that breathing is really me."

She could still picture Sameer, beaming as he stirred the apparently "simple" *karahi* chicken curry, sniffing the aroma that was sweet and pungent, caught up in wonder with the process that Maya was never herself going to feel.

Maya plucked the sunglasses off the bridge of her nose and adjusted them on her head. A four-seat dining table made of a darker mahogany wood was situated in front of the french doors that led out to the back garden. Lena sat in one of the chairs, looking at her phone. Although Lena had, through the requirements of the business, acquiesced to owning a mobile phone many years before, she pushed at it with thick, clumsy fingers as if still not entirely comfortable using something small enough to fit in the palm of her hand.

Maya's mother was a stout woman, with thick-rimmed black reading spectacles and a face that was far friendlier than it was traditionally attractive. Of course, when Lena's face wasn't friendly, it was kind of terrifying. She barely glanced up as Maya came into the room, remaining focused instead on her phone where she was typing a message with her thumbs. Judging by the manner her thumbs were thumping the screen, the phone may well have offended her.

"Honestly, I do not know what we are paying Sameer's lawyer for," Lena said without looking up. "It seems that I am doing all of the work. The preliminary hearing is on Wednesday. I trust you will be coming?"

"Of course," Maya replied.

Lena finally put the phone down and got up to greet her daughter with her customary large bear hug. She did so wearily, and Maya could see the strain of current events in her face. She wore a dark, shapeless *kurti* that Maya hadn't seen before. It made her look like she was in mourning.

"Has Dad been in touch?" Maya asked. It was strange how Maya still called Goldie Sharma "Dad." Biologically, he was just that, of course. But, if she included her toes, Maya may well have had enough digits to count the number of times she had seen him in the last two decades. "Is he helping with the fees? I could . . ."

Lena gave a curt shake of her head at Maya's offer of financial help. "Goldie has been in touch, given a little. It has always been his way to do just enough to win his seat at the table, then sweep in like he is the savior."

Lena crossed over to the cooker and stirred one of the pots—some sort of dal, Maya judged. "Looks like you're cooking to feed an army," she observed.

"I didn't know if you would be bringing Veer," Lena said, her eyes still on the pot. "That boyfriend of yours eats like he is hollow in the legs, that one."

Maya winced. Ah, there we go. "Fiancé," Maya made herself correct her mother, something that took a personal force of will to do. It was necessary, however, to draw that line in the sand. "We're engaged now. Veer is my fiancé," she said tersely.

At the cooker, Lena snorted derisively. "I assumed you wouldn't be going ahead with that foolishness, not with what is happening."

Maya was shocked. She had come expecting a fight of some sort or another, but outright dismissal . . . ? They stood in silence for a few seconds, and suddenly she wanted to weep like a five-year-old on the playground because this was her mother, the woman who had birthed and raised her, who was supposed to stand by her, no matter what her choices. Maya clawed her fists together, her muscles constricting with the effort. Finally, the pain broke the noose of hurt and betrayal tightening around her until she could breathe again.

"You mean because my alcoholic brother just killed someone?" Maya's head snapped up, taken aback by what had come from her own mouth. They were harsh words that she normally would have chastised herself for bringing up when her mother was in so much pain already, true though they were.

Lena dropped the wooden spoon back into the pan with a splatter of yellow dal and rounded on her daughter. Maya's face was a mask of contrition, but Lena didn't see it. "How dare you!" Lena cried, her plump cheeks quivering like jelly. "You selfish girl."

I just stated facts, Maya wanted to say, but instead what came out of her mouth was a whiny protest. "I'm not a girl," she said, which made her sound just that. "I'm an independent and highly successful woman who can do as she pleases." Maya cringed a little when she realized she was quoting Veer.

Lena advanced, and Maya found herself taking an involuntary step backward. "How can you do this to me at a time like this? Your brother is about to go to prison, and all you want to do is bring even more shame down upon this house. Whatever did I do to deserve such children?"

"How can marrying the man I love be shameful?" Maya said. She stretched out her fingers and battled a mad desire to itch and itch and itch until her skin lay in bloody shreds at her feet.

Lena made a strange wheezing sound as if she'd been running. "You know," she accused Maya. "You know what you are doing."

Finally, Maya found the voice she had been looking for. "What, because I'm fucking Indian? I'm not Indian, I'm American, and American women can marry men twelve years younger than them because American society doesn't have its head up its damn ass."

Lena raised her eyebrows, her anger tempered by her daughter's foul-mouthed display, but by no means halted. "Well," she said, "you certainly curse like an American woman. And you never learned that in this house."

"Dad used to curse all the time," Maya said, struggling to contain the incredulous tone in her voice. "But it's okay for him because he's a man, and what's okay for men isn't okay for women. Isn't that right?"

Lena bridled indignantly. "Not at all."

Maya wiped the sweat from her forehead. It was too warm in the kitchen. She began to pace in front of her mother and casually flicked an arm in her direction. "You're right, Mother, of course you are. Because it's not okay, for instance, for a man to cheat on his wife, is it? You took advantage of being in America then to throw his unfaithful ass out, didn't you? I'm sure that would have been just as easy back in the villages of good old India. And then you went and married a Mexican man because that's okay for Lena Jaitly. But heaven forbid your daughter, born and raised in America, should enjoy any of the freedoms of living here." She stopped, breathing hard, but she still had one word left. "Hypocrite."

Maya turned and found Manuel standing in the doorway to the kitchen. He seemed frozen as if his face had just that instant been unexpectedly and painfully slapped. Suddenly she felt sick with guilt. Had he heard the bit about marrying a Mexican? She wanted to apologize for saying that, for everything to be all right and for her not to feel so furious with her mother. She wanted to start again and to calmly lay out her reasons. She wanted her mother to listen. Yet all she could do was walk past him to leave.

Maya's face boiled as she again navigated the meandering path at the front of the house, having swapped the humid heat of the kitchen for the dry, itchy rays of the Californian sun. She felt guilty and humiliated, and not for the first time after a conversation with her mother in recent months.

It really wasn't fair, she thought balefully as she fumbled for her car keys, and it felt like the way she was treated would never, ever change.

Chapter 9

"Okay, so you've got this," Sameer's attorney said.

Sameer had spoken to him several times, yet the man's name kept escaping him. Mark . . . ? Maybe it was Matthew. He was a graying, middle-aged man with glasses and what appeared to be a large mole on his nose.

Sameer's head hurt; it had hurt for more than two days now. The walls of the courthouse's interview room weren't helping. The color reminded him of cat vomit, which made him feel a little sick himself. Which made his head hurt more.

Sameer had spent so many days in sterile, dour, depressing rooms like this one since his arrest. The criminal justice system didn't do interesting rooms, apparently. He suspected that he wouldn't have minded the fact so much if he still had alcohol to occupy his mind. Drunkenness was great for not caring about your surroundings, as was the need for a drink in the first place. A lack of alcohol could easily fill up his thoughts and had done so quite nicely—if painfully—after his arrest. But that had cleared up surprisingly quickly, and now Sameer was left with only silence and dull rooms.

Mark or Matthew handed him a sheaf of papers. "Mr. Sharma, I'd like you to look at this transcript to be sure that it is faithful to the statements you gave the morning after your arrest."

Present at Interview:

Detective: Sergeant Devon Harris
Detective: Greta Anderson
Suspect: Sameer Sharma
Attorney: Matthew Traverso

DETECTIVE HARRIS: Mr. Sharma, were you involved in a motor traffic accident yesterday evening where a Nissan sports car left the Central Freeway and overturned on the exit ramp?
SHARMA: (Inaudible reply)
DETECTIVE ANDERSON: Mr. Sharma, as you did with your name and age, we will need every answer to be loud and clear for the benefit of the tape.
SHARMA: Yes.
DETECTIVE HARRIS: Can you tell us what happened?
SHARMA: I was giving her a lift home. Her friends had let her down and . . . we were friends, you see, friends from work.
DETECTIVE HARRIS: Who were you giving a lift home, Mr. Sharma?
SHARMA: Ruchi.
(A shuffle of paper)
SHARMA: Miss Ruchi Thomas, the deceased.
SHARMA: It's a shit word, don't you think?
DETECTIVE ANDERSON: Sorry?
SHARMA: *Deceased.* What a bad way of saying *no longer living.*
(TRAVERSO attempts to subdue his client.)
DETECTIVE HARRIS: Do you feel bad about it, Mr. Sharma? Do you feel it was your fault? After all, a blood test shows that you were well over the legal limit.
TRAVERSO: My client's feelings are hardly relevant here, Detective.
DETECTIVE ANDERSON: Do you think it was right to leave the scene with Ms. Thomas trapped in a burning vehicle?
TRAVERSO: Again—
SHARMA: I tried. She . . . she was stuck. The fire.

(TRAVERSO asks for a five-minute pause, as SHARMA breaks down.)
DETECTIVE HARRIS: So, Mr. Sharma, would you please give us
your version of events.

"Sameer? Sameer?" his attorney—his name was Matthew after
all—was saying sharply. "Did you hear what I was saying? With this
damning evidence, I'm afraid there's not much we can do." He stee-
pled his fingers and touched his fingertips to the outside of his flared
nostrils.

Sameer realized, belatedly, that the attorney had been expecting
some kind of affirmative reply. When one hadn't been forthcoming, he
continued anyway.

"The charge is 'DUI Manslaughter Gross Negligence.' The 'Gross
Negligence' is the important bit; it could mean up to a ten-year sentence. They contend that you must have driven recklessly to end up
where you did and that you fled the scene and left Ms. Thomas to die."

How did he say all of that so evenly? No judgment in his tone. That
even tone was worse than hearing distaste—Sameer had decided so the
first time he spoke to Matthew. If you could hear the distaste in someone's voice, well, you knew where you stood with them. The possibility
of being disliked was always worse.

"You are to plead 'Not Guilty' to this charge," the attorney continued. "But as this is a preliminary hearing, we will have the opportunity
to offer to plead to the lesser charge of 'DUI Manslaughter Ordinary
Negligence,' based upon your assertion that the accident happened
when you took your eyes off the road and that you only left the scene
after attempting and failing to rescue Ms. Thomas. You left to attend
to your own injuries—which you had every right to do—and then you
turned yourself in there. If a 'Guilty' plea is accepted on that charge,
maybe you get just two years. Four, at the worst."

Sameer nodded.

"In all likelihood, the prosecuting team will be ready for this, and there will be some argument before the judge decides whether to accept your plea or continue with the 'Gross Negligence' charge."

"What are the chances they'll go for it?" Sameer asked.

The attorney hesitated, not meeting his eyes. It was brief, but telling. "It depends," he answered.

"On what?"

"How keen the judge and the DA's office are to make an example of you. The stomach they have for spending money and time on an actual trial. To be honest, not a single witness to the accident has come forward, only people who turned up after it, when your car was on its roof and at the bottom of the exit ramp. And you weren't there."

"Which doesn't look good."

"Which doesn't look good," the attorney agreed. "If you had veered the other way and hit the divider, or if you had hit the side of the freeway just about anywhere other than down the exit ramp, we'd have a better argument. We could say it was a momentary loss of control, perhaps something on the surface of the road. But making it all the way down an exit ramp . . . It looks more like dangerous driving, or that you were too intoxicated to tell the difference."

Sameer *had* been too intoxicated to tell the difference, so what was the point of this?

The attorney had one of those big, firm beer bellies he carried proudly like a badge of honor. He stroked his belly now, his face unreadable.

"So," Sameer said, "by pleading 'Not Guilty,' we're bluffing, then?"

The attorney raised his eyebrows in response but didn't speak. Sameer could feel anguish, like a toxic chemical, flooding his bloodstream. He had spent half his life lying and bluffing, creating falsehoods and false appearances for the benefit of others, and he was so, so tired of it all. He should have been a damn lawyer.

∾

"Lena, so good to see you!"

The asshole was wearing sunglasses to his son's preliminary hearing. "Goldie," Lena replied, attempting to inject as much acid into her tone as she could. "You look . . . the same."

Lena's ex-husband grinned as if taking her words as a compliment. Thick gold chains hung around his neck, as well as some stupid scarf. The aviator sunglasses he wore were oversize, and his unbuttoned shirt lacked a tie and showed too much hairy chest. At least he had shown the decency to wear a suit. It looked new and expensive, although possibly purchased from some sort of retro outfitter that specialized in 1980s recreations, like a bad version of something the actor Shashi Kapoor might have worn in the movie *Kabhi Kabhie*.

His hair was cut a little shorter than when she had last seen him, now spiked where it had once been slicked back. It made him look like an aging rapper.

Goldie glanced over at Lena's current husband. "Looking good, Manuel. Still farming in the village that is Fresno?"

Manuel smiled politely. If Goldie's tone had meant to cause offense or get some sort of rise, it was never going to work. Not that it had stopped Goldie from trying for the last decade. "As little as I can get away with," Manuel answered equably.

A blonde woman wearing a tight red skirt, black ruffled top, and gold stiletto heels forced her way through a group of people that stood just inside the entrance of the courthouse lobby. Her skirt stopped about six inches too high on the leg for anything that should be worn to a courthouse. Of course Goldie had brought one of his floozies to his son's hearing—why not?

The woman, who towered over Goldie by about half a head in her high heels, leaned in and kissed his cheek when she arrived. Her lips left behind a red mark, something that Lena sure as heck wasn't going to be pointing out.

"This is Sheryl-Ann," Goldie said. "Sheryl-Ann, this is my ex-wife, Lena, and her husband, Manuel."

Sheryl-Ann thrust a long-fingered hand topped with dress-matching—and patently false—nails toward Lena. "Lovely to meet you."

Lena took the offered hand, partly out of shock.

"We met when I sold Sheryl-Ann's house," Goldie said, then proceeded to rattle off the listing. "Exclusive two-bedroom apartment in North Beach with balcony and bay views."

Sheryl-Ann smiled affectionately as he spoke. Lena, on the other hand, shuddered, reflecting that each of Goldie's girlfriends could be named by their house listing.

As they moved across the marble floor, Lena seethed. "He's treating his son's hearing like a social gathering. I bet he only brought her because he knew we'd be here. Fourteen years, and he's still the same."

Manuel put a hand on her shoulder and squeezed it. "It's his way, my sweet. It's how he copes."

Lena cast an irritated glance at Manuel. "You're far too generous a spirit, husband."

The lobby was busy, and Lena wondered how many of these people that she had never seen before were present for her son's hearing—and if any were from the family of the woman, Ruchi. They neared the large oak double doors that led into the court itself. While the lobby was impressive, the doors themselves were just plain intimidating. Serious things happened beyond those doors. Lives changed.

Lena and Manuel veered off and took a seat on a bench along the wall. It was going to be a few minutes yet before they opened. She spotted Maya almost the moment that she and Veer came into the lobby. Maya saw Goldie and his latest squeeze almost straightaway, and Lena witnessed her change direction. They started to cross the lobby until

Maya locked eyes with Lena and came to an immediate halt. She saw her daughter lean in and speak to Veer for a moment, then the couple sidled over to the other wall, opposite the one where Goldie, as always, appeared to exist happily in his own world, either unaware or uncaring that the daughter he hardly ever spoke to had just avoided him.

And her mother.

So, there they were, three parts of the family lined up against three different walls of the courthouse, and one more in a cell somewhere nearby, awaiting his fate.

~

Suddenly, Goldie's voice, from Sameer's first day at high school, almost fourteen years ago, was sharp in his head.

"It's a big day, son," Goldie said as they drove along in his silver Mercedes. The car was starting to look old now, inside and out. Now that he lived with Goldie, he had started to notice the car's flaws. A dent in the front nearside panel had been uneconomical to repair, and the once bright pattern on the seats was fading, especially in the front. Down in the foot, a lack of car mats had seen the carpet wear through in places, and there was a general smell of years-old cigarette smoke having worked its way into the upholstery.

"The first day of a new year in a new school is your first day as a man," Goldie continued. "You get me, eh?"

"Yessir," Sameer replied with his standard answer.

"School before now was different. Junior high, middle school—they're friendly, safe environments. You hear me?"

"Yessir."

They drove through the Mission District, the extensive graffiti they passed seeming to alternate between ugly black tags and stunning pieces of wall-size art.

"But high school is a whole different ball game. High school is where it gets serious, where you start to sort out life's winners and losers."

Sameer was pretty sure his father had never been to high school. Hadn't he grown up in India? Did they even have high school there? Sameer knew better than to bring up any contradicting point of view, though.

"So, I think it's time I start to share something with you, son. It's the Sharma code of wisdom, and I got it from my dad. It's not written down anywhere," Goldie said, prodding the side of his own head with the index finger of his nondriving hand, "but is passed down from Sharma man to Sharma man. So, it belongs just to us."

They were approaching the high school now, which looked like a decaying colonial-era building, or someone's best effort at recreating one. It had the air of a grand-looking shithole, and the kids outside looked like they might be on day release. Sameer remembered his old school, which had looked a lot nicer than this one.

"Are you ready, boy?"

"Yessir."

"Rule One is that you have to assert yourself, because no one will do it for you. Be your own man, Sameer Sharma. But be a man, be someone that people notice. You understand me, eh?"

"Yessir."

They pulled up to the sidewalk.

"Whenever you walk into a room, do what you want to do, not what everyone else expects of you. Whatever happens to you in this life, make sure it's because you made it happen, not because you let it happen."

∽

As Sameer stepped into the courtroom and took his place on the stand, it didn't take him long to spot them all, though the room was surprisingly full. His dad was the easiest to find, with his aviator shades and something in blonde and red sitting next to him. He grinned and held up a hand in acknowledgment to Sameer.

Then Sameer found Maya and Veer, Maya looking anxious while Veer stared straight ahead. His successful sister and her trust-fund musician boyfriend. Fiancé now, Sameer had learned. He guessed the car accident had put a dent in their special night. Of course, if he had turned up to the restaurant like he was supposed to . . .

Sameer pushed those thoughts down, along with a rising sense of nausea that they were bringing, yet he couldn't pull his eyes away from the two of them. So perfect, even in the midst of the disappointment they were no doubt bringing their two families. Everyone always looked at Veer Kapoor—pretty little prick that he was! A part of him wanted to hate Veer so much for everything he had, a man who was always the center of attention. Well, everyone was noticing Sameer now, too. He was finally the center of attention.

His eyes slid across the audience—was that what they were, like they had turned up for the taping of an episode of *Judge Judy?*—and found Lena and Manuel last of all. His mother looked ill, and Sameer realized how all the different parts of his family were sitting apart from each other. Families, more than anything else, appeared to adhere to the laws of entropy. There was something terribly sad about that.

The judge read out the charge, but Sameer hardly heard it. His eyes were darting from face to face, scanning the room for Ruchi's relatives. He had never seen them before, but it was easy to spot them. They were huddled in a corner, their faces naked with grief. There was Ruchi's father, sitting ramrod straight. His eyes were bright with unshed tears, and he was holding himself like a marionette on tight wires. There was her mother, a pink-and-purple paisley scarf wound tightly around her neck, now clutched to her mouth to stifle her sobs. There was her sister, Rhia, a young woman, maybe in her late twenties, again wearing the Burberry plaid coat he had seen her wearing in a newspaper picture.

Seeing her, oddly, felt a little like seeing a recognizable pop star or movie star in a department store. He found himself staring at her with fascination, desperate to catch her gaze. She did look over eventually, eyes blazing at him in wrathful recognition. He looked at her beseechingly, trying to telegraph his penitence, but Rhia quickly looked away, unable to stand the sight of him.

~

"Rule Two, son, is that women are the most beautiful and wonderful creatures in the world, but they are just not the same as us—in the same way a colorful parrot is a beautiful creature, more beautiful than maybe any other bird. But you wouldn't let a parrot make your decisions for you. You get me?"

"Yessir."

"And, just like a parrot, if you tell a woman what to think and what to say enough times, she'll repeat it back to you. Remember Rule Number One: be your own man, Sameer."

~

The judge eased into her seat in the courtroom and picked up the papers before her.

"Sameer Sharma, do you understand the charges laid out before you?"

"Yes, your honor."

"And how do you answer the charge of 'DUI Manslaughter Gross Negligence'?"

He sucked in the tiny bit of breath that he would need to speak the four words that were expected of him, the words that were needed to carry on this crazy charade, this game where Sameer should pretend that he didn't deserve to have the full weight of the law thrown at him.

Where he prolonged the agony and suffering of Ruchi's family because the system allowed him to.

All of a sudden, Sameer felt so utterly tired of all the games, and the breath he had taken was fast leaving him that, in the end, he had only enough left inside to speak three of those four words.

"Guilty, your honor."

Behind him, he heard his sister gasp and his mother's sharp intake of breath, like a wounded animal.

Chapter 10

"Look how they sensationalize things," Veer heard his father, Harry Kapoor, say as he sat reading the newspaper at their large kitchen table with its eight elegant chairs. "Ah, I tell you, I cannot read this newspaper anymore. *India West* used to be a respectable read." With that, he folded up the newspaper and tossed it disdainfully down on the table.

While Pinky wore her advancing years well, Harry—who was older than his wife and had hit the big "six-zero" the previous year—was very much beginning to look his age. His hair and mustache were still quite black with only a fleck of gray, but his once-plump face now sagged with wrinkles, and there was a creeping frailty about him that had not been there even a couple of years before. He wore a tailored suit that rivaled any in London or Paris with a starched white shirt, even though it had been more than fifteen years since the billionaire businessman had stopped making his daily commute into the office. Unable to sit still and enjoy his early retirement as Veer was sure his mother would have preferred—on second thought, perhaps not; Harry Kapoor with nowhere to focus his energies would likely have driven Pinky mad—he had instead started becoming involved in several charitable endeavors. Some of these were local to the Bay area, while others were focused back in India, where Harry had grown up.

Harry wore no tie—his only concession to this semiretirement—but Veer spotted the shiny brown wing tips on his feet. His dad was fastidious about shoe polish.

Out of the corner of his eye, Veer watched Pinky extend her left arm to get the newspaper that Harry had discarded—she had to stretch; the glass-topped table was excessively big—while Harry reached for a letter beside him on the table. He waved it toward his son. "I'll need you to look over one or two charges on your credit-card statement for this month before I pay it off. Remind me to show it to you before you leave, would you? Can't be too careful; people will try to rip you off wherever they can."

"Sure," Veer answered, observing his mother's frown—as deep as her Botox would allow. Harry, like many Indian businessmen, was not ashamed to look for deals and watch out for hidden charges, but Pinky Kapoor found such sensible behavior where money was concerned distasteful—embarrassing, even.

While Pinky thumbed through the paper—obviously looking for the page that had incensed her husband—Veer continued stirring the gray pot in front of him on the induction hob, marveling at the astonishing white-and-grayness of the entire Kapoor family home, something that had passed him by when he actually lived there. *Lena Aunty's kitchen is so much more homey than our own,* he mused.

"'DUI Killer Sentenced,'" Pinky read aloud, then darted her eyes across to Harry, who raised his eyebrows disapprovingly and pressed his mouth into a thin line. Veer, turning back to focus on what he was doing, felt his stomach sink, and his appetite for the dal he was making for the three of them suddenly diminished.

"'Sameer Sharma,'" Pinky continued, "'the twenty-nine-year-old San Francisco resident who fled the scene of a motor vehicle accident and left a female friend to die in a blazing car wreck, has today been sentenced to twelve years in jail.'"

"Enough, Pinky," Harry grumbled. "We do not need to be hearing this with our lunch."

Pinky, however, was not deterred. Veer could not see the grim look that his mother wore as she continued, but he had seen it plenty of times before—the particular expression that meant she planned to push on through his father's rebukes and displeasure—and he knew it would be there. "It goes on to tell you about the effect on the family. The girl's sister, Rhia Hussain, is quoted as saying that her sister was a 'sensible person' who 'would never knowingly have gotten into a car with some-one who was unfit to drive.'"

Veer found himself unable to stop from stirring the dal faster with the wooden spoon that was, unsurprisingly, dyed gray.

"'She went on to call the whole incident a "horrible waste of life," "a tragedy my family will never recover from," and, like many others involved in the case, she can't help but wonder if her sister would be alive today had Sameer Sharma made more of an effort to free her from the car or, at the very least, tried to contact the emergency services straightaway.'"

The spoon turned an even faster circle as Veer tried to take deep breaths and ignore his mother, pretending to be too absorbed with making lunch to notice. It was excruciating.

"'Is twelve years enough when a bright young woman has lost her life?'"

"Pinky!" Harry snapped. "Veer came to make us lunch, not to hear this."

Pinky Kapoor put down the paper in a slow, deliberate way. It was a massive room, one end of which was all glass, looking out across the grounds toward San Francisco Bay from the mansion's vantage point high in the wealthy Oakland suburb of Piedmont. "Maybe he needs to hear it." She mumbled the words, but she mumbled them just loud enough. Pinky was the queen of the under-the-breath comment.

Well, that was that; she was not going to let him avoid this conversation. Veer turned around.

"Poor girl," Pinky said, looking at her son.

"Poor Lena," Harry pointed out.

"Hmm," was Pinky's rather noncommittal reply.

"She's your friend," Harry chided gently, his ire from a moment before having evaporated instantly. Harry Kapoor was an imposing man, but he had never had a temper. "Have you even seen her since Sameer was in the hospital?"

Pinky's nostrils flared, but she drew herself upright, manicured nails digging into the bone china of her teacup with a scrape.

Sniffing fastidiously, Pinky looked over at her son. The moment—the confrontation Veer had thought was coming—seemed about to be passing, so he took the opportunity to begin serving what he had described as "musician's dal" into bowls. Veer's mother had not looked impressed by the name of the dish.

"Is that supposed to mean 'dal on a budget'?" she had asked when he arrived and told them what he would be making the three of them. "Dal is already supposed to be a cheap meal—how does one make it cheaper? Remove the lentils?"

"Maybe it means 'dal with alcohol in it,'" Harry had said, smiling goofily at his son. "You musicians like drinking, don't you? Whiskey, perhaps?" he had added hopefully.

"Now, now, Harry," Pinky had said in a rebuking tone, "you know what the doctor said."

"'Don't have any fun, Harry,'" Veer's father had grumbled, holding up both hands in boyish surrender. "That's what that miserable man said."

Veer watched them indulgently now as they returned to a little back and forth about menial matters, the storm having passed just to the proverbial west of them. He loved them both with an intensity that came on like a dull ache in his heart, and he tried to remember if they had enjoyed so much banter when he was younger. Their relationship had been different when he had been growing up.

Their marriage had been an arranged one—Veer's mother married off at sixteen in Delhi, after her father had died owing a lot of money. She had been wealthy once and intended for a childhood sweetheart from a respectable but much less affluent family. With her mother and siblings faced with destitution—and the existing marriage arrangement likely to be made forfeit—a young, wealthy businessman who had made his fortune in America swept in. His name was Harry Kapoor. Of course, that wasn't his real name, but an Anglicized modification of *Hari*.

Although far from unkind, Veer's father had treated marriage and the birth of his progeny like one of life's checkboxes. Pinky, in turn, had invested most of her time in acting as a prominent figure in local social circles and, later, in her son's upbringing. All this allowed husband and wife to avoid each other—something that had not been too difficult in their vast McMansion. It seemed to Veer that only when Harry took early retirement on his doctor's advice did the couple ever properly spend time together. And, surprisingly, it turned out that they got on rather well.

Veer sat down with them, and they started to eat. "Musician's dal is your traditional dal *makhani* but without butter. We starving musicians have to rely on fresh sharp spices and clean herbs to impart the rich flavor, rather than expensive cream." He chuckled contentedly at his wit.

Pinky stirred her spoon idly through the smoky-sweet dal and looked at Veer fully in the face. "Your father's right, though," she said reflectively, "this must be very hard on your Lena Aunty. Are she and Maya . . . talking?"

Veer kept his eyes on his food. "No, not as far as I know."

"As far as you know?" Pinky pushed.

Veer suppressed a scowl. "Maya doesn't usually want to talk about it, and I don't make her."

Pinky put down her fork with a sigh. "Son, that family is under so much pressure right now. Maya should be with her mother at a time like this, supporting her."

"Rather than being with me?"

"If it's keeping them apart, son, then yes."

Veer shook his head irritably. He began tapping on the table. "You'll try any angle, won't you? You just don't want us to be together."

"I want you to be happy, I want Maya to be happy, and I want Lena to be happy," Pinky said. "And I don't believe this can happen with this . . . relationship of yours."

"Because she's older than me," Veer said, looking straight at his mother.

When Pinky answered, she met his gaze. "Because she's twelve years older than you, Veer. It's not so long ago that she would have been almost old enough to be your mother, do you realize this?"

Pinky set her lips together and nodded her head sharply, as though giving herself permission, then said combatively, "And, because her brother is a drunken deviant and a coward who left a woman to die in a burning car. I wanted for you somebody sweet, and young—maybe the daughter of one of our Silicon Valley set. There you go, I said it." Pinky held the handle of her flowered bone-china cup of chai firmly.

"So, Maya is not a suitable kind of girl." Veer thundered, enunciating every word like a boxing announcer at a WWE tournament. "And, she has a mind of her own, eh? I know she was not what you were hoping for, but . . . She's. The. One."

Pinky made a strangled sound. Harry looked stricken.

Veer did not move for what seemed like an eternity. "Tell me, do I bring shame on you?" he asked, gritting his teeth.

"Never!" Harry interjected, rippling upward from his chair.

"Never," Pinky agreed, her nostrils flared. "You've always done what you want, and we've always been proud of you, even if the band hasn't exactly . . ." She trailed off under a signal from Harry's raised eyebrows;

Veer's father had always been the most accepting of his music career. "We've trusted your judgment," Pinky added, almost convincingly.

Veer pushed his food away and stood up. He narrowed his eyes, and his bone-piercing gaze swept over Pinky. "So why can't you do that now? You've known Maya since she was a child, and Lena Aunty is supposedly your closest friend from high school. Why can't you just be happy for us?"

Harry shot Pinky a look, and they locked eyes, confusion written large on their faces.

"We are happy for you," said Harry, his tone appeasing. "What your mom is worried about is that people will talk . . ." He didn't finish the sentence. The Kapoors were used to an envious and admiring chorus from their friends and associates, not being reduced to a tabloid-type cliché. In a region known for its crush on all things tech, they relished their image as a power couple, generous in giving to their charitable endeavors while being attentive to their only son.

Veer drummed his long fingers on the table, keeping his face closed and withdrawn.

Pinky pressed one fluttering hand to her forehead, refusing to meet Veer's eyes.

~

It was a weird day for Maya. Jenny, the HR person at Holbeck Consulting, the company where Maya worked as VP of sales and marketing, had gotten engaged.

First of all, it was weird that they even had an HR person, as it seemed like only yesterday—okay, it was in fact, about four and a half years ago—that Maya's boss, Tim, had headhunted her from the same company he had left when starting his business six months before. Maya had been part of an extremely small staff then, and the whole company would meet most weeks in a tiny conference room. No chance of that happening now, as they would need a small theater to hold a meeting for everyone who worked at the company these days.

It was also weird because Jenny was a robot. She had a personality vacuum that she—luckily—filled by being exceptionally good at her job. Maya had heard more than once about the fantastic Rob, Jenny's fiancé, but had never met him and had started to think that he didn't exist. Or perhaps it was that Rob was the name Jenny had given to her vibrator.

Either way, Jenny was now apparently marrying Rob, and—most likely because Jenny didn't have any friends or, as far as Maya could discern, any life outside of work—her shower was happening over an extended lunch. The place Jenny had found for the celebration was nice enough. The menu was a little bland for Maya's tastes and the seating arrangement a touch tight, but they had all packed nicely into a few adjacent booths. A central bar was the restaurant's prominent feature, and Maya was drinking more than was a good idea, even considering that it was a Friday afternoon.

Sameer's sentencing had taken place on the previous day—it had been even worse than the preliminary hearing, and Maya had been among those there to see her little brother receive twelve years in jail. She knew that he had gotten off lightly in some ways—that someone else lay dead because of his actions, yet it had still been devastating to her. It occurred to Maya it might be the last time she saw Sameer outside of prison for a very long time. He would be more than forty when he got out. What chance of a good life, a good career, would he have then, as an ex-con?

Not that Sameer had been making the most of his life, but he had been holding down an office job and living in his own place. Maya always held on to the hope that things would get better for him, that he would start turning up to things more, that he would grow up. In little moments of fantasy, she had always imagined him coming back to them. That he would quit drinking, find a nice girl, that they would meet in Walnut Creek on the weekend once or twice a month and have a family meal with their mother and Manuel. Like ordinary, decent, functional families did. She never went quite as far as to imagine Goldie there—some things were just going too far into the realm of fantasy— but she wanted her brother back.

Maya sighed, picked up her napkin, and proceeded to carefully accordion fold it one way, then the other.

And yet her sorrow over Sameer was not the only reason that Maya was on her third glass of chardonnay before the food had even arrived. It was that look on her mother's face each of the three or four times their eyes had met outside and then inside the courtroom. The look that called her daughter a traitor for loving the man that she did. The next look that said, *How can you be so selfish at a time like this?* And then there was the *My children are ruining my whole social standing and probably half of my business* look.

And, as Maya drained that third glass and eyed the pizza that had just been laid in front of her—which she suddenly had no appetite for—a realization struck her: Lena would never admit that she was wrong. Maya's mother had lived more of her life in America than in India, but her particular brand of stubbornness was, as far as Maya was concerned, a uniquely Indian one. She wouldn't ever be able to see Maya's marriage any other way.

The thought chilled Maya, driving cold, sharp points into her stomach and stirring up the chardonnay, helping to make time seem like a terrible thing at that moment. The endlessness of it, stretching out toward an indefinite horizon, her mother's mind never, ever changing, immovable like granite jutting out of an ancient landscape.

Maya looked up from her pizza, which was now making her feel intensely queasy. Two women who looked Indian to Maya sat over by the window. One looked away as Maya caught her eye, but the other stared a moment longer before turning to lean in toward her lunch partner and talk conspiratorially.

Maya threw bad vibes their way. In fact, if there had been any chardonnay remaining in her glass, she might have been inclined to head across and throw that over one of them, too. Of course, a little ironically, that might have been the chardonnay speaking.

"You all right, Maya?" Jenny asked from across the table through a mouthful of arrabbiata pasta—about as adventurous as the HR manager tended to get. "You look . . . unwell."

Maya was on her feet, suddenly and without explanation. Reaching the restroom, she was glad that someone had left the cubicle door wide open, as the half second it would have taken to open it would likely have made all the difference. As it was, most of the chardonnay and accompanying bile made it down the toilet bowl.

Before leaving the restroom, she obsessively checked her shoes and clothes for signs of splatters—nice—and, although the worst of the queasiness had been left behind in the cubicle, it had been replaced by a little dizziness and a growing headache around her temples. Maya made her excuses from as far away as possible without having to shout, sure that she was giving off the stench of vomit, then almost ran for the door to thwart the efforts of two colleagues who moved forward for the customary goodbye peck on the cheek. Sure that everyone would be remembering the way she had been knocking those glasses of wine back, Maya headed out and took a short cab ride back to her place.

The cab driver was mercifully not a chatty one, and soon she was being greeted by Vittor, the dapper-looking sixty-something Maltese concierge of small stature and build. Dressed in a black, double-breasted coat and tie, he added a certain character to the otherwise soulless modern building that was her apartment block.

"Wait, Miss Maya," he called as she tried to hurry past, "you have this in your cubbyhole." Maya stopped and crossed to the desk where Vittor held out that day's copy of *India West* to her.

～

Veer let himself into the apartment two hours after leaving his parents' home in a thunderous rage.

Come to the apartment, Maya had texted. I need you.

Are you ok? Veer had messaged back.

Just come. I'll say when you get here.

As Veer walked through the door of Maya's apartment—their apartment, really, since Veer had moved in six months ago—he was met as usual by a large piece of modern art, hung above a crimson velvet seat in the hallway. The painting looked to Veer as if some devious person had spent half an hour flicking several paintbrushes at a canvas and then slapped a $2,000 price tag on it.

Veer was supposed to be the artist in the relationship, but Maya seemed to get a lot about art that he didn't see.

Maya had once asked Veer whether he felt like he had to be the talented one in any relationship, whether—intentionally, or otherwise—he looked for lovers who didn't have his artistic flair. He had been angry with her for about two days after, perhaps angrier with her than he had been at any other point in their relationship. How could she accuse him of being so shallow? And then, grudgingly, he had come to acknowledge that Maya was 100 percent right; the space occupied by the creative person in any given room had to be his space. He needed the mystique, the certain sort of respect that such a status afforded. He hated that particular little truth, but there it was.

Maya wasn't in the lounge, although there was a newspaper on the ottoman—that same stupid *India West* newspaper that his parents read . . .

Shit!

It was laid open on the second and third pages. Dammit. He was such a self-obsessed idiot; he should have realized that Maya would have read the article his mother had been reading, too. Veer peeked into the little kitchen but found it empty, save for half a glass of water on the counter.

"Maya?" he called out. "Sugar?" On one of the many occasions that everyone else's opinion about their respective ages came up, Veer had teased Maya, calling her his sugar mommy. It had kind of stuck.

A nervous feeling crept over him like a bundle of firecrackers was pushing its way into his stomach. He doubled back and headed into the other hallway, which had the main bedroom at the end. The half-empty glass in the kitchen came back to him, and horrible, stupid thoughts began to race through his head. "Maya?" Veer called again, his naturally melodic voice catching in his throat.

His heart started thumping in alarm when he saw the suitcase out on the bed. Where was Maya? The door to the balcony was open, but he couldn't see her out there. That stupid fear gripped him again, horrible thoughts that at once terrified and shamed him.

He thought of how he understood Maya better than she realized. He knew she liked her legs, her breasts, but that she wouldn't wear sleeveless dresses because she thought her upper arms were "so rolypoly." He knew she slept on her stomach, but that she liked to sit on the sofa with her legs curled up when they watched a movie because she was afraid of spiders running across the floor in the dark.

Veer jumped, suddenly aware of a presence behind him. Maya was standing in the entrance to the en suite bathroom, something small and white in her hand. She looked . . . well . . . disheveled, which was unusual for Maya, who, even in her casual jeans and T-shirt, always looked put together.

"You okay?" Veer asked. "You're home early."

"Got sick at lunch," Maya replied. She wasn't looking him in the eye.

"I saw . . ."—Veer's eyes flicked across to the partially packed suitcase—"the paper."

Maya took an unsteady step toward him. "Let's go," she said.

He closed the distance, looking down for the thing she had been holding, but that hand was now behind her back. "Where?" he asked.

Maya put her other hand up to his face, though it restrained him as much as it caressed as he tried to lean in. "I wouldn't," she said, "I think I've still got sick breath." There was something in the tone of her voice, in the way she held herself, that made Maya feel far away from him at that moment. "Paradise," she said in response to his question.

Veer was confused, so he went on instinct and ostentatiously batted his eyelashes at her and said, in his cheesiest voice, "Paradise is where you are, baby."

A small, sad smile reached Maya's lips, though not her eyes. "No, the town of Paradise, dumbass. In the foothills of the Sierra Nevada mountains."

Veer grinned and opened his mouth to make another wisecrack, but Maya slapped his cheek. It was a light slap, but it shocked him into silence. "I'm serious," she said. "Tim has a home there that he sometimes uses on the weekends. I just spoke to him, and he says it's ours for a couple of months, at least. We could just . . . get away from everyone and everything."

Veer looked down at the suitcase again. There was something about this collusion with her boss that annoyed him. "I don't think we should run from this. You're not responsible for your brother's mistakes, and no one has any right to tell us what we can do with our lives and our love. Not your parents, not my parents, not any of their friends or goddamn social circle. Besides, won't it just look like admitting we're wrong?" He shoved his hands into his jeans and frowned.

Maya took a step back from Veer, her shoulders dropping. "I don't care anymore."

"And you've got your work, and I've got gigs coming up."

She brought her hand out from behind her back and thrust it toward Veer. A white piece of plastic with a small window in it containing a blue cross. "And I have your baby inside me."

Chapter 11

Maya loosened her seat belt and turned slightly sideways to face the driver's seat of her Tesla Model S as they emerged on the Oakland side of the Bay. Veer had insisted on driving as if being pregnant suddenly made Maya incapable of doing so. It would have been offensive if it hadn't been so darn cute.

Veer glanced over and she smiled at him. All his opposition, his caution, had melted at the sight of the pregnancy test in her hand. She didn't think that anyone could have been more thrilled at the thought of fatherhood. "Yes," he had said as he held her, "let's start a life away from all of them, from all of this bullshit."

"This feels so good!" she now cried out, causing Veer to jump a little at the wheel. "This morning we were San Francisco residents, and that was all we were going to be."

They were approaching the split between the freeways, which would send them north along the coast and ultimately up toward Sacramento, and deeper still into wildfire country. "And now a new home, maybe a new life," Veer said. He winked at her, lines deepening on either side of his brown eyes with their ridiculously long eyelashes.

Okay, they were getting carried away, but why the hell not? "Even though I'm going to be working . . . remotely, I feel like all this weight has just left me," Maya said.

Veer reached over and touched her stomach. "Well, it's about to come right back on, I'm afraid."

Maya laughed and gave him a playful punch in the arm. "You'd better be nice to me when I start swelling up. Seriously, though," she said with a sigh, "it's so good not to give a damn about any of them for once. Not your mother, not my mother, not . . . Turn the car!"

"Huh?" Veer said, still in the middle of nodding and agreeing with her.

"Turn the car," she screamed. "Take MacArthur Freeway!"

"But—"

"Do it!"

Veer did as he was told, negotiating the sudden change of lanes admirably, given the short notice and near hysterics of his passenger. "What's the matter?" he asked loudly over an enraged chorus of horns behind them. "That'll add twenty or thirty minutes to the journey."

"More than that," Maya said, trying to look apologetic and failing. "I've got to see Sameer before I go. At Santa Rita Jail."

Veer nodded slowly.

Maya took a deep breath and said carefully, "And Kookie Aunty. The last time I saw her was last year."

Veer clutched the steering wheel tightly and looked unimpressed.

"What?" Maya said. "I haven't seen her since she arrived, what with work and everything else. I can't move away and not see her. Anita Aunty, too. It'll be a quick visit. I promise," she said in a rush of words.

"I don't know why you all make such a fuss about that crazy old woman."

"Veer!"

"I'm kidding," he added quickly, "although I still don't agree with you." He shrugged impatiently. "You realize that you can't say anything to her, and especially not to Anita or Chintu Uncle, or even Selena if she's there."

Maya frowned at him.

"In fact, are you sure it's a good idea at all? If either of our mothers ever discover we were there just before we fled the city, they'll . . . Well, it'll probably involve some sort of public flogging for Anita." Veer gripped the steering wheel with two fists, a frown twisting his mouth.

He had a point.

Maya turned to look out the window as the suburbs slid by below them, her chin in one hand. She let out a long sigh and spoke. "Is it right to be leaving with my brother just sentenced to jail for the next twelve years?"

Veer didn't reply for a moment. When he finally drew in a breath to say something, Maya—still gazing out the window at the fat fluffy clouds that lay on the Californian blue sky like globs of whipped cream—cut him off.

"You probably mostly think of Sameer as my useless brother who never turns up when he's supposed to and barely manages to hold down a job. He wasn't always that way, you know."

"No one's always that way, Maya," Veer replied, biting his lip at the reproach he could hear in his voice.

"He was a really funny teenager," Maya continued as if she hadn't heard Veer's comment. It was an easy thing for an only child with a billionaire dad to make judgments about the life choices of the poorer, averagely dysfunctional majority. "He used to make me laugh by mimicking Mom." She chuckled sadly. "He was so good at that. One time he did this impression of Mom where she had fallen asleep during a Mindful Meditation class, waking up to discover that everyone else had experienced flashes of wisdom and were flushed with feelings of serenity, while she'd snoozed and drooled. He had me crying with laughter doing that. And he always smiled. It was, like, his default expression. A cheeky little smile."

Maya turned back to Veer. "There are seven years between us, but when he got to fourteen, fifteen maybe, he'd started to grow up a bit more, to become his own person. I was already away at college, but it was always so good whenever I came back. He wasn't just an annoying little shit anymore."

Maya cast her mind back and remembered a roadside restaurant . . . dammit, she couldn't even remember where it was, not even the name, just that it had been on the way back from Limantour Beach, about a one-and-a-half-hour drive up the coast. The trip had been Goldie's idea—that being the first long weekend of the summer, they would have a day out together, like a proper family. Goldie had been in an ebullient mood, and even the jaded twenty-year-old Maya had to admit that her father's good humor could be infectious at times.

Goldie and Lena had both been surprised at the number of cars parked at the entrance to the remote spot at this time of year—May being typically cool and blustery—until they wandered toward the northern edge of the beach and realized with horror that it was a popular area for nude sunbathing.

Thirteen-year-old Sameer led the way; then he came back red-faced and grinning. "They're naked!" he shouted in a hoarse whisper.

"Stop looking!" Lena had raged at both father and son, who had ogled at the dozens of bare bodies—some of whom had given them dirty looks, snatching up towels and bits of clothing, while others had simply ignored them—and Maya had dragged Sameer away. The Sharma family had hurried back to the Mercedes-Benz that Maya's mother so hated, and that Goldie had wasted so much of the family's money on, according to Lena.

Maybe because she wanted to end the day on a happier note, Lena had made Goldie stop at a roadside diner on the way home—a rarity for a culinary control freak. Maya had seen the glint in her teenage brother's eye while he pretended to study the menu as the waitress arrived.

"I know what I want," Sameer said quickly as the waitress took out her notebook, cutting in front of Goldie, who always ordered first. "I'd like the burger with no dressing, please," he said, throwing emphasis on certain words. "Skin-ny fries, please. Lots and lots of skin. And a side of naked slaw. I want it totally naked, okay? As naked as you can get."

There was shocked silence around the table, the moment seeming to hang precipitously before the whole family burst into hilarious laughter, leaving the waitress at first confused and then increasingly irritated.

Maya was smiling at the memory, but as Veer glanced across at her, the smile fell.

"Then Mom and Dad broke up, and he went to live with Dad, and . . . that messed up our relationship." She turned and rested her forehead on the cold glass of the window, feeling the need to hide the single tear that was beginning to mark a path down her cheek. "I'm not sure I've really seen him smile since then."

Veer leaned over and squeezed Maya's hand tightly.

Maya took a shaky breath and said in a low voice, "Veer, I still want to see Kookie Aunty after I visit Sameer."

"Go see Sameer first," he said. "Then, I'll drop you at Anita's, and maybe it would be better if it was just you that went in to meet Kookie? At least then only one of our parents can call for the public flogging." He tapped the battery indicator on the dashboard. "We're a little marginal on battery, so I'll go and find somewhere to plug in for half an hour."

～

The Santa Rita Jail where Sameer was being held pending a transfer to somewhere more permanent was humming with activity when Maya arrived. Thank goodness it was still visiting hours; otherwise, she would've had to come back the next day. She was shuttled through various checkpoints and patted down by a female officer before being led to a dismal-looking waiting area. A dozen or more plastic chairs were bolted to the floor, and a flat-screen television was mounted on brackets in a corner near the ceiling. The air was sticky, and the floor felt grimy under Maya's sandals.

It was shocking to see her little brother in the garish fluorescent light. Her head was still half picturing him as a smiling, acned boy when she saw the guard walking a disheveled, orange-jump-suited man with ankle shackles and handcuffs into the visiting area.

It took Sameer some time to spot his sister where she sat waiting at a table, and when he did, his eyes went wide.

"I didn't expect you. Come to gloat, did you?" Sameer said as he sat down opposite her, his voice unexpectedly gravelly, like prison had already forced an extra Y chromosome or two upon him.

The words were harsh, accusatory, but he didn't look at her as he said them; instead he fidgeted with the zipper on his jumpsuit.

"Why would you say that?" Maya hissed back, his words cutting her like a blade of ice. "Why would you think that is how I feel? You're my little brother. We were . . ."

Sameer looked up, met her eyes. "We were what?"

"Close once," Maya mumbled, the words feeling like a lie as she spoke them. The difference in their ages lay between them like a chasm; she wondered if those years would ever operate between them as a bridge.

Sameer coughed out a bitter laugh. "I must have missed that." He was now running the zipper of his jumpsuit up and down in short frantic spurts.

Maya gathered herself, drew in a breath, and squared her shoulders—prepared to say what she had come to say. "I'm leaving San Francisco," she said, "with Veer. We're heading upstate and getting away from . . . well, everything, I guess. Everyone. I can't pretend to understand how you must be feeling . . . the accident, Ruchi." Without giving herself a chance to think, Maya leaned forward and laid a hand on Sameer's forearm. "I just . . . I wanted to see you before I go. You know, in case it's a while until I see you again."

Maya saw Sameer's surprise and . . . something else. Envy, perhaps? She realized belatedly that *heading upstate* was not the best choice of words and meant a whole different thing for him now.

"I'm not the only black sheep, then," Sameer said, pulling away his arm. "I half thought they might leave you alone, seeing as I've already done just about the shittiest thing a child can do to their parents, so I didn't think you and Veer would seem so bad after that. Mom's even managed to drive the favorite child away, huh?"

"Favorite child?" Maya repeated back.

"You always were her favorite," Sameer said, "even before I went with Dad."

Maya shrugged. "If I was, then that was because she wanted to make me into her perfect Indian-daughter image." In her mind's eye, Maya could see her mom berating her because she thought her skirt was too short to wear to school. Rather than fight her mom, it had been easier to wear the longer skirt, then dive into the restroom as soon as she arrived at her junior high school and roll up the skirt to show off her tanned legs. So, too, with her mom's rule about "no makeup until you get to college." Maya would leave the house garden-fresh, no makeup, hair swirled into a topknot and pinned with a lacquered black barrette. Once inside the girls' restroom, she'd let her hair down and emerge with a full face of expertly applied makeup, lips moist and shining with red lip gloss. "She would say to me, 'Just get married to a suitable boy, then you can do whatever you want.' And by *suitable* boy she meant an arranged match with an Indian man of her choosing. You don't know how hard I've worked to carve out a life that was my own." Maya's voice rose with the last words, trembled slightly, and Sameer looked nervously left, then to his right, but no one paying them any attention. He spoke his next words in a deliberately hushed tone.

"You should get out of the city," he said. "Get away from here. Leave the whole fucking lot of them behind and never look back."

∼

"Listen, Maya, did I ever tell you the story of when Anita transferred from Lady Irwin College to St. Stephen's at Delhi University?"

Anita spilled the tea that she was in the middle of pouring for Maya, veering suddenly sideways so that a great pool of the hot beverage started to spread across the antique coffee table. They were sitting on Victorian-style, high-backed armchairs that were arranged in a rigid circle around the table.

"Anita, what are you doing?" Kookie exclaimed. "This table was your father's mother's table. It's an heirloom!"

Anita's eyes slid away, and she put the teapot back down on the serving tray. "I'll get a cloth."

"I'm sorry again for intruding unannounced," Maya said as Anita returned. "You should not have to be serving me tea when you have just come home from work."

"Nonsense, Maya," Kookie said, reaching forward to clasp Maya's hand for at least the sixth time since she had arrived. "It is so good to be seeing you."

"I had meant to come before, but . . ."

"I know, I know," Kookie interrupted. "You are a working girl."

Behind Kookie, Anita had to cover her mouth as she mopped up the tea. Maya couldn't suppress a small smile but at least stopped it from becoming a laugh. Kookie carried on, oblivious, as always, to her faux pas. "You modern, successful women are an inspiration to all of us. We older ones must be provoking you to go and make your mark, so work must be coming first, even more so for a woman than for a man."

"And it doesn't take much to pull an Indian woman's achievements down," Maya said with a glance up to Anita, who had finished mopping up and was pouring Maya's tea again. Anita gave her a sympathetic look as though she totally understood.

"This is true," Kookie said, nodding sagely. Then: "Now, what was I talking about?"

Anita stood up, having finished pouring. Her eyes went wide, and she shook her head vigorously at Maya, her diamond nose pin glinting once, twice, three times in the light as she did so. This time, Maya couldn't suppress her laugh. Kookie looked confused but chuckled along, anyway.

"Weren't you congratulating Maya on her engagement?" Anita suggested, thinking on her feet. Despite herself, Maya cringed.

"Ah, yes," Kookie said, even though the subject hadn't come up once since Maya had been there. She looked quizzically at Maya. "Who is he again?"

"Veer," Maya said. "Veer Kapoor."

Kookie brightened at the mention of the Kapoor name. "Harry and Pinky's boy?"

"Yes," Anita confirmed as she made her way back to the love seat and sat down next to Kookie. "Although he's not been a boy for a long time." Maya appreciated Anita's efforts.

Kookie nodded. "Good match, Maya. And you know the family, never a bad thing if you need to . . . hold him to account for anything."

"No worries on that one, Aunty," Maya said. "He's about the kindest man I've ever known."

"Oh, they all are, to begin with"—Kookie sniggered—"until they are having you where they want you."

"Mother!" Anita chastised, though Maya just chuckled.

"No, really, Aunty, I'm not sure my Veer could be mean if he tried. Funny, stupid, sarcastic, maybe infuriating—but never mean."

Kookie leaned forward in her chair, hungry for detail. "So, I know how you are knowing each other, but how did it . . . ?"

"At a party," Maya confessed. She had a faraway look in her eyes as if peering down the misty corridors of memory to find the exact point in time. "Oh . . . almost eighteen months ago now."

Kookie sat back in her seat, hands clasped together in anticipation. "Oh, a party. This is sounding exciting already."

"I was there, thinking to myself, 'I'm too old for parties.'"

"Nonsense," Kookie said. "The older we get, the more we are needing of a good party to cheer us up. Young people have all of the health and all of the beauty. Why are they needing parties to make them happy, too? Now, do the needful and tell an old woman all about falling in love."

"I had just been through a big breakup," Maya began. She omitted the word *divorce*, although its presence still hung there like a cloud on a still day as she fumbled for her next words. Anita knew, Kookie may well have known, yet there was something instinctive inside—having grown up believing marriage was sacred and quintessential to an Indian woman's well-being—that she couldn't bring the word to her lips, even though it had been a young, foolish, and mercifully brief coupling that she felt only mildly responsible for. "My . . . ex was the perfect match, or so everyone kept telling me, until I believed it myself and was ready to put my qualifications—my new degree—aside and be a wife to him. Five years my senior and a doctor, no less. Our astrological charts even matched."

Kookie inclined her head sagely at the last part, then frowned. "What was going wrong?"

"He had a temper," Maya answered, her voice determinedly casual. "He knew he did, too, but found it shameful to look for help. Heck, he even brought out the worst in me, as well. The arguments we used to have. Perhaps I would have gotten out earlier if I hadn't been so young, if I had understood that these things only ever get worse, never better." Maya pinched the bridge of her nose like she was in pain.

"The day he raised his hand as if to strike me was the very same day I left him." Maya swallowed hard. "That's the one small comfort I can take. I kicked him in the groin and hightailed it out of there." Her lips quirked into a smile, even though the back of her throat felt clogged with phlegm.

"Maya." Anita jerked back, surprised. "I'm sorry. I never knew that part of it," she gasped.

Maya's mind flashed to another moment just after all this had happened. A kick in the groin and a dramatic exit are never the final act, not where marriage is concerned. The divorce, the legal side, dragged the final entrails of the relationship out in a long, painful act that ensured that everyone got a good look at the rotten insides.

Maya had started working with Tim, kick-starting her career like a two-fingered salute to her estranged husband and the society that would have seen her beholden to him, there to produce children and keep house. Her ex had waited just long enough, it seemed, to lay claim to her new earnings by way of support. She had been distraught, not so much because she begrudged the money—although she *really did* begrudge the money—but because it somehow kept them bound together when all she wanted was to fly free of him.

He was a *doctor*, for crying out loud. It was ridiculous, and she had forgone any attempt to pursue him financially precisely because she only wanted to be rid of him. Panic had gripped Maya, and she had finally come undone on the sofa in her mother's lounge, the air filled with the sharp smell of sizzling cloves and garam masala bubbling away in the kitchen.

"I'll never be rid of him," she had wailed.

"Think of it as a donation," Lena had said to her soothingly, stroking her gently on the back. "I send money to a blind girls' school in rural India every month, but I never notice it go, and it never stands out to me on my monthly statement, but I feel better for knowing that I do it."

"I won't," Maya had grumbled sullenly, sniffing back her runny nose.

"You feel better for not being with him," Lena reasoned. "Isn't it worth it?"

"It's my keeping-the-asshole-at-bay fund," Maya muttered, although the thought made her grin a little.

"Your charity for deadbeats," Lena had tried, joining in. It was an awkward effort, but Maya had appreciated it. In fact, she had laughed and coughed out her last few sobs all at once, falling into her mother's enfolding arms. Lena was a good hugger.

Maya now looked down at her clenched hands, the memory bringing with it a wave of doubt about everything that she and Veer were about to do. Her mother could be so . . . un-Indian at certain moments, yet at other times she worked twice as hard as anyone else to fit in, and if her children conflicted with that, then woe betide them.

"So, I was not in the best frame of mind to be attending a party," Maya now went on, smiling her gratitude to Anita, "but I had finally given in to all those people telling me I had to, you know, 'get back out there.' I think I only went to make them all shut up." Maya touched her lips with a finger, her expression dreamy as if she had drifted into her past.

"It was an enormous penthouse apartment, not so far from where I live now. A friend of Tim's, I think. That's my boss. It was a sort of a half duplex, where the lounge reaches up to two stories and a balcony looks down from where the bedrooms are. And there was this giant-size wooden sundeck and an infinity pool."

Kookie nodded along, looking like she wished that she could have been at the party, too.

"Everyone had been encouraged to bring swimwear, although I hadn't gotten the message, and I wasn't much in the mood to be hanging out in some stranger's apartment half-naked, anyhow."

Anita nodded her agreement; Kookie looked a little disappointed.

"I hadn't even been there an hour, and I was already making plans to leave. I've . . ." Maya looked bashful for a moment but pressed on after a glance at the two older women. "I've always been proud of my body, I've always worn what I've wanted to wear, even if my mom often hasn't approved."

Kookie shrugged supportively, and Anita gave her mother a sideways glance.

"But, for the first time, I felt . . . frumpy. Like I didn't belong in the clothes I was in. I was looking at these younger women—many of them prancing around in bikinis—and the men, too."

"In bikinis?" Kookie asked, appearing genuinely confused.

Maya laughed. "No, I mean a lot of the men were in swimwear, and they were . . . comfortable with themselves and looked like they belonged there. And me, I was single again at thirty-four and . . ."

The room was still as the other two women waited for Maya to continue, held by the sadness that had just spread across the glassy surface of her dark-brown eyes like ink through water.

"And then I heard an acoustic guitar playing. I had been halfway to the door, thinking that I should at least find Tim and tell him that I was going, but so desperate to escape without having to make excuses or explain myself, to run home and eat an entire carton of Ben & Jerry's."

Anita chuckled, while Kookie looked a little baffled.

"The guitar was coming from outside, by the pool, an area I had been avoiding for most of the time I had been there." Maya paused and sipped her tea; Kookie's irritation at the delay was visible.

"I've never been very musical, but do you know how sometimes a combination of—I don't know . . . tone and melody, I guess—just stops you from doing whatever you're doing? How music can interrupt everything else?"

Mother and daughter nodded.

"I had to stop. I had to go back and see. And there he was, Veer Kapoor. I don't know how I hadn't seen him before then. I mean, it was a big place, but it was still just an apartment, and somehow Veer had arrived and set up outside with a stool, a guitar, and a microphone, and

I had missed all of this. I recognized him straightaway, even though it must have been years since we had been in the same room."

"Kindly stop, Maya, *beti*," Kookie interrupted. "I must be asking, was Veer Kapoor the entertainment?"

Maya laughed. "Yes, basically. I think the guy who was throwing the party had seen him play a few weeks before. Sought him out. Veer's in a band, but he probably plays more gigs on his own."

"For money?" Kookie asked, incredulous.

"I think it's good he wants to work, even if he doesn't need to," Anita put in quickly. Maya thought this, too, although she had since come to understand that his "income" from gigging was heavily supplemented by leaning on the credit card that his father paid off at the end of every month.

"But . . ."

While Kookie was struggling for comprehension, Maya went on. "I watched him for a few songs, but I stayed inside where he couldn't see me. There was something familiar in the way he played, even though he was only playing cover songs. It was like his guitar style and his singing had his own character about it." Maya shrugged. "I suppose that's not such a strange thing. Like I said, I'm no musician." Maya cocked her head to one side as if she was listening to something.

"I had never thought of him as more than Harry and Pinky's son. Nice enough—I mean, I had always liked him—but just some rich boy who was going to lead a rich boy's life where no particular skills were needed. It was weird that he should be singing and playing a guitar and . . . that I should love it so much."

Maya held both palms upward in a very Indian way. "But I'm no stupid girl, not infatuated like I could see so many of those pretty young things splashing flirtatiously around in the pool were. And, although I thought maybe I should go over and say hello, I still wanted to be out of that place and away from those people."

"So you left?" Kookie asked, sounding almost enraged.

"Yes," Maya said. "I left and took the elevator down and went to look for a cab or call an Uber."

Kookie sat back, looking like she felt cheated. Even Anita did the same.

"And I had just hailed one when a voice called my name from the building's entrance. It was Veer."

Maya's audience almost squealed with excitement.

"He was out of breath, like he had run down from the top of this very tall apartment block, which he had. 'Maya Sharma,' he called after me. 'I thought it was you.' I remember feeling a little guilty then, like maybe I should have stayed and said hello to him after all, even though we hadn't seen each other since we were younger. 'Hi, Veer,' I said, probably sounding every bit as tired as I felt. I indicated the building behind him and said, 'Aren't you supposed to be playing up there?'

"He walked up to me, and now that I was seeing him close up, sweating and panting, I realized that he had definitely matured since the last time I saw him.

"'I wanted to say hi,' he said. I laughed and pointed up to the top of the building that we stood outside of. 'Did you really just run all the way down here to do that?' I asked.

"I remember how he laughed when he realized how absurd it sounded. But then he answered, and he sounded as if he was surprised to be saying it, 'Yes. Yes, I did.'"

Anita and Kookie were both leaning forward in their seats. "That's romantic," Anita said.

Kookie glanced over at her daughter and then back to Maya, "So, you said he was all sweaty? I am thinking that this is the important detail here."

Maya laughed and continued. "Yeah, we just sort of stood there looking at each other until the cab driver broke the spell by shouting out to me—something along the lines of 'Are you getting in this car, or what?' It shook me out of the moment, and I reflexively moved to get into the cab until Veer reached out toward me, even though he was still a few feet away, and said, 'Hey, you want to take a walk with me?'"

Kookie shook her head and, misty eyed, repeated in her stilted accent: "Hey, you want to take a walk with me?"

"I shook my head at first," Maya said. "Told him I was just going to head home. Said it was one of those nights, you know, where I'm just feeling all a bit too old for it. He was insistent, though, said something about cheering up people who were having a bad day being a talent of his."

"So, you went with him?" Kookie asked.

"I went with him," Maya agreed. "And we ended up down near the water in Rincon Park, talking beneath Cupid's Span."

Anita laughed, her nervous twitch gone, and Maya nodded at her in agreement. "Cheesy, I know."

"Not at all," Anita said. "I like it." She turned to her mother to clear up the uncertainty on the old woman's face. "There's this sculpture of a bow and arrow in this park next to San Francisco Bay, it's called Cupid's Span. You know, after the old god of love."

"And what did you talk about?" Kookie asked.

"Now, Mother," Anita chided. "Let poor Maya have some secrets."

"Well, I'll tell you something he said that night that made me feel a whole lot better," Maya answered, her expression a little distant. "I was telling him about all those women in bikinis at the party—pretty young things with tight skin and all that time ahead of them. I thought I might be insulting him, as he wasn't so much older than some of them."

Maya looked at the other two women, a glassy sheen appearing over her eyes. "I'm twelve years older than him, but sometimes I swear his soul is much older than mine is. He said to me something that's never going to leave me, whatever happens between us. He told me that beauty is something you grow into and not out of."

~

With apologies, Kookie went off for a nap just before Maya left. It seemed that Maya's story had worn her out.

"I know that she seems good most of the time," Anita said to Maya once Kookie was safely off in her room. "But she is definitely at her best when company is around, and you're one of her favorite people." Maya flushed, her smile renewing itself, "As she is mine."

"At least we managed to avoid the story about Lady Irwin and St. Stephen's," Anita said and rolled her eyes.

Maya gave her a quizzical look.

"Never mind," Anita said hurriedly.

"I really enjoyed telling you both that story about when Veer and I reconnected," Maya said. "I've never been able to tell anyone that story before."

Anita hugged her as if picking up on the underlying sadness beneath the statement. To her own surprise, Maya hugged her back so hard that the slight Anita gasped. When they came apart, Maya felt tears streaming down her face.

"Oh, my dear," Anita said, "it'll be all right, you'll see. They will come around eventually." Anita was probably the world's worst liar, and they both knew it.

But Maya went along with it, nodding her head as she looked at the floor. "I know, Aunty, I know."

Chapter 12

By the time he entered his midteens, Sameer had a fair idea of what living with his father was going to look like. Sometimes he felt like an island, with no one to turn to. Other times he felt worthless, belonging to no one.

"You wanna put me one of those bagels in, too?" Tracy said, eyeing sixteen-year-old Sameer with her usual level of disdain from where she leaned against the kitchen doorframe. Her short denim skirt, barely eight-inch-wide tube top and sequin-speckled leather jacket looked ridiculous at seven in the morning. In Sameer's opinion, the outfit had looked ridiculous last night, too, but this effect was made all the worse by the smeared remains of last night's makeup—the rest of which was most likely still on Goldie's pillow.

"Do it yourself," he answered, barging past her. Tracy was already smoking a cigarette—she seemed to have breakfast covered.

"You little shit," she hissed after him.

Sameer turned back to face his father's latest squeeze. "You little slut," he retorted, then belatedly noticed Goldie standing in the doorway to his bedroom.

Tracy turned her glare from Sameer to Goldie. "You wanna teach this one some manners?" she said and stormed out of the apartment. As soon as the door slammed shut behind her, Goldie crossed the hall, obviously furious.

"How dare you talk to her like that, you little runt. You have no respect." He pulled back his hand as if to slap Sameer, but appeared to change his mind at the last moment and let it hang there for a few seconds before it fell to his side. He heaved an exhausted sigh and looked heavenward as if to seek divine guidance in the momentous burden of having to be the father of a sixteen-year-old boy.

"But she treats me like a slave," Sameer whined, "and she doesn't even live here." He was having breakfast on the mottled Formica kitchen table on which sat a greasy bag of day-old bagels and a box of cornflakes.

"Don't you talk back to me!" Goldie hollered. After a moment he carried on, his tone indignant. "I've been seeing Tracy for two months now."

"Well done," Sameer said. "That's more than twice as long as the last one."

This time the slap made contact. It wasn't the first time that Goldie had slapped Sameer in the last year and a half since the boy had come to live with him, but this one had more force than any of the previous. Perhaps, in some messed-up way, it was because Goldie saw him as a man now, more able to take a hard slap. The physical truth was just about the opposite, however, as Sameer was a late bloomer and among the smallest of the boys in his grade at school.

"You've no respect for me, either, boy. What am I to do with you?"

Sameer didn't know why he had said what he said. If there was one thing he respected about his father more than anything else, it was his ability to snare almost any woman he set his sights on. Granted, the women that Goldie set his sights on were all of a similar type—blonde, with short skirts and a lot of makeup.

Sameer stared listlessly into his bowl of congealing cereal. His spoon had clattered to the dingy brown linoleum floor when Goldie struck him. He picked it up and wiped it on his sweater.

Sameer's respect for his father's conquests came mostly from the fact that he still had yet to get so much as a kiss from a girl himself.

This was another way in which he seemed to lag behind his classmates. Of course, as far as Goldie was concerned, his only son had no such trouble with the ladies. Sameer couldn't even begin to imagine the look on his father's face if Goldie ever realized that he had never even gotten to first base with a girl. "Are you a gay, boy?" would likely be the first words to come out of his mouth. Not that Sameer had any problem with anyone's sexual orientation, but he knew his Dad well.

"I'll tell you what, boy," Goldie said. "You can walk yourself to school today. Maybe that will teach you some manners."

Sameer let out a groan. It was a long way to walk to school. He grimaced, waiting for another slap or rebuke about his attitude, but this time Goldie only glared. "Dad," Sameer said carefully, "it's the first day of the spring semester, and I'll be late if I have to walk."

"Should have thought about that, shouldn't you?" Goldie said, seemingly satisfied with this consequence.

It really was a long walk to school, and Sameer was a sweaty mess when he got there. Worse, the thought that kept bouncing from side to side in his mind was *Mom would never have made me walk*.

Lena was not past punishing her son for rudeness, but she would never have countenanced making him late for school, or having him wandering the streets at any time, especially when a passing cop might have picked him up for truancy.

In fact, he was so late that the doors were locked and one of the secretarial staff had to let him in. Mr. Partridge, the headmaster, caught Sameer as he hurried to his math class.

Wearing a leather-elbowed tweed jacket with brown loafers, Mr. Partridge had the air of someone who thought he should be running a prep school in New Hampshire, rather than a high school in one of San Francisco's less affluent areas. Before Sameer could explain himself, he was slapped with after-school detention. It was his first detention of any sort.

Sameer fretted about it the whole day, wondering how his father would react. Of course, he could point out that he had only been late and got detention because the bastard had refused to take him to school. However, there was no doubt that Goldie would consider such a comeback as insolence. Not for the first time since he had chosen to live with his father, Sameer wondered if he had made a rash and stupid decision.

As the bell rang for the end of school, Sameer's bottom lip quivered. He suddenly had a deep pang of wanting to speak to his mother. She always put on this fake, doggedly cheerful voice when she knew he was feeling low, as if she could bulldoze him into being happy—but he had only just spoken to her the night before last, so their weekly phone call was some way off. Of course, Lena had initially been on the phone almost every other night when Sameer had first left with his father. Sameer remembered the constant hounding from her being irritating, but now he thought about it, maybe it wasn't the hounding but instead Goldie's grumpiness about the ex-wife he couldn't stand always calling up that had made Sameer push his mother away. Eventually, they had agreed to just once a week. He could still hear how miserable his mother sounded on the other end of the line when they did talk.

It was a shame, because Sameer had the feeling that by the time he got home from his detention, he would be in dire need of some of his mother's particular brand of bulldozing.

Sameer slouched as he walked to the detention room, his slight frame curving forward, hands dug deep into his pockets, dwelling on how there was now a blemish on his otherwise spotless school record. Sameer Sharma had never once been held behind, or even so much as lost a little of his lunch break for any sort of punishment. He was a good student who took his work seriously—certainly a lot more seriously than many of his classmates—and he studied hard, mostly getting good results.

Now, however, he was one of the bad people.

~

The two sets of doors had become familiar by now. Two clangs followed by two thuds. His cuffed hands behind his back, Sameer took his seat in the cramped prisoner transport. Sometimes it was a large van, as it was today, and sometimes it was a bus. Sameer preferred the bus, as he could see out of it. He had thought that it would be the bus today, as today was the big ride to his new home. Today was the twelve-year ride.

There were seven other figures in the back of the van already, and Sameer found himself pushed uncomfortably close to a large, hard-eyed black man with a smooth bald head and a smartly trimmed beard. The man didn't look up as Sameer came in and sat down, yet, Sameer felt like he might be upsetting him just by sitting there. He had an odor of unwashed clothes and a sour smell of sweat. Sameer's insides shook with cold and fear.

As the first of the cage doors clanged shut, Sameer looked up and caught the eye of a twenty-something white man almost opposite him. Like the man next to Sameer, he had a beard and no hair on top but was different in every other way. Sameer could see where the shaved hair was just starting to grow back, and the beard was red, long, wild, and tufted. Tattoos erupted out of the neckline of the man's top onto his chest and neck, a seemingly unplanned mishmash of a spiderweb design and what might have been Latin writing in a font that recalled the signage used by Nazi Germany.

The man fixed Sameer with a piercing stare.

Clang. The second door of the cage swung shut.

"Hey, Mustafa," the tattooed man said, "who'd you blow up then?"

"Quiet in there!" the corrections officer shouted as he slammed the first of the outer doors shut with a thud.

The man chuckled to himself and continued to look at Sameer, who turned away just a little too late. The last door thudded shut.

"Are you staring me out, Mustafa?" said the red-bearded, tattooed man. "Is that what you're doing? Are you a tough one?"

Sameer kept his eyes on the floor, and after a moment, the man's eyes must have slid across to the burly giant next to him.

"You got something to say to me, too?" the large black man next to Sameer said in a thick baritone voice. Apparently, the smaller tattooed man didn't, although Sameer didn't glance up to check what was going on.

The van had been driving for less than a minute when the rain began to fall, making the loudest noise Sameer had ever heard rain make on the top of a vehicle. It was even worse every time the van stopped—presumably at lights or a junction—like the roof was made of corrugated tin.

It was a short ride to his new home upstate, and soon he could hear gates opening and security shutters rolling up and back down again. The eight of them were paraded off the van, straight through a small door, and into a light-gray painted breeze-block corridor. There, security personnel waited to check them in. The stench of stale food mingled with the darker stench of sewage assailed Sameer's nostrils, slipping inside and down his throat.

Twelve fucking years of painted breeze-block rooms and stinking corridors.

Panic gripped him, filling him in a way it hadn't done since that first night and morning following his arrest. Somehow, the whole process of being charged and tried and sentenced had swept him along with it. Only now did the yawning span of time ahead of him truly become apparent.

Lena had been allowed to approach him as he left the courtroom following the sentencing—which had occurred ten days after the preliminary hearing. There was no interview room or visitors' space, just a row of bench seats on one side of a broad, marbled corridor—and, for once in her life, his mother had seemed short of something to say to him. "It'll be okay, son," she had said weakly, visibly cringing as she spoke the words.

At the time, he had taken some small, spiteful pleasure in her discomfort. *One thing you can't fix, you stupid cow of a woman.* Yes, even then he hadn't truly conceived the fullness of how screwed he was, so that scoring private points over his mother took precedence over panic.

Hold it in, you idiot, he thought to himself now, pinching the skin of his forearm painfully and concentrating as fully as he could on that. He was not a worldly-wise person—and not a natural criminal—yet Sameer knew enough to understand that losing it right now would be the worst possible start to his time in prison.

Sameer's mind went blank as the pain in his arm washed over him, making him yelp as he stumbled toward a door leading to a cell block. A long-suppressed memory began sneaking up on him then, trying to claim him, even though it was thirteen years in the past.

"Your first time in here?" the teacher had said as Sameer tried to find a seat. It wasn't that detention was full, but rather that there were no other students in the room, and Sameer was faced with an overabundance of seating choices.

"Why don't you come down and sit in front of me? It'll probably make things a bit easier."

Sameer hadn't seen the teacher before. He was younger than he had expected and wore beige slacks with sneakers. He had sandy hair, a freckled face, and small gray eyes.

Since Sameer didn't recognize him and had no previous experience for reference, he wondered if they got special teachers in for the job of after-school detention. With that thought, another small wave of panic washed over him—just the latest in a set of panic attacks that had been hitting him throughout the day, happening almost every time he remembered his detention and the fact that his life was, basically, ruined. Under the desk, he stretched out his left arm and used his right hand to pinch the skin on his forearm. He did it until it hurt, and that nervous feeling inside his belly receded just a little bit.

"I'm Mr. Barr," the teacher had said when Sameer arrived at the front of the classroom. "James Barr to my friends and family, but as you're a student, I'm afraid it's plain old 'Mr. Barr' to you." He winked at Sameer.

"I'm new to the school, and I don't believe we've met," he continued, glancing at a sheet in front of him. "Mr. . . . Sharma, is it?"

"Yessir," Sameer replied reflexively.

"Ah, so you're not in here for a lack of manners, at least," Mr. Barr joked.

"Tardiness," Sameer replied, gulping convulsively.

"Tardiness?" Mr. Barr asked, a discernible note of surprise in his tone. "A repeat offender?"

"No," Sameer replied. "My first time."

"Dammit!" Mr. Barr exclaimed, slapping his sheet of paper down on his desk. "So, they've got us both here wasting time for that crap— while the real criminals walk free, I'll bet."

Sameer couldn't help but give a cautious grin. Mr. Barr was likable, if a little odd. "I guess so, sir."

"Have you ever been in detention before . . ." Mr. Barr glanced down at his sheet again. "Sameer?"

Sameer shook his head, "No, sir."

"Well," Mr. Barr said, "don't worry. Your life's not over or anything. I believe there may even be a few ex-presidents who got detention once or twice."

Sameer smiled more openly this time, the knot that had been sitting in his stomach all day loosening slightly. "I'm not sure my dad will see it that way, not that he cares too much about what I'm doing."

"High expectations, huh?" the teacher asked.

"More like minimum inconvenience," Sameer answered, surprising himself both with his quickness and his honesty.

"Ah, well," Mr. Barr said as he took a seat. "You got homework to do?"

Sameer took his seat and began to open his bag. "I do, sir. Shall I just find something to work on?"

Mr. Barr looked at him for a moment. "Can do, if you want," he said. "I mean, I've got quite a few papers to mark, and I guess I should be getting on with that. Then again, seeing as they've got us both here against our will—and for a dumb reason to boot—it feels like doing work is a bit like letting them win. Wouldn't you say so?"

Sameer nodded slowly, a little unsure where the teacher was going with this.

Mr. Barr rummaged around in the desk in front of him and brought out a small box, holding it up for Sameer to see. "Do you play chess?" he asked.

Chapter 13

Veer sat on the sitting area floor, his sock-covered feet tucked under him in a yoga position. He bobbed his head in time with the music coming through the large pair of headphones and scribbled notes on a small-ruled notepad.

Taking the headphones off, Veer glanced at the cell phone that lay on the coffee table in front of him. *In a minute,* he thought to himself, before getting up and heading into the kitchen.

Veer made himself a kale-spinach-mango smoothie. He drank the smoothie, slowly. He washed up the glass and the smoothie maker, taking his time to make sure that they were properly dried before they went back in the cupboard. Eventually, he decided he could not put things off any longer and went back to grab his phone.

"Veer?" Pinky's voice sounded brittle on the other end of the line. Vulnerable. "Son?"

"Yes, it's me."

The crack in Pinky's voice quickly disappeared. "Are you okay? Where are you?"

"I'm fine, Mommy, we're fine."

"You . . . you left." Her tone was thick with accusation.

"We had to; it was too much," Veer said, his voice defensive.

"Too much for her?"

Veer did not answer, taken aback by the resentment in his mom's tone. Did his mother really blame Maya for taking her cherished son away from her? For God's sake, that was absurd. But that was what Maya had been trying to tell him, he realized. Those four words—*too much for her?*—acted like a lens on his brain, bringing into focus the rather obvious fact that Pinky Kapoor was always going to make a battleground of the space between herself and a prospective daughter-in-law. Even Maya . . . maybe especially Maya. He thought back to when he had first called to tell his parents he was proposing to Maya. His mother said she worried because of the age difference, and because Maya was a divorcée, but all he had heard was blah, blah, blah. It was making sense now—the blessing and curse of Pinky knowing Maya forever meant that she felt betrayed by Maya. Et tu, Brute?

Veer gripped the phone in the palm of his hand and tried to control his breathing.

Pinky took his silence as a warning and changed tack.

"Where have you been living?"

"Not now, Mommy." Veer still bristled but forced himself to relax. He could picture the expression of aggrieved anxiety etched theatrically on his mother's face.

"I can't know where my son is?"

"We're not so far; we just needed to get out of San Francisco for a while."

"Only for a while. You're coming back, yes?"

"I don't know," Veer snapped shortly.

"I haven't seen or heard from you in over two months. Your mother, who gave birth to you and raised you."

"You're hearing from me now." Veer's voice had taken on an edge, and its tone interrupted Pinky's flow.

"Are you well?" she asked after a few moments. "Are you eating okay?" Veer rolled his eyes; for an Indian mother, you could be eating better no matter how much you ate.

"We're fine. We have a nice place."

"But how do you afford it? You haven't used your credit card, and I know you haven't been making your music."

He hadn't used the credit card because they had access to the account and would know straightaway where he was making his purchases, and Veer knew they would check. The second question, though, that was more of a surprise. "You spoke to my bandmates?"

"One of them. The one with the tattoo on his neck. Your father was in business with his father, back before this music was ever a thing for you."

"Wow," Veer said, his voice acidic, "the network never fails, does it?"

"And I know her flat hasn't gone onto the real-estate market," Pinky continued, ignoring Veer's comment. In fact, it was almost as if she were trying to prove the lengths they had gone to.

"She does have a name, you know. You've known Maya all of her life," he said through clenched teeth.

"Which makes it even worse. Our families have been so close, we've always thought of Maya as your elder sister—not . . . not your paramour," Pinky said with an irritable clatter of crockery. She must be making chai for herself; his mother always claimed the brewing process was therapeutic for her.

"Makes what worse? That she makes me happy? That she loves me and I love her? And, I have never thought of her as a sister, never." Veer was shouting now.

"She'll probably never bear you a child—a good strong son to take forward your family name," Pinky retorted, her voice aquiver. "So old, and a career woman like that."

Veer was silent for several moments.

"I'm sorry, I'm sorry," said Pinky quickly, her voice quivering. "Please don't hang up, please don't disappear on me again."

A voice sounded quietly on Pinky's end. "Who is it, my dear?"

"It's Veer," she whispered, though Veer still heard her distinctly.

"Is he okay?" Veer heard his father ask. Even in the background and over the phone, Veer could hear the strain in it, the worry. It seemed so wrong, as Harry Kapoor never worried about anything. This cut him deeper than anything else that had been said during the phone call.

"I've got to go now," Veer said decisively, feeling his emotions pulling at the threads of control. "Just know that we're fine. We've got a place; we're managing for money. I'm working—"

"You're working?" Pinky interrupted, sounding far too shocked for Veer's liking.

"Busking, gigging, teaching," he said, the words falling into the cavernous silence of his mother's unspoken disapproval, her—albeit correct—assumption that these things brought in only a pittance. "And Maya's managing to work remotely, too." He hated that he felt the need to add that, that they could only be okay if Maya was bringing in money as well. "All of us, we're fine," he finished. He took a long slow breath from deep inside his chest, like blowing out a candle in slow motion.

"All of you?" Pinky questioned, and Veer realized what he had almost given away—the piece of information he and Maya had agreed that neither set of parents yet deserved to know. The whole thing had been easier when they discussed it, the two of them alone in the lounge as the hour crept toward midnight, egging each other on by remembering all the ways that their parents had been unfair toward them . . . cruel, even. Now, hearing his mother's voice, it seemed that they were now the cruel ones, that there was something almost spiteful in keeping the knowledge of a grandchild from his own mother and father, and from Lena and Manuel, too.

"I'll call again, okay?" he said crisply, then cut the line, feeling—as he always did after important conversations with his mother—a little like he had come off second best.

Maya woke up on the futon in the lounge to the sound of an Englishman's voice, which sounded at once well spoken and rather rude. It took her a few moments to realize that the TV was on, and then she remembered that she had been watching a TV movie, one of those guilty pleasure movies full of terrible actors and with a predictable plot that somehow still felt comforting and familiar, like a favorite blanket that was worn and disgusting and should just be thrown away.

She must have drifted off in the middle of it, and now there was an Englishman with craggy features and dark-blond hair in a restaurant kitchen, shouting at lots of terrified-looking junior cooks. Maya shifted her weight, alternating which leg she held out straight and which leg she curled under her body, trying her best to combine comfort and balance. No one had told her about how a developing baby could upset your center of gravity.

Veer's voice floated through from the sitting area next to the kitchen. It was probably what had woken her up. He was making that phone call to his mother. She could hear the annoyance in his voice, then a horrendous screeching sound, as Veer must have pushed his chair back across the floorboards.

Panic gripped Maya like an invisible fist punching the air from her lungs, while on the TV a short junior cook with round glasses lost his temper with the churlish Englishman and took off his cook's jacket, throwing it onto the floor and storming out of the kitchen. Was Pinky right now persuading her son of the foolishness of what they were doing? Veer could be a softie; it was one of his many endearing qualities, although it could also mean he was giving away their very private location to his mother right now. If anyone could afford to hire a bounty hunter or gang of mercenaries to come and forcibly extract their son, it was the Kapoors.

Geez, get a hold of yourself, Maya.

The doorbell rang and made Maya jump in her still half-asleep state, its trembling, serrated-edge sound the only sharp and unsettling noise in the chalet-in-the-woods home that they had made theirs since leaving the city. Checking her mouth for drool and quickly but ineffectually mussing her hair, Maya righted herself a little like a Weeble toy and went to answer the door.

"Sarah!" she exclaimed, carefully keeping the irritation from her voice. Sarah McKesson was a middle-aged retiree who lived with her husband, Derek, in the next house over. They were not quite "next door," being a few minutes' walk along a dusty track, but they were the closest neighbors Veer and Maya had.

Maya liked Sarah, but the woman did have the worst timing in the world. Indeed, one of the first few times she had called round to the house, Maya had been midorgasm. Since then, Maya had learned to at least close the blinds, something that had not been such a worry when she had lived on the forty-second floor of an apartment block overlooking San Francisco Bay.

"Honey, I didn't wake you, did I?" Sarah asked, holding a china teacup in her hand.

"No, no," Maya replied, unconsciously trying to rearrange her hair again.

"This isn't a come on," Sarah said with a brief eruption of laughter, reaching out to place a familiar touch on Maya's forearm with one hand, while holding up the teacup in the other, "but I've come over to borrow a cup of sugar." The woman had dyed-blonde hair that was short at the back and the sides but curled like a fluffy beehive on the top. Wearing tight jeans and a formfitting lime-green blouse, she reminded Maya of Peg Bundy, the iconic housewife from *Married with Children*.

Her hair jiggled about the top of her head as she laughed. "Derek won't do coffee with less than three sugars in it. I'm always telling him he's poisoning himself into an early grave."

"Sure." Maya smiled back. Sarah, as had been her way since day one, made to cross the threshold without invitation.

"I can't really invite you in," Maya added hurriedly. She leaned in and lowered her voice. "Veer's on the phone with his mother."

Sarah raised her eyebrows. Although Maya had not exactly furnished her with all the details about Pinky, her fifty-something neighbor had proved adept at reading between the lines from day one. "Oh."

Maya moved out onto the doorstep, quietly closing the door behind her. Tall fir trees loomed in every direction, doing much to hide an almost cloudless azure sky. "I know what she's like, Sarah," Maya said, her voice still hushed. "She's probably reeling off a list of gorgeous, desirable, twenty-somethings to him right now."

Sarah coughed out a small chuckle before remembering to look sympathetic.

"Of course, she's been trying that with Veer since well before we got together," Maya told her. "But, I mean . . . look at me, Sarah." She swept her arms downward across the small pouch of her belly that was clearly evident. "Those vacuous bimbos might start to look tempting."

"Nonsense," Sarah replied a little too loudly. "You're a beautiful flower . . . with another little flower inside you." The woman meant well, but her protestations did nothing to help. In fact, although the women were not in any way similar, seeing Sarah always made Maya miss her mother, reminding her that her child's grandmother was not yet even aware of their existence. There was something irreconcilable about hiding from their families and missing them all at the same time.

Maya sighed, exhaling a long, slow breath. "We're in a bubble here, Sarah. And we've been so lucky, my boss so understanding. I mean, he's let us have this place almost rent-free. But it's like limbo in some ways, and we'll have to face what's waiting for us back in San Francisco at some point."

"If it was up to me, you'd stay here with us forever," Sarah replied, with only a hint of *Stepford Wives* in the way that she said it. "You are much better conversation than Derek ever is."

Maya giggled, as always finding Sarah's company a tonic, even if she tended to groan a little inside when she first saw the woman heading up the front path. Derek, Sarah's husband, was a gruff—if kindhearted— man with a barbecue obsession. Maya had always assumed they were together under the opposites-attract rule.

The door popped open and Veer stood there, the phone call evidently finished. "Hey," he said, eyeing Sarah suspiciously, which made Maya flush guiltily. Veer did not enjoy Sarah's company as much as Maya did.

"Sugar," Sarah exclaimed, as if she were swapping the word for an ashamed expletive.

"She's come to borrow some," Maya put in quickly. She scrunched her face and looked up at Veer. "That was quick."

Veer gave Maya a noncommittal smile and a shrug, then turned to Sarah. "I'll get you some," he said, waving away the offered cup. Veer came back less than a minute later with a tiny ziplock bag full of sugar and the air of a man in a hurry to be rid of their neighbor.

"Didn't know you were a Gordon Ramsay fan," Veer said with a wry grin as Maya came back into the lounge and found the futon again, Sarah having left.

"Huh?"

Veer indicated the boorish, sandy-haired English chef, who was at that time shaking a plate of fish rather violently under some poor cook's nose. "The TV chef."

Maya shook her head. "Oh . . . no. I fell asleep. How was she?" she went on, unable to keep the edge from her voice.

"Oh, a completely changed person," Veer answered nonchalantly, taking a seat by her feet, then idly beginning to massage them. His magic fingers let out her tension like undoing the knot of a balloon. Perhaps it was the rough calluses on his guitar-playing fingers. "She's seen the error of her ways and can't wait to accept both of us back with open arms."

"Really?" Maya asked with round innocent eyes, her fears having made her momentarily gullible.

"No, of course not," Veer said, rolling his eyes. "She's the same old Mom. But I'm glad you made me call. She was relieved to hear from me, I think."

"You didn't crack and tell her, did you?" Maya asked nervously.

"No . . . Well, it almost slipped out at the end there. But no, I didn't say."

"Good, cause I would have been pissed if you had."

Veer frowned and stopped massaging Maya's feet, but he did not say anything in reply. Maya instantly felt a little guilty for saying it. On the one hand, she did not want to be the horrible ogre stopping him from spreading the good news to his family, but she also knew what both of their mothers would be like if they knew they were about to become grandmothers for the first time. Maya was determined that their impending little arrival was not going to be used to paper over cracks that had developed in the relationships with both mothers.

Maya slid away from Veer slightly, pulling up her gray vest top to expose her belly, which no longer took a lot of exposing, being right at the point—now in her fourth month—where her nicely curving stomach was about to become a plain old bump. She needed some new tops and some new dresses. A sari would be a good idea, Maya supposed, but she had never taken to dressing like her mother.

"She's just the same, you know," Veer said. "It's like, I don't know . . . like they can't change, or something." Veer ran his fingers through his hair in an agitated gesture, rumpling the overlong black curls.

He exhaled loudly, then jumped up as if an alarm clock had gone off. "Shall I make some lunch before I head out?" he asked, going back into the kitchen.

Maya nodded happily in assent. Sometimes, she wondered if Veer thought that he needed to feed her a certain amount of food before the baby would grow big enough to be born. Still, she wasn't complaining.

"Are you playing this afternoon?" Maya asked, getting up from the futon and flopping down on a cream-colored leather couch. It was an expensive piece of furniture and sweaty against her skin, often squeaking when she moved around on it. She shifted her weight to one hip and massaged the other, while the calfskin couch farted out of an imperfect seam.

"Yeah, I reckon so. Not the bar in town, I think they need a rest from me. Chico, perhaps."

"How could anyone need a rest from your music?" she said sweetly—and dutifully. Veer had occasionally played at local bars back in San Francisco—for fun, rather than for money. Now it was his only source of income, and although it was not quite a living, the money he made minimized the need to dip into Maya's savings. A couple of times Maya had casually suggested she could rent out her San Francisco apartment, but Veer had dissed the idea, determined to fend for his growing family himself.

"Oh, I don't give them too many of my songs," Veer said with an ironic grin. "Mostly just covers of the Jonas Brothers."

"You should," Maya said. "It's like you're inspired here. You've been writing so many songs, and . . . I don't know, it's like you've found your voice, your style." Maya hugged her mug of coffee with clenched hands. She knew Veer had been waiting for a big break—*to be discovered, baby*, is how he put it as he winked at her, the absurdly long eyelashes fanning across his cheekbones—but now with money tight, she wished he would get a steady job and sometimes overcompensated for these thoughts by slathering on compliments about his songwriting.

The job conversation was not one that Maya was ready for today. Pinky had never approved of Veer's music, yet she had never stood in the way of it. *Dammit*, she chastised herself. *Why am I forever comparing myself to his mother?*

Chapter 14

"You've got a little"—Lena pointed surreptitiously toward her husband's mouth—"drool coming out."

Lena and Manuel were standing toward the edge of a vast tent—certainly the largest Lena had ever seen at a private event—watching the bride-to-be, Esther Vora, dancing in her *chamak-dhamak*, razzle-dazzle finery. Flanked by two young, pretty women, Esther was nonetheless doing a very good job of being the center of attention.

Manuel slapped a hand to his face and pulled his fingers across one corner of his mouth. The fingers brushed plenty of salt-and-pepper stubble but came away dry. He looked at his wife, who was grinning.

"Ha, funny," Manuel said, raising his voice to be heard above the bhangra music that blared out through rented speakers at the *Sangeet* night, the traditional music-and-dance party. It was the first of two events that would be held ahead of the *Pheras*, the actual wedding ceremony itself. "I was just admiring them."

Lena raised her eyebrows.

"The dancing . . . they're very good."

"No one digs a hole for themselves like you do, dear husband," Lena said.

"It's impressive, that's all. The way they're all . . . in time."

"Just stop now."

Manuel stepped closer to his wife and took her arm lightly. "No one moves like you do, though."

"Ha!" Lena barked. "No way I'll be taking to the floor tonight. For one thing, no one wants a freight train running through the middle of the dance floor."

Lena felt Manuel's frown—he hated it when she was self-deprecating—and her lip began to tremble as they stood in the half-light toward the edge of the huge tent.

"What is it?" he asked.

For a moment, Lena just continued to stare intently at the dance floor. On a raised dais behind them, a DJ adjusted the knobs of his stereo equipment, turning the volume up high. "It's never going to be like this for Maya," Lena said eventually, "is it?" She caught Manuel's eye and knew what he was thinking. "Yes, she had a small traditional wedding the first time around, but it ended badly. Now, even if she were to want a big fat Indian wedding, with all her family and friends, it's not possible. How could it be? With the Kapoors and all their friends disapproving of the match . . ." She shook her head sadly. "And my Sameer. He will be in his forties when he gets out. What marriage prospects will he have then as an ex-con? Even if he does find a half-decent girl, there could never be a big wedding after what has happened."

Lena turned toward her husband and waved her hand to indicate the crowd behind them. "I always wanted this for my children, and being here tonight reminds me that it will probably never be. I just want to get through this night. This is why we are standing over to the side, out of the way," she said, and pushed her hair back behind her ears, as if irritated by it hanging there.

Manuel turned and indicated the nearby buffet table. "Oh, I thought we were just naturally drifting toward the food." His expression was a tad pleading, but Lena scowled back at him.

"I couldn't possibly eat anything," she said, "not with all these eyes on me. Their judging looks are bad enough, without stuffing my face while they watch." Lena had glanced at the buffet on the way in and had already noted that she could have done much better—and probably for half the money, too, she would wager.

"Are they watching me, too?" Manuel asked a little petulantly, a hand slipping to his stomach. "We didn't eat a proper dinner."

A meaty hand slapped Manuel in the upper arm.

"Ow!" he exclaimed. "I don't see anyone watching you. They're all watching the dancing and not being judged by their wives for it."

Lena sighed. "How long have we been married?"

"Is it an odd number or an even number?" he retorted playfully.

Lena resisted the urge to hit him in the arm again. "All these years, all the events we've attended together, and you still don't understand Indian society, do you? Just because they don't let you see them looking, it doesn't mean that they aren't looking. Just because you can't hear them talking, it doesn't mean that they aren't dirtying your name behind your back. It's when they let you see the looks and hear the comments, that's when it's time to get genuinely worried."

"When they're about to run you out of town, huh?"

Lena's only answer was to raise her eyebrows at her husband. His glib reply was not too far from the truth. He was the kindest, most supportive man, despite his irreverent sense of humor, but he still did not get the complexities of a social life, perhaps because he had never really had one before they met.

"I won't let them run you out of town." Manuel now winked at her. "I promise."

Lena was taken back to the farmer's market she used to visit as a vendor about ten years ago. In many ways, Manuel did not look all that different from when she'd first met him—his face still had the same rugged brown attractiveness she had noticed when she set up her very first curry stall beside his. How kind he had been, how encouraging, this unassuming farmer who came all the way up from Fresno to sell his lettuces, onions, cabbages, and spring fruit. He always appeared comfortable in his own skin: easy, relaxed, and in his element at a time when Lena had felt so completely out of hers.

"Hello there, how can I help?" he'd said. She was struggling with the faded-red awning that stretched over her boxes of homemade samosas, spinach *pakoras*, paper cups of steaming-hot tea, and flat squares of Indian sweets.

And just like that, with his muscles rippling underneath his smooth skin toasted golden brown in the California sun, he had her.

Lena leaned toward Manuel and rested her hand on his chest; the warm smile he returned to her was guileless. Bless him. Men were so often like children, and Manuel was the particularly innocent child who bumbled along happily, assuming that everybody just got along. It was often the case that she could not bring herself to ruin his perfect little bubble. Indeed, Lena sometimes wished she could live in Manuel's bubble, but the best she could ever do was to be beside it, enjoying all that blissful ignorance by association.

"Go on, then," Lena told her husband as he continued to edge toward the buffet table, a hopeful look in his eyes. "But don't you over-indulge, you hear me? I'll be cooking when we get home."

He stuck out like a sore thumb at Indian society gatherings—not just as a Mexican, but also because his idea of "smart casual" was more "shabby casual"—yet he never showed the slightest hint that he understood this fact. Lena had become used to the sneering—it was her life, and she had chosen it. But, tonight, they sneered because of a son who was now in prison and a daughter who had vanished from sight along with the "crown prince" of the Bay Area. And that was hard to take. Talk about a cursed family.

Suddenly, Manuel's mouth was by Lena's ear, his manly musk briefly interrupting the aroma drifting over from the food. "I think we're in trouble, sweetheart, because Pinky's over there, and she keeps looking straight at us."

~

"You're staring, my flower petal," Harry Kapoor said calmly. He was standing behind his wife, almost a whole head taller than her.

"What?"

"You're staring at Lena. Either go and talk to her or stop staring at her."

"Look at her," Pinky said, almost as if her husband hadn't spoken, "standing there as if she doesn't have a care in the world." Pinky scowled.

"I'd say she probably has some pretty big cares at the mo—"

"Chatting away to her husband, playing around with him, while here I am, worrying about Veer every minute of the day."

"It looked like she hit him a moment ago."

"She's letting her daughter ruin our son's life, Harry, letting her hide him away from us, and she feels like she can just turn up here at this *Sangeet* and rub it all in our faces."

Pinky's voice trembled as she finished speaking, and she took a long, steadying breath. She had been getting better each day in dealing with her grief, although there were moments like this when the magnitude of what had happened—the son she had doted upon from the moment he was born fleeing the city and closing her out of his life—welled up like a pot trying to boil over.

Pinky had experienced that sadness—she felt as if her chest was banded with iron straps of sorrow—the day after Veer and Maya had left. She winced now at the memory of turning up at Anita's house unannounced after finding out that her son and that . . . that *usurper* had been there the previous afternoon. She had been unable to control herself—furious, throwing accusations followed by the humiliation when Chintu, Anita's always mild-mannered husband, had thrown her out of the house. It was a shame that still snapped its little teeth at her.

She felt her husband's hand lightly touch her elbow. It brought her out of the memory but did little to distract Pinky from either of the two targets for her anger and indignity. "I mean, husband, how can she have the nerve to show her face?" The voice that Pinky heard as she spoke seemed to be turning the accusation both inward and outward.

"We should dance," Harry said, his tone that of the de-escalator. "Look, everyone's going up."

"Don't be ridiculous," Pinky said. "This isn't a time for dancing."

"It's a *Sangeet*," Harry said, his voice becoming ever so slightly firm. "We're the Kapoors, flower petal, and when someone invites us to a *Sangeet*, they expect us to honor them with a dance."

Harry moved around to stand in front of Pinky and held out his hand. He had the insistent look on his face that had made Pinky melt on more than one occasion throughout their marriage. "They will stare," she mouthed at him, smiling tightly as the music began again, drowning out her actual words.

"They had better," she thought she heard him say back. Harry had been retired for so long now, it was sometimes easy to forget the force the man had once been, how his mere presence in a room—however big or small the space—had always commanded a certain respect. She drew attention in one way, he in another.

Pinky took her husband's hand and was led onto the dance floor. It was mostly older couples, and she saw Anita and her husband on the opposite side of the floor. Anita wore a green-and-gold sari and a bindi on her forehead that made her dark-kohl-lined eyes look even bigger. Chintu's bald head was thrown back, as if laughing at something tremendously funny that his wife had said. His dark-blue Nehru jacket was unbuttoned at the neck and bulged around his belly.

She had not even noticed that Anita was present, but then it was perhaps the biggest tent she had ever seen at a *Sangeet*. Esther Vora had evidently inherited her mother's penchant for making a statement. Pinky managed to catch her friend's eye. Anita saw her and waved jauntily; a content smile played on her lips, and even her left eye was not twitching the way it so often did. Pinky forced her lips into an uncomfortable smile and managed a quick flick of the wrist in reply. She should have been happy to see her friend enjoying herself, she knew this, yet to see nervous Anita so carefree and unconscious of how she looked while Pinky—confident, elegant Pinky Kapoor—felt so awkward and judged by every pair of eyes, well, it only served to heighten her own nerves. She could feel a migraine coming on.

But then she started to feel the music, swaying her body and taking small steps, holding that posture she was famous for. Pinky's body almost seemed to pulsate and flow as she moved with none of the stiffness that many of the other older dancers around her did. She knew how good she looked, more like a twenty-something than a fifty-something. Harry, unfortunately, had never quite managed the same gracefulness, but he did an adequate job as he turned and slowly spun back and forth before her—like he was a hunter, circling and readying himself to move in for the kill—and seeing him dance always made her smile.

She does have a name, you know. You've known Maya all of her life.

Pinky's step faltered, her dancing becoming briefly out of time with the music, before she recovered and flowed back into the rhythm. This had been happening ever since she had spoken to Veer. The call had caught her off guard, and she had said what was in her heart—thoughts that were bound to antagonize her son, who could still be sensitive and tetchy, even at the age of twenty-five. They had always been so close when he was little; yet once Veer had become a man, an invisible line had developed, one she was forbidden to cross. Not that Pinky hadn't continued to try, anyway, believing that she should still be able to guide him as she always had. Now, endless replays of the call came back to her unbidden, forcing her mind to again and again play out the conversation she wished she could have had instead.

Which makes it even worse, had been her answer to his complaint. Pinky had seen Maya like the older sister Veer had never had. She was Lena's daughter, for crying out loud, so would always have been like family for them—just not like this. Never like this. Pinky remembered

127

throwing the girl a great party at the Piedmont mansion when the house had only recently been completed, celebrating Maya's graduation. It had taken Maya two attempts to get through college, as the girl had changed course after her first year—always one for making rash decisions—but Pinky had congratulated her for her persistence and thrown Maya an event that the Sharmas could never have managed themselves.

Because she was like family. And now this was the thanks she got.

The Sharmas had been late arriving to their own party, she recalled, and Veer had stayed out of the way in his room, playing the guitar that he had only recently taken up and already begun to master. When Maya arrived, he had finally joined them and, Pinky remembered with an icy chill down her back, Veer had followed the young woman around like a puppy dog all evening. It had been cute, with him ten years old and Maya twenty-two. If only she had known.

Why could they not see how betrayed she felt? Maya should have known better than to bring this disgrace upon them.

In the tent, the bhangra rhythm shifted, the beat suddenly cut through with something more modern and remix flavored—a horrible cacophony to Pinky's ears—and she was relieved to see the other women begin to peel away from their partners and leave the floor. In their place, most of the young men now moved onto the floor, forming themselves into a rough line. Pinky stepped away, thinking that she might find Anita and see if she had brought Kookie with her. The old woman had a way of lifting her spirits.

When she turned, Pinky saw them all—the couples who had left the dance floor—looking at her. It reminded her of a movie they had watched once, years ago when she had been pregnant with Veer. In the film, a man suddenly realizes that he is in a world almost entirely populated by aliens disguised to look like people. While he is walking along the street all the aliens pick up on it. They stop what they're doing and all turn to stare at him at once.

In the film, the aliens continued to stare, but at Esther Vora's *Sangeet* the moment only lasted for a fraction of a second, the people around her slipping perfectly back into conversations, back to watching the dancing or to heading for the buffet or the bar. Once, she might have dismissed it or assumed that it had everything to do with the way she danced, or the fact that she was goddamn Pinky Kapoor, the one they called a peacock—yes, she knew about that, and she reveled in it. Peacocks were the grandest of the birds, and everyone loved staring at them. She had always liked the staring.

Not tonight, though. Tonight she did not strut past them. Tonight she bowed her head and walked quickly toward the back of the tent—where there were fewer people and more shadows. From the corner of her eye, over to the right, Pinky caught sight of Lena, who saw her, too, and half raised a hand as she passed. She ignored her erstwhile best friend—not that she wanted to talk to her, anyway, but to do so would be to give everyone something else to gossip about, to blacken the Kapoor name with. She could hear the whispers following her to the back of the tent, spreading among the women—those aging lionesses—the curious, pitying stares that seemed to say, *Not only is her future daughter-in-law-to-be twelve years older than her son, she is sister to a man who killed a girl in a DUI!*

We shouldn't have danced, Pinky thought.

She caught her husband's eye, saw him laughing and slapping backs as he turned to leave the dance floor. He had every right to enjoy himself, yet Pinky felt a flash of annoyance pass through her nonetheless. Harry missed his son but showed little if any of Pinky's horror about what Maya was doing to their only child, who could have had his pick of any of the suitable young ladies present. If Pinky had anything to do with it, he still would.

Chapter 15

"Hey, holmes, whaddup *ese?*"

Sameer stood against the wall in the exercise yard, the same spot he had occupied during all his previous outdoor exercise sessions, one foot against the wall, hands in his pockets, trying to look small and inconspicuous. He had known very little about prisons before ending up in one, but he knew enough to understand that the exercise yard was an important place, that the benches and the weights would likely be someone's territory—a place you didn't want to find yourself accidentally competing for. If he had any choice in the matter, Sameer might have preferred staying in his cell for the entire length of his sentence, watching TV. He had already developed a habit with terrible TV shows, the latest being repeats of Gordon Ramsay's *Hell's Kitchen*. Mostly, he enjoyed seeing the blunt-speaking chef lose his temper, although the actual cooking part was sometimes interesting, and he found himself wanting to try some of the recipes, which was ironic, as he had rarely done more than stick a plastic tub in a microwave for years now.

Thinking of cooking had made him think of his mom, fondly remembering those halcyon days when she made mutton curry and spinach paneer for him. Pangs of regret would open up within him when he thought like that, a hollow feeling like hunger. He had been so angry with her for so long, so used to that feeling—living off it, being sustained by it. Yet, somehow, he could no longer even quite put into words the shape of that hatred.

And what had it achieved, huh? It had taken a beautiful soul out of the world, stolen her from her family. The pale face with the deliberately pursed lips of her sister, Rhia, in the courtroom visited him almost every time the lights went out. He remembered how she had met Ruchi at work once and seemed not to stop smiling, dimples dancing in her cheeks, yet the last time he had seen that face, it had appeared set into stone.

That was the legacy of all that righteous rage he had harbored for Lena Jaitly, for his annoyingly successful sister, for . . .

"Holmes, you with me?" The man who had spoken and was leaning against the wall next to him was called Gus. He was white with a tattooed shaved head, over six feet tall and muscular, with large, well-manicured hands. In contrast to the way he had greeted Sameer, Gus didn't look in any way Hispanic, his accent placing him as coming from somewhere much closer to New York and the Eastern Seaboard, which made the way he spoke the Mexican slang sound kind of stupid. Not that Sameer was about to tell him that.

"You know," Sameer replied, "just . . ." He didn't know quite how to finish his sentence. *Trying not to be noticed; hoping I could just stand here and that no one would bother me for the next twelve years.*

"Trying to stay out of the way?" Gus said. "I get it. I'd be scared if I was you."

Sameer glanced up at Gus, but quickly looked away again, not wanting to meet the big man's gaze. On the other side of the yard, close to the weights area, the same pale, tattooed man who had given Sameer a hard time in the van on the way to the prison was waving his arms and talking loudly to some of the white prisoners who were lifting weights.

"Way I heard it, you're in here for getting some girl killed in a car wreck," Gus continued. Sameer didn't say anything, though he couldn't stop a lump appearing in his throat, and he quickly swallowed it. "Maybe you were acting like some *naco* piece of shit, I don't know, but it just sounds like bad luck to me."

This time, Sameer glanced and met Gus's gaze. He was looking at Sameer intently, discolored chipped teeth flashing against leathery skin. Sameer just nodded and lowered his eyes.

"Not like most of these cholo bitches," Gus went on with a general wave of the arm. "Pretty much every one of them did something bad enough to mean they belong in here."

"What did you do?" Sameer asked, wishing that he hadn't the moment the words were spoken.

Gus's face darkened for a second, and Sameer's stomach tightened—this was why he was trying not to talk to people—but then the big man's expression loosened slightly again. "I killed someone," he said, "and I sure as hell meant to kill the *pinche* piece of crap. Was pushing my little bro into dealing drugs for him. Wasn't taking no for an answer." He shrugged. "What you gonna do, holmes? Can't let that shit go."

Despite his reasoning, there was something chilling in the way the big man said it. All the same, Sameer shrugged back. It seemed like the best thing to do.

Across the yard, the pale skinhead with the Nazi tattoos was hassling a black prisoner who had passed too close to the weights. "He's been doing that every day since he got here," Gus observed. "He's a little weasel, wants to impress his big white friends and make sure they look after him."

"That one scares me," Sameer admitted, then wondered whether he should have. Gus raised his eyebrows, which were like light-colored caterpillars and almost invisible from where Sameer stood. In fact, Gus seemed a pretty hairless person, with not a vestige of hair on his head and hardly any fuzz on the other exposed body parts. "He hassled me in the van on the way here," Sameer continued, now feeling the need to explain, "called me *Mustafa* and all that. What does that even mean?"

Sameer finished with a small laugh and Gus joined in. "That one's not scary," Gus said once he had finished laughing. "That one will be dead within a month if he doesn't change what he's doing, no matter the friends he thinks he's making. Trust me on this one, *ese*, it's not the noisy ones like him you got to be worried about."

"But I should be worried?" Sameer asked, swallowing hard.

Gus pushed off from the wall with a grin, leaned forward and pointed a finger at Sameer, indicating his posture—one foot against the wall, huddled down to look as small as possible. "Just because none of these cholos has been hassling you yet, doesn't mean they ain't watching you. They might leave you alone for a month. We've all got nothing but time in here, ain't nobody in a big hurry. But they all sizing you up, holmes, and you wanna be thinking about what you gonna do when the time comes."

The bright, delirious morning sun rose in the sky and cast the bleak shadow of the prison building onto the yard. Sameer shivered.

Later that night, when the bell for lights out clanged, he was trapped in the darkness. The web of memories rolled over him, like a broken film that stuck in the projector, slapping the machine with every revolution of the wheel.

"Hey there, jailbird."

Sameer remembered he had looked up from his phone as he sat on the steps in front of his school. He had been looking at the text on his mobile phone for about the twentieth time in the last ten minutes. It was marked as from Dad and read: Held up at work.

His father was supposed to be picking him up to go out for pizza straight from school—which was very rare for them to do, but Goldie had promised. What was Sameer supposed to do with *held up at work*? Sit and wait on the steps, he guessed, although Sameer's school was in a neighborhood where hanging around in front of the building for too long after the school day was over would eventually attract the wrong attention.

The voice belonged to Mr. Barr, the teacher who had overseen his detention a couple of months before. They had played two games of chess—the first of which Sameer had lost heavily, although he put up more of a fight in the second game—and then Mr. Barr had let him go fifteen minutes early.

The whole experience had left Sameer hoping that he might have some lessons with the school's new English teacher, but his classes had continued to be taken by the old fossil Mrs. Blakely, who was of the opinion that every child was a complete Philistine unworthy of and unable to appreciate classic works of literature. The fact that she was in most cases correct . . . that didn't change the fact that she sucked as a teacher.

Mr. Barr broke into a grin as he approached along the sidewalk, a briefcase in one hand. "Keeping out of trouble, I trust, Mr. Sharma?"

"Yessir," Sameer replied automatically.

"If only all the other students were as polite as you," Mr. Barr said, arriving to stand over Sameer. Today, the teacher was in faded boot-cut jeans, white Nike sneakers, the usual white shirt, and a worn beige corduroy jacket. Somehow, his outfit was at once academic and bohemian. "You do realize that hanging about after school doesn't improve your grade point average?"

The evening shadows gathered softly around them. "My dad's running late," Sameer explained. "Held up at work. We're supposed to be going for pizza."

With uncanny timing, his phone chimed its message tone: Stuck with a big client, it read, going to be very late. We'll do pizza another day.

"Pizza's off," Sameer said, unable to keep his shoulders from slumping. He stood and turned to start the walk home.

"You know what's in here, Sameer?" Mr. Barr called out. Sameer turned back to see the English teacher lifting the briefcase he was holding in one of his hands.

Sameer tried to look interested, but it was a briefcase, and in his experience, briefcases didn't tend to include anything interesting.

"This," Mr. Barr said with exaggerated pomp, "contains the script for the end-of-year play."

"*A Midsummer Night's Dream?*" Sameer asked, pushing the hair back from his forehead. It felt like a safe guess.

Mr. Barr shook his head.

"*Romeo and Juliet?*"

"No Shakespeare," Mr. Barr hooted.

"*The Importance of Being Earnest?*"

"They wouldn't let me," said Mr. Barr mournfully.

Sameer chuckled.

"Man," Mr. Barr said, "I wish you were in my class, Sameer Sharma. You've already mentioned more plays than any of my students have even heard of. But you still haven't guessed it."

"Oh no," Sameer said, adopting a horrified expression, "it's not *The Little Mermaid*, is it?"

Mr. Barr pulled a look of mock horror. "No . . . Jesus, no. No musicals."

Sameer shrugged, out of ideas. "What is it, then?"

"*Our Town*," Mr. Barr said. "I think I can do something with that." He started up the steps. "First of all it's detention duty, then it's the damn school play. They sure like sticking it to the new guy around here."

The teacher stopped at the top of the steps and turned back around. "Mr. Sharma," he said, "I was going to order in something to eat. If you want to volunteer as my coproducer, then I could make it pizza."

"I don't know," Sameer said doubtfully. He liked the teacher, and he enjoyed English—as much as he could with Mrs. Blakely trying to ruin it—but coproducer for the school play sounded like a lot of commitment. More than that, it sounded like a good way to become a target, and as an academically inclined South Asian kid from a one-parent family who never had any money and lived in a dive in a shady area of town . . . well, he had enough of that in his life already.

"There's a whole bunch of extra credit in it," Mr. Barr tried again. "And I may even be prepared to hack into the school computer system and delete that detention that's blotting up your permanent record," he added with a wink.

Chapter 16

The visitor hall was like a depressing version of an airport departure lounge. Make that an even more depressing version of an airport departure lounge—and Lena hated flying at the best of times. Flying was so unnatural, so . . . out of control. Right from that moment when the sudden acceleration of the plane forced her back into her seat—a feeling like the aircraft was panicking, as if it had suddenly become aware that there wasn't enough runway—Lena found that it completely disagreed with her.

And yet, the worst part of flying was always going through airport security. Lena hated the constant feeling of anxiety that arose within her as she tried to remember whether there were any liquids in her hand luggage and whether she had removed all metal items from about her person, separated her devices. The apparent insanity of having to place her tickets and her passport into a box when—once the security people had done their thing—that same box was pushed into a big line of other people's boxes, so that anybody could grab all that important stuff and vanish in moments. And, of course, Lena was always the one who got flagged for an extra pat-down, a swipe with a wand, or a wipe of the fingers with that funny bit of paper. Apparently, she had the look of a middle-aged drug mule. Or, at least, that was how she felt when it happened. It was the indignity of it, the way she suddenly felt dehumanized as these oh-so-serious people carried out their business across her private body.

The visitor hall at the prison was just like this, except no one looked excited to be going on holiday. Everyone—except, perhaps, some of the children—just looked as stressed and depressed and humiliated as she felt.

Manuel had wanted to come in with her, but Lena had asked him to wait in the parking lot, at least for this first visit. It was the right thing to do, as she did not even know how Sameer was going to react to her, let alone to Manuel, who he had never approved of. All the same, there was a pretty big part of Lena that wished her husband was with her as she stood in the line for a visitor ticket, spoke to the corrections officer at the desk—whose job was apparently to show a complete lack of patience toward anyone who hadn't visited before—and then submit to a body search that made the ones administered by airport security seem entirely respectful.

"Do you have to do that?" Lena said as the female officer—who had already made her remove her *kurti* behind the barely adequate "privacy" of a mobile screen—reached forward without warning and roughly pushed a gloved hand up and under her bra.

"If you want to see your son today, ma'am, then yes, I do," the officer replied in a monotone.

Having finally cleared security, Lena went through to a featureless white hall, with rows of seats facing each other, and cameras mounted everywhere on top of dirty, smudged windows.

There was at least a kids' corner—a communal space with a collection of shabby-looking toys and grimy half-finished puzzles where children could go when their energy became too much and the visiting spouses or grandparents wanted to be able to talk properly with their incarcerated relative. Lena saw that there was a small television screen attached to the wall in the kids' corner. This one obviously had cable service, although the last person to watch it must have been an adult, since the channel was turned to that snarly British TV chef's show. She hoped for the children's sake that the sound wasn't up.

She spotted the heavy door through which the prisoners—one of whom, it still seemed so crazy, was her son—would enter. She found a seat close to the door, but not too close, and looked around at the other visitors.

Some of them looked like normal families, she guessed, many likely the wives and children of inmates, judging by their age. Many others, however, looked . . . How did they look? Lena struggled for a while to frame the thought until, finally, all she could come up with that didn't feel in some way prejudicial was, "Not her sort of people."

Then again, maybe now they were her sort of people. The sort of people who had relatives in jail. Who had children in jail. She glanced around, seeing if she could spot any women her age. Would she see herself in them? Would they have left containers of food at the door of Ruchi's sister, Rhia, and for her parents, as she had done more than once in the last few months? She felt like a criminal herself when doing so, stealing quietly up to the door to deliver a mixed-vegetable curry—always a safe choice when you could not ask what someone preferred.

She had wanted to help, to do something to assuage the guilt over what her own flesh and blood had caused.

A loud buzzer went off, interrupting her train of thought. It was a shocking sound, a little like an alarm, and the heavy door slid open. The scariest-looking bunch of men—most wearing blue-gray overalls—that Lena had ever seen in one place began to file into the room.

And, tucked amid all these scary men, standing out in orange overalls instead, was her little boy. Sameer.

A host of memories from thirteen years ago rushed through her brain on repeat, like tumbleweeds through a desert.

"I want to speak to him," Lena had said over the phone, keeping her voice flat. "I want to speak to my boy. I haven't spoken to him in nearly two weeks and I hear he's helping out with the school play. I want to ask him about it."

"Eh, I told you," Goldie replied in his usual lazy, belligerent drawl, "the boy comes home late, sometimes he goes to the shop. He's got, you know, puberty or something. He needs his space. He doesn't always tell me where he's going, when he's going to be here. It's how we roll 'round here, I'm not his keeper."

"You are his bloody keeper, Goldie. That's what being the father of a minor involves. Being his bloody keeper!"

"Don't you shout at me, you bloody fat cow, you."

"Oh, save it, you ridiculous man," Lena barked back. "I don't have to take your put-downs anymore. Do you want me to come over?" Although Lena asked it like a question, it was absolutely, totally, and utterly a threat. "I'll do it, you know. I'll come over there right now."

She was raising her voice, and she hated it when she raised her voice with Goldie. Ever since the divorce, she had adopted a businesslike tone with him, one that she always hoped sounded ever-so-slightly condescending. Somehow it seemed crazy that this man had once seemed so far out of reach for dumpy, plain-looking Lena. He was her "friend" at Delhi University, where, even then, Goldie had been one of the jocks and fancied himself a player. She caught him on the rebound from his "princess," the dream girl who had done a little modeling and came from a respected and moderately wealthy family. Lena had known at the time that this was exactly what it was and hadn't cared, relieved to be on the arm of a charmer like Goldie.

The rebound relationship had turned into marriage and a two-year-old Maya before Goldie's second failed business. He'd left the university with what amounted to barely a passing grade and moved them to America—the Bay Area, in particular, as this was where Lena's old school friend and wife-of-a-billionaire, Pinky, resided. The move, she knew, was as much to avoid Goldie's mounting debts as in service of any quest for a new life.

"Don't . . . Look, we'll set up times for a call; how about that, eh?"

Goldie hated it when she went over to his apartment, so it was a damn good threat. She had never completely understood why he hated her coming over so much, guessing that it was some combination of embarrassment about the crap hole of a place he had ended up living in and the possibility that she might meet one of his pathetic Barbie-doll girlfriends. Lena had followed through on the threat twice before—both times when Sameer had been too busy to call her—and had no real desire to do so again. For one thing, going to that apartment reminded Lena of how her son would rather live in squalor than come and reside with her. She wished that she could summon the courage to confront Sameer about it, but as bullish as she could now be with Goldie, Lena wilted at the thought of her son's harsh rejections.

"We'll set up a time, eh?" Goldie went on. "And I'll tell Sameer he's got to be here."

"When it's good for him," Lena added quickly. It was always a balance, being the absent parent. There was a fine line between being in her son's life enough and being an inconvenient drag. Of course, it seemed that Sameer had two absent parents. It just so happened that one of them lived with him.

~

"Look at me, son."

Aside from the first moment that their eyes met as Sameer had walked into the visitor lounge, he hadn't looked at Lena once. It was a strange experience, finding your son unable to meet your eye. He appeared thinner, although his hair was as mussed as ever.

The orange jumpsuit that had been issued to him was a few sizes too big, and he had to roll up his pant cuffs, so when he sat down, it revealed the ankle of his still chicken-like legs. Goldie had called him "chicken legs" a few times when he was younger, she remembered, and she knew the taunt had stuck with Sameer, making her feel a little ashamed of having just had the thought.

"I thought Dad was coming," Sameer said, still not looking at her.

The derisive snort came out before Lena could think to stop it, and then Sameer did look at her. "What?" he said, crossing his arms in a defensive gesture that she had seen many times before.

Lena could have said a hundred things about why she did not think that Goldie would be making the effort to visit his son any time soon, but she just shook her head and looked at the ground, the best course of action for the moment.

The longer she sat there, it still did not get any easier to see Sameer in the orange jumpsuit. He had never had the best dress sense or, for that matter, cared much about style. Not like his sister. Or his dad. Goldie cared deeply about style; it was just that his was a style that was about thirty years out of date.

No, Sameer was more like his mother in that way. Lena cared little about her appearance. She had taken more care with it when she had been married to Goldie, but only because not to do so would have elicited critical comments.

Sameer had owned a faux-leather jacket a few years back, she remembered. He had truly liked that jacket and always seemed to be smoothing it and looking down at it when he wore the thing, even when it had become old and cracked and tatty. She could not quite remember now when he had stopped wearing it. The thought made her suddenly very sad, and she had to shake her head to clear the emotions that were threatening to overwhelm her.

"How are you doing here, son?" Lena asked. "Are you coping okay?"

Sameer just looked angry, his brow furrowed, his breathing shallow and tense, and for a moment she didn't think he would answer. Then his features relaxed slightly. "I'm okay," he said. "It's not too bad so far."

Lena was not so sure she believed the statement—something in the way his body was hunched into his jumpsuit. She had always been able to tell when Sameer was lying. "That's good," she said awkwardly. "I can . . . They said on the way in that we can send you things, little things to make life easier here. Is there anything you would like?"

Sameer glanced around nervously, his gaze skipping from face to face like a pebble over water. "No, it's fine."

"There must be something," Lena pushed. "Just ask. I want to help."

Sameer sat there looking awkward for a moment. When he finally did speak, it was in a sort of hiss between clenched teeth. "Shut up," he said.

Lena was shocked. "What's the problem?" she asked.

Sameer leaned in toward her just a little, and Lena leaned forward in response. "People are listening," he whispered. "If they know you'll bring stuff in for me, they will start tapping me up for it."

"Oh," Lena answered as she sat up straight again. She honestly didn't understand what he meant, but his demeanor was enough to make her realize that she shouldn't push the matter any further. She changed the subject. "So, we've been looking into an appeal. We might be able to get your sentence reduced."

Sameer slouched back into his chair a little, his shoulders dropping. "You don't get it, do you?" he said.

"Get what?" she answered. "Look . . . if there's a chance. The attorney I spoke to was talking about the possibility of halving your sentence. That's six years of your life back."

For the first time since he was a little boy—perhaps since the day that Goldie left—Lena saw tears starting to form in her son's eyes.

"Is it?" he said. "In here, out there . . . I'm still the person who left a woman to die in a burning car."

"Oh, son," Lena said and started to reach out a hand toward him. She checked herself, not so much because of any reaction from Sameer—though he did flinch a little—but because she found herself glancing over at a corrections officer who stood nearby. She had expected the guard to shout, "No touching!" but, throughout the visitor hall, kids were jumping on their fathers, and the guards didn't seem to be interfering with anything that was going on; perhaps she had just seen too many movies.

By the time she had rid herself of the feeling, the moment was gone.

"Yes, Sameer," Lena said, "you did this thing. But you did not mean for her to die, and if you had kept trying to get her out, you, too, might be dead. You are paying for what happened, but what good is it to keep you away from the world for longer than necessary? And what good is it to consume yourself with guilt? Guilt is useful for five minutes until you accept what you have done. After this, it is only a hindrance."

"You always think you can fix things," Sameer said, the words an accusation, "but it's too late to fix things. I'm broken. We're broken." The tears were now beginning to run down Sameer's face. "This is your fault, too, you know."

"What do you mean?"

"You left me with him."

"With who . . . ? Your father?" Lena said. "You chose to go with your father, Sameer. What was I supposed to do? I just wanted you to be happy. Anyway, what does your father have to do with it?"

Sameer was trembling a little when he answered. "I could have told you. I would have . . . been able to . . . tell you."

"Tell me what?"

In a split second, Sameer had changed again, and whatever moment had been there was gone, and so, too, was his inclination to say any more. He turned quickly away, and wiped his eyes dry on the yellow-orange sleeve of his jumpsuit. Then he sat back in his seat. His chair was the same distance from hers as it had been a moment before—it would have been impossible for Sameer to move it—yet now he seemed so much farther away.

"What do you do with yourself?" Lena tried. "What are your days like?"

"Boring," Sameer answered coldly, his arms crossed.

"Do they not give you things to do?"

Sameer's brow furrowed, and again the face went a death-mask blank. He turned his head away, then his features relaxed as he swung back to look at Lena. "There's . . . um, a cooking course." Lena inclined her head, and Sameer gave a nonchalant shrug. "I think they just want to train us so they don't have to employ so many cooks," he went on. "Save money."

"If it keeps you busy . . ." Lena answered cautiously. A business course might be more useful for him.

Sameer's look became faraway. "Remember how I always used to hang around in the kitchen when you were cooking?" He pushed out his lips, made a raspberry noise.

"My little taster," Lena agreed, reminiscing.

"More than that," Sameer went on. "I watched what you were doing. I . . . I wanted to know. It seemed like magic, to make something that tasted that good."

Lena sat, tongue thick in her mouth. It felt like perhaps one of the nicest things her son had said to her in the last fifteen years. She tried to speak, but whatever the words were going to be, they got caught in her throat.

Then Sameer's wistful face fell, and she knew that the moment had passed even before he spoke. "Then Dad and I left, and that was that." Lena touched the back of his hand lying on the table.

"You probably shouldn't come again," Sameer said, averting his gaze once more. "It's . . . this place is going to change me." He made a hand gesture to indicate the other inmates in the hall. "These are my people now; this is who I am now. You don't want to see it, don't want to be a part of it. You're a respectable Indian woman living in California. Go be with your own people."

Chapter 17

For the first time since Maya and Veer had come to Paradise, Maya genuinely wished she was somewhere else. She had missed her mother at times, but always wanted Lena in Paradise with her, rather than wanting to be back in San Francisco or Walnut Creek. But, she should right then have been on the small stage at Esther Vora's *Sagan* and, although Maya would not be cutting the slimmest, most desirable figure with her Heffalump bump, she found herself craving the feel of a tight-fitting *lehenga choli* on her body with matching gold jewelry, and the sight of a woman in the mirror who shone with the unmistakable sheen of cosmetics—rather than merely the homely glow of the little life growing inside her.

Sarah had told her about her motherly glow at least a thousand times, it seemed. Against expectation, the compliment was starting to wear thin. Today she wanted a crowd, too, rather than the stillness present inside the chalet's walls, punctuated only by the occasional gust on what was a warm and windy day in Paradise.

Had she been at the *Sagan*, she would have been dancing—all fourteen bridesmaids for Esther had prepared a dance that they would have performed together at this prewedding ceremony. Although Esther had been more of a frenemy than a friend lately, and Maya wasn't even sure she would have attended the wedding, she closed her eyes and in her mind's picture she could see herself—chin held high, long blonde-streaked brown hair caressing her body with circular movements, and her *lehenga* swish-swishing around her legs as her henna-adorned feet moved in quick rotating circles on the wooden floor.

Her mind jumped to the awkward conversation she'd had with Esther to let her know she was not going to be attending her wedding. "Virry, virry awkward," as Kookie would have said in her delightful distortion of English grammar.

Esther had professed mild dismay at Maya leaving town. "We'll miss you, Maya darling," she had trilled as she made perfunctory noises and hung up, and Maya could feel Esther's mind whirring as she thought of which potential bridesmaid-to-be would be rapidly replacing Maya.

"Hey!" Veer snapped as he returned home, guitar in hand. "What do you think you're doing?"

Maya was at that moment on top of a small step stool, reaching a feather duster up into the corner of the kitchen. She was wearing bright-yellow rubber gloves and had tied a spotted handkerchief around her head to keep her hair in check; the overall effect made Maya look like she was posing for the cover of a sixties housekeeping magazine. Cleaning was a coping mechanism, a way to take her mind off things . . . and it had not been working so well. "I'm dusting cobwebs," she replied petulantly, knowing that the duster was not the thing Veer had a problem with.

"I mean, what do you think you're doing on the stool?" Veer fumed as he rushed over to his fiancée, tossing his guitar to the sofa on the way and holding out his hands as if Maya was about to topple at any moment. "If you fell . . ."

"Pregnancy hasn't made me an imbecile," Maya snapped back as she stepped down, pointedly not taking the offered hand.

Veer cast an eye around the room, which now smelled of synthetic pine forest and tangy lemon. It was not like they lived in squalor, but clutter usually got the best of him. The fact that Lena had failed to adequately instill her homemaker qualities into her daughter meant that both Maya and Veer were housekeeping-challenged. Yet the room was almost sparkling. "You all right?" he asked.

Maya gave a noncommittal huff. "It's Esther Vora's *Sagan* today," she told him.

"Oh," Veer answered, doing so in the way Maya had noticed men did when they had no idea what a woman was talking about but didn't want to admit it.

"I would be up there on the stage if our families would just accept us," she said.

"Is that where you want to be?" Veer asked. He did not sound hurt, at least not yet.

"I want things to be normal," Maya answered. "Like they were, but . . . just with you and me together. I . . ."

"What?" Veer pressed after Maya's barely underway sentence had just hung there for a few seconds.

"It's stupid." Maya shook her head.

"Good, tell me," Veer said with a note of insistence. "I get tired of bringing all the stupid in our relationship."

Maya rolled her eyes. "I was sitting here earlier, before I got the gloves on and the duster out, and I was just imagining—like a daydream or a fantasy—being at Mom's house, with our new baby. And your mom and dad were there, and everyone was laughing and happy." Maya's eyes had misted up a little, and she tried to blink it away. "Even Sameer was there, so I know it was all bullshit, but—"

"But it's how it should be," Veer put in with a lopsided smile. "Don't feel embarrassed for wishing that our families would just act like normal people." Veer took Maya's hand and rubbed it reassuringly.

"This repeated questioning of our choices. The people who believe we are doing something wrong." Maya's nose stung with impending tears. "Did you ever wish you were just American growing up? Some of the other kids had such simple lives, it seemed."

Veer's smile faded like sunshine leaving the room. "I can see why you would say that, but I've always loved our big Indian community, even though I don't see right now how any of them will come together. Sometimes I wonder if Lena and Pinky have formed a super-mom-team to come and find us, just so they can try and tear us apart again."

Maya nodded her agreement. "Seems sad that's the best we can hope for."

~

"What the hell is this, Harry? Why are we all the way back here?" Pinky demanded, jutting out her chin as everyone stood for Esther's entrance. Harry leaned in to hear her over the racket made by the unnecessarily large number of *dhol* drums that Esther had hired for her procession into the venue.

It was Esther Vora's *Sagan*, which was being held in a hall of moderate size on the Piedmont estate belonging to the Dhar family. Esther was marrying the middle son, Faisal Dhar, who Pinky had always heard was by far the least dynamic of the three Dhar boys.

The Dhar family were exceptionally wealthy, their business ventures being even more numerous than—although not overall as valuable as—Harry's had been, and their estate was very much a statement of their wealth. Pinky, who was more of a quality than a quantity person, wondered what the hall on their grounds was used for when it was not the venue for their son's *Sagan*. Correction: the Dhars' daughter-in-law-to-be's *Sagan*. For, although the *Sagan* was traditionally an event held by the groom's family and an opportunity for the bride's family to honor the groom with a token, a *sagan* of cash and clothes, the stamp of Esther Vora and the wedding designer she had hired was all over it. The Dhar empire would likely be at least one business down by now, as surely even they were not liquid enough to fund this wedding without having to sell off a few assets.

149

The hall was a change of venue from the *Sangeet*. The *Pheras*—the wedding ceremony—was scheduled to take place the next day back in the tent the *Sangeet* had been held in, and she guessed that the only reason for the change of venue for the *Sagan* was because the tent was getting a complete makeover, ensuring the decor for Esther's wedding events were different each time.

Although the hall was a little underwhelming from the outside, on the inside it was almost as if one of those outlandish TV interior decorator personalities had been let loose with instructions stating, "Do not leave any inch of any surface untouched." It was all a bit much for Pinky's tastes, but it certainly gave the impression of money having been spent. Which, of course, was probably the point.

Pinky had known very little control over her own wedding, which had been a kind of halfway house—impressive, but hurriedly arranged when financial misfortune had hit her own family and the match with Harry had saved them all from the gutter. The young Pinky had not been impressed by her sudden and unexpected fate. The only saving grace was that her friends from Delhi—both Lena and Anita—had been there to hold her upright when she found her feet faltering during the unending cycles with Harry around the sacred fire. How dizzy and disoriented she had felt when the mingled smell of crushed marigolds and burning incense had overpowered her. She could still feel Lena's large, warm hand stroking her back when silent sobs racked her thin shoulders, Anita's tremulous voice coaxing her to eat, pushing tiny sips of water in her trembling mouth.

What a strange life. People said that the past and the future didn't exist, but they did. Just not at the same time. The past was right there, if you wanted to look at it. Pinky's worst secret fear was thumping right below the surface—people looking at her as she toppled from grace, like she and her family had all those years ago, when her father's bankruptcy was splashed across the *Hindustan Times*, *Times of India*, and *Indian Express*.

Sometimes, she would say that it was a miracle that she and Harry had worked out so well. But then she looked at the younger generation—her son now a classic example, with his divorced bride-to-be—and she wondered if letting them sort out their own love lives was really for the best. And to think Lena had allowed that to happen, instead of controlling her own daughter better.

It was one thing to let her daughter's own reputation and morality fall by the wayside, but to let Pinky's family be brought into it . . . her only son. Pinky had been putting her neck out for Lena since they were teenage schoolgirls together; did that mean nothing to her?

She pressed her spine into the back of the chair and knotted her fingers into a brown labyrinth, tried to stop her head from swimming. She did not know Esther Vora all that well, although Esther's mother had been a close acquaintance before succumbing to aggressive lung cancer when Esther was not quite yet an adult. It had been because of those cigarettes that she endlessly smoked—usually through a cigarette holder like the woman thought she was in an Agatha Christie novel. "Cancer sticks," Harry called them. Pinky had never really decided if she liked Esther's mother, but she had always respected certain things about her. From what she could tell, the daughter had inherited her mother's taste for lavish ostentation.

Of course, if Esther had held a smaller, more intimate *Sagan*, Pinky could have found a way not to be offended if they had not been invited. What was far worse than not being invited, however, was to be invited and not included in the "designated seating" list for friends and family.

It was an insult to them, however well they did or did not know either of the families involved. They were the Kapoors, dammit. Harry had been more important than anyone else in the whole hall, could have bought almost all of them out himself, and they were left having to ask someone to move so they could sit together at the same table near the back.

They found themselves opposite an oddly dressed couple—the man was wearing a navy velvet *angarkha* with a heavy gold chain on top of it, and the woman was clad in a fussy brocade *salwar-kameez* in shades of yellow and green, the *dupatta* of which kept sliding off her shoulder and onto the burnished wooden floorboards of the pavilion. When Pinky had politely opened a conversation with them, they had turned out to be just about the most snobbish grocery-store owners she had ever met. Pinky swore that if the woman looked down that long nose of hers just one more time at her . . .

She fixed her gaze on Harry, waiting for some kind of explanation as to how they had found themselves in this situation. "Well, we don't actually know her that well," Harry finally answered her silent question. Only in recent years had they become like this, as if they could read each other's thoughts. Harry's breath tickled his wife's ear as he put his mouth close to it, fighting to make himself heard over the drums. Even with all the noise masking the inflection of her husband's voice, Pinky could tell he was not convinced by his words.

"Well, we bought them the *thaal*," Pinky said, tapping the box by her feet as Esther and her entourage swept past them. The groom and his family were already seated around the small stage and dance floor at the other end of the hall. Very far away, it seemed. Pinky thought that perhaps this was in part because, even though the hall was a small one, it was packed with people. Every few steps, the whole entourage posed for someone to take photos of them, like they were entering along a red carpet. Pinky strained her neck as she politely clapped along in time to the drums. Yes, there undoubtedly was a strip of red carpet that they were walking along. She could see it.

"You got the silver *thaal*?" Harry asked between some very non-rhythmic claps of his own.

"Of course," Pinky answered. The procession was almost at the front of the hall, and the groom's family had stood up to receive the bride, her family—of which there was only Esther's father—and friends.

"I thought you were joking about the silver *thaal*," Harry said. "That's a five-hundred-dollar platter."

"But Esther is a woman of taste and she will appreciate it. It will stand out well among the gifts." In her mind, Pinky added, *And I bet that sour-faced harpy opposite us bought them a kilogram of rice and a sack of garam masala from their storeroom.* How she could not wait to see her face.

Harry did not look convinced, but neither did he push the matter. She had trained him well. The drums finally stopped causing what Pinky considered to be a rather infernal racket, and people began to sit down.

"I haven't seen Lena and Manuel," Pinky said. "Or Anita."

Harry shook his head.

"Perhaps they haven't been invited," Pinky theorized, unable to keep a slightly hopeful note out of her voice. Anita would be a welcome friendly face, but she did not want to see Lena. They had not spoken since Veer and Maya disappeared, and it felt strange for them to have gone so long without speaking, even though she absolutely, definitely did not want to speak to Lena. At such a public event, having to talk to her in front of everyone would only be a further humiliation. That said, both being at the event and not talking—as had been the case at the *Sangeet*—was just as likely to set tongues wagging.

More than that, though, was the fact that if she and Harry had been invited and Lena had not . . . well, that would say something, would it not? That the Sharmas are to blame for Maya and Veer's engagement. That Maya was an older divorced harpy who had lured her son into this disgraceful situation. Pinky's eyes narrowed, and she nodded to herself. It would also take a little of the sting out of the debacle with the seating arrangements.

They moved almost straight onto the gift giving. Traditionally, the bride's family—and maybe also friends—would offer gifts to the bridegroom and, by extension, his family. Here, there was less distinction about who was giving the gift and who was receiving. The most import-ant part was the gifts.

Indeed, it was Esther who seemed to have the most hawklike eyes on who was providing what gift. Not that Pinky paid much attention; she was fairly sure that their gift would outdo any other. She and Harry were a little slow joining the queue, it took far too long to reach the front, and when they were almost there, Pinky turned around and saw her husband's eyes go wide.

Harry glanced at Pinky and quickly away again, trying to find something else to look at. His eyes settled on some pretty young thing, which, for many other wives, might have been a source of jealousy or anger. The game, however, was already up; Pinky knew Harry's gaze was only a distraction tactic.

She searched the room in the direction that he had been looking—toward the stage area where the gift giving was going on—standing on tiptoe and craning her neck over the throng of people bustling around the front of the hall. She was about to give up and interrogate her hus-band when she saw it.

She saw . . . them. Lena and Manuel sat just two—yes, two—tables away from the stage. And, with a terrible clang, Pinky dropped the silver *thaal* onto the floor.

∼

The last week for Lena had been a roller coaster of thoughts and feelings.

Visiting Sameer in prison had been shocking at first: impersonal, degrading, humiliating—and that had been before her son had turned up. For the first time, she had felt like the mother of a felon, rather than merely the mother of two children who had, in their own ways, been disgracing her.

And there had been another lesson learned in the last week, too . . . Something along the lines of *Be careful what you wish for.*

In spite of feeling heart-wrenchingly sad that Maya and Sameer were absent from the festivities of Esther Vora's wedding, Lena had not been able to keep herself from scrutinizing the spread at the *Sangeet*, which had been lackluster at best. As might have been the case with any professional, Lena had been a little upset at not being approached in connection with the catering for Esther Vora's wedding.

It was, of course, ridiculous. Lena certainly was not set up to cater to the scale that Esther's wedding was going to require, and having employed a wedding planner, Esther may have had only limited involvement in choosing suppliers. Then again, Lena had ruminated, if she was anywhere near as much of a control freak as her mother . . .

And there it had been, that poisonous thought: *Of course she wouldn't ask you. Your son is in prison for manslaughter, and your daughter has shamed the son of one of the community's most wealthy families before disappearing with him.*

But then Esther Vora had called. "Mrs. Sharma?"

"It's Jaitly," Lena had replied acidly to the unrecognized voice on the other end of the line. She had been divorced from the man for fourteen years, yet there were still occasions when his surname followed her around. It was bad enough that her kids had to have it.

"Oh . . ." Her snippy reply had stumped the voice on the other end of the phone, which was becoming vaguely familiar. She knew this person, and perhaps they were not selling something, after all. "Lena?" the woman tried.

"Yes."

"It's Esther . . . Esther Vora. You were at my *Sangeet* a few days ago."

"Oh . . . oh, Esther. Yes. Sorry." It was a miracle she and Manuel had been invited at all, Lena had thought, but now the invitations to the *Sagan* and the *Pheras* were probably about to be withdrawn.

"I need your help; we're having a bit of a catering disaster."

And there it had been: her way back into some vague sort of acceptance. There were other very important things on her mind—other than Sameer, there was the fact that her daughter had fled town and was not returning her frantic calls or texts. She'd been often awake in the middle of the night, and Lena was not a woman to pass a sleepless night for any slight cause. Esther's call meant she would have to set her familial worries aside for now.

The next few days had been harried, but she had managed to deliver an acceptable spread for the *Sagan*. Aside from adequate payment, Lena had received the much better recompense of a spot for her and Manuel among the friends and family members at the *Sagan*.

"You are Lena?" one of the women at Lena's table asked a few minutes after they had been seated. Lena did not recognize her, although she might have been a part of the groom's family. She knew that Pinky had known the Dhar family to some extent before the wedding, but Lena and her family had never been wealthy or respected enough to mix in that higher circle. Being a last-minute addition to the family-and-friends area at the *Sagan*, Lena and Manuel had probably been fitted in wherever it was possible to squeeze them. Indeed, it had occurred to her more than once that it might even have been at someone else's expense.

"Yes. Yes, I am," she answered.

"I am Faisal's shameful aunty who no one speaks of," the woman said. She was probably a little older than Lena—with short brown hair and round tortoiseshell glasses—although at their age it was becoming harder to tell who was older than who, since some people wore their years better than others.

Lena smiled awkwardly, not quite knowing what to say in response.

"I have already inspected the spread you have kindly laid out for my nephew's sake at such short notice." Round glasses went on, and she leaned across conspiratorially. "In truth, I only turn up to these things for the food. If it tastes half as good as it looks, then I shall be sure to recommend you. I think it's incredible what you have done in so little time."

What Lena should probably have said was "Please do not recommend me to anyone . . . ever," as the experience of the last few days had left her never wanting to cater anything bigger than a family birthday party ever again. Instead, she smiled and nodded her embarrassed thanks, happy at just the thought of her name being passed around in a positive sense once again.

Soon after, Esther made her entrance, and that was when Lena noticed Pinky and Harry sitting toward the back of the hall. It was a relief, she realized, to be sitting so far from them, but the feeling soon turned to something a little like guilt, before finally mellowing into a wider sadness. She had always loved spending time with Pinky and Anita at public events and gatherings—how they would laugh together and feel like teenage girls for a few hours—and she wondered if things would ever be quite the same again.

But then the gift giving began, and—like everyone else in the hall, she guessed—Lena began to worry that her rather boring gift of department store vouchers was not enough or, at least, not thoughtful enough, and that it would pale in comparison to the other gifts. Ridiculous, she realized, considering the huge service she had provided with the food, but she sometimes felt that worrying about these sorts of things was in her Indian DNA, passed down through many generations of people for whom impressions were everything.

She found herself watching intently as all the gifts were presented, trying to figure out what they were, as it was not always immediately obvious from where she was sitting. Lena was so wrapped up in this that she did not notice as Pinky and Harry joined the line.

The hall went eerily silent in the wake of a loud metallic clang—almost in anticipation rather than reaction—and everyone, including Lena, turned to see Pinky with a stricken look on her usually regal face. She was looking at Lena, but quickly looked away again, while Harry stared stoically straight ahead and put a comforting hand on his wife's back. Slowly, Pinky bent down and picked up what looked like a silver *thaal*—a beautiful-looking serving plate that, if Lena knew Pinky at all, probably cost several hundred dollars.

Even from where Lena sat, she could see that the thing now had a long dent running through the middle of it.

Lena tried to catch Pinky's eye to offer her a sympathetic look but, irritatingly, Pinky was doing an excellent job of avoiding her gaze as she continued to move up the queue. When she finally handed over the dented silver *thaal*, Lena—staring but trying not to look like she was staring—could not fail to notice the devastated look upon Pinky's face.

It is still a beautiful thing, Lena thought charitably, doing her best not to be irked by the way that both Pinky and Harry were blanking her and Manuel. They had not talked at the *Sangeet*, either, and she had almost felt thankful for that—not wanting to be drawn into another altercation with Pinky, yet somehow their refusal to look her way in the well-lit hall was needling Lena, bringing heat into her cheeks and beginning to ruin her first good mood in a long time. Screw that stuck-up peacock of a woman who could only lord it over her because a billionaire businessman had taken pity on her ruined family all those years ago. But for that piece of luck, Lena told herself, there would be nothing to make Pinky any more special than Lena was.

Once the gifts were done, Esther Vora's father—a tall, severe-looking man with bushy side-whiskers who wore a black achkan and white silk pajamas, and had not smiled once all day as far as Lena could tell—applied the *tikka* to Faisal's forehead, and Lena realized that she was about to be called into action. She had offered to clear things away before the dancing started.

"Just go and slim down the food, will you?" she said to Manuel, who wanted to be helpful but, as usual, had no idea how to be so. He looked at her with a quizzical expression, and his hand went subconsciously to his stomach, a mix of temptation and fear spreading across his features. "I don't need you to eat it!" she cried out, rearranging her features into a patient mask. "We need to consolidate the two tables of food into one table—more room for the dancing. So, I need you to double up the plates and so on."

"Right . . . Okay." Manuel hesitated and scratched the side of his nose but, thankfully, started to amble toward the buffet. Lena bustled over to the small stage, knowing that she was undoubtedly going to have to head back to help him in a few moments. He was the most wonderful husband, if only she had managed to train him in domestic matters a little better.

Lena got onto the stage just as Esther's father and Faisal were finishing up. She hurried to tidy up the wrapping from the gifts and the incredible mess that had been made in just a matter of minutes with the *tikka* material—vermillion powder, clay, sandalwood paste, *diyas*, and crushed marigold flowers. Glancing back toward Manuel, she saw him pick up a plate, look at it, bounce his gaze frowningly to the table, then put the plate down again.

Oh, for . . .

Panicking, Lena started throwing the *tikka* things wherever she could—using anything that looked like it might hold or contain the refuse to be carried away from the area. People were already getting up from tables, and the pundit was glaring at Lena, clearly wanting to move his laptop and briefcase out from where it was being stored in the wings, so that he could leave for the next wedding ceremony he was performing.

"What the hell are you doing?" came a voice from behind her. Lena looked up and saw Pinky standing over her, a frown darkening her chiseled features.

"Sorry?" Lena asked, glancing uneasily at Pinky. She followed Pinky's eyes to the floor where, unthinkingly, she had placed the quickly swept-up *tikka* mess onto a dented silver *thaal*.

The dented silver *thaal*. "Oh—" was about as far as Lena got.

"It's not enough that you let your daughter shame my only son," Pinky began savagely, her voice matching her armor of moral certainty, "or that you have the gall to show your face after your son killed a young woman"—she thrust an arm toward the *thaal*, which, in fairness, had been pretty well ruined before Lena had come along—"but now you have to insult me in this way."

Lena tried to speak but was cut off. Not many people could cut Lena off, but Pinky's voice was already so loud and so shrill that it could probably have broken glass. "Is this all I am to you, a place for the trash? Is this what four decades of friendship means to you?"

The blood rushed through Lena's ears like fire hoses. The outrage that she—like almost everyone else—had to be humble in front of Pinky Kapoor let loose the dam of anger that had been rising within her for months. "Friendship? Friendship?" she roared. "If friendship means lording it over me for almost all of those four decades, always being made to feel inferior to Pinky the Bloody Peacock . . ." Lena turned around and kicked the *thaal* across the stage. Pinky's face contorted at the mention of the nickname that everyone used behind her back. Lena was not much of a sportswoman, so the plate did not go far, but still the point was made. "Well, you can go and stick that friendship right up your tight . . ."

Lena did not finish the thought. Instead she stormed from the stage and past Manuel, who stood with two half plates of food in his hands and his mouth wide open.

Chapter 18

"Wey, whaddup, *ese?*"

Wey was Gus's name for Sameer. Apparently, it was street slang for *dude*, or so Gus said. He could be calling Sameer a chicken-legged mofo, and Sameer would have been none the wiser. Even during his time at school when he had still given a damn about any of the lessons, languages hadn't been his strong point. And, anyway, he doubted they would have taught Fake Gangster.

"Whaddup?" Sameer replied, making some sort of effort to meet the big man on his own level. The first time he had done that, Sameer had been worried that Gus might think he was making fun, or something, and it made him think of the restaurant scene in the film *Goodfellas* with Joe Pesci: "I amuse you? I make you laugh?" Not that Gus and Joe Pesci shared too many physical similarities.

Gus had seemed genuinely pleased, though, so Sameer had kept up with it. Anything to keep the big man as a friend, as hanging around with him was keeping trouble away, he was sure of it. Sameer felt lucky to know Gus. He was odd and just about as far as he could be from anyone Sameer might have befriended outside of prison, but no one messed with Gus, and he had come to understand, that meant that no one laid a finger on him.

Having just returned from his cooking class, which was doing a great job of breaking up his week, Sameer was outside his cell on the overhead tier of their wing, standing on what was a sort of gantry-style walkway that ran the entire perimeter of the upper level.

Gus looked past him, through the door of the cell, and at Sameer's latest cellmate, Chad, who was sitting on the bottom bunk. The big man's glare said, *Get out, now.*

Chad—apparently named after the drummer of the Red Hot Chili Peppers—was already Sameer's fourth cellmate. He was an idiot, but he was on a short stretch for robbery and looking to do his time as quietly as possible. Sameer was kind of hoping that Chad was going to stay.

Being an idiot, Chad didn't understand Gus's glare straightaway, not until the big man added, "Move it, *mala copa.*" That was a new one for Sameer; he might have to ask what it meant. He had a feeling that Gus didn't always know what the words he used meant, either.

Chad jumped up, catching his head on the metal bed frame, and hurried out past them.

"We need to talk, *chavo,*" Gus said once Sameer's cellmate was gone. *Chavo* was another unfamiliar term—and instinctively Sameer pinched the skin of his own arm. Something in the way Gus's meaty hand invited him to step back into the cell caused a nervous fluttering in Sameer's stomach. Bad things happened during "private words" in cells.

Gus stepped into the doorway once Sameer was through, blocking the escape route. Sameer tried to think . . . Had he done something to offend the big man? As they had spent more and more time together, he had relaxed around Gus, although never entirely. Something in Gus's manner always carried a small undercurrent of threat.

His pale, weirdly hairless form providing a hulking presence, even standing in the doorway as he was, Gus pointed to the cell's one chair, which coupled with the small desk against the far wall—evidently there so that inmates could keep up with all their important business, Sameer had thought wryly upon first seeing it. "Take a seat."

"You all right?" Sameer squeaked, doing as he was told. He cleared his throat to speak again, this time meaning to sound less like a frightened child, but found that he didn't know what to say.

"You been on kitchen duty, eh, holmes?" Gus said.

"Well, yeah . . . It's cooking class, actually," Sameer answered, wincing inwardly at the fact that he had felt the need to correct Gus.

"That's what I meant," Gus said, reaching up lazily to push against the top of the doorway, reminding Sameer of the temporary steel supports used in the renovation of old buildings.

Understanding started to dawn on Sameer, and he could not believe that he hadn't thought of it sooner. Everything in prison was an angle, about what you had access to, what advantage you could bring. "Look, they're crazy careful with the kni—"

Gus interrupted him merely by taking a step into the room—noticeably reducing the space inside it. "You've gotta keep on with it, you get me, holmes?" he said with an urgent insistence to the way he spoke that wasn't usually there, not even when he had menacingly told Chad to leave the cell a few moments before. "Don't go flunking out."

"Like I said," Sameer pressed, feeling it was better to get this straight right now, be honest and upfront about it. "There's just no way I could get so much as a milk pan out of that kitchen."

Gus's eyebrows furrowed, and he cocked his head slightly to one side. He was looking at Sameer like he was stupid. "Wha . . . ?" Those monstrous shoulders shrugged like mountains moving. "Why would you do that?" Gus asked, the fake gangster persona slipping ever so slightly for a moment.

"Well . . ."

"You told me your mom's a cook."

"The regular San-Fran-Bay Curry Queen," Sameer joked, breathing a small sigh of relief. The conversation wasn't going where he'd thought it would, which was good.

Gus frowned like he didn't quite get what Sameer was saying, but he nodded anyway. "You should follow in your mom's footsteps," he said. "Become a great chef or something, own your own restaurant."

A pseudo-primal instinct activated itself within Sameer, making him feel annoyed where he had been on the verge of terror only moments before. No one had the right to tell him to respect his parents or what to do with his life. Gus wasn't much older than him, and he was making him feel like a teenager. "Oh, I don't know," Sameer replied, getting to his feet, now feeling that he didn't want Gus towering over him so imposingly. As it turned out, standing up didn't make all that much difference. "We're just . . . different. Me and Mom. With the cooking, it was something to get out of my cell, you know."

"You got to have a plan for when you get out of here." Gus poked a finger at him. "Or you'll slide back into the same old shit, be the same old *naco* who drove drunk and got a girl killed." That felt like a slap in the face, almost as hard as Gus's actual hand could have delivered. Aside from that initial discussion he had shared with Gus, they didn't talk about the shit that had landed them where they were. It was almost like an unspoken rule.

"That's years away," Sameer said, feeling stung. Gus's words were true, and Sameer had tortured himself with those thoughts often enough, but he hadn't had it so plainly expressed by anyone else since the trial.

Gus's beady eyes looked like they were misting up. Surely not. "It'll come around, your release, and you'll be just about old enough to have a life still, wey. To be something other than a killer." His chest heaved as he said the words. "Me . . . if they ever let me out of here, I'll already be an old man by then."

Sameer's mouth worked, trying to find the right words, but no sound came out. He had never seen Gus look vulnerable in the way he did now. He watched the man's Adam's apple pulsing in and out, swallowing something back and pushing it down inside.

"Whatever shit made you into that idiot in the car," Gus finally went on, "you got to put it behind you; forgive those you need to forgive—including yourself—and only think about what's ahead."

"Yeah," said Sameer, in a low and unconvincing voice. He listened to the voices of the other inmates in the yard, shouting and cursing and laughing, as he looked through the window of his cell. Gus left, and suddenly Sameer was transported back to the school hall with his teacher, as all around him, the momentary quiet of the cell was swallowed up by the darkening summer sky.

"Do you think this table will take things over too much in the middle?" Mr. Barr asked Sameer as they stood on the school hall's small stage. Sameer was drawing the tattered and stained heavy red curtains back across the stage. They looked as old as the main colonial-style school building itself.

"I think it's good there," Sameer answered as he closed the curtains just in front of it. "It's like an anchor," he said, "or . . . something that everything else can move around."

He had come to realize that a lot of the point of putting on *Our Town* as the school production was that it needed very little in the way of props and sets. Which did then beg the question about why he was still needed as a coproducer. The only real logistical issue still outstanding was going to be sourcing almost thirty sets of the early twentieth-century clothing that they would need.

"I know what you're saying," Mr. Barr said, even though Sameer could tell by his tone that he wasn't quite convinced.

It was a strange position that Sameer found himself in during those first few weeks of working on the school play. On the one hand, he had possibly the coolest English teacher in the history of teaching seeking and, apparently, valuing his opinion on just about everything to do with the play. He got to adapt a script, which sounded like something that someone working in Hollywood did. He had a real say over choosing the cast, too, and this gave him power over all those popular drama kids who usually wouldn't give him the time of day.

The whole thing did, however, make him look like a bit of a teacher's pet, and it wasn't like the bullies needed any more ammunition to give Sameer a hard time with.

"I want to start thinking about lighting, too," Mr. Barr said. He waved a hand toward the space beyond the now-closed curtain, where a geriatric lighting rig was fixed to the ancient ceiling. "We've not got a lot of static options out there, and I'm afraid of messing with the positions of the lights on the rig, just in case I bring the whole thing down."

Sameer finished with the curtains, giving them his customary uncertain look.

Mr. Barr continued as Sameer crossed to the table just in front of the stage. "So, we need to work out what happens on the stage around what we want to do with the lighting, at least a bit, or we'll create a problem if we try to do it all the other way around."

"Uh-huh," Sameer said. He was feeling a little strange this afternoon . . . distracted. Realizing that he hadn't been listening properly to what Mr. Barr had just said, he hoped that the teacher hadn't noticed.

"You okay?" Mr. Barr asked.

Apparently, he had. "Yeah, I'm just . . ."

"Come on, out with it."

Sameer still felt reluctant to speak.

"Look, Sameer, I could probably get fired for this but . . . you know, what the heck. I've got a cheap bottle of wine out back and"—he put on a silly southern accent—"there ain't no one in the school but us sad-ass theater producers. Do you fancy a small glass of the stuff to celebrate the end of Phase One, before the real craziness begins? Then you can tell me what's up if you want to."

Sameer was unsure, but he didn't want to end this last evening of "just them" on the low note of having refused such an invitation. He'd had alcohol before, and if he was going to be honest, he did want to talk to someone, and—lame though it might be—Mr. Barr was just about his only option.

"My mother's calling tonight," Sameer said as Mr. Barr rummaged around in a plastic carrier bag, producing a bottle of wine and two plastic glasses. The teacher indicated a thick crash mat, the sort usually seen in the gym. Sameer could only guess it was there for stage stunts, although he didn't think it was going to be needed in their play.

"She lives in . . ."

"Danville," Sameer finished.

"That's right. Nice."

"A lot nicer than where I live."

"Is it bad that she's calling?"

"It used to be. I . . . I don't know, I blamed her about the divorce. And mostly it was just awkward, you know? Like, you live together all these years, and you just talk all the time. Mostly about the usual stuff. Then you're talking on the phone once or twice a week, and suddenly you have to find something to say. And . . ."

Sameer paused as Mr. Barr handed him a cup of the wine and they sat down on the edge of the crash mat. "And it always felt so false, you know? Plus, she would have to tell me that she loved me ten times at the end of the call like I'd missed it the other nine."

Mr. Barr laughed.

"It's been better lately, since I've been doing the play, because now we organize a time, and at least I'm prepared and I can think of things to say, you know?"

The teacher took a large swig of wine, downing almost half of his cup. Sameer gulped down his and tried not to cringe. He wasn't a fan of wine, he decided.

"So, why's it a problem tonight, then?" Mr. Barr asked.

Sameer took a breath, not quite believing that he was going to say it out loud. "The last time she called, I was out, and . . . I was actually thinking of calling her myself. I . . . I think I might see if she'll let me move back."

The wine cup stopped halfway to the teacher's mouth. "Wow, that's big."

Sameer took another gulp of the wine, which wasn't so bad this time, and nodded his agreement. "I just thought it would be different, you know . . . living with my dad. I thought we would get that quality time we never had before, but he's always at work, and half the time, he brings a different woman back to the apartment with him. Sometimes we have pizza in front of the TV, but that's about it. Mostly he pretends I'm not there."

Sameer took another swig and forged on, the words flowing like . . . well, like they said wine sometimes did. Next to him, Mr. Barr lay down, his head propped up on one arm.

"I miss my sister. I've, like, only seen her twice since I moved in with my dad. I miss my mom's cooking. I also miss just living in a nor-mal house. Our apartment is a shithole." Sameer slapped a hand over his mouth, eyes wide. "Sorry."

"It's just us here," Mr. Barr said casually, tapping the mat, indicating for Sameer to lie down next to him. Sameer's head was beginning to swim a bit, so it seemed like a nice idea. Suddenly—he didn't quite see how—the bottle of wine was in Mr. Barr's hand, and more wine was being poured into his plastic cup.

"I guess I never gave my mom credit," Sameer said as he propped his head on one arm, just like the teacher was doing. "But she made the house . . . a home, I guess. Our apartment is chaos and always such a mess.

"I don't . . . kn-know whether I will shay it tonight but . . ."

"You'll have to move schools again," Mr. Barr pointed out.

"Don't worry," Sameer said with a lazy, alcohol-affected grin. "It won't . . . won't be before . . . the end of the year. I can . . , f-finish the play." Words were starting to become difficult for Sameer, yet the teacher was halfway through his second cup of wine, and he thought he should keep drinking, though he decided to turn his gulps into sips.

"This will be the last time that it will be just the two of us," Mr. Barr said.

"I know," Sameer said. It was the other reason he had been distracted. He wasn't looking forward to having to share his favorite teacher. It was like having a clever older friend who he looked up to and who genuinely got him. Now there would be needy drama kids clamoring for his attention.

"Drink up. We should make this special," the teacher said.

Sameer didn't know what he meant, and he wasn't sure that he wanted to down the rest of the wine. He did as he was told, however, and immediately regretted it. Nausea flared for a moment, then settled back down again, replaced by a glowing warmth in his cheeks and a slightly spinning ceiling.

Later that night, Sameer had sat on his bed. He'd curled himself into a ball, trying to push himself into the wall, trying to scrunch into it and disappear. Goldie had begun slamming his fist against the bedroom door. The tears had dried up, which was the worst thing. Crying had been a way of getting the feelings of fear and revulsion for all that had transpired out of himself, bleeding hotly out of his blinking eyes and washing away what boiled riotously inside him.

Now the emotions had nowhere to go and they were threatening to overwhelm him.

"Sameer!" Goldie barked from outside his bedroom door. "It's your mother."

"I told you, I don't want to speak to her."

"Boy, you come out here and speak to your mother now, eh. Do it, or I swear I'll . . ."

Goldie did not finish the threat; he did not have to. His father could be enough of a general shit if he was pissed at someone, without having to do anything specific. Lena was probably threatening to come over and sneer at the life Goldie was providing for their son again; Sameer could hear the dread in his father's voice.

Sameer got up and had to stop for a moment as pain lanced briefly inside him. It had been a long, awkward, and often painful walk home, and he was scared—scared that he was damaged inside, scared that he would have to go to a doctor and everyone would find out what had happened.

He opened the door and glared at his father, who glared just as intently back and thrust the phone out at him.

"What?" Sameer hissed impatiently down the phone. He wanted her gone, wanted to be back in the room. No, what he wanted was not to be in this crappy apartment at all. To be back at home in Danville, going to his old school with his old friends, with no . . .

He almost burst out crying. He felt it like a raging howl held inside him. Lena had said something, maybe about homework or not speaking or . . . something. He had missed it. After an awkward silence, she spoke again.

"How's life with your father going? Is he treating you well?"

"What's that supposed to mean?" The words came out before he even thought them, bursting forth in place of the howl that had been there a moment before.

"Is . . . Is he spending time with you? Not always at work or . . . out with someone?"

Yes, he's always at work or out with someone. You left me with this selfish shit and now . . . Now . . . "If you want to ask about Dad's life, then you should be speaking to him."

"I just mean that—"

"Look, if that's all you've got to say, then I've got things to do—"

"The school play?"

What? *She knows. Oh-oh-oh* fuck, *she knows.*

"Your father told me when I missed you the last time . . . he said you were helping out with a school play. Was that why you were back late from school today? I think that's grea—"

"I hate you."

Sitting now on the top bunk in his cell, as Chad snored quietly below him, Sameer rocked slightly backward and forward, his knees drawn up to his chest. The conversation with Gus was hanging around at the edge of his thoughts, prodding at him. Not so much the well-meaning message that the big man had given him—although Sameer had been relieved that he wasn't being asked to procure Gus a weapon—but his own, almost visceral reaction to the words.

Don't tell me how to feel about my own mother, he had raged internally. *You don't know shit. She left me, left me with a father I couldn't talk to, with a sister who looks down upon me, and a new school where . . .*

Maybe he had been feeling this way for too long.

Chapter 19

"You're quiet," Manuel remarked to Lena as the two of them crossed the San Francisco–Oakland Bay Bridge, heading into the city from their home in Walnut Creek. She had been withdrawn, she knew it. She also knew that her husband understood why, despite the apparently innocent tone of the question. Here was an invitation to speak about it.

The argument with Pinky had been playing over and over in Lena's mind. She did not want it to, but the words and the feelings of impotent rage kept coming back to her. She could not get them out of her head—addicted to the rush of fury that every mental rerun brought with it.

What was most interesting about it was that, half the time, Lena was thinking about things she should have said and done to defuse the situation, instead. She regretted her outburst, partly because she was embarrassed by the memory of it, but also because she had hurt Pinky. However much the woman deserved it, they went back so far, and now Lena had said certain things that she could never take back. She should have taken the higher ground.

"And the other half of the time," Lena explained as they drove through the San Francisco streets several minutes later, "I think of all the things I could have and should have said to put that prim, tight-ass, fu—frustrating woman more firmly in her place. Dammit, all I did was use her dented plate to quickly pick up some rubbish."

"Would that have made you feel any better?" Manuel asked placidly from the seat next to her.

"No . . . it's not about . . . Just shut up, okay?"

Manuel did not react to her snappy reply, not so much as a twist of the mouth or a crease of the brow. He just kept driving, looking at the road ahead. It had the desired effect.

"Actually, there is this third feeling," she told him. "It's not anger, it's not shame. It's . . ." Lena strained to describe this other feeling that had taken longer to reveal itself than the other two. "Relief."

"Uh-huh?" Manuel pressed gently after Lena had been staring off into the middle distance for a few moments. Giving the feeling form had been a little stunning for her—a sort of revelation.

"It's like telling Pinky those things, those . . . truths, I guess," she explained, "has lifted this weight from me. Something I've been holding on to for years, and for better or worse, I've let go of it." She drew in a deep breath that filled her ample chest. "I feel lighter."

"Are you sure about this?" Manuel asked several minutes after they had left behind the towering glass and steel towers and the surrounding buildings had become smaller, older, and progressively more tumbledown.

Lena sighed. "No . . ." she answered, "and yes. I mean, I have to do something, don't I? If I never get to have a proper relationship with my son ever again and I didn't try something? Well, then I can't blame anyone else but myself."

"Very wise words, my wife," Manuel said with a grin. "It's just, you know . . . this?"

His timing was impeccable as they pulled up outside the small hall that they had hired for the afternoon. It was one of those buildings that a Realtor might try to spin as a "development opportunity," then look slightly ashamed about it.

Lena inclined her head to indicate that she got Manuel's point. "If I want to understand his world," she said, "then I need to reach out.

Sameer put me onto this idea, how he is taking up cooking in prison. And food . . . food is what I *do*. With food I can relate. Seeing him going to prison and Maya disappearing, I've felt so helpless these last few months. I needed to do something."

The last few words caught in Lena's throat, coming out as more of a croak.

"And you are," Manuel reassured her, reaching out and lightly clasping her forearm.

Just over an hour later, they had set themselves up inside and were in business.

"This is making me realize how we never come into the city anymore," Manuel said, wringing his hands in delight.

Despite his reservations when they arrived, Manuel had soon started beaming, and Lena was beginning to find it mildly irritating. "We never came into this part of the city," she said crossly as she ladled out a generous helping of a *masala* dish of her own devising.

"Maybe you never did," Manuel retorted. He had been charged with the rice, as he could not tell a Balti from a korma until he put it in his mouth and, Lena had her suspicions, perhaps not even then.

"Second-Chance Curry"—Manuel's name, and she'd had her doubts—had been a resounding success . . . sort of.

The small hall was in San Francisco's Mission District and was blessed with an abundance of flaking blue paint, a sagging window unit, and a decrepit peaked roof. Cobwebs hung from the ceiling like long, dangling veils. It had a small, shadowy attached kitchen with rotting countertops and clogged plumbing that delivered only a brown and sludgy liquid. But, for now, it worked in a pinch. The vendor had been happy to rent it out for just three hours on a one-off basis and had not seemed in the slightest bit interested in what it was going to be used for. The event had been much busier than Lena had expected, especially considering their last-minute effort with a couple of posters and flyers to advertise it.

"Ha!" Lena said. "You're the biggest country bumpkin I've ever met, husband. As if you ever came into the city before you met me. I'll bet Danville was like a metropolis for you."

"I used to come to a market two blocks over every week."

Lena raised an eyebrow in reply, one that said: *Doesn't that just make you the urbanite?*

"I can't believe it's going so well," Manuel commented gaily.

"Uh-huh," Lena replied half-heartedly.

"Isn't it?" Manuel turned to smile at a man whose skin was dirty and who had a ruddiness that might equally have been sunburn or years' worth of alcohol. His scraggly beard and clothes were ingrained with the same dirt as his skin, and in a perverse way, like a young woman who has slathered her face in makeup, his age was hard to determine.

"Yes, it's going well," Lena eventually replied, once she had served the man with some dal, having described what each of the dishes was. She had been doing that a lot.

"We're feeding lots of people," Manuel pointed out, obviously not convinced by the words, perhaps because of her dispirited tone. "And some of them really look like they need it."

"Hmm," Lena hummed pointedly. "Maybe that's a part of it. We put up a sign saying that this is for ex-cons, and I'm not saying that anyone here is, er . . . coming under false pretenses. In fact . . ." She nodded to a group of four men in the far corner of the little hall who were all hunched forward over their plates and talking in what looked to her like a conspiratorial manner. "I'm worried that those ones over there are planning their next heist right now."

Manuel chuckled. "You think we should ask for proof that the people coming in for food are the real deal? Prison tattoos to get in?"

Lena deliberately ignored the joke and replaced one of the pots of *navratan* dal on the burner in front of her.

"You know, it's funny," she went on after about a minute. "Maya was the one I was always trying to get to learn to cook, and she was terrible at it. Always had an excuse, something else to do every time I was trying to show her a new dish. Have you seen the pokey little kitchen she has in that expensive apartment of hers? I'll bet it's only ever the microwave that gets used in there.

"But it's Sameer, isn't it, who now says he always had an interest in cooking? And I never saw that. I wanted him to be the successful businessman and her to be the good Indian wife, the cook. How wrong can one woman be?"

"Come now—" Manuel began.

"And yet it was Maya who became such a successful business-woman." Tears now welled in her eyes, but at least the line for curry had temporarily gone quiet. "And I never told her how proud I was of what she had accomplished. And now she's . . ."

A burly, dark-haired man of about thirty with a face ravaged by childhood acne—some of the craters still visible beneath a close-cropped black beard—came in, and Lena quickly rubbed away the tears and recovered herself while Manuel spooned out the rice.

"I tried hard to be a good mother," Lena went on quietly, once the man had moved on. "Although sometimes I think I was trying hardest to be a good wife for Goldie, like I had something to prove for getting the Sharma boy—a better match than anyone had hoped for me. Then, once he and Sameer went, I was trying my hardest to make a living and get the business going. Did I miss bringing up my children somewhere in between? Perhaps this last year has been some sort of comeuppance for that."

Manuel reached over and squeezed his wife's arm again. "You are a force, Lena Jaitly," he said, "but you are not that powerful."

Lena smiled in appreciation at his effort, even if it did not really help. "You know," she said a little distractedly as a tiny wizened-looking woman accepted her plate and moved on, "Sameer was trying to tell me something the other day, something bad, I think, about living with Goldie. He closed off before he finished, then that's when we got onto the cooking talk and . . . I just feel like I don't know my kids as well as I should. I look down on Goldie, but . . . What is it they say about getting your own house in order first?"

"Maybe I'm biased," Manuel said gruffly, "but I think you're too hard on yourself. Goldie is an asshole," he added with a raised eyebrow. "Everyone knows that."

"Yeah, well"—Lena shrugged—"this was what the Second-Chance Curry thing was about . . . feeling like I could connect. But I'm not sure it's working the way I wanted."

Manuel looked thoughtfully out at all the people still eating in the small hall. "Second . . . Chance . . . Curry," he said almost to himself, rubbing his chin in that way he did when an idea was coming. "Maybe Sameer should be our example. He's learning something he can take with him when he gets out of prison. Instead of just feeding the ex-cons, why don't we teach them to cook at the same time?"

She liked that. She liked that a lot.

It had been a heck of a day for revelations, and this new one was blowing Lena's mind wide open. As she began to pack away her used chafing dishes, *Magnum P.I.* played on an old-fashioned television set mounted on the wall behind the area where they had set up the buffet. Lena's brain whirred. Not just with thoughts about teaching convicts to cook, either. Other things were coming more sharply into focus. It was time that Lena started taking a more direct approach about her missing daughter, too.

Chapter 20

"Road trip!" Sarah squealed as Maya started up the Tesla, which purred gently to life. She had owned the eco-friendly all-electric car for a couple of years and had become used to how quiet it was when she drove around, but the lack of that enthusiastic petrochemical roar upon turning the ignition was something she still found disconcerting.

"Let's go to town!" Maya joined in using her best country-boy accent, and then turned off the engine again.

Sarah gave her a quizzical look.

"What, you've never seen *The Lost Boys*?" Maya asked, dismayed that her amusing eighties pop-culture reference was being missed. Veer would have gotten it, and he wasn't even alive in the eighties. "It's, like, one of my favorite movies."

"Honey," Sarah answered, "I'm old enough to have seen most eighties movies in the cinema, but I was more a *Breakfast Club* kinda girl."

Maya nodded her approval to that and started the engine again. She should be careful, she supposed, as the battery was low, and she and Veer had run the thing dead in town once before already. Paradise was not quite the electric car–friendly town that San Francisco was. She pulled off the drive of their house in the south of Paradise. They lived far down the lane, some way beyond the point where the tarmac road just sort of gave up and became gravel, so that a slightly heavy foot on

Maya's part caused the clutch on the car's automatic gearbox to spin up the wheels.

"Sorry," Maya apologized, "I've hardly driven these past few months."

"Don't you apologize," Sarah replied with one of her mischievous grins. "I might have been a petrol head in another life, you know. Derek does all the driving, but you should ask him who won when he took me go-karting on our third date. He's never taken me go-karting since, let us just say that."

Maya laughed. Sarah might seem like a fussy busybody sometimes, but she had a way of making Maya relax whenever she found herself in the older woman's company. They headed north—the only direction to head in, as the road slowly merged with the rest of the landscape the other way—soon coming to the junction with Pearson Road. Turning left, they headed into the center of Paradise, an almost impenetrable wall of fir trees hemming them in on either side, broken only by turn-offs onto other roads and the occasional track into some dwelling or other building.

"Blossom Baby Store is the only place in town for baby stuff," Sarah told her as they drove, "although sometimes the market gets a few sleep-suits in. I guess we're lucky even to have that in our little town, and not to have to go all the way into Chico."

"I don't know if we'll get much," Maya answered. "I just want to get in the mood, you know?" Sarah gave a lazy nod of agreement. "I feel like, so far, being pregnant has mostly been about vomiting and weight gain. Two things I always thought were mutually exclusive. I need to feel like a mom-to-be."

They carried on in silence for a while, but Sarah kept eyeing Maya with sideways glances as they drove along. Eventually, as the trees suddenly receded and they came to an open area dotted with a mix of commercial and industrial lots alongside the road, Maya had to say something. "What?" she asked, starting to feel paranoid.

"Well . . ." Sarah began, with a rare hint of nervousness in her tone, "you just tell me if it's none of my business."

"Oh," Maya said with a wry chuckle, "I'm going to love this, aren't I?"

"I was just wondering if you had spoken to your mother yet?" the older woman pressed on.

Almost against her will, Maya found herself deflecting a little. "Well, I've been looking at how Veer's communications have been going with his mother, and it doesn't fill me with confidence about talking to mine."

"What do you mean?" Sarah asked.

"Um, Pinky—Veer's mother—is probably one of the scariest people I've ever met."

Sarah raised her eyebrows as they pulled into a parking lot, where the pastel-painted baby store lay just across the way.

"Don't get me wrong," Maya added hastily, "she was, like, my Pinky Aunty most of my life."

"Aunty?"

"Not actual aunty," Maya exclaimed with a laugh. "Veer and I aren't cousins. It's just what we call our parents' friends . . . Aunty and Uncle, to show respect and proximity."

"Oh, okay." Sarah still sounded a little confused but didn't stop Maya from carrying on.

"I always loved Pinky Aunty, but sometimes she had this stiff and unrelenting way about her, like she could be made of stone if she wanted to be. And Veer . . . you could always tell how protective she was of him."

"From what you've told me, no shit," Sarah agreed, always sounding funny when she swore.

"But, if Pinky is the scariest woman I've ever met, then my mother is probably the most stubborn. What's the point in talking to her if I know how the conversation will go?"

Sarah shrugged noncommittally. "I get what you're saying, and I'm thrilled to be going baby-clothes shopping with you, especially as I'm not sure if I'll ever get to be doing this for a grandchild of my own. But I can't help thinking about your mother down in San Francisco. I feel . . ."

"Guilty," Maya quietly finished for Sarah, when it seemed she would be unable to finish the sentence for herself. Sarah's only answer was a sad smile—Maya knew from their earlier conversations that their only son couldn't have children. Maya felt the day's joy draining out of her already.

"True, this might be my mom's only chance to do something like shop for a grandchild's baby clothes," Maya stated somberly. "I'm nearing forty, and Sameer's life is on hold for the next twelve years." Then she remembered that last conversation with Lena. *I assumed you wouldn't be going ahead with that foolishness . . . not with what is happening.* The guilty moment passed. "But I feel like she's the one who's made her bed with all of this.

"You know what, Sarah?" Maya said, her voice cracking slightly, tears being pushed back from the threshold. "I always did my best to be a good daughter for her. Worked hard, married a nice Indian boy. Got divorced, of course, because it turned out he wasn't such a nice Indian boy, after all. And that wasn't my fault, like our dad being such a shit wasn't her fault." She could feel her teeth grinding before she said the next words. "But it was never enough."

～

Maya and Sarah left the store with three onesies: one blue, one pink, one yellow. Sarah seemed to think that they needed to be covered for any eventuality, which made Maya wonder what the yellow one was for. No matter, she didn't believe in any of that gender-stereotyping nonsense. She would be perfectly happy with a boy all in cerise pink.

"I never knew you were divorced," Sarah said as they placed their meager purchases in the back of the car.

It took Maya a moment to remember that she had mentioned that fact just before they went into the store. "Another life," she answered, a little distantly, "or it feels like it. But not when you're Indian, I guess; that stuff sticks with you forever."

"And you said your mom was divorced, too?" Sarah asked as she opened the Tesla's door. They both climbed in before Maya answered.

"Yeah. The thing with Indian society, even here in the US, is that if a woman leaves a man, he gets all the sympathy, especially if she cheats or leaves him for someone else. Then she's a wicked whore."

Maya activated one of the controls on the Tesla's touch screen before turning to Sarah and continuing. "If the man cheats, or if he leaves his wife, then surely she did not do enough to keep him. She must have let things slide in the bedroom or in the kitchen department. Maybe she's too fat and unattractive, or a lousy cook or housekeeper."

"You want to grab some tea and cake, or something?" Sarah asked her. "My treat. You know the place over on Skyway?"

"Veer knows the town so much better than I do," Maya admitted shamefully. She had never been so helpless back in San Francisco.

"Just keep along Pearson," Sarah told her as they pulled out of the parking lot. "I'll tell you when."

Soon they were climbing out of the commercial center and passing low hills, which sprang out of the land and were dense with underbrush. Maya could see Sarah looking thoughtful again. "Is that how it was when your parents got divorced?" the older woman asked eventually. "Like you were saying before about always blaming the woman?"

Maya nodded. "My mom's always been a big woman, so that didn't help perceptions, I guess. People always shamed her for letting herself go, although she kept an immaculate house in a coveted zip code to offset things." Sarah looked puzzled, so Maya went on. "These things matter. Honestly, everything about outward appearances matters where

I come from. The size of your house, the make of your car, and whom you're dating or marrying is everybody's favorite topic. It's what Veer and I came up here to escape from." Maya moved the air conditioning vents to shoot on her face and neck and looked out the window at the hot, cloudless November day.

"Then Mom went and met Manuel rather than age quietly and gracefully as a divorcée," Maya continued. "A non-Indian. A Mexican, even. And yes, there's enough racism around, even among us immigrants. It's been hard for Mom, always being on the outside," she mused. "I do get that, I really do. Probably worse because one of her best friends is Pinky Kapoor, wife of one of the Bay's richest men, who could never put a foot wrong in our social circles. But that's just it, Sarah, that's what I don't understand. Why can't she empathize with me more?"

Reaching the end of Pearson Road, Maya turned right onto Skyway Road, another of the town's big thoroughfares, which linked it to Butte Meadows in the north and, the other way, to Chico in the southwest.

"Oh, Maya," Sarah said after a few moments, her tone affectionate. "Don't take this the wrong way, and I know you'll get there soon, but until you've had a child of your own, you will always be a child yourself in some ways."

Maya knit her brows but was not exactly offended. "What do you mean?"

"Do you know what the number-one thing is that any parent wants for their child?"

"I don't know," Maya answered a little impatiently. "Health? Happiness? Safety?"

"A better life than they had. Not to make the same mistakes."

Sarah didn't say any more than that, and about a minute later, they pulled up in front of a café that looked quaint and inviting in an old-fashioned sort of way, with blue painted shutters and a door looking out onto a courtyard area. Blue-checkered tablecloths brought out the blue of the shutters.

Maya could feel a vein pulsing in her forehead as she sat in the driver's seat. She, like her mother, had been divorced, and had left a man who didn't make her happy. But she hadn't let that stop her and had worked hard to become successful. Now, she was in a relationship that had caused her to become the proverbial talk of the town within their close-knit local Indian community.

Sheesh. Like mother, like daughter, huh?

Sometimes, Maya felt like a halfway house of a halfway house. Not merely a child of Indian parents growing up in America, she had been born back in the motherland—Indian by the place of her birth, as well—although she could scarcely remember the short time that she lived there. She had often felt adrift in a way that Veer or Sameer never could, a mongrel mishmash of identities, and had at times been jealous of those kids who were more American than Indian. Sometimes she had even resented her parents' generation for their strong sense of who they were.

Yet she was far more like her mother than she had realized. If Maya was any one thing, she was coming to understand, it was her mother's daughter.

Chapter 21

It was a beautiful ceremony. The sacred fire was a little like everything else, huge under the wedding *mandap*, or pergola, and Pinky had been able to feel the heat from about halfway back in the rows of seats.

Pinky stared unseeing at the grand columns where sprays of hibiscus, marigolds, and fragrant jasmines wilted in the heat and fire smoke. She had been feeling so miserable, so embarrassed, so . . . powerless. Veer had stopped returning her calls, and her rich Silicon Valley friends were sad and outraged for her, but in such a tsk-tsk-isn't-it-terrible-that-Veer-and-Maya-have run-away manner that left her feeling brittle and defensive. Could her angst possibly be because she had fallen out with her best friend over Maya and Veer's choices? Harry was angry, too. She could tell by the way that she had hardly seen him for the last couple of days—something that could easily happen when it was just the two of them rattling around in the mansion. Pinky was not sure whether he was angry at her for the outburst itself, angry with Lena for her words, or just at the whole situation in general, and right now, she could not be bothered to ask. It was just easier to keep avoiding him.

Pinky took her sunglasses off and chewed on the stem. They had been happy less than a year ago. Their handsome, talented son did what he wanted, but he did what he wanted well and would one day have his pick of all the most eligible Indian women in the Bay Area. He'd never been one of those high school jocks who was consumed with girls in short skirts and getting at what was underneath them. Instead, he'd matured into a poster boy for the Sensitive Male club, and she had been so proud of what an amiable and upbeat young man he was.

Somewhere in front of her, a woman cursed the heat. A baby cooed. Pinky looked at the fuchsia-and-orange swaths of organza fabric cascading to the *mandap* floor in pools all around Esther, and the colors started to smear together as she gazed, eyes blurring.

She was not so ignorant or self-obsessed as to not realize that her objections to Maya and Veer's marriage might sound traditional and outdated to a younger generation. Still, there were things you could never appreciate until you had watched a child grow up yourself. Until you had invested years in hoping and dreaming for them. Until you saw the same mistakes that you yourself had made as a foolish younger adult being played out by the next generation. She knew that Lena would appreciate that fact. *It's this wretched generation gap,* she remembered Lena complaining when Maya had changed majors and her mother was upset at the one full year of wasted tuition. *Why can you not rejoice that I found my path?* Maya had huffed at her in return.

As for Veer, every time she reproached him, it made him more incensed. He wasn't returning her calls or responding to her text messages. And, when she trawled through her social-media pages, she found they had been erased of any traces of Veer. He had deleted and blocked her. The pain of the online snub was like a vicious, nagging paper cut. He had cut off all ties with her as if to say, *You may have raised me, but your input is no longer the primary influence on me.*

And here she was bemoaning Lena for her inability to control Maya. If she was brutally honest with herself—and Pinky usually felt that the world was brutal enough, without her help—she knew that she had looked down upon Lena. Not because she and Harry were so wealthy—which was what Lena no doubt thought—but because Lena had in some ways stopped being a parent when Goldie and Sameer left. Maya was already at college, Sameer only around on occasional weekends, and Lena had found her business . . . her new baby. She could not mother Sameer properly and had not continued to mother Maya as she should, and look what had happened.

Pinky dug her painted nails into the flesh of her hand, reproaching herself, even as the realization about how wrong she had been continued to bloom. For all the time Pinky had, she had been as powerless as Lena, for all the money they had, she and Harry had been unable to locate the couple.

Sucking her teeth to hide her panic, Pinky tried to hold back a sob. It felt like she was hovering on a precipice, and on the other side was a screaming abyss of despair unlike anything she'd experienced before, even during those times of true grief—when her dad died, or when the family business turned out to be bankrupt—and, if the separation had taught her anything, it was that she couldn't bear Veer not talking to her. She felt her emotional foundations shifting; how empty her life had felt, bereft of the usual pattern of Veer and her speaking every Tuesday and Thursday, and their Friday lunches together in Pinky and Harry's home—him calling her Mommy the way he did, which thrilled her soul to its very center, his warm, lively presence that she had taken for granted. Having been so sure of herself and her actions for so long, it was amazing to realize that much of her strength, decisiveness, and confidence derived from Veer and her being a family together.

So, what if it turned out that Maya had the starring role in his production of *Happily Ever After*? At least Maya was sharp and smart, and not ludicrously unsuitable like a porn artist or a stripper. Immediately, Pinky's thoughts flitted to her Silicon Valley friend Asha, whose son had dropped a bomb by announcing he wanted to marry a pole dancer. Tsk-tsk, poor Asha.

Pinky's heart lurched as if at the sudden scurry of a black, hairy tarantula, overcome with the sobering realization that things could be worse. In that moment Pinky felt a shift, as quick as a delicious bite of *kulfi* melts in the mouth: it suddenly occurred to her that she could make peace with it. If she was ever to see her son again, be a family again, she had to accept Veer's decision.

Pinky leaped up from her seat, making little puffing noises through her lips. There was something she must do, something that went hand in hand with her newfound position on her son's choice of partner. Whatever it took to repair the rift with Maya's mother—her lifelong friend, Lena—she must do it as a first step toward a reconciliation with Veer. It took some time to get her alone, but eventually, she managed it.

"A word, please, Lena Jaitly," Pinky said, biting her lower lip.

$\sim$

Lena had felt Pinky's gaze on her throughout much of the ceremony, had done her best to ignore the heavy weight it seemed to add to the back of her neck, determined as she had become over recent days that a falling-out with Pinky Kapoor—however long and deep their friend-ship—was not currently the most pressing issue in her life. It wasn't the most pressing issue in her life when she got up that morning, and then, as she arrived at the *Pheras*, Lena had received a phone call that had at least doubled that sentiment.

Yet it took Lena off guard when, fully half an hour after the cere-mony had finished, Pinky had suddenly emerged out of the crowd, an intense, serious look on her face.

They were a little way from the tent, near a small grove of cotton-wood trees. Manuel looked uncertainly between Pinky and Harry—the other woman's husband was hanging back a few yards, and with a deep inner breath, Lena squeezed her husband's arm, giving him permission to move away. Harry and Manuel fell into step with each other as they walked away from the women. They looked odd—the tall, thin Harry and the smaller, still wiry Manuel—men who had never been easy in each other's company, if not for want of trying.

"Wonderful food at the *Sagan*," Pinky remarked brightly.

"Thank you," Lena replied stiffly. The compliment had thrown her a little, especially after the rather formal way Pinky had asked to speak to her. Lena's chin lifted, her hackles were being raised . . . and, by heck, she was going to fight. Not because she gave a damn what Pinky Kapoor or anyone else thought, but more because she wasn't planning to take any more abuse from anyone. In fact, wasn't worrying about what everyone else thought what got them to where they were now?

"I've always respected the way you took something that you were good at—your passion—and made a successful business out of it," Pinky said, looking Lena straight in the eye.

Lena became very still. In the distance, having been egged on by some of the guests to make a repeat performance of their turns around the fire, so that everyone could get more photos and video, the couple completed their first circuit again.

"You provided for your family," Pinky continued gravely, "after . . . you know, Goldie. Unlike me, who has been provided for all of my life." There was a fragile honesty to the way that Pinky was speaking, which was further disarming Lena.

"Every time I speak to Kookie Aunty," Pinky went on, looking off to a space above Lena's head, "I'm reminded how old we all suddenly find ourselves to be, how little time there literally is when it comes to it, how ill-health can rob us of even that. And I wonder if I have not done enough with my time." Pinky exhaled, then fixed her gaze on Lena. "I know I could have been a better friend to you at times," she finished, holding her tiny clutch bag in front of her with trembling fingers. They had been sixteen years old the last time Lena saw those fingers tremble in that way. Although still slender with pink polish on acrylic nails, the fingers were beginning to wrinkle with age.

"Ah, Pinky, that was a long time ago," Lena said desperately. Pinky was apologizing for past slights—perhaps the time when Pinky did not stand up for her at the cards night in her home, or before that, with the married man who had found license to place a too-familiar hand about Lena's waist when it became widely known she was a divorcée. There were times when Pinky could have spoken up, when the word of a Kapoor would have carried weight and provided much-needed support.

Lena was grateful for the olive branch being offered, but it was unsettling to see the regal Pinky so humbled, even though there had been times in the past few weeks when she had fantasized about it. An image surfaced: Lena in the days after Goldie—and Sameer—left, when Pinky would come over, open the blinds, fling back the covers under which Lena was hiding, and say, "Let's go for a drive." She would get in the car with Pinky, and they would stop to get hot-fudge sundaes—a familiar ritual from their college days in New Delhi—from Mel's Diner. Pinky would park at the beach, where they would stare out at the ocean for hours on end, neither of them saying a word. Lena wasn't sure when the grief lifted, when the heaviness lightened, and daily life began to overshadow the pain of the divorce, but eventually she began to talk and giggle again with Pinky, and later, when she met Manuel, let love in.

They had been looking silently at each other for several long moments, as Faisal and Esther came onto their third circuit, their steps progressing at several times the original ceremony's speed—more a celebratory dance than the original solemn commitment. Lena's podgy, phone-poking fingers had knitted with Pinky's ringed ones, and she had not even noticed it happen.

"Our children," Pinky sniveled, wiped her eyes and nose on the *pallav* of her light-pink sari with a silver border, and looked down.

"That reminds me," Lena said, withdrawing her fingers only to reach up and wipe a tear gently from her friend's cheek, careful not to smudge her makeup. "I took a certain liberty." She glanced over to where their two husbands were walking a slow circle farther up in the distance, trying to look like they were having a riveting conversation and yet, all the while, eyeing their wives like hawks. Had they gleaned that it was safe to come back to them yet?

"Liberty?"

"I was fed up with being ignored. With not knowing where they were or how to get ahold of Maya if there was an emergency."

"Veer has stopped answering my calls and has blocked me on social media, although we did have one brief conversation sometime back," Pinky admitted as Faisal and Esther began their penultimate circle around the fire.

Lena raised her eyebrows. "At least he has spoken to you. How are they?"

Pinky looked ashamed. "I'm sorry, Lena, I should have . . . Even with how everything has been, I should have thought to let you know. I just assumed that Maya . . ."

"It's okay," Lena told her. "But she hasn't." Lena swallowed the lump in her throat. "She must be really mad with me."

It was Pinky's turn to reach out a hand. "To be honest, *fine* is about as much detail as I got out of him. And that they are not so far away. That's about all I know."

"Well," Lena said, clearing her throat as cheers erupted and camera flashes went off with the couple having finished their steps around the fire, "hopefully we will know more soon." Behind Pinky, their two husbands were now heading back down toward them. "I thought it was time to take charge of things a little, so I've hired a private investigator to see if he can track them down." Lena paused, then spoke softly, "He has a reputation for being discreet, so I'm not concerned about that."

"Ha!" Pinky let out a small wry laugh. "Great minds, eh? Harry and I did the same thing a few weeks after they left." Her lips pressed together and pushed into a pout. "I should have mentioned—"

Lena waved away the attempt at an apology; they had been in a different place then.

"But it was no good," Pinky went on. "A total waste of money. So, I wouldn't be too hopeful."

"He's gotten back to me already," Lena put in. "Called just after I arrived here."

Pinky's shoulder brushed Lena's, her and Lena holding each other up, the way they always did. She could feel the hope in the way her friend's body sagged just a fraction.

"They're close, Pinky," Lena said. "Only up in Paradise, just a few hours' drive."

"Thank goodness," Pinky breathed, a hand coming up to her breast.

"There's no landline to call, I'm afraid, but there is something else." Lena's gaze bore into Pinky, intent on her friend's reaction to the next words she would speak. "Maya is pregnant."

Chapter 22

Maya made a noise that was somewhere between a shout and a scream. "We're not ready, Veer! We have no family, no support network, and barely half of the things that we need. We've got, like, three baby onesies. We don't even have a crib!"

"The baby isn't due for another four weeks. We've got time." As Veer spoke, Maya turned fierce eyes on him.

"Do you get anything about pregnancy, Veer?" Maya said, breathing through flared nostrils. "The baby could come at any time."

Do you get anything about pregnancy? There was a buzzing sensation in Veer's ears. It was a hurtful thing to say, even if the implication was rooted in truth. He had been to as many of the prenatal classes as he could, yet Veer still didn't feel that he "got" pregnancy. The coming birth, the arrival of a new little person into their lives—it was all very mysterious to him, and he didn't feel like he had a handle on any of it.

Worse still, he didn't feel that he had time for it, as it seemed now—with Maya working less than she had when they first moved to Paradise—like he had to spend all of his time either working or looking for ways to make money. Maya thought that he had cut up the credit card that his father had always paid for—Veer had said that he was going to get rid of it, and Maya had assumed the rest—but it still sat at the back of a drawer in the bedroom, calling out to him like a siren whenever things got hard, when the panic of making enough money even just for them, let alone to buy things for their new arrival, filled him with an increasingly familiar trepidation. Always the thing that scared him most was when he imagined the expression on Maya's face when he let her down.

Geez, he missed being able to use that credit card.

"Look," Veer said, holding up his hand as if to ward Maya off, "I've got a two-hour lesson this morning, so why don't I get a few things afterward?"

"We should be getting things together," Maya said, scowling, "That's how it's supposed to be." Veer wondered if she was thinking about Lena, how she might be getting things with her.

As much as Maya had been adamant in not telling their parents about the pregnancy, that pregnancy was soon to become a genuine new life. "If they cannot accept us, then how can they accept our child?" Maya had asked many times, often sounding more like she was trying to convince herself than trying to convince Veer. "They do not deserve to know," she'd once said at her most angry.

Veer didn't want their baby's impending arrival to be a dirty secret, not when he wanted to shout it out loud and gloriously to the world, but he wasn't ready to share it with his parents, either. Not until his mom could accept Maya. Veer loosened his clenched fists and relaxed his shoulders. He could get so furious, especially with his mother, but that boiled kettle always cooled over time.

With Maya, though, as her stomach had swelled and the life inside her had become so much more than an abstract concept, he could tell that her mother's absence, the total lack of communication, was taking its toll.

"You know how carsick you get these days," Veer replied now in a placating voice.

Maya's morning sickness, which had persisted for much of the pregnancy, had finally abated, only to be replaced by a horrendous form of projectile travel sickness. Despite multiple scrubbings, the Tesla had not smelled the same since the first time it happened. "Best to stay here. Derek and Sarah are next door if you need anything."

Derek and Sarah, in Veer's view, were about as different from the younger couple as it was possible to be, but he knew that they were good people at heart and eager to look out for them. If you asked Veer, Sarah could be a little too eager, assuming the role of surrogate grandmother-to-be in Lena's absence. The woman even reminded him of Maya's mother a little, which he thought was why the two women seemed to have bonded so much. Sometimes it irked him slightly.

Maya put down her empty smoothie cup on the coffee table with a loud clatter. "I'm not sure I like the idea of you going shopping for baby things on your own," she responded, her chin jutting out mutinously.

"Hey," Veer said, pretending to look offended. "I've been to all the classes, and I happen to have a very babyish sense of style and taste. Infantile, you might say."

Maya laughed. She didn't look convinced, but the panic seemed to have subsided a little, at least. His humor was great for deflection and buying time. Veer couldn't stop himself from peeking at his watch, and Maya evidently noticed. "Go on," she said, "you'll be late for your lesson."

Leaving the house, Veer felt a sense of satisfaction from lifting Maya's spirits, something he was always good at. But the feeling soon faded, as he remembered the way Maya had spoken—scornful and lacking faith in him.

Do you get anything about pregnancy, Veer?

~

Veer had discovered several months back that teaching guitar paid a lot more than gigs in bars did. At first, he thought of it as selling out, but had quickly found that passing on his knowledge was extremely rewarding, especially to those students who were genuinely interested in learning, as opposed to those who were just taking the lessons to please their hipster parents.

Unfortunately, that morning's student, Neal, fell into the latter category. Still, he was a weekly two-hour lesson, and Veer didn't turn such a gift down. No, sir. And, even better than that, Neal's father was a school principal and had mentioned the previous week that the current guitar tutor who gave private lessons through the school was set to move to Colorado next month. Hint, hint. If it worked out, he could make a good living just through the lessons at the school.

Neal was frustrating Veer this morning, however.

Veer was a more patient teacher than he had ever thought he might be. He believed that everyone could learn to play a musical instrument, and that they could come to it their own way. It was the end result that counted, and Veer was not one for musical theory, which seemed like placing shackles on something that was all about freedom and expression. Feeling.

But then he had started teaching and realized that, for those who weren't quite naturally born to it, some sort of musical structure could be useful. And there was no substitute for practice. Lots and lots of practice. Something that, despite his claims to the contrary, Veer didn't think that fifteen-year-old Neal ever did.

"I just can't get it," Neal complained, shaking the guitar slightly in his frustration as he stumbled awkwardly over the relatively simple scale that Veer had given him to do. It was a wonder that Neal's father had been dropping hints about the potential teaching position at the school if his son was the only evidence he had seen of Veer's teaching abilities. The boy was far from being one of his successes. "Can't I just do chords?" Neal asked. "I'm good at chords."

Good was stretching it.

"Practice is the key," Veer said calmly, thinking that he must sound like a broken record. Neal snorted. The boy looked the part of the guitarist, with his streaked-blond, floppy-fringed hairstyle, his rolled-bottom jeans, and his designer sneakers. Although his house wasn't quite the Kapoor mansion, it was a large four-bedroom home that must have been worth well over a million, and Neal—an only child—had a huge room that was obviously kept tidy for him by either his mother or a maid. Veer remembered those halcyon days.

He realized that Neal probably thought he was just a poor guitar teacher—scraping out a living because he had failed to make the big time. Not for the first time, the thought stung, curdling some of the acid in his stomach. Perhaps because that's just what he was now. A part of him wanted to say, "But I am Veer Kapoor! My father's a damn billionaire who could probably buy half this wretched town!"

Sometimes I'm a little too much my mother's son, Veer thought to himself wryly. Although, he was coming to realize, he was also too much Harry Kapoor's son. Not like his father, but a consequence of him . . . The trust-fund kid who had never had to worry about money. Watching Neal silently practice his fingering, Veer started to understand that being a guitar teacher—or gigging over in Chico—was not going to show anybody that he could step out from underneath his father's shadow. He needed to do something more.

At the same time, however, there was the weight of responsibility of the here and now. The possibility of a steady teaching job hung like a worm-riddled but still very juicy carrot, especially as he and Maya were trying harder and harder to find ways not to have to return to San Francisco. Eventually, Tim was going to want his house back, too.

"Are you in a band?" Neal asked, like Veer's thoughts had been written on his face.

"I was," he answered, "back in San Francisco."

"What, you just never made it big?" the boy asked. If Neal knew the question was rude, he didn't show it.

"Never?" Veer said, in mock anger. "I'm only twenty-five, you know. It's not too late."

Neal looked back at Veer, his expression serious. Apparently, Neal felt that twenty-five was far too late.

Veer scoffed. "Yeah, whatever."

"So, why did you move to Paradise?" Neal asked, his arms resting comfortably across his guitar, practice apparently forgotten for the moment. "I'm guessing it wasn't for the live-music scene?"

Veer studied the guileless fifteen-year-old for a long moment. "My fiancée is pregnant," he said eventually. "Our families don't approve of us."

"So, you're on the run?" Neal asked with a mischievous grin.

"Something like that."

"Why don't your family like it?"

"Maya, my fiancée, is older than me."

Neal gave a locker-room nod of approval. "Bagged an older chick, good going. She hot?"

Veer laughed and rolled his eyes. "Let's play some guitar, shall we?"

"Yeah, she's hot," Neal continued, ignoring Veer's suggestion. "Else why you going through all this trouble? Giving up your music, teaching me because my dad wants me to be like Eric Clapton. Who the hell is that, anyway?"

It was the first time that Neal had admitted what Veer had long suspected, that the guitar was not really the boy's dream, but his parents'. He should have been annoyed, but he found himself laughing along and not caring so much. Money was money. Yet there was something in the way the boy spoke about Veer giving up his own music and teaching that stung. It shouldn't have, but it did.

"You scared?" Neal asked. The question caught Veer off guard. "'Cause I'd be scared if I'd gotten some chick pregnant."

"She not just some—" Veer tried to protest, but Neal, who apparently hadn't finished, cut him off.

"Because that's, like, life over, you know? Game over, man. Suddenly you're responsible for this other life, and your life isn't yours anymore."

Veer regarded the floppy-haired young man. "You've really thought about this, haven't you?"

"Me," Neal carried on, although he now looked down at his guitar again and began to find the fingering for the start of the scale, "I'm going to be wearing a condom. Con-tra-ceptive, that's the key. No way some girl's taking the rest of my life away from me." The look that Neal gave Veer before he returned to playing the scale was a pitying one, and it left Veer feeling more like he was the teenager in the room, his love life more an object lesson for Neal than his guitar tutoring was ever going to be. "Still, if your fiancée is much older than you," he added, eyes down at his stumbling fingers, "then I guess she knows what she's doing, huh? She'll probably help you out."

~

"Can I help you?" a voice behind Veer said, making him jump.

"Um . . . Yes," he said. "Crib."

It was one of those obvious statements, as he was standing in the Blossom Baby Store in Paradise, right before an extensive display of cribs. And that was the problem. Had there been only one or two cribs—maybe even four or five cribs—then Veer might have felt slightly more in control of the situation. He could at least have made an ill-educated guess and kept the receipt for a quick swap or return if it was wrong. Instead, he found himself facing a mass of what must have been at least twenty-five or thirty cribs, and the whole thing was a little overwhelming.

Not for the first time recently, Veer felt out of his depth.

"When's the baby due?" the woman asked knowingly. The shop assistant—or owner, maybe—looked to be in her late fifties, with a head full of tightly permed steel-gray curls. There was something maternal about her—the fuller body shape, the white woolen cardigan that could almost have been handmade, and her capable, efficient manner.

It should have been reassuring, yet her appearance only served to make Veer feel more out of place.

"Four weeks." Veer answered, shifting uneasily on the balls of his feet.

"Four weeks?" The woman repeated back to him. She gave him a look that said, *Wow, you're leaving it late.*

Veer crossed his arms defensively, his short sleeves pulling tight against his biceps. Great. This woman with the orderly row of curls marching across her pink shiny scalp, who was probably a grandmother to a lively brood, also thought he had no idea what he was doing. *Well, there's a line for that today, lady.*

"Why don't you start with a bassinet?" the woman said. "They're a good option for a newborn."

Veer nodded gratefully, already feeling a little silly for getting so wound up inside. A bassinet sounded musical, so straightaway the idea of it was appealing. More orchestral sounding, perhaps, than rock and roll, but he could work with it. The woman moved them along to one end of the section, where there were several smaller-looking, basket-shaped beds. Veer put his hand on one of them and shook it slightly, worrying about the fact that its legs didn't seem entirely stable. At least, not as stable as he guessed the crib would have been. He wondered about whether to bring that up, or whether it was going to sound stupid.

"Is this your first?" the woman asked.

Veer nodded. "Yeah." *It's that obvious, isn't it?* To be fair, Veer had always had a youthful face and probably didn't even look his twenty-five years.

"The downside of the bassinet is that it will probably only last you a few months before you'll be wanting to put baby in something bigger. So, it's an extra expense, but in my opinion a worthwhile one. The little ones get lost in a great big crib, you know? A bassinet just seems cozier. Also, they're better for putting the baby down during the day. And, if space is something you're worried about, a bassinet takes up a bit less than a crib."

They all seemed like good reasons to Veer and, helpfully, there were fewer bassinet options to choose from. His emotional roller coaster was climbing carefully upward again. "Yeah," he said, the warm feeling of confidence seeping into him. He cleared his throat noisily, trying to sound like the woman hadn't just completely led him to the decision, like he'd had at least half an idea of what he was doing when he walked through the door, "I'll take the bassinet."

"The portable bassinet?"

Um . . . "Yes, that one."

He liked the bassinet the woman had shown him, which had a Bluetooth speaker built in to play music. The father of twins he'd met at the prenatal class had told him he would go insane with "Twinkle, Twinkle, Little Star" on repeat nightly, so Veer had a plan: his baby would go to sleep listening to Veer's music instead.

Veer went to the counter to pay. "Boy or a girl?" the woman asked conversationally.

"We decided not to find out," Veer replied.

"Ah, that's nice," the woman said, nodding approvingly. "I'm sure it will be a lovely surprise, whichever way it goes. Don't you worry now, becoming a parent is like a duck taking to the water. You'll do great because the first time you lay eyes on them, all these instincts you never knew you had just kick right in."

Veer smiled politely as she took the payment. She meant well, he was sure, yet her words were having the opposite effect of what she intended, and he left the store desperately hoping that he had made the right choice—what if his instincts never kicked in? What if he was broken in that way . . . ? Parentally challenged? Those butterflies that had been fluttering away in his stomach all day just did not seem to want to quit.

Chapter 23

When the doorbell rang, Maya knew exactly who it would be.

"Hey there, Sarah," Maya answered the door in the too-casual tone she seemed to reserve primarily for her next-door neighbor. Outside, a warm breeze was swirling around the tall trees that lined either side of the lane. The wind tossed Sarah's honey-blonde bangs around her face, and she reached up with one hand to pat her hair down.

"How's the little 'un doing, honey?" Sarah asked before Maya had even fully opened the door, her eyes round and shiny like a Disney character. Sometimes, Maya swore the woman only came over to see the bump and not her.

"Oh, you know," Maya replied more tiredly than she meant, her hands clasped over her swollen belly like she had only just been rubbing it for luck, "making me look fatter by the day."

"Nonsense," the older woman replied in her raspy voice, inviting herself in as always. Not that Maya minded most of the time, although it did clash with her sensibilities, the rules of behavior that had been ingrained into her as an adolescent that you called and asked before you dropped in. Paradise seemed to be a your-house-is-my-house town. "*Pfft*. You are glowing," Sarah continued. "Pregnancy suits you." At least she knew to say the right things.

Maya found herself following Sarah down her own hallway, which was the only part of the building not modernized in a previous round of work—probably when Tim had taken possession of the property—so it had what must have been the original stone cladding on the wall and classic parquet flooring. Maya had broken the flooring up with a long runner rug, which Sarah always managed to trip over, like her feet were making a complaint about it. Veer said that he liked the paneling and the stone cladding in the hall and wasn't sure about the runner. Veer would never be making any interior-decorating decisions.

"Coffee?" Sarah asked as they reached the open-plan living area and the kitchen.

Maya wasn't sure whether Sarah was asking if she could have one or if Maya wanted one. "Um, I've been trying to cut the caffeine out, so I don't give the baby an in-the-womb coffee addiction. To be honest, morning sickness got me half the way there. Would you like one, though?"

"You sit down," Sarah said, waving her over toward the sofas. "I'll do it."

It was like a little dance they did, a ritual so that Sarah could set about making herself a drink, not once appearing—Maya noticed—to have to search for where anything was. It occurred to Maya that Sarah may well know the kitchen better than she did, and that made her think of her mother.

"I may not be much company," Maya warned. "I've been in a foul mood all morning."

"You should spend an evening with Derek when his football team has just lost, honey," Sarah answered. "That man can pout for America. I can't imagine you're ever less than a bundle of sweetness." The twinkle in Sarah's eye let Maya know she was being at least a little ironic. "You're a woman, after all, and it's well known that we're all sugar and spice."

"I flipped out this morning. Said some mean things to Veer," Maya confessed. It felt good to confess; shameful, but good.

"And I'm sure he was completely undeserving," Sarah replied, spooning sugar into her coffee. There was a reason that Sarah was all sweetness.

"Those three little one-pieces we got together, an infant seat, and a diaper pail, that's still the only baby stuff we have," Maya explained.

"Really?" Sarah turned to her, evidently shocked. She was confessing to the right person.

"Not even a crib yet."

"I feel another road trip coming on." Sarah pressed her palms together gleefully, a little like she was praying.

"No chance!" Maya exclaimed, puffing out her cheeks in an expression of nausea.

"Oh yeah," Sarah said, her expression drooping as she poured boiling water into the french press straight from the tap. Maya hadn't known that the tap could even do that until she had lived at the property for almost three months. "The travel sickness."

"Did you have anything like that when you were pregnant with Jeremy?" Maya asked. The couple's only son was older than Veer and lived on the other side of the country, so Maya had never met him.

"Oh no," Sarah chirped. "I worked right up until two days before he was born."

What was it with the older generation and their tendency to make the younger one feel inferior by treating pregnancy and childbirth like it had been a minor interruption to their schedule?

"That's the way it was in those days, honey," the older woman continued as she swilled the french press around, like she was encouraging the coffee to brew faster.

Please don't tell me again about how you didn't have pain relief, Maya thought. She was planning to have as many drugs as the doctors would allow while that huge lump in her belly made its way out of her body.

"Did I ever tell you that I didn't have any pain relief with Jeremy? Not one bit of it."

Maya nodded and tried to school her features into a neutral expression. There was no malice intended, Maya knew that, but Sarah did like to flaunt that particular piece of information rather a lot. Her mother had been proud of the same fact—no pain relief with Maya, although Sameer had been a more difficult birth. No surprise there, then.

"Anyway," Maya moved the conversation on, "Veer said he would stop by the baby store later. So we'll see what he comes back with, I guess."

Sarah came over, coffee in hand, and sat next to Maya on the sofa. A box of assorted chocolates that Veer had brought home from his last trip to the grocery store sat temptingly nearby. Like a starving woman, Maya shoved a white chocolate truffle into her mouth, then picked up another, studying it.

"I hope he doesn't try and buy anything too important," Sarah said. "Like a crib. He is a man, after all." Although Maya found herself slowly nodding along as she popped the second chocolate in her mouth, she felt a little sorry for Veer. For one thing, he was right now being tarred with a brush meant for Derek.

"I feel a little embarrassed," Maya said, her mouth full of chocolate. Her eyes widened at how good the strawberry was. "I was a bit harsh. I did that thing where I took out all my worries on him, rather than just the ones that were his fault."

Sarah took a long sip of her drink, for which she had used about twice as much coffee as Maya would use when making a pot for both her and Veer. No wonder the woman was so . . . perky.

"So, what are these other worries?" Sarah asked.

Maya quickly snatched up another chocolate and threw it in her mouth to prepare herself for what she had to say next. Pushing down the results of a brief nauseous moment, Maya finally gave her reply. "It's your fault, actually."

Sarah raised a faux-offended eyebrow.

"It's what you said when we went shopping and got cake afterward," Maya went on, scrabbling in the box for another chocolate, something to take the taste of the last coffee-flavored one away. It seemed to Maya that Sarah gave her a baleful look as Maya hurriedly stuffed her fourth chocolate into her mouth. Key lime truffle. She was already a whale; a few chocolates were right now only a drop in a very big ocean. "About still being a child until you have had one of your own."

"I said that?" Sarah asked a little guiltily, gold hoop earrings jangling as she shook her head. "Sounds harsh."

"Well," Maya pushed on. "It was more about wishing your child a better life than your own."

Sarah laughed. "Jeremy didn't make the same mistakes as us. He made a whole load of his own. Still, it's working out well. He's even speaking about adopting." There were specific reasons, Maya knew, that Sarah had been thrilled to have a pregnant next-door neighbor, beyond just the usual. Jeremy was gay, something that Derek had struggled with—although, apparently, father and son were never exactly peas in a pod. Sarah's only complaint was that she might never have a pregnant daughter-in-law to shop with . . . Cue Maya Sharma!

"I think that's why my mom was so harsh on me . . . on us and the relationship. I guess I was so angry at her for not supporting me, I just didn't see it at first. She thinks I'm making all the same mistakes that she did, and things have been so hard for her."

"Are they mistakes, though?" Sarah pointed out.

"No, I'm sure as I can be that they're not. But . . ."

"It won't stop her worrying."

"I thought my mom was trying to control me, trying to make me into the perfect Indian daughter," Maya said. "Maybe she is, but only because she thinks that's the best way to protect me."

"I can relate," Sarah said with a raise of her smudged penciled eyebrows. "It took Jeremy's entire childhood for Derek to accept that he was not going to have the son he thought he was going to have. Manly, like him. You know, completing DIY projects together, kicking back with some brewskis before a round of golf. I'm still not sure he's ever really grasped it . . ." Sarah's voice trailed off.

"Is it still difficult between them?"

"It was never easy between them. It was difficult the first time Jeremy picked up a hammer or tried to use a drill. Or swung a golf club, for that matter. Our son was never going to be a builder or a golfer, or anything at all like his father, really, and that was difficult for Derek straightaway. Not that he said anything much, mind you. But it was there, in his eyes. We want our children to be newer versions of us."

They sat in silence for a moment, Sarah cradling her mug, Maya weighing a growing queasiness in her stomach against the thought of another chocolate. "Imagine if my mom never saw her grandchild because of . . ."—she gestured with one of her hands toward the empty space, as if it somehow contained all their family disagreements, their anger, and their disappointments with each other—"all this silliness." Anger was, in its way, an empty thing, Maya had come to realize, and so often when it went away it left only regret, whether you were proved right or not. This seemed truer the older you got; vindication was not what it used to be.

Sarah, unusually, didn't say anything, instead raising an eyebrow that might have been agreement, or might equally have been meant to say, *Don't be silly, everything will be just fine soon.* Her neighbor's silence unnerved Maya just a little.

"I should go," Sarah said, and returned a half-drunk coffee to the kitchen.

"Maybe I'll make that phone call, eh? That one I've been thinking about making for months now," Maya said, then grunted an "oof" as the baby somersaulted in an unusual display of daytime acrobatics.

"Like I've said before, that one's your decision alone, honey." Its possibility had hung in the air around many of their conversations. "Oh," Sarah added, reaching out to touch Maya's arm. "I almost forgot,

Derek's barbecuing tonight, which is no big deal, because he barbecues three times a week usually. That man does like his fire and his steak. He's out there burning twigs again right now, and in this breeze, too. One day my silly husband will burn down this whole town, I swear it. Anyway, I thought we could invite the pair of you over. The year probably doesn't have too many barbecues left in it."

"We're both Hindu," Maya told her.

Sarah looked back, seemingly confused. "Can't you eat at other people's houses? Or are barbecues not allowed?"

"No," Maya replied with a laugh. "We don't eat meat from cows."

Sarah playfully poked her arm. "I know that! If you come, it'll save me from having to eat barbecued steak again."

Sarah left, the house falling quiet behind her, save for the sound of the rising wind outside. The house always seemed a bit more silent after Sarah left. It was just Maya and the phone gripped in her sweaty palm, and Maya spent a good couple of minutes running opening lines around in her head—none of which were remotely satisfactory—while she found her mom's number and unblocked it on her phone.

No hurry. She would call her mom tonight, or tomorrow. When she was ready.

Maya moved to put the phone on the side table and get some food, but it rang suddenly, as if the act of unblocking her mom's number had caused it to ring. The instrument vibrated in her hand, causing her to jump and let out a small gasp. She brought the handset up again, turning it to see a still-familiar number on the glowing LED screen.

Chapter 24

Lena dialed the number, her hands shaking as chai dribbled onto her varnished cherry-hardwood floor. She should have finished her afternoon tea before making the call.

"Mom?"

"My girl," she said hoarsely, tears filling her eyes in an instant, like someone had loosened the screw holding them back.

She could hear that Maya was crying, too. "I was going to call," her daughter sobbed on the other end of the line. So many months since Lena had heard that voice. It sounded crystal clear as if she were in front of Lena and not many miles away, being listened to through a receiver. It made Lena's heart ache like someone had reached inside and squeezed it. "How did you . . . ?" Maya began to ask. "I only just . . . never mind."

"I need to tell you—" Maya went on.

"You're pregnant," Lena interrupted without thinking. Dammit! In her enthusiasm, Lena had stolen her daughter's thunder. She waited for more questions.

"Yes," Maya gushed. She sounded surprised, but not, Lena thought, angry. "Did Veer . . . ?"

Lena glanced at the tattered business card, smudged with *haldi* stains, clutched in her sweaty hands. A. R. Frane, Private Detective, specializing in finding missing persons. Now was not the time to tell her daughter about the lengths she had gone to in order to find her.

"No. Is he okay, Veer, your . . . fiancé?" Lena hadn't meant to pause as she said it. Again, she braced for Maya's tone to change, for the defensiveness to come, the walls to go up. Was it because she deserved it? That she had frozen her daughter in place, the woman from months ago who she had hardly seen—even when right in front of her—as she obsessed over Sameer's trial?

"He is," Maya answered, her voice throaty with emotion. "Okay, I mean. We're all good, and we're not so far away. The baby is due soon. I'm—"

Maya appeared to stop herself. What was she going to say? That she was sorry Lena had not been told sooner?

"I'm sorry I missed your pregnancy," Lena said the words because of a need to fill the growing space, maybe because she did not want to make her daughter say it instead. Lena had not known the words were an apology when she said them, but as they settled in their place, she knew that they were just that, and fancied she could feel some of the tension drain away on the other end of the line.

"We're-in-Paradise," Maya offered, blurting three words out almost as one. "Maybe you could come and see us. You and Manuel. Pinky and Anita, too?"

The last part was a question, Lena realized. Maya was wondering how things were between Lena and Pinky, and maybe within the broader Indian society at large. Lena flinched. Anguish rose in her chest like a wave in an ocean—that her daughter, living away from family and friends, a baby on the way, should even have to worry about that.

"That would be nice," Lena answered, feeling like she should have managed a less bland reply. "A road trip upstate, eh?" she added, trying to be jaunty. Then, after another moment: "Pinky Aunty and I are closer now than we have been in a long time."

The moment the words were said, Lena thought she did not like how they sounded at all. Perhaps her daughter would think she meant they had been planning and plotting together, bemoaning their wayward children. "Just pay no mind to any rumors you hear about Esther Vora's *Sagan*," she added wryly.

"Oh, okay," Maya replied, sounding confused. "To be honest, we have heard almost nothing of home here. It's like being in another world."

"Must be nice."

"Most of the time." There was a note of sadness in her daughter's answer.

"I almost forgot," Lena piped in brightly. "Are we to be blessed with a boy or a girl?"

"We chose not to find out," Maya answered.

"Ah, a surprise. That will be lovely. Was Veer not keen to see if he had a son?"

Maya gave a small laugh, and Lena again experienced that invisible hand clenching tightly around her heart. How long since she had heard that note of brightness that was her daughter's laugh? "Veer is excited," Maya told her, "but I think he sometimes forgets that we have a new human being coming into our lives soon, and all the upheaval that will bring."

Lena chuckled along. "He is only a man, poor thing. I doubt Manuel would have been any better."

Maya laughed again and, as their mirth settled with what seemed like an easy, natural rhythm, Lena finally felt the weight beginning to lift from her chest. Maybe now, her daughter would call her every two days, as she'd always done. Maya would share her pregnancy stories, questions about her growing belly and food cravings and worries about childbirth. Now, her daughter would be her daughter again. Yet she did not want to move past this point with anything unsaid, no secrets hiding to rear their ugly head and trip their healing up again.

"I . . . um, I hired a private investigator," she told Maya. Lena had been going for "confession," yet it came out almost like a boast. "I thought I should say."

The silence on the end of the line stretched for what seemed like a yawning great chasm of time. "I get it," Maya finally replied.

"Huh?"

"Maybe I wouldn't have understood five or six months ago, when this big lump in my belly was not even showing," Maya said. "But I get it now. Your . . . instinct to protect."

"Oh . . . Well, yes."

"But call them off now, will you?" Maya added wryly. "Now that I know, it would just be kind of creepy knowing they're out there."

Lena laughed, dislodging a tear of relief that had been waiting to fall. "Yes, of course."

"Good to talk to you, Mom," Maya said softly.

"And you, my daughter."

Chapter 25

"You like to barbecue, Veer?" Derek asked, pointing a skewer at him.

"Um . . . no, Mr. McKesson."

"It's Derek, Veer. Just Derek."

"I'm good with dal," Veer offered. Derek McKesson, Sarah's husband, didn't look impressed. They were standing by the barbecue, the aroma of the chicken—featuring Derek's "special marinade"—spiced now with the faint smell of woodsmoke on the breeze and mingling pleasantly with the apple trees in the McKesson backyard. It should have been heaven, but Veer wanted to be just about anywhere else.

"You can tell a lot about a man by his barbecuing. Trust me, Veer, if you're living out in these parts and planning to stay here, you will want to know how to barbecue. And how to set fires, like in a woodstove. Watch and learn, Veer, I'll steer you right."

"Stay here?" Veer said uncertainly.

"In Paradise, of course."

"Oh, well . . . I guess we'll see," Veer replied with a tight smile. He found himself not wanting to be railroaded by anybody. Wasn't that why they had left San Francisco in the first place?

Paradise had been fine at first, but for Veer it had mostly been about living in a bubble with Maya—no family, no friends, or anyone else they knew. That was what had made Paradise special for Veer. If he was honest with himself, Veer was struggling to keep his attention on his hosts this evening. Even though the older couple meant well enough, Maya found it easier to be around them than Veer did.

"What did you get a bassinet for?" Those had been Maya's words when he had proudly returned home with his purchase from the Blossom Baby Store. She had known what it was without Veer telling her—and he had been practicing a whole speech about this mysterious piece of newborn sleeping architecture.

"It . . . er, takes up less space," he had replied.

"And we'll have to go back and buy a crib anyway when the baby outgrows it, before you know it," Maya had complained. "Geez, they saw you coming."

Geez, they saw you coming. What a hurtful thing to say to the father of her child.

"This barbecue chicken's fantastic, Mr. McKesson," Veer said as they ate at a sturdy wooden bench-seat table in Derek and Sarah's backyard, which had the air of eating dinner out in a national park somewhere. It seemed like the thing to say. He noticed Maya grin at the respectful-yet-awkward way he added, "ah, Derek."

"McKesson," Maya said. "Is that Scottish?"

"Yes," Derek replied, looking pleased that Maya had asked. "My grandparents moved over when my father was young, a few years after the war."

"Which war?" Veer asked.

"Ah, bless you," Sarah said, reaching over and touching Veer's hand. Then she looked over at Derek. "It was the Civil War, wasn't it dear?"

Derek ignored her, the steeliness of his gaze instead falling on Veer. "After World War Two."

~

Veer looked uncomfortable, Maya thought, although she supposed he hadn't spent as much time around the older couple as she had. She was used to their constant mild bickering, something she found endearing, although she could see how it might be mistaken for tension if you didn't know them.

They sat among the trees in the McKesson backyard, the older couple having chosen to keep most of the mixture of oaks, apple trees, and taller redwood trees, where many homeowners would have cut them down for space. Insects chirped, and fireflies flitted among the grass and looming trees. Already the soft, warm shadows of twilight were falling on the valley; only high above did the sky still gleam pale blue, outlining the black lace of the treetops.

Maya hadn't realized how much she could love a place like Paradise until she and Veer had fled San Francisco, even if she had only seen a few hundred yards of their own road for some time now. She had ached for the familiarity of family and friends, yet Paradise had done its best to console her, to show her that the world did not begin and end in San Francisco Bay.

"How did shopping for baby things go earlier, Veer?" Sarah asked solicitously.

"He got a bassinet instead of a crib," Maya cut in with a wry tone and an inward eye roll.

"What's a bassinet?" Derek asked. "Can you sleep in it?"

Sarah's eye roll was entirely external. "If you'd had any say in it, Jeremy would have slept in a hammock between two trees."

Derek nodded approvingly, playing along with his wife's sarcastic remark. "How nature intended."

"Money's getting tight," Maya went on. "It would have been better to go straight to a crib."

"I can take it back," Veer grumbled a little sullenly. "I just . . . I don't know, I thought maybe we could get the crib once we were settled back in the city."

Maya's eyes narrowed, squinting as if trying to comprehend what Veer was saying. "In San Francisco?"

Derek pushed his cutlery together on his plate and limbered up, rolling his shoulders. "I think I'll go and see about putting some wood on, maybe start a pot of coffee."

"We should get back," Veer cut in, making to rise himself. "Thank you so much for dinner," he added—although, for all the brightness in his tone, he may just as well have been thanking the IRS for collecting his taxes.

$\sim$

"Well, that was rude," Maya said as they walked from the front of Derek and Sarah's property and out onto the road. She'd barely had enough time to bid farewell to her neighbors, so she could keep up with her fiancé. "We didn't even offer to help clean up."

The evening was still full of the birdsong that always filled the trees close to sundown, and walking along the track, the couple were in semidarkness. There was no street lighting, which, for some reason, only ran about halfway along their road from the Pearson Road end. All the same, Maya could still make out Veer's dismissive wave of his hand. "Sarah never lets a guest tidy up, you heard her say that."

"That's not the point, though," Maya pushed. "You can't just leave . . . You embarrassed me."

Veer stopped and turned to her. His features were hard to make out in the fading light, but his posture was rigid. "I embarrassed you?" he hissed, emphasizing the first and last words. "Did you have to go on about the crib thing like that?"

"It's just Derek and Sarah," Maya answered back. "And, anyway, it's true. Money is getting tight, and we'll have to be careful."

"We're fine," Veer growled, like the words were nails being dragged across a blackboard, and the way he turned away to carry on walking was, Maya thought, telling. Maybe it was the right time, maybe it wasn't, but what the hell . . .

"Have you thought any more about Neal's dad's offer?" she asked, walking a pace or two behind Veer. "That would be a stable . . ."

"Stable!" Veer huffed disdainfully.

"Yes," Maya pressed pointedly, "stable."

"You're saying the money I bring in isn't enough?" Veer said the words like an accusation. "That I don't work hard enough?"

Geez, he was touchy tonight. "No. But it would be more money and more stable. I thought you were interested in it. A real job." Although it would not be visible in the shifting purple sky until they were almost in it, their own driveway neared.

"A real job!" Veer exclaimed, briefly throwing his face skyward. "You sound like my mother." Ouch. "And if I do," Veer went on, "then it's just like we're committing to staying here, in this two-bit little town with our all-American neighbors."

"I thought you liked Paradise," Maya said, her voice becoming brittle. This attack on Paradise felt like an attack on their lives there. And, by extension, on her. It made a lie of the happiness she had been feeling. "What's wrong with Derek and Sarah, with our place, our lives here?"

Veer stopped walking and turned back again. "It isn't ours," he exclaimed. "We've been here six months, Maya. How much longer do you think your boss will let us stay in his house on such a low rent? Or working a fraction of your hours remotely, for that matter? Never seeing clients when that was half your job? Have you even spoken to him about how it affects your maternity leave?" He paused; even in the poor light, Maya could see Veer's jaw shifting, turkey-like, in and out, back and forth. "It's like you're living in some fantasy . . . some la-la land. And you talk about me and 'real jobs'!"

That hurt, and Maya tried to find a way to tell Veer how unfair he was being, even if a part of her knew that he had a point. Before she could, though, he went on.

"You've missed your mom. I know you have. And now that she's called and you're talking, we should finalize where we want to be once the baby's born."

"Of course I've missed her. And I realize I've been unfair to her, too. But it doesn't mean I just want to run straight back home to Mommy the moment things get tough."

Veer took a step toward Maya, his dark shape looming over her. "What's that supposed to mean?"

"I didn't mean . . . You are being a bit childish, you know," said Maya. She could feel the heat rising in her cheeks.

When Veer spoke again, his voice had dropped to being barely above a whisper. Somehow, it made his words all the worse. "And that's the problem. I'm your fiancé, the father of your child, yet sometimes you still treat me like I'm a child. Like I'm not ready to be a father. Like I can't do what it takes."

With that, Veer turned around and stalked up the drive toward the house, leaving Maya with her mouth working up and down uselessly like a stoned goldfish, trying to form the right reply and saying nothing until it was too late and he had disappeared into the darkness.

Chapter 26

It was the year 2005; Tiger Woods had won both the Masters and the Open Championship, Hurricane Katrina pounded the Gulf Coast, and Sameer was a ghost, sliding through a world that never touched him. Couldn't touch him. Yeah, that was it. The world couldn't touch him; he was immune to it. He walked to school—he always walked to school now, and Goldie never questioned it. Not once.

The streets slid by on the walk, and Sameer never really saw them, never remembered passing any of the once-familiar landmarks. He weaved between the crowds of kids as he walked through the school gates, almost none of whom had ever known his name. All those people who never even knew he existed. So maybe, in a way, he didn't.

It no longer mattered if he sat at the back of the class or at the front of it because he took no real part in any of his lessons, and no one—not even teachers he thought had once liked and valued him as a student—seemed to notice. By never raising a hand or taking part in class discussions, Sameer thought he might slowly be becoming invisible to the others there. Maybe if he didn't turn up, no one would notice. Maybe he could go anywhere he wanted, do anything he wanted, or even just die in a ditch. Who would know?

"We still good for the extra session tonight?" Mr. Barr asked as he passed Sameer putting books in his locker.

Oh yeah, he would notice. "All good, Mr. Barr."

"Great." The English teacher touched his arm in that way he always did now, and an uncontrollable wave of fear and revulsion shot through Sameer. Had Mr. Barr always touched him that way? Before . . .

Sometimes he fantasized about quitting, but the thought of the explanations he'd have to give—to Mr. Barr, his dad, even his mom—choked the words he might have said.

The day passed too quickly—it always did on the days when there was rehearsal. Tonight was even worse, though, as it wasn't even a proper rehearsal night. Sometimes, rehearsal nights ran so long that he could sneak away before it was just him and Mr. Barr. Sometimes.

But tonight it was a stage-management run-through, and it would be just the two of them.

~

"It's not enough," Winston Woznicki said when Sameer handed him a twenty-dollar bill on the way home. They were standing on one of those random street corners that made it look a little like they were in a war zone. The buildings on the plot next to them had been half demolished—or maybe only ever half-built, strewn with pile drivers and construction hoists—and the fences stopping kids from running across it were now mostly fallen. Plants grew stubbornly among the rubble, and the whole place was a litter dump—from candy wrappers to dog shit to suspicious-looking needles.

Winston Woznicki, whose name when you said it in full made him sound like a dollar-store superhero, was only a year older than Sameer but already looked like he was in his twenties. He stood over six feet tall with not a hint of lankiness and sported the closest thing to a mustache that the school would let him get away with. "What do you mean?" Sameer asked. "I just want a cheap bottle of bourbon; it shouldn't be more than fifteen dollars."

The older kid sneered. "Yeah, and you look about twelve years old. Maybe if you looked your age, I would take a five-dollar profit on buying you illegal alcohol. But from you, I want at least ten bucks."

Sameer sighed and handed over the extra five dollars. Woznicki emerged from the dilapidated liquor store with boarded windows only about a minute later and handed Sameer the bottle in the traditional brown-paper bag.

"Pleasure doing business with you," Woznicki said. "You want to make it a regular thing?"

Sameer peered into the bag at the bottle of bourbon. "Same time on Friday?"

"You're on," the older kid said and turned to leave. After a moment, though, he turned back to Sameer. "Is that just for you?"

"Oh yeah." The reply was a little too enthusiastic.

"I think you might have a problem there."

"You have no idea," Sameer answered, ignoring the familiar blackness in his stomach. He looked away, plucking helplessly at the fabric of his shirt.

Winston Woznicki shrugged and carried on his way.

~

"So, there you have it," Lena said as she sat opposite Sameer during an early morning visit in the prison visitor hall. "Your sister is pregnant—very pregnant—I'm going to start up a charity for ex-cons to learn cooking while running a soup kitchen, and I no longer have to kill Pinky Aunty."

Lena's last comment made Sameer's mouth turn upward just a fraction, and he saw her make a show of narrowing her eyes and scrutinizing him. "Was that a smile?" she asked.

"I doubt it," Sameer replied, although both sides of his mouth curled up slightly this time.

"It's you that inspired us, taking your cooking lessons in here," she said. "How are they going?"

Sameer frowned. "Slowly," he answered, "I feel like we have to go at a snail's pace for all the people who can't even toast a Pop-Tart."

"Well, I expect you have a head start on all the others," Lena joked, "being the son of the Bay Area's curry mogul."

They laughed together at that.

"I do like it, though, and not just because it gets me out of my cell more. Some of us are even going to be prepping lunch for our wing once we're finished here."

Lena's face lit up; Sameer could not remember when he had last seen Lena look proud that way. It caught him a little off guard. "Where's Manuel?" he asked to change the subject, looking around in an exaggerated way. "I thought he was going to come this time."

"I didn't know how you would feel about your sister's good news and what I was planning to do," Lena said in a low voice, looking down at her chipped nails. She regarded him warily. "You stuck in here. I just didn't want Manuel to be another . . . provocation."

Sameer shook his head. "I've been so angry, haven't I? I've been angry, and I've been drunk for too long. All I've done with my life is get a girl killed."

Lena reached out and touched her son, and for the first time in years, he didn't flinch away from her. "There's time. Aside from having you and Maya, everything significant I've done in my life has come since, what . . . my late thirties? You'll still have so much time when you leave here, and we'll be ready to help if you need us to."

Sameer smiled weakly back at his mother; he wished he could find the same level of enthusiasm. There was such a long, yawning gap of incarceration that stretched out before he could become something other than a convict, before he could do any of the things his mother was helping him dream about. All the same, he looked forward to seeing her and was sustained by her visits. "It will be okay," he said, gently patting her hand before withdrawing his own. He watched her confidence falter for just a moment and felt relief when the smile returned a moment later.

~

"You seem in a good mood, *ese*," Gus observed as he and Sameer walked at the back of a group of prisoners along a narrow corridor, painted battleship gray, which had steel cell doors to either side. No wonder the convicts were depressed so much of the time, Sameer had been thinking to himself. Surely a little uplifting yellow couldn't hurt. Pastel pink or cornflower blue? Gus was right—he was in a light, almost carefree mood. A rare feeling in a place where you could never truly relax.

"Good visit with my mom," Sameer answered. While most of the group—including Sameer—were on their way to the kitchen to make lunch, Gus would be heading on a little farther to the administration building.

Gus grinned knowingly. "She glad you're following in her footsteps?"

Sameer couldn't help but scoff a little. "They're big boots to fill."

"Don't be rude about your mom!" Gus snapped.

"Oh, I didn't—" Sameer said, paling a little. For once, he hadn't been making a disparaging remark about his mother's size. "I just meant that she's a bit of a cooking legend. You know what, my dad hasn't come to see me once in here. He always said what a 'useless cow' she was. I'm starting to realize that she's worth ten of him."

"I was just playing with you, holmes," Gus said, waving his large hands in the air. "You're as easy to mess with as my brother; I think that's why you remind me of him."

"I do?"

"Right from that first moment I saw you in the yard, holmes. You looked lost like my little bro always did in any situation he was unfamiliar with."

"This the one—"

"I killed the piece o' crap over? Same one. Only one."

"Does he live back east?" Sameer asked, thinking about how this was only the second time Gus had mentioned him. "Not get much chance to come see you?"

Gus's face darkened again, and his big, expressive shoulders slumped. "Doesn't want to see me."

"But—"

"Well, it was kinda my fault he was getting targeted. Remember I said there was a dealer trying to make him sell drugs for him?" Sameer nodded, although their only previous conversation about Gus's brother had been way back when Sameer had first come to the jail, and he didn't really remember. "I was already working for the *pinche* motherfucker," Gus went on. "But Ray—that's my bro—he was clever and good at school and not a part of all the shit I let myself get involved in. You know . . ." Gus trailed off and went quiet for a moment. They were almost at the end of the corridor, where most of the prisoners—including Sameer—would be scooting off to head into the kitchen.

Gus stopped and turned to Sameer, almost causing the prison guard who was walking at the back of the group to bump into them. If it had been any other prisoner except for Gus, the guard might have barked at them to keep moving, but instead the guard just looked put out and stared at the wall like he was pretending not to listen. "Some people just aren't destined for much. That's like me: I'm a piece of crap, and I know that. But those that can be, they got to make the most of what's given 'em. Ray's a doctor now, not living in some crack den or dead five years ago over a dozen wraps and two hundred bucks, you know?"

Gus started moving again, rounding the corner to where the guard at the front of the group was already unlocking the kitchen door. "And, anyway," he added, "now I've got you to look after, at least until you get out of here and go start your own restaurant or something."

Sameer found himself looking up into the most genuine, unguarded smile he had yet seen on Gus's pale, smooth, and often terrifying face. There was hope there, and expectation, and all of it seemed to be focused on him. Sameer felt at once grateful and self-conscious.

"Come on, Gus," the rear guard said testily, "that filing won't do itself, you know."

Sameer watched the big man disappear down the corridor to filing duty at the office, which was seen as just about the best work duty a prisoner could get, partly because old Ms. Fischer, the septuagenarian administrator, had a thing for butterscotch sweets and always brought a pack into work with her, sharing them freely with guards and prisoners alike. In prison, these little treats became huge pleasures to cherish.

"My mom's starting a charity, Tyler," Sameer told the man working next to him, once they were set up in the kitchen and preparing for lunch.

"That so?" Tyler answered distractedly in his mildly southern drawl, absorbed in the slicing of a capsicum pepper. He was doing it well, if at about a tenth the speed that Sameer could have sliced it. Tyler was the same age as Sameer, with short, tightly packed dreads, and he was in for possession of cocaine, with another three years left on his sentence. You did not always know what someone had done when you met them in prison—at least not straightaway—but they were usually quick to volunteer how long they had left inside. Those that did not do so were never expecting to make it out again.

Sameer liked Tyler, mostly because he took the cooking seriously, even if he did not have what Sameer would think of as a "natural talent" for it. "She wants to teach ex-cons to cook. I think me doing this might have inspired her, you know?"

A flicker of a wry smile played across Tyler's lips. "You think they gonna let me out early, so I can learn to cook with your mom instead?"

Sameer laughed breezily, "You can always ask."

While Tyler continued carefully slicing his pepper, Sameer moved to his left where some chocolate had been slowly melting in a pan. The weeks of cooking lessons were all coming to a head for the inmate wannabe chefs, who were today tasked with cooking lunch for their fellow prisoners on the wing. Only around two-thirds of the initial class had stuck with it—or, more accurately in many cases, behaved well enough within the kitchen or in the rest of their prison life to be allowed to continue with the lessons, which, they were reminded during every session, was a privilege.

The whole idea and logistics behind teaching prisoners to cook was, Sameer himself had to admit, kinda nuts. The knives were obviously the biggest part of the deal, with a set for each inmate to be found in individually locked and see-through cases that were mounted to the wall along one side of the kitchen, the keys for which were attached to Ted—the beefy ex-army chef who taught them. They were allowed to access them only one at a time, which slowed things down a lot as Ted spent half his time going to and from the cases, plus no one left the kitchen until every knife was back in its proper place. It would only take one missing knife, and no one was going to be doing any more cooking, that was for sure.

"What ya doin' there?" a voice asked at his left shoulder. It was Earl, a scrawny, rat-faced man who thought he knew everything about cooking because his mom ran a diner somewhere in Hicksville, USA. In Sameer's opinion, the fact that Earl's mother owned a deep-fat fryer and was a fair flip with a spatula did not make Earl a chef with the right to boss everyone else in the kitchen around. Earl felt it did.

"Brownies, for dessert," Sameer answered, trying to put as little inflection into his voice as possible so he could minimize any conversation with Earl. Besides, he needed to get them into the oven and give Tyler a hand.

"But what was that you were putting in there just now?" Earl pressed, poking a finger at the jar on the side, the contents of which, a few moments before, Sameer had been sprinkling into the brownies.

"Cardamom," Sameer answered with a sigh, wishing that he could have had some seeds to crush himself, but even the presence of a small jar of ground cardamom in the kitchen had been a pleasant surprise.

"Why the fuck would you do that?" Earl growled.

"It's how my mom does them," Sameer answered, trying to ignore the idiot's superior tone. "They're delicious, you'll see." Earl pretty much thought he was Ted's number two in the kitchen and had been stressing about prepping lunch like the whole thing was somehow going to reflect on him. As far as Sameer had seen, his extreme stressing had only put everyone else on edge and slowed things down. Earl was mostly running around like a headless chicken, although, come to think of it, he had seemed disappointed when Ted had put Sameer on brownie duty, while Earl himself had been sent to the griddle. Which was fitting, Sameer thought.

"That's not how Ted taught us," Earl insisted. "And it's not how my mom made them, and she had the best brownies in the county, everyone knew it."

Sameer turned off the heat and pushed the pan away to let the mixture cool a bit, all the while trying to count to ten in his head. When he turned back, the smaller man was looking at him intently, his brow furrowed. Earl was not cut out for the stresses of kitchen life. "You've ruined the brownies," Earl went on through gritted teeth, "gone and put your Paki-shit flavors in 'em."

"My parents are from India, Earl," Sameer answered with mock over-patience. It was that or tell him to fuck off. "Different country. Now, why don't you go flip some burgers just the way momma does."

Earl's face reddened, and Sameer realized that he probably shouldn't have added the last bit.

"Earl!" It was Ted, his commanding voice cutting through all the kitchen noise. "Need you to come slice more onions over here."

The only person in the kitchen Earl appeared to respect was Ted, and he scurried back toward his station.

"Shouldn't have taken the bait," Sameer complained half to himself as he moved back next to Tyler. The other man had continued his slow slicing throughout the whole exchange, keeping his head down the way people did in prison when conflict came into their vicinity.

"Dude's a prick," Tyler answered without looking up. The words and the accompanying shrug seemed to sum up the situation well enough, and Sameer turned back again to find the trays he had already laid with greaseproof paper ready for his brownies.

There was a sudden intense pain in his arm.

"You fucking ruined 'em," Earl hissed, and the man's stale coffee breath hit Sameer's nostrils. Sameer looked down and saw manic-eyed Earl holding the handle of a knife, but no blade was visible because all of it was inside his arm.

It was surreal, like the whole thing couldn't possibly be happening, not over fucking brownies, but then Earl's hand came out and forward again.

Chapter 27

Sometimes, a good night's sleep wipes away bad feelings, Veer reflected, standing in front of the espresso machine as the tender bitterness of coffee beans fluttered up to his nostrils. A new day could be a new start. We could be so angry when we went to sleep, so full of righteous indignation—because being right was important, wasn't it? Yet we could wake up to find that the whole darn thing didn't matter. It wasn't important, not in the grand scheme of things. Not compared to all the blessings that life had heaped upon us.

Not when we loved someone.

That didn't happen for Veer when he awoke in the morning on the couch, following the barbecue at the McKessons' place the night before. He still felt like he was right. He still felt annoyed with Maya for treating him like an imbecile. For complaining about the bassinet to the McKessons and then talking about their financial worries in front of the older couple. It . . . *belittled* him.

Veer mixed the beans within the water, and the ground coffee became one with the steam. The scent alone rejuvenated him. Sipping the coffee, attempting to overcome the inertia of the recently awake, Veer did have to concede that—*perhaps*—he had overreacted a teensy-weensy little bit about the job. A steady music tutoring job at a school had seemed like a gift when he had first heard about it—regular money doing what he loved. Well, sort of. Writing and recording songs, gigging—these were the things he loved the most. But, if it was music tutoring or packing bags at the market . . .

And yet, Veer was right that accepting the job would be a commitment to staying in Paradise for longer. And *that* had never been the plan. Not that there had been a plan when they had packed up their things in a matter of a few hours and fled San Francisco all those months ago. They'd left in March, and glancing at his watch, Veer saw it was November 8, so it had officially been eight months.

Maya didn't appear to be up, which was odd. Even throughout the pregnancy, she was an earlier riser than him, as if her nine-to-five body clock—in career-girl Maya's case, often eight-to-eight—had never left her. Veer recalled coming in the previous night, not speaking a word to one another. He had been determined not to break, not to be the one who began conversation again like everything was normal, like it was okay for her not to consider his feelings.

Veer stretched, wincing just a little at the dull pain in his back. He wasn't sure why he had slept on the couch when there were other bedrooms with beds in them, even if the beds weren't made up.

Finishing the last dregs of the bitter beverage, Veer imagined Maya in the comfy bed, right now sleeping the peaceful sleep of the just, dreaming happily, safe in the unbreakable conviction that she was right and that her fiancé was being an idiot. He almost gave in to the urge to go and wake her, just to bring her out of that inaccurate dream.

And yet he was drawn to see her, asleep or otherwise. There was a tiny little ache inside, which had been growing since the moment he had opened his eyes. He wanted things to be okay. Preferably for her to apologize and see the error of her ways, *then* for everything to be okay, but with each passing moment and every swelling of that ache inside him, he would take "okay" in any form that it came to him.

Dammit, Veer, you weak-minded fool.

Any moment now, he was going to crack and just go in there. Just to catch a look at her. If he did, he knew that every last scrap of righteous indignation he had left would crumble. He would probably even end up apologizing, for crying out loud. That was when Veer had a fantastic idea.

∼

It had been horrible sleeping on her own, if spacious. At one point, Maya had spread herself out on the bed in a star shape, which had been fun for a while, but she found that pregnancy made her crave human contact and closeness with Veer when she had expected that things would, if anything, have gone the other way.

What is his problem? Maya had known quite a few men in her life, not an immodest number, she liked to think—certainly more than her mother ever needed to know about. Still, of all the men she had known, Maya would have figured Veer Kapoor the most stable. She had always felt that she knew where she stood with him.

He's always been so chilled out, she thought as she filled the kettle to make her own damn cup of tea. He always took life's highs and lows so well, and he had been so relaxed about the pregnancy. *Too relaxed,* Maya had thought more than once. *Yeah, maybe that's the problem—perhaps it's all just catching up with him at once.*

Maya put the kettle on and found her mug and a tea bag. She considered that maybe she shouldn't have freaked out at him the previous morning. Perhaps it had set him down a path to questioning their life in Paradise. Maybe it had made him think that it would just be easier to go back to the city and the support network there.

She had put Veer up on a pedestal in some ways. The thing was, pedestals tended to be narrow ledges that were hard to stay balanced on indefinitely. Occasional falling off—the odd bout of idiocy, perhaps brought on by excessive external pressure from one's fiancée—was only to be expected, perhaps even healthy. Even Manuel—who Maya viewed as an almost perfect example of a good and honorable husband, full of kindness and compassion—could sometimes be unreasonable or stubborn, so her mother said.

Then again, Lena Jaitly was, as Maya knew all too well, a hard person to please all the time. She grinned inwardly, irony spilling over her thoughts like water released from behind a dam of ignorance. Like mother, like daughter, eh?

Like father, like son, came the next thought. Goldie's behavior and Sameer's acting out could be thought to be related. Her heart ached with thoughts of Sameer. Maya slapped a palm to her forehead. Why hadn't she thought to ask how Sameer was doing when her mother had called?

She had thought of her brother so much in the last six months or so. She remembered, with a pang, how he had looked when she had visited him in jail—the face she'd seen on him, she'd never seen before. Everything had been burned out of him, he was looking inward, looking helplessly young, looking old. She wanted to promise that she would never fail him again. Sometimes Maya forgot that he had been left with Goldie Sharma as his only role model. Her mother could be hard work, overbearing, even suffocating, but at least she cared. *Enough to send a private investigator after us,* she thought with a sheepish grin of pride.

Mug in hand, Maya wandered over to the side window. The Tesla was still there. *So, he hasn't left me and taken my car with him.* She caught herself and grimaced. Not only was it not funny, but it was unfair to Veer.

She walked to the back of the house, noticing how noisy the wind was in the almost-silence of the chalet, with only her bare footsteps padding along to compete with it. The wind swallowed up all other noise: her footfalls, the beat of her heart.

Maya couldn't see him out in the garden, or taking a walk down by the creek bed, which he often liked to do. Tim, her boss, had been much more merciless with the trees in his back garden than Sarah and

Derek had, so that they had an excellent view of the small and usually dry river valley below them.

Maybe he had gone for a run down there, hopefully trying to see if he could sweat out a Y chromosome or two. *Hee, hee.*

No sign of him there, either, although something did catch her eye, far to the left of what she could see. It looked like a blot on the horizon, and it took several moments to pick it out correctly against the glare of the autumn morning's sun.

It looked like smoke, and Maya's forehead puckered.

Suddenly, a great gust of wind blasted the glass in the window in front of her, making Maya jump. It was double glazed, yet she saw the window shudder at the impact. Alone in the quiet house, she again heard the howl the angry wind made as it bullied its way through the trees and around the chalet's structure.

Outside, a flock of crows swept by, their wings shaking the air. Maya rubbed her eyebrow, wondering what sort of idiot would be setting a big fire like that with the wildfire season barely over.

~

Veer had made incredibly good time, mostly because he had jogged the majority of the way. Now he was sweaty and gross, despite the strong wind that kept finding him as he went. At least the run had cleared his head a bit and put him in a more positive mood. It would be lunchtime by the time he got home again, but he and Maya would have something wonderful to eat, and either way, things would be okay. Maybe they wouldn't even *need* to say anything about the previous night—just silently put it behind them.

He understood now—Veer Kapoor was often the last person to understand anything about himself—that last night Maya had touched a nerve that was already exposed and raw within him. That the life he had led before Paradise had not prepared him for where they were now. Earning money—an underlying prerequisite of any worthy male—was extremely difficult with the skill set that he had equipped himself with. He could not be solely relied upon to provide, at least not to give them any degree of comfort. They only survived now because Maya had continued with what amounted to contract work for her company and because they paid her boss only a bare minimum of rent.

Veer was angry because she had blundered into his own shortcomings when she had complained about the bassinet. He needed to take the school tutor job and man the heck up. Stop letting his fear rule him.

The Holiday Market on Skyway Road was limited compared to the overstocked stores you would find all over the San Francisco suburbs. Yet, Veer had gotten used to shopping there and appreciated it—it felt quirky and different. He also loved renting DVDs from the little kiosk located on the same commercial plot as the store—which made him feel giddy and nostalgic for a bygone era.

Veer picked up some skewered kebabs and fries, one of Maya's favorite meals. The shop assistant eyed all the food that Veer loaded onto the conveyor belt. She was eighteen or nineteen, he guessed, with short hair dyed jet black and cut into a wavy bob. There was a hint of crimson on her lips, about as much eye shadow as the store would probably let her get away with, and a discreet gold stud in her nose.

Once he would have thought of her as cool and mysterious, would have been drawn to her—the kind of girl he liked to pursue or be pursued by. "You gonna want some bags?" the girl asked with a demure yet knowing smile.

Veer nodded, not having brought even one bag with him. "Yes, please." He watched the girl as she got two bags out and wondered what her story was. Probably lived with her parents, maybe even born and raised in Paradise. She looked too hip to stay in such a small town all her life, though. Was she saving up, perhaps, trying to get a deposit for an apartment rental in Sacramento or San Francisco? Or Yuba or Redding, at least? Somewhere where she could explore her potential, whatever that potential happened to be. Veer found himself suddenly concerned with the girl and her future, determined that she wasn't going to be spending it in Paradise. Dammit, maybe he was starting to think like a parent, after all.

The girl—Aimee, he had now noticed on her name badge—looked up as she passed the bags to Veer and caught him staring at her. She blushed a little, and he found himself feeling a little embarrassed, like she might think he had been staring purely out of attraction. Not that she wasn't pretty.

"Didn't I see you playing in a bar in Chico one time?" Aimee the checkout girl asked as she scanned his food through.

"Probably," Veer answered, "but I don't do it anymore."

Aimee tilted her head in a question.

"I teach guitar mostly now," Veer explained.

"Oh, really?" she said. "I've only just started learning to play, but it's hard. Do you have any . . . space?"

Veer was pretty sure he was being chatted up, a thought that made him feel oddly vulnerable in a way he never had before, like even the idea of it was somehow unfaithful to Maya. He would be the world's worst cheating husband if a girl asking for guitar lessons had him prickling with sweat. That was a comforting thought, at least.

Yet he was drawn to this cool young girl if only from the desire to see her become someone, to have a great life.

"I'm probably going to start a teaching job," he answered, not knowing for sure if that was true, yet also not wanting to make promises he couldn't keep. He finished stuffing the last of his purchases into the bags. "So I'm not taking anyone on until I know if it's happening. Sorry."

Aimee looked crestfallen.

"But I'll . . . let you know if that changes."

As he walked toward the doors, Veer tried to put the encounter straight out of his mind and focused on the unpleasant task ahead—walking back with the two heavy shopping bags. Buses ran nearby on Skyway, but they only ran into Chico—totally the wrong way for him. *That's Paradise for you,* he thought and grinned at the absurdity.

Just as he got to the door, a man came running into the store. A messy-haired, overweight white man wearing a Harley-Davidson shirt, he was sweating heavily and trying to take in enough breath to speak. When a word finally came, it was the only word that was needed.

"Fire!"

Chapter 28

The sun was beginning to inch its way into the sky by the time that Lena left the house to go to her restaurant—she had delegated so much of the day-to-day running, yet still found her diminished role was almost a full-time job. Singing off-key to an old eighties Lata Mangeshkar song, she felt amazingly light despite the burdens she still carried.

Pulling up in the Kebabs & Curries restaurant's parking lot, Lena spotted a familiar sensible suburban hatchback. She checked her watch to see that it was eleven thirty—the restaurant had only been open a few minutes, and the day had already brought them some welcome customers.

"Anita! Kookie!" Lena gushed as she entered the restaurant to find her friend and the woman's mother sitting at a table and enjoying an early lunch. "I hope the staff are treating you well," she added, throwing a mischievous look at the waitress, "or I shall be sure to have them whipped."

"They have treated us like royalty," Anita said hastily as she stood to greet her friend. Anita was not always the best at telling when someone was joking.

Kookie frowned at Lena for a long moment, confusion finally growing into the sparkle of recognition. All the same, her name came out more like a question. "Lena?"

"Aunty, you look well," Lena lied. She looked older, even since the *Pheras*.

"You look well," Anita said, her tone conveying a good deal of surprise. She tipped her head toward Lena appraisingly, and the diamond nose pin on the bridge of her nose glimmered.

Lena did look well, she knew. She was done looking like the victim, with feeling guilty or somehow inappropriate if she allowed herself a smile. Now, she had something even more powerful. "What I feel is hopeful," Lena replied a little cryptically as she took a seat with them, and the comment lit up Anita's face. She was a pretty woman when she smiled; Anita's face had always been transformed that way.

"That's good," Anita purred appreciatively, although her eyes begged the question, Why?

"Everything is looking up," Lena told her, her face brightening. "I have a purpose, my son is looking much better than he was, and . . ." Lena paused. Once upon a time, Anita would have been one of the first people she would have told about Maya's pregnancy—shortly before most of the rest of the world—yet she had held the news close to her chest. Not so much for shame, but privacy. Her own, and the absent Maya's, too. "Can you keep this to yourself?"

"Yes," Anita replied automatically, her expression one part confused and at least four parts rapt.

"My daughter is soon to have a baby."

One of Lena's favorite things about Anita was that the woman was an open book, and she looked on patiently as she watched the various connotations play themselves out across her friend's face. "That's . . . great news," Anita said finally, grabbing Lena's hand across the table and squeezing it.

"Oh, a baby!" Kookie squealed, also belatedly, pressing her palms together in excitement. "A child is such a blessing, no? Who is it that is pregnant?"

Lena chuckled sadly, while Anita just looked embarrassed. "Maya," Lena said.

"Oh, she is being such a nice girl, that one." Kookie frowned, looked momentarily distant. "With Veer, am I right?"

Anita looked back to Lena, seemingly apologetic at the mention of Veer.

"It's okay," Lena said. "I'm . . ." It was too much to put simply. "Things are going okay."

"You and Pinky seemed better at the *Pheras*," Anita pointed out, leaving the debacle of the *Sagan* unspoken.

"We are," Lena said with a smile. "And at least one of us should have let you know that," she added with a tinge of guilt. Lena looked at Kookie, realizing that poor Anita had enough on her plate, without being left hanging about the problems of others. The longer life went on, the more difficulties it managed to heap on many of them. *Still, all the more reason to smile when we can.*

Then Lena's phone rang and, a few seconds later, the smile fell from her face.

~

"Manuel! Manuel!" Lena screamed. She bounded out of the car, leaving the door open in her panic to collect her husband on the way to the hospital.

"They're flying him into Zuckerberg," Manuel said, bursting out the front door of their single-story Walnut Creek house. "Here, I'll drive."

It seemed to Lena that the traffic getting out of Walnut Creek was as bad as she had ever seen it for the time of day. Every now and again she would shift in her seat or wriggle her neck and shoulders, as if her clothing was making her itchy, yet none of it did anything to ease the fear thudding in her chest.

"We'll be on the freeway soon," Manuel said with a strained note of encouragement as he looked over at his wife, "and everyone else will be going the other way at this time of day, so we'll make good time then." He reached across and placed one of his rough, calloused hands reassuringly on hers for a moment.

Manuel was right, and soon they were heading west on the freeway, the sun shining on their faces and forcing them to put the visors down.

It promised to be a beautiful, warm, and breezy day—quintessential California, which didn't seem right at all. It was a gorgeous morning, and her son was in a helicopter or already at the hospital, perhaps dying, maybe already dead. How could it be such a gorgeous morning if that was happening? She had seen him only a matter of hours ago, had sat right opposite Sameer, and he had seemed . . . a little better, at least. And "a little better" had meant a lot to Lena.

Had she touched him before she left him at the prison? Sameer had never been a hugger—since before his teens—but it seemed important suddenly that she should remember if she had touched his hand or his arm, if she had felt his skin against hers.

Don't think like that, Lena told herself, resisting the urge to slap her hand or pinch herself as punishment—so tightly wound were all her muscles, so ready was her body for actions it couldn't take. Those were goodbye thoughts, the thoughts of someone who had already given up on her son.

Lena looked past Manuel and up to the left, taking in the scenery to ease her frantic mind, which felt like it was losing its shape, unraveling like a poorly made sweater. Some of the hills of Piedmont were visible from the elevated highway, and she knew that the Kapoor mansion was up there somewhere, among all that lush greenery.

She thought of calling Pinky and began to fumble for her cell phone, just as Manuel glanced over. "Anita will have called them already," he said, evidently reading her thoughts.

Lena slumped back in her seat again, finding at least a shred of comfort in the fact that such an idea had even presented itself to her. She needed her friends, she realized, perhaps more than she had known. Yes, she had been ready to let Pinky go if need be, if that was what had been required. But maybe she had also been taking those lifelong friendships for granted, simply because they had always been there, and she had become too used to the support they brought with them. It was moments like these—like her divorce all those years ago—that showed the true value of friendships.

Lena bit her lip so hard she tasted blood.

Only as they picked up signs for the Zuckerberg Hospital did Lena begin to realize the irony of where they were going. Zuckerberg was a big hospital with a major trauma unit, so a lot of patients were sent there, yet she still found herself thinking about that night less than a year ago when she had been called and informed that her son had been in a car accident. Lena felt panic rise like bile in her throat—it was as if this place was trying for a second time to claim her son.

He had been okay then, only a little beaten up, yet death had been there that night, and much in Sameer's life had been taken because of it. In all of their lives. Her son was paying the price for it again today, she realized.

Dammit, leave him be, Lena's thoughts raged as the huge hospital building loomed up out of the city landscape. She clenched her teeth and tried to think of a prayer in the Hindu tradition in which she had raised her kids, but that they no longer followed.

Dear *Bhagwan*, have we not all suffered enough?

Chapter 29

"I came as quickly as I could," Pinky said with a catch in her voice. "Anita called me. I think she was going to drop Kookie Aunty off to her neighbor's before she came." Lena nodded, while anxiety snarled and snapped and gnashed at her like a rabid dog.

Pinky had burst through the waiting room's double doors in a fussy flurry of movement—still a peacock, even when she didn't mean to be, albeit a peacock in a panic. Visible beyond the slowly shutting doors, the tall, thin figure of Harry Kapoor loped down the corridor after his wife. He was much leaner than he had once been, for sure, but Harry could never be described as athletic, not how Manuel had been and, in many ways, still was.

As she watched him—her mind oddly detached, as it had been for some time now—Lena recalled a vague memory of Harry from around the time she had first met him. Back then, and for quite some time after, she had known only a plump, sweaty man, back when all he did was work, eat unhealthily, and—only occasionally, so Pinky had told her—sleep. Harry had never suffered one of the health scares that usually brought such men to their senses. However, a doctor's warning during an annual private healthcare screening had set Pinky on the warpath and ensured that Harry was never going to get his hands on any *gulab jamun* ever again.

Now, it was hard to picture the Harry that had once been, yet Lena had a momentary image of it before the double doors closed on him.

"What's the news?" Pinky asked as her husband reached the doors and followed her through them. "Have they said anything about how he is?"

Lena got to her feet to greet her friend, surprising herself a little when she found that she could, indeed, stand on them. "No, not much news at all, really. They have police guarding the area where he is, and the doctors we do see aren't the ones who have been dealing with him." She indicated the double doors some way to her left that led out of the other side of the waiting area. "There's a receptionist out there, but it doesn't seem like anyone tells her anything, either."

Behind Pinky, the usually quiet Harry grew stern as he listened to Lena's report. "It's not right that they won't tell you anything. You've been here, what, over an hour?"

Lena and Manuel both nodded.

"Is this because he's a"—Harry paused for just the briefest moment—"convict?"

"It doesn't seem to be helping," Lena replied cagily. She glanced at the phone clutched in her tightly clenched fist, her fingers white and numb with the pressure. Nothing from Maya. She'd called her to tell her what was going on with Sameer, but it had gone straight to voice mail.

"Right," Harry said, tossing the jacket he was carrying onto one of the seats. "We'll see about that." He strode purposefully across the waiting area and out through the far set of doors in a way that brought back another memory of the man Lena had once known—the fierce businessman who got things done.

Pinky lifted her hands in a hopeless sort of gesture, assuming a look that wasn't sure whether it wanted to be apologetic or not. "He's . . . I think he might be about to bring out the 'Don't you know who I am?' It doesn't happen as often now as it used to."

Manuel shrugged. "It can't hurt."

"Unless he gets himself thrown out," Pinky said, taking a seat next to Lena and reaching to take her friend's big hands in her tiny delicate ones.

Lena looked into Pinky's eyes, her own glistening with wetness. "I feel like I'm coming apart, Pinky. Why is my baby in there? It feels like I'm trapped watching some horrible movie, and I can't look away from it. I want it to end; I want it over. But what is 'over' going to mean?"

Harry appeared again through the double doors to their left.

"There's news," Harry called out, "and the doctor needs to speak to you."

∽

"Your son was stabbed multiple times, Mrs. Jaitly. He lost a lot of blood, but he is stable for now. We're hopeful."

The doctor, Manuel, and Lena were sitting at a table in a small office. The doctor was in his forties, with gold-rimmed glasses and black curly hair that was beginning to show signs of gray. He had an air of privilege about him as if he'd studied at Johns Hopkins or Stanford, as probably his father had and his father before him. It should have been disturbing how easily Lena found comfort in these old stereotypes of what an American doctor should be; yet, right now, all she wanted was to be reassured.

"One wound was very deep," the doctor said—*Dr. Carter*, his name badge read, like the former president. "And it looks like this is the cause of a complication."

"A complication?" Lena asked.

"Sameer's left arm has suffered some severe trauma, and it looks as if an artery in the arm has collapsed, restricting the blood flow."

"What does that mean?"

"It means that the lower half of Sameer's arm is not getting the flow of blood that it needs to keep it healthy. The limb is beginning to die, and in six, maybe eight hours at the most, the limb will become too far gone to save it."

"Is there anything to be done?" Manuel said, regarding the doctor with a serious, thoughtful look. Lena sat upright in her chair, hope radiating from her face like warmth from an electric heater.

Dr. Carter exhaled. "This is why we are talking to you. I have my opinion, but you are Sameer's family, and I felt you had the right to be involved in the decision.

"We will have to operate either way, which is a risk to his health in Sameer's current condition. He is relatively stable now, yet not completely out of the woods. If we remove the arm"—Lena gasped and clutched her chair tightly—"then we guarantee we only have to operate once."

"But you can try and save it?" asked Manuel solemnly and determinedly.

"To pick a figure out of the air, I would say there is roughly a twenty-five percent chance the limb can be saved. But a dying limb does not do the rest of the body much good, and it will be a little while until we can be sure if it has worked. And, if it hasn't, he will still need the operation to remove it."

"Could you not, I don't know, try your best to repair it and make a decision there and then?" Lena asked desperately.

Dr. Carter gave a small, kind smile. "Hedge our bets; the best of both worlds?"

Lena nodded.

"In my opinion, given Sameer's delicate condition, I would take the arm and know I'm giving the patient the best chance of survival. But then I make these sorts of calls almost every day and never for someone I know and love."

~

"Ah, Lena . . . Manuel. How the hell is he?" Lena's ex-husband had arrived while they were in the office with the doctor. Even in the waiting room, Goldie was wearing his stupid aviator sunglasses, and Pinky's cheeks were mottled red as if his arriving on her watch somehow made her to blame.

Lena barely noticed as she walked into the room like a zombie, one foot sliding slowly in front of the other, her gait unsteady, as if she only maintained her balance through her gradual and tottering forward motion. Her look was far away, and Manuel stepped behind her, a supporting hand on her upper arm.

In a delayed reaction, she looked up at Goldie, her eyes slowly focusing on him, her expression suggesting that maybe she hadn't understood his words.

"What did they say?" Pinky asked, her tone gentle.

After a brief moment in which Lena still hadn't spoken, Manuel took over for her. "He's stable. They're hopeful he'll pull through."

"That's good then, eh?" Goldie said. "I thought from the look on your face—"

"They're going to amputate his arm," Lena said, half shouting the words. The deep silence that followed them was only disturbed by the electrical whirr of a vending machine selling chips and candy bars.

"Which one?" Goldie asked. It was a question that seemed equal parts sensible and absurd.

"The left," Lena answered.

"He'll . . . he'll be deformed," Goldie said.

Lena looked up sharply at him, and even Manuel's eyes narrowed, yet Goldie didn't seem to notice. He turned and went to sit down on one of the uncomfortable waiting-room chairs, his legs splayed out straight in front of him as he studied his boots. Lena pinched the bridge of her nose to ease the ache forming behind her forehead and moved to take her seat beside Pinky.

Chapter 30

Anita arrived a little after Goldie, bringing a very welcome home-cooked meal in little Tupperware boxes. Lena saw her start—her nose pin twitching—when she saw Goldie, evidently realizing she didn't have a box of breakfast goodies for him.

More to save Anita's blushes than out of any concern for how hungry Goldie might be, Lena offered him her box. "Here," she said, "have mine. I can share with Manuel."

Goldie flashed a look at her, one that she imagined said: *You of all people are the one offering to give up your food?*

Of course, his look might not have meant that at all, but as far as Lena could tell, even around a decade and a half after their marriage ended, he still thought she was a stupid, fat cow. Nothing she had learned about Goldie in the years since had made her believe that he was a better person. Then again, maybe today of all days she should give him the benefit of the doubt.

Lena shook the box at him as he hesitated. "Go on," she said, "I'm not sure I'm all that hungry, anyway."

Her ex-husband took the offered food with a small nod of thanks. On a whim, she sat down across from him, struggling—as she had been throughout the day so far—to fit her ample bottom comfortably into the plastic seats that had obviously been made for San Francisco's gym generation.

Goldie cast an uncomfortable glance at her as he opened the Tupperware box and scents of fried potatoes and cardamom were released from where they had been held captive. Lena found herself briefly thinking about what an excellent cook Anita had become over the years, then about what a strange thought it was to have while her son was lying somewhere in a room nearby, perhaps being prepared for surgery to remove his arm, perhaps fighting to cling to life.

"He's only been in that prison a matter of months," Goldie complained suddenly, pulling Lena from her thoughts.

"How long does it take to make an enemy?" Lena replied.

Goldie looked sharply across at her. "Do you know who might have done this?"

"I only saw him earlier today, and he didn't say anything to me. I mean, he said it was bad in there, but he seemed so much better in himself than the last time I had visited. He seemed . . . like he was starting to accept things."

"Accept things?" Goldie asked.

"Yeah. To take responsibility."

"He had a car accident, Lena," Goldie argued. "Now my only son is going to be some cripple for the rest of his life. And he's got to go back into that place as a cripple." Every time Goldie said the word *cripple*, it sounded a little like he was coughing it up, as if it stuck in his throat a little.

"He got into a car after he had been drinking, Goldie."

"Big deal," Goldie said with a shrug and shoveled a spoonful of food into his mouth. He carried on speaking as he chewed. "Who doesn't do that sometimes, eh?"

"And a young woman died as a result," Lena said. Even after all these years, Goldie's belligerence and self-centered view of the world could still shock her.

"People die in car crashes," Goldie reasoned. "People die in car crashes every day without someone going to prison for twelve years, getting stabbed, and losing their arm for it. Who the hell does that help, eh?"

Lena could only stare at him with her mouth hanging open in shock. Goldie carried on shoveling food into his mouth and chewing noisily, either unaware of the look she was giving him or determined to ignore it. It was like they were married and living together all over again.

When Lena spoke next, she had taken time to make sure she could moderate her voice and keep it to the waiting-room level. "I don't want our son to be in prison, Goldie, any more than you do. I don't want him to be lying in there with them about to remove his arm. I don't want to think that he might not make it out of there alive, or that even if he does, he'll still have to go back to prison again.

"But don't you think that he was out of control? Don't you think he was going nowhere and just wasting his life? Always drinking too much, always . . . angry. Why was he always so angry?"

Goldie didn't look at her. Instead, he kept looking at his food, chewing for far longer than seemed necessary.

"Maybe all this can still end up having a positive outcome. Maybe he can come out of prison and find something to do with his life. He'll only be about forty, with so much of his life still ahead of him. And today, when I was with him, I think he started to realize that."

Goldie put his spoon down and placed the Tupperware tub on the chair next to him before turning an enraged look at Lena. She remembered that look. The savage eyes. The compressed lips. The start of a snarl on his face. When Goldie Sharma took his time to say something, that was when he was truly annoyed.

"Ay, Lena, you do speak some shit. Our son, my son, is going to be a useless bloody cripple. There is no silver lining, he is never going to do anything useful ever again, and any woman worth having will never want him."

Lena froze, realizing that everyone else in the room was looking at them, while really trying not to look at them. Except for Manuel, who was most definitely looking at the both of them, and his face had gone hard in a way it almost never did. Lena had about a hundred comebacks ready for Goldie, maybe a thousand ways to tell him what a useless, unhelpful shit of a man he was. But, looking at Manuel, she remembered that now was not the time and reined that familiar anger and contempt back in.

Suddenly, the doors to their right burst open, and another family walked in, because—such was the way of things—theirs wasn't the only world being destroyed or hanging in the balance that day. Just like on every day in every city across the world, tragedy was waiting for someone. A white woman, almost as large as Lena was, walked at the group's head, with her husband and children following, her eyes red rimmed and her hands shaking. Ever polite, Anita and the Kapoors stood up and moved along toward the left-hand set of doors so that the new family could sit down together.

Lena was glad that they were tucked away in a small waiting room in some more remote part of the hospital and not in the much larger and more public space near the main part of the trauma unit. It was strange when the other family came in, as the space had felt like theirs up to that point, although she hadn't realized that.

The other family's presence pulled Lena back from her growing anger and frustration with Goldie. Instead, she just stayed where she was, dispirited and deflated like a balloon with a small leak. There was no safety in numbers or comfort to be had in knowing that others were going through a situation similar to her own, she mused. On the contrary, it made her feel that her family's problems were less significant if they were happening to others, too. And, if their problems didn't matter all that much, then maybe the world cared a little less about what happened to her son. Somehow, maybe the powers that be, the unseen gods, might be less inclined to save him. *Stop it,* she told herself, a hand reaching to pinch her arm, then stopping just short. If she got into that he's-going-to-die mode, everything would spiral into a dark hole of depression. She needed to stay positive, upbeat.

Lena turned expectantly as another doctor in a white coat—a gaunt man with a long white beard and fierce eyebrows—came out and spoke to the other waiting family.

There was a primal wail of grief from the mother, while the father flinched at the news the doctor had given them. Lena tried not to look at them directly, yet there was nothing much else to focus her attention on. Out of the corner of her eye, her mind took in the details. The middle-aged, overweight woman with pronounced blue shadows under distinctive opal-black eyes and scanty brown hair pulled into a sad knot at the back of her neck. Lena saw her dissolve with a horrible, guilty fascination, the woman's legs giving way beneath her while being pulled into her husband's arms. One of the boys started to cry quietly, tears trickling slowly down his cheeks, while a younger boy turned his head from one member of his family to the other in apparent confusion.

Lena extracted herself from the uncomfortable seat and walked over to look out the window, suddenly desperate to be far, far away from this family's pain, terrified that she might be looking into her own future. As she passed them, Lena noticed the various states of discomfort of her own family and friends who waited with her as the very human drama played out just a few feet away from them.

Everyone looked away from what seemed like an unbearably private moment. Manuel had put earbuds in and would be listening to a Spanish meditative chant, she knew, his features schooled into a mask of sympathy. Anita avoided looking at the other family, too. She went to a corner of the room, put one palm against a wall, stood on one leg, and held her ankle in the other hand as if doing a stretching class for one. Harry and Pinky—man and wife for so long—each held the exact same expression. They radiated the sort of cool, calm detachment that someone who didn't know them might think showed a lack of concern. In reality, it was just that they were as professional in every aspect of their life as they had been in business and in socializing in San Francisco Bay society. For them, proper behavior was seldom switched off.

She looked at Goldie, always the odd one out in the room. He was scowling, appearing vaguely annoyed by all the commotion, as if it encroached upon his own issues. Lena remembered that other people's problems never really diluted his own. She suppressed a sigh, finding herself almost jealous of her ex-husband right then.

A few moments later, the other family moved away and took their grief with them, leaving five friends and one ex-husband in limbo again.

In the bare room, Anita's cell phone rang shrilly. Lena froze, perfectly still at the window. Moments later, Anita came running to Lena, her eyes darting like tiny fish. "I have to leave," she gasped. "Kookie's disappeared. I left her at my neighbor Deepa's house." Her chest was heaving with every word. "They think she slipped out through the backyard gate. It was unlocked."

$\sim$

When Sameer's surgery finished, Dr. Carter himself came out to see them.

"It was a success," the doctor said with just the right mix of optimism and gravity—he had likely done this sort of thing many times before.

"A 'success,' as in, my son doesn't have an arm anymore?" Goldie asked testily.

The doctor gave a small, professional nod to acknowledge Goldie's comment, then returned all his attention to Lena. "We were able to do more to repair some of his other wounds during the surgery," Dr. Carter said. "And, in my opinion, we've gone from a seventy-five percent to more than a ninety-five percent chance that your son will pull through this. I'm even surer now that the decision to amputate his arm was the right one, however hard it must have been." He glanced back over toward Goldie for emphasis.

"We had to remove the arm at quite a high point," the doctor continued, "so it's about three inches above the elbow."

Goldie's face was pale, and he turned to stalk off across the waiting room. The television that was situated above and to the right of the vending machine had been turned off when they arrived. It was now on and playing the news, and Goldie stopped in front of the TV and stared up at it.

"When might I see him?" Lena asked.

"He's still a little out of it from the anesthetic," Dr. Carter answered. "And, either way, he needs rest right now. But I promise that when he's awake, we will see how he is, and I will make sure that you get to see him as soon as it's possible."

"Could I go in and see him while he's still sleeping?" Lena asked, beseechingly. Somehow, his pulling through would not be completely real for her until she could see him. "I promise I won't disturb him."

Dr. Carter smiled kindly, then looked slightly embarrassed when he answered, leaning in to speak confidentially—even though it was only him and those there for Sameer in the waiting room. "I'm afraid I will have to have a quick word with the gentleman guarding him," he said in a comforting tone, "but I'm sure I can make that happen very soon."

"Dr. Carter," Goldie grumbled once the man had disappeared through the double doors that led back to the reception desk, wards, and theaters. "Wasn't there a Dr. Carter in that TV series? *ER*, wasn't it?" He scoffed out a disparaging noise. "I think that's all this doctor is," he said, "just an actor. How could he not save my son's arm?"

For some reason—perhaps because relief had eased the tension to allow for other emotions—this was the point at which Lena started to lose her patience with Goldie. "For the love of . . . Will you just let the arm thing go, Goldie? Our son is still alive, isn't that what matters? What are you even doing here? You never went to see him in prison."

Lena paused in what was about to become a tirade, having expected Goldie to rage back at her, most likely with the word *fat* coming early in his response. Instead, he was looking up at the TV again.

"Are you even bloody listening to me?" Lena asked.

"Eh, Lena," Goldie said, as if he genuinely hadn't been listening to her. "That town you said Maya had gone to, what is it called again?"

Lena huffed, irritated by what had to be the weirdest of deflections. "Paradise," she snapped. "Why?"

Chapter 31

There was a lot more smoke—so it seemed to Maya—than there had been only twenty minutes before. What had been a vague smudge on the horizon not so long ago had now become thicker smoke, rapidly increasing, being blown past and even overhead. She could tell that it was windy outside, and the smoke moved fast, making it hard to tell where exactly it was coming from.

She wished that Veer had at least left a note. She wished more than anything else that they hadn't argued the previous evening, whoever's damn fault it was, and that was seeming to matter less and less now. A stubborn part of Maya still wanted to be angry at him, not to be the one to pick up the phone and call or message him, but that inner voice was being drowned out by her rising fear for him, for what was going on, for her own situation with all that goddamned smoke nearby.

Maya picked up her mobile phone and stared at it, waving it back and forth slightly as it flickered between having one bar of signal and no bars at all. Considering how widespread the town was, and how it was in the middle of nowhere, the mobile coverage around Paradise wasn't so inadequate, Maya had always supposed. However, they were out on the edge of town, and it often varied day to day between a barely usable signal and no signal at all, with very occasional shocking moments of a clear two or three bars that were always far too short lived.

She pulled up WhatsApp so that she could use the property Wi-Fi, rather than the basic cell signal. The call just rang and rang with no answer. If Veer was doing this on purpose, she might have to kill him.

"Screw this," Maya said, her voice eerie in the otherwise quiet house, and ambled off—in her usual duck walk—to put some clothes on. A couple of minutes later, at least now dressed but still looking far from her best, she headed to the outside of the house, holding up her phone and slowly rotating around while trying to get a signal.

Straightaway, she came to realize that the wind had picked up tremendously; gusts that must have been above fifty miles an hour were bending the pines over to the southwest at a thirty-degree angle, causing several unsecured objects to fly across the yard. She watched a white plastic chair go airborne a little north of the creek and slam partway through the chain-link fence on the western property line. The chair hung there, quivering in the wind right where the fence caught it, appearing to levitate a foot off the ground.

The smudge on the horizon was no longer a smudge at all, but a thick, charcoal-black smear, as if a child had taken the side of a black crayon and spent several minutes rubbing it vigorously across the sky.

As soon as Maya got about fifty feet from the back of the house, two clear bars of signal appeared on the phone as she held it in front of her. She brought Veer's number up in her contacts and rang it again, watching those two bars suspiciously for as long as possible, while she slowly brought the phone up to her ear. Maya's heart was beating fast, and her chest moved tightly as she counted off the rings . . . one, two, three, four . . .

Come on, dammit!

"Hey there!" *Yes!* "This is Veer's answering machine." *Oh, for fu—* "Leave a message for the luckiest father-to-be in the world after the beep . . ."

Damn you. That was new, recorded since the last time she had left a message on his cell phone a week or so back. All of Maya's anger leaked out of her, and when the beep sounded, the first sound to come out of her was a sob.

~

Sarah was already approaching the front of the house when Maya returned from the back garden, her wind-whipped hair looking like an abandoned swallow's nest, she was sure. As much as it was a relief to see her, the long-time resident's worried expression only deepened Maya's panic.

"Maya, honey," Sarah called. "Looks like there's a big fire nearby."

"I've seen it," she replied. "I was just out in the back garden, and the sky to the . . ." Maya began to cough—a tickle in the back of her throat, similar to way she felt when spring allergies set her off.

"Could you tell how far?" Sarah asked as she reached her.

"I don't know," Maya replied, breathing hard to get her coughing under control. "The big black blotch is just on the horizon, but . . ." She looked upward, where every break in the tree cover showed thick gray tendrils of smoke rising to stain the sky. She was catching snatches of an acrid odor, and ash was drifting down like snow, settling on her eyelashes.

Sarah looked at the house. "Where's Veer?" she asked. "Is he in the house?"

"Um, no," Maya said, finding herself embarrassed and reluctant to tell the truth, despite the situation. "He went out walking."

Sarah looked over at the Tesla, mild confusion on her features. "On foot?"

"Yep," Maya replied with a shrug and a roll of her eyes. "I can't get through to him," she said with a small tremble of her lips. She kicked at the grimy, sooty ash landing on her foot and felt hope deflating like an old balloon.

Sarah hugged her. "You want to come in with us, honey?" she offered.

Maya nodded gratefully.

"Anything you need to get from the house?" Sarah asked.

Maya grabbed a coat, although the morning air was warm, despite the wind. The smell of smoke was mixed in with it, and Maya wondered a little ridiculously if some of the warmth was from the distant fires—which, if things were that warm, might not be so distant. The pair of them waddled over—really, it was Maya doing all the waddling—to the McKesson house. Maya realized about halfway over that it would have been a lot quicker in the car.

When they reached the house, Derek was outside loading things into their little SUV. "Have they given the evacuation order?" Sarah called out to him as they walked down the front path.

"No," Derek replied, "but I want to be ready if they do."

Sarah gave out an exasperated huff. "And how will we hear the telephone if neither of us is in the house?"

Derek stopped halfway through loading a plastic jerrycan of what might have been water or, Maya supposed, might have been fuel. Although putting more fuel into anything during a fire seemed preposterous, so maybe not. "Ah," Derek answered, looking like he felt foolish.

"Ah," Sarah agreed. "You men, too busy being useful to actually be useful." Derek looked wounded by the comment.

"Is there some sort of system?" Maya asked in response to Sarah's comment about the evacuation order. She was appalled with herself for not having thought about that before.

"Paradise has something called the CodeRED system," Sarah explained. "It's set up to call the landline when the evacuation order is given. Doesn't cover all of the town, but I know we're on it, I checked a few years back. Don't you worry, Maya," she said reassuringly, "they'll let us know if we need to get out."

Chapter 32

"This is Melvin Stein reporting from just outside of the sleepy town of Paradise in Butte County, California, where a fast-moving wildfire seems to have started this morning somewhere in the area to the northeast of town on Concow Road.

"The smaller town of Pulga has already been evacuated, and we believe that evacuation has begun in the town of Paradise itself, as high winds drive the wildfire toward the town, with reports suggesting it may already have reached the outskirts on the northeast of the town.

"Fueled by vegetation that was tinder-dry after years of successive drought, this fire comes late in the season when many might have hoped that this fire-prone part of California would be able to feel relatively safe for another year. However, reports suggest that this is a potentially dangerous fire given the high winds today that are gusting to over fifty miles per hour in this part of the state.

"Right now, the town of Paradise is braced and preparing for the worst but hoping for the best, and willing these high winds to die down or, at the very least, show a change of direction that might spare the town the worst of the fire.

"We'll keep you updated as things progress here in Paradise."

～

Lena was white faced, her hand flying to her mouth as she watched the wall-mounted television—as was everyone else in the waiting room. Except for Goldie, who had decided that this was the time to get a Coke out of the vending machine. Had Lena not been so distracted and shocked, she might have kicked him.

"Oh, my goodness," Pinky said, scrambling to pull out a mobile phone. "I'll phone Veer and see how things are with them."

Lena nodded gratefully.

"Won't they need to keep their phones clear for calls from the evacuation system?" Harry asked.

Pinky scoffed. "I don't think our city-born child will be signed up for the fire-evacuation system, Harry," she said. Then, looking over at Lena and Manuel, added thoughtfully, "Of course, your Maya might have had the sense."

"Like you said," Manuel said, "they're city people, so I wouldn't count on it."

Pinky took herself off to a corner as she tried to call Veer. Meanwhile, Lena felt Manuel's concerned look as she sat, her hands clasped together in front of her face so hard her knuckles had turned white.

Manuel gently took his wife's shoulders and turned her to face him. "It's okay," he said, "it looks from the news like they're aware of what is going on, and I'm sure they'll get everyone out if they need to."

"I can't . . ." was all that Lena managed in reply. She felt as if a great weight on her back dragged her toward the earth.

Pinky scurried back into the center of the room and called out, "Straight to voice mail." She looked down at the phone again, her fingers tapping nervously on it. "I'm sure I've got Maya's number here somewhere."

This, rather than her husband's reassuring words, seemed to give Lena the jolt she needed, and she returned to her bag to retrieve her mobile phone. Panic only seemed to accentuate the clumsy way that Lena went about using her phone, and she jabbed furiously at it until eventually it submitted and brought up Maya's number.

Almost everyone in the waiting room seemed to hold their breath for the long seconds that Lena held the phone to her ear and waited. The tension was infuriatingly broken as Goldie opened his can of Coke with the characteristic click and hiss.

"Maya!" Lena called out loudly, causing Pinky—who was the closest to her—to jump a little. As she tried to listen to the phone, Lena screwed up her face, seemingly trying to push it harder into her ear. "I can't hear you," she said loudly. "Maya, are you okay, do you know about the fire?"

A few moments later, Lena took the phone away from her head and stared at it. Slowly, she looked up and at those around her. "She's gone. The line was so bad, I'm not even sure if she heard me."

"I should go," Harry said, "drive up there. Bring the kids safely back."

Goldie gave a small chuckle. "You've got to be kidding, eh, it's more than a three-hour drive from here to there."

"So?" Harry demanded.

Goldie took a sip of his can. "So, this will probably be over one way or the other before you can even get there."

"We don't know that," Manuel said. "It depends on the wind; it depends on lots of things. And, either way, I don't think that's a reason not to try. They might need us." His head turned sharply to look at Lena, evidently realizing that he had just included himself in the venture.

Lena nodded slowly. "You should go," she said, then turned to Harry, "both of you. I appreciate you being here, Harry, but I've got my friend Pinky." She excluded Goldie, who didn't seem to notice. "And maybe they will need you."

Harry was still looking at Goldie, his eyes narrowed. "You do have a point," he said and began to stroke his chin. "It's hours in a car."

"Lance," Pinky said.

"Lance," Harry agreed, as if Pinky had just pulled the thought out of his mind. Then, to everyone else, he said, "I used to own a helicopter for, you know, avoiding traffic. I let the pilot I employed buy a controlling share in the thing when I retired, so that he could run it himself. I still have a stake, and he owes me. Lance will take us."

The last four words were a statement of fact, which, Lena remembered, was how Harry Kapoor had once been known to conduct business. "You want to come, too?" Harry asked Goldie gruffly as he pulled out his cell phone and moved off to make the call.

"I'll stay here," Goldie answered, "for when the boy wakes up."

∼

"Look at him," Lena said. "Do you think he's going to spring out of bed, defeat you with one arm and make a miraculous escape?" Although her words were sarcastic, Lena's tone was that of a woman coming undone.

The police officer guarding Sameer was, however, unmoved. "No, I do not, ma'am."

A little hysterically, Lena wondered if he took that same attitude and brand of comment back home with him at night: *Pass the mashed potatoes, husband. Yes, I will, ma'am.*

Dr. Carter had come to tell her that she could see Sameer shortly after Manuel and Harry had departed on their mission to Paradise. However, he had warned Lena that her son was still extremely groggy from the general anesthetic and the overall trauma of the attack. It wasn't until she was halfway to the room that Lena realized she hadn't seen if Goldie wanted to come. For his part, he hadn't made any effort to do so. When she arrived at Sameer's room and found him handcuffed to his bed, Lena had been unable to stop herself from making an issue of it.

"Stupid, then, isn't it?" Lena growled at the officer, just to have the last word, but then focused all her attention on her son. There was something a little cyborg-like about him as she approached, surrounded as he was by wires and machines, and with a stump where his left arm should be. It was as if the world and that damn prison had dehumanized him somehow, taken away a part of his humanity, a little of who he was.

Despite all of Dr. Carter's warnings, she crumbled, her body swaying slightly as she took in the state of her son, and suddenly wished that Manuel was there with her. Or Maya.

Lena let out a whimper like a hurt dog, unable to stop it, and the noise caught Sameer's attention, who she'd assumed was deeply under.

"Mom," he croaked, peering at her like someone with terrible eyesight attempting to focus without glasses.

Lena swiftly closed the gap to his side and took a chair. She went to take his hand but realized that she had come up on his left side, where there was no hand to take anymore. Glancing at the other hand, which had a tube coming out of it, she elected to rest her own hand on his chest, instead, knowing that she could not bear to sit there and not make contact with him.

"Sameer," she said, the simple act of calling her son by his name like the sweetest music to her ears when the possibility of never again doing so had been dangerously present so very recently.

"I . . . They . . ." His voice was a harsh whisper, coherent thought and expression a challenge, but Lena felt she knew what he was going to say.

"I know, son. But they had to do it. It saved your life, and that's all that matters."

"I . . . I didn't want to let him do it, Mom. I'm sorry."

"You don't have to be sorry. It had to be done."

"He touched me, Mom, he did things."

"They operated on you. They . . . they had to take your arm to save your life."

"I wish I'd never done the play."

Although still confused, Lena froze, an instinctive feeling, like the hairs were standing up on the back of her neck. "Play?"

"Detention," Sameer breathed, his eyes rolling back in his head a little. "I met him in detention."

"Who did you meet in detention . . . ? Do you mean in prison?"

"School . . . detention . . . Mr. Barr." Suddenly, Sameer lifted his head a little and looked straight at his mother, a measure of lucidity appearing to find him. "I didn't want him to do it," he cried, sounding like a wounded animal. "He touched me, he . . . made me do these things." He laid his head back again, staring at the ceiling, voice falling to a whimper. "Don't tell him. Please don't tell Dad."

Lena leaned forward. "Not tell Dad what? Did something else happen in prison?"

Sameer seemed exhausted by his outburst, and his eyes had lost focus. "Yes . . . no. That's not . . . what . . . I mean."

"It's okay," Lena said, "you can tell me later."

Sameer closed his eyes, and Lena thought he was going back to sleep, but several seconds later, he spoke quietly once more, his voice almost a whisper. "He raped me, Mom. He was my teacher . . . and he raped me."

Chapter 33

The initial reaction in the supermarket had not been one of great panic, despite the manic shout of the man in the Harley-Davidson shirt.

Veer found himself feeling as much an outsider as ever as he looked around at the other faces in the store—including young Aimee over on the checkout—to get some clues as to how to react to this news. The response among the customers and staff in the Holiday Market was mostly one of pragmatism.

"Where is it?" asked the person who had been waiting behind Veer at the checkout, a tall woman in her late fifties or early sixties with overly permed ash-blonde hair, her figure hidden beneath layers of tweed and thick cotton.

"Don't know for sure," the man in the Harley-Davidson shirt answered, looking a little put out that everyone in the store hadn't just thrown their arms in the air and run screaming for the door. Veer was with him on that. "There's a lot of smoke in the sky everywhere north and northeast of here. Maybe east, too. And I mean, a lot."

A man emerged from behind some shelving close to the checkout. He had the look of a store manager. "I've just seen that they've evacuated the area out where the mobile-home park is, but that's right over on the eastern side of town. There's no word of a general evacuation yet, and no activation of the CodeRED system." He looked at Aimee for emphasis. "I don't see any sense in shutting up the store and going until someone tells us to."

Veer turned and continued to head for the door. He didn't necessarily agree with the store manager, even if the man was probably a seasoned resident of Paradise. And, anyway, he wanted to see this smoke for himself.

Veer was some way out into the parking lot before he could turn and get a good angle past the building and the thick column of fir trees that stood sentinel beyond it. Once he could see, however, his eyes bulged as he gaped at the sky. Rising up from the high ridge to the east was an incredible column of smoke—it stretched from north to south as far as he could see, rising straight up as a solid wall that appeared to have no end. Its plume widened until it mingled with the clouds above, forming an oppressive ashy dome.

Veer hesitated for a moment, caught between two decisions—one arguably of the heart and one of the head. He wanted to get back out onto Skyway and start heading toward home and Maya as soon as possible. Yet a small exchange with some random checkout girl called Aimee pulled at Veer's moral center, and he realized that he couldn't leave without running back into the store and warning everyone else. Maybe he would look foolish, but right then, his conscience didn't care.

"I think you've got to see this," Veer called out once he was back through the sliding doors of what was one of the town's biggest grocery stores. He hoped he sounded as confident and authoritative as he wanted to. In a sense, all those nights fronting the band and playing gigs around San Francisco had prepared him for this. "It looks awful out there and not so far away."

Aimee glanced over at the store manager, who was still where he had been when Veer left, talking to the lady with the tightly permed hair. Something silent crossed between the checkout girl and her manager—perhaps a mutual assessment of whether Veer was worth listening to—and then they both started to move over toward the doors. It was a ridiculous feeling to have at that moment, yet Veer felt a little proud of having gotten the locals to listen to him when Harley-Davidson-shirt guy had failed. It was a feeling that somewhat tarnished his Good Samaritan efforts.

Turning, Veer led the little group back out of the supermarket and into the parking lot.

"Jesus," the store manager breathed as he saw the full extent of the smoke on the horizon, "I ain't never seen anything like this. Why haven't they issued the CodeRED evac?"

The man had clearly, at some time, been military. Either way, Veer now realized that his reasons for getting the people in the store out to the parking lot hadn't been entirely selfless, as the reaction of the manager of the Holiday Market had just confirmed that his panic wasn't merely that of a city boy not understanding the situation.

The store manager turned back around to Skyway Road. "Looks like people are leaving, anyway," Veer said.

"You get home now, Aimee," the store manager called to his checkout assistant.

A thought occurred to Veer then. "Hey," he said, "have any of you got a car here?"

"We both live close by," the store manager said, "so we walk."

"I've got my little Chevy," the woman with the permed hair told him.

"I don't suppose you're heading toward the east on Pearson at all?"

The woman shook her head. "I'm just up on Bille, I'm afraid."

"Even if you could take me a little way down Skyway," Veer said, hating that he sounded like he was pleading, "end of Pearson, say?"

The woman took a step or two away from him, shaking her head and doing a sort of negative jazz hands. Her eyes had gone wide, and she glanced back toward the horrible black smudge that was now the sky at just about every point east and northeast of where they were. "I'm sorry," she mumbled and turned to head off toward her car.

Veer noticed that Aimee and the store manager had already started back toward the store, and he found himself alone in the parking lot, with two bags of purchases and a terrible feeling building in his gut. He dropped the bags—why the heck was he even still holding them? He pulled out his phone to call Maya, pleased to see that he had a couple of bars of signal. And a voice mail, too . . .

Bringing the phone up to listen, all Veer could make out after several seconds of silence was what sounded like a single sob—it was Maya's sob, he could tell that much. His heartbeat pounded so loudly in his ears that he had to strain to hear through the rush of anxiety that washed over him, so he listened to it a second time to be sure that he hadn't missed anything at the start.

Veer took a long look at the unsettling orange-tinted sky as he called Maya's cell phone—not that he expected it to have a signal. Sure enough, it went straight through to her voice mail.

"There's a fire, Maya," Veer said into the phone, "and everyone seems worried. I'm on foot and out on Skyway, so I'm gonna try to come and get you, but you should get to Sarah and Derek for safety first, yeah."

Veer almost took the phone away to press the red button on the screen and end the call, but he paused, the phone still a centimeter or two from the side of his face. "I love you, Maya. I love you so much."

This time, Veer brought the phone down and ended the call, noting that the battery was under 50 percent. It had been important to say, even though he knew what saying it the way he had said it meant, the way it let all those fearful feelings in and the way it was letting his cruel imagination think that the last exchanges they would ever have might have been angry ones.

Pushing those thoughts aside, he forced himself to breathe deeply and started jogging at a slow pace, concentrating on keeping it steady enough that he could hope to maintain it—it was some distance back to where they lived. And, as he sped, cutting down on a dirt road heavily overgrown with weeds and coarse grasses to save a few seconds getting onto Pearson Road, his mind whirred with thoughts that were suddenly more urgent.

Dammit. He had to reach Maya and let her know that nothing was more important than their little family. Screw his parents. Screw their so-called friends. He would stay here in Paradise and work in a school if that was what Maya wanted. For all the confusion about today, that had an air of clarity to it. After he found Maya again, nothing would ever be more important than the three of them.

Coming back to the moment and the task in front of him, Veer's mind raced, thinking of all the ways he might deviate from the main road . . . yet he kept going back to the fact that staying on the road was the best way to go. It would only take hitting one obstacle he didn't expect—one fence there was no way around or over, a piece of rough ground too difficult to cross—and he would have wasted tons of time.

A blizzard of ash began fluttering down from the sky, and Veer spent the first few hundred yards after making the call trying to flag down a lift, but only two cars stopped, and neither of those wanted to head east and toward the direction of the fire. Understandable, he guessed.

Now, on Pearson Road, the traffic that he did see was all heading west. Some waved or pointed or even blasted their horn at Veer, pointing desperately for him to head back the other way. One man even stopped.

"You don't want to be heading that way, partner," said a wizened-looking man with a thin black mustache and a pointy chin. "I've just come from out on Pentz Road, and I've never seen anything like it. The fire is massive, friend, and fast, real fast, and heading straight for the town.

"I ain't waiting for no evacuation order, I'm heading out to Chico until I know what this thing is doing. You wanna do the same. I'll give you a lift if you want."

The genuine look of concern on the man's face when Veer said that he was heading back toward his pregnant fiancée made the pit of his stomach drop away.

Thunder, flame, and smoke ruled the world, and an ominous orange glow like the final moments of a winter's sunset lit the sky, but it wasn't until he crested the hill that Veer got his first glimpse of what was happening on the eastern horizon since leaving the parking lot at the Holiday Market.

Veer was not at all a religious person, but as he looked at the approaching fire and smoke column, the only words that came to mind were godly: *holocaust, qayamat, apocalypse.* Holy crap! He had just come to understand in a way that he hadn't truly grasped up until that moment just what deep shit the whole town of Paradise was in.

Chapter 34

Every time Maya tried to call Veer, she had to find the right spot in the McKesson house for a signal. What was worse was that this spot seemed to move around every few minutes or so. She had tried texting and sending WhatsApp messages, too. The WhatsApp messages were sending but never looked to be received and read—those two pesky ticks not turning blue for her—and the texts came back with an alert saying they were "Undeliverable," whatever the hell that meant.

"No answer again?" Sarah asked as she came into the lounge and saw Maya staring in frustration at her phone.

"I'm so worried about him, Sarah," Maya said. She paused for a moment; despite her fear and the seriousness of the situation, there were certain things that her upbringing still made it difficult for her to admit to someone who wasn't family. "We . . . argued last night. The last words I said to him . . ." Maya's voice broke down for a moment, and in the pause, Sarah closed the distance between them and clasped Maya's hands. "They weren't good ones."

"Now, now, honey," Sarah soothed, "there is no need to be panicking like this. Fires are not the most uncommon thing in this part of the state, and we've always been all right before."

Maya's eyes met the older woman's. "Has it ever been this close before?"

Sarah hesitated, and it was Derek who took over as he entered the room. "Was it 2007 or 2008?" he asked his wife. "That one was a bit scary."

"Yes, yes," Sarah said, then turned to Maya. "Maybe you could try the house phone to make a call?" she suggested.

Derek scoffed at that. "Sorry, but we've got to keep that open in case the evacuation order comes through."

Sarah shot dagger eyes at her husband but didn't go as far as contradicting him. Although not knowing where Veer was was almost more than she could bear, Maya did not want to endanger them all by missing the evacuation call. The fear not only curdled her stomach, but it also made the muscles in all her limbs feel like they wanted to spasm at the same time. It was like the worst itch in the world, and it made her want to scream.

"I need some air," Maya said. "I might go out to the front and see if I can see anything, or maybe find someone and see if they know anything."

"I'll join you," Sarah said and turned back to her husband, pointing an accusing finger at him. "You stay here in case the phone goes."

The first thing that struck Maya as she stepped out of the front of the McKesson house was how much more ash was falling everywhere than had been the case when she had first stepped out into it. Not only was it falling more thickly than before, but it was also falling in bigger pieces—great big flakes in black and gray.

The second thing that struck her was how it seemed like the sun was starting to go down, drawing out the sky in otherworldly reds and yellows. The air had grown thick and black with whirling smoke and departing birds, which looked like an apocalyptic signal, largely because that was what always happened in movies.

"I ain't never seen anything like this," Sarah said, her usually reasonable diction failing her for a moment. The older woman took her eyes from the sky again and met Maya's fearful gaze. Maya saw Sarah's expression, and unadulterated panic pumped through her body. Her chest heaved, and her hands fluttered uselessly over her belly.

"What are we going do, Sarah? Where's my Veer?" she whimpered. As if in answer, Maya's phone beeped once, and the voice-mail symbol came up on the screen.

"Veer?" Sarah asked as, just a little up the road, a green pickup truck pulled off one of the drives and sped north toward Pearson, spinning up gravel as it went.

Maya listened to the message, her eyes moving up to meet Sarah's halfway through. "He was on Skyway," she said. "He's coming back on foot. He . . . he sounds scared, Sarah."

"Call him!" Sarah said, and Maya did so, but it only rang and went through to his voice mail again. Her mouth moved wordlessly for a moment, then she canceled the call and almost threw her phone down in anger. "Dammit, dammit!" Maya screamed, shaking the thing in her fist. "Why isn't he here with me? Why?"

Holding a hand over her mouth, Sarah had stepped back a few paces. Her momentary panic-driven rage ebbing away, Maya followed the older woman to see what she was peering at.

Looking between the nearest trees and toward the tops of more distant ones—although maybe only half a mile away—Maya could see flames dancing behind them, writhing and reaching skyward, at once lithe and furious and deadly.

Sarah swallowed with an audible gulp. "Okay, we've got to evacuate, screw the CodeRED system."

They started back down toward the house, and Derek met them at the door. "Is it the evacuation order?" Sarah asked hopefully.

"No," Derek answered, "but we can't wait any longer. Everything past the creek is on fire."

"It's even closer than that to the north," Sarah told him. "Come on."

They had scarcely gotten out of the door before they were assailed by a hurricane of smoke, sparks, and cinders, which nearly blinded and suffocated Maya. She doubled over in a coughing fit, shuddering at the fury of this fire that was consuming their slice of Paradise. Maya felt herself heaving for breath as Sarah thumped her hard on the back. She placed a hand on Sarah's shoulder and ducked, spitting out a glob of dirty sputum.

As they scrambled into the waiting car, Maya caught Sarah glancing back at their house, the look on her neighbor's face suggesting that she was contemplating the possibility they might never see it again.

"Do you think it's getting close?" Maya asked from the back seat as Derek turned north along the lane that led closer to the center of Paradise. It was the only way out by road—and, in all practicality, by foot as well—yet going that way felt counterintuitive as it seemed, if anything, to be taking them in the direction that the smoke was telling them they didn't want to go. *But Veer is this way,* Maya reminded herself.

"Hard to tell," Derek answered honestly, peering beyond the windshield.

With the smoke blowing thickly at ground level now, Derek couldn't drive at more than about fifteen or twenty miles per hour. Already the light outside was like nighttime with soot everywhere—in the sky, on the windows of the car, on the driveways and lawns they passed.

Derek started to fiddle with the knobs of the radio, but needing to keep a better eye on the road due to the poor visibility—even with his headlights on full beam—he gave up with what he was doing. "Sarah," he said, "would you bring up the police band?"

Sarah calibrated it for a few moments, twisting knobs back and forth before a crackly but official voice could be heard. It was hard to make out clearly.

"That's it," Derek said. "Just clean things up a little if you can." The voice crackled momentarily, and they lost it altogether for a few seconds. Sarah adjusted it some more, and when it finally came back, the voice was a lot clearer.

"Just south of Pearson, coming across the canyon . . ."

Sarah looked at Derek, the alarm clear on her face. "Oh my god," she said, "that's close."

"Yeah," Derek answered, his voice still relatively steady. "If it's coming from the east, which it sure seems to be, that's got to be our little creek and canyon they're talking about."

"All traffic on Pearson needs to be stopped . . ." the voice continued.

"Stopped?" Sarah and Maya both exclaimed together.

"What do they mean *stopped*?" Sarah added.

"Listen," Derek said, "they could be talking about any part of Pearson in any direction."

They listened some more, although the voice had halted for the moment.

"Oh no," Maya breathed, looking between the husband and wife toward the extent of what she could make out in the full-beam headlights. Derek began to slow the car, which had only been doing about twenty miles per hour, anyway.

"No," Sarah said, her voice having gone up half an octave from where it usually was. For the first time, Maya could hear real fear in the woman's voice. "Is this the backup to get out onto Pearson?" They had hit a line of cars, and they were still some way from the end of the lane. "Why? Are they stopping people from getting out?"

"I'm sure it will start moving in a minute," Derek said, his voice having adopted a firmness that Maya could tell was designed to quell his wife's growing hysteria. It seemed to work for Sarah but wasn't doing an awful lot for Maya.

It hadn't seemed like things could get much more terrifying, yet the darkness around them grew even deeper and the smoke thicker. Oddly, Maya felt comforted when the first car joined the line behind them. At least they weren't the last car anymore.

That comfort lasted about thirty seconds when Sarah spotted something out of the passenger window. "Oh no," Sarah said. "Not good. *Not good.*"

Maya followed her gaze through the blackness to their right, somewhere beneath the orange glow that hung vaguely in the sky through the smoke. "Is that . . . ?" she began.

"The fire," Sarah finished for her.

It began as a small orange glow somewhere among the trees, but within just a minute or two, they could see great pillars of fire consuming whole trees that combusted like a Kuwaiti oil-well fire. Huge, white-hot, and intense, the flames were staggering in height, like monsters spilling forth from the very mouth of some biblical Hell. Nothing in the surrounding area was burning as hot as this massive collection of pine-tree trunks and dense undergrowth, and it could be felt within the car in stifling waves with each new gust of wind that blew it toward them. The constant roar from it sounded like fifty hot-air balloons firing their propane burners all at once.

Maya shuddered and pressed her knuckles to her lips. She felt like a thick woolen blanket was smothering her.

A sliver of relief came as the line started moving again. Sarah turned around and reached out a hand. Maya took it. "You hang in there, honey," Sarah said, seeming to have calmed slightly, even though the fire was growing ever closer.

"I think we've got another problem," Maya said, her voice trembling as recognition dawned.

"What's that, honey?" Sarah asked a little absently.

"I've just made a mess in the back seat of your car," Maya said.

Sarah patted her hand before drawing her own one away. "Don't worry, honey, we're all pretty scared, and you've got a good excuse."

"No," Maya said more strenuously. "I mean that my water just broke."

Chapter 35

"Are you in pain? Shall I call the nurse?" Lena asked, reaching out to place a hand on Sameer's feverish brow. He started up, his eyes bulging with a fear that lit its own terror within her.

"Hush, I'm sorry. It's nothing, *beta*, only me." Lena spoke soothingly to him, her jaw working to find a magic balm.

Sameer had fallen back to sleep after his initial confession to Lena, and she had just wanted to sit next to his bed for a while, watching him and trying to figure out what it all meant—although she was also desperate for news of what was happening in Paradise.

At the same time, however, she hadn't wanted to know a single thing. The news reports weren't going to tell her how her little girl was doing; all they were going to do was show sensationalized pictures of the fire's devastation. So, she had stayed there, and no one had come to kick her out, and lost in her thoughts, somehow half an hour had passed, and Sameer had woken up again.

Sameer looked about uncomprehendingly.

A dingy curtainless window faced a compound wall. Its white-wash—as Lena knew from many hours of staring at it—was covered with unintelligible black graffiti. From cracks in the plaster at its base, poppies struggled from the mud. There was an exhaust vent in the room's upper-left corner, with a fan that provided ventilation. Outside the glass double doors, the policeman standing guard stretched his arms and belched loudly.

Sameer groaned and pulled at his restraint, closing his eyes and shutting her out completely, like he always did.

This time, Lena was not having it. She came to Sameer's left side, reaching across to take his square-fingered right hand in her chubby fingers and bringing it to her cheek, caressing it. Caught by surprise, Sameer let Lena stroke his hand, before eventually pulling it free from her grasp.

He skewed his jaw to one side, turning his face away from her.

Lena crawled beneath the sheet and lay down next to him, only barely touching his shoulder where the dressing began. He smelled lightly of Old Spice aftershave and blood and fear.

"Sameer, my *beta*," she said, her voice tremulous, "I've made many mistakes with you. I don't want to make any more."

They lay together like stalks of corn in a field. Lena looked up at the solitary utility light strung from a cobwebbed, cracked ceiling. Her heart was beating very fast.

She put a trembling hand lightly on Sameer's right forearm. If he spurned her now, how would they ever find their way back to each other? "Tell me about that day . . . the day when you got detention," she whispered.

She felt Sameer grow still beside her. But for the rise and fall of his chest, he might have been made of plaster.

Then he took a deep, shuddering breath, and slowly he began to speak.

"I'd never gotten detention before that day," Sameer said, "and I remember feeling like that was it, you know? My life was over." The man in the hospital bed, who had lived as many years again as the schoolboy who had felt so marked by getting detention, gave a bitter little laugh. "Man, the shit I've pulled since then, the bad things I've done—illegal and legal—that little boy wouldn't worry so much about one detention if he could see me now." His voice changed. "Of course, that's where it all started to go wrong." Sameer's voice was barely above a whisper.

"Why did you get that detention?" Lena asked. She eased to the side of the bed and lifted herself a little so that she could look at Sameer. All she could see of his face, his profile, was stony.

"I got into an argument with Dad," Sameer answered.

"What about?" Lena asked, her voice faltering. She watched him, her brow knitted with concern.

"Women," Sameer said with a certain wryness. "After a while, it was always about women. I thought he was the coolest when I first moved in with him. There was always some new woman, always pretty and blonde and younger than him, not . . ."

"Like me?" Lena finished in a rush of words, filling the awkward pause.

Sameer looked away, embarrassed.

"It's okay," Lena said. "You were what . . . fourteen or fifteen years old? I know as well as anyone what a teenage boy thinks an attractive woman should look like. And your father, for all his faults, he was a handsome man. I was so thrilled when we were first married. All the other girls in our social circle in Delhi wanted him, yet pudgy Lena Jaitly got him."

Sameer looked back again, surprised.

"Oh yeah, I always had a little bit extra on me," his mother said, a dip in her voice as if awaiting his judgment, "even back then."

Sameer sighed heavily and shook his head. "Yeah, if I think about it now, it all comes down to that. Isn't that strange?" There was a catch to his voice. His face fell, cheeks and eyes and mouth changing shape and dissolving, and it caved into itself like a dying flower as he began to narrate his story.

Lena could feel a wave of nausea washing over her as the story went on. Something was falling into place. Pieces of a puzzle forming a picture.

The pungently acrid smells of disinfectant overwhelmed Lena's senses, and suddenly she tuned in to the strange cries and groans sounding all through the hospital. She felt sick as she tilted her head to see him; now, it was all coming together in her memory. "The school play?"

For a little while, Sameer stared off into the distance as if he wasn't going to go on. Just as Lena was trying to find something to say, he started speaking again fast, as if forcing the words out through a small hole in some invisible personal wall he had just breached. "And then he got me drunk, and he raped me . . ."

Lena was chewing so hard on her lips, she tasted blood. Her heart was about to explode out of her body.

"And nothing at all changed otherwise, except that the play's rehearsals went from being my favorite time of the week to the worst time," Sameer continued. "But I couldn't say anything, do you understand?" he said, voice now trembling. "How could I ever say anything? Dad would never have looked at me the same way again." He looked like a pathetic little boy, with large, hollow eyes and pale cheeks, instead of a grown-up man.

Lena wanted to sweep Sameer into her arms and onto her lap and rock him back and forth like she used to do when he was little. She wanted to protect him, to be there in a way that she hadn't been able to when he was a boy. After this was over, they would take Sameer back to prison. He would be where she couldn't look after him again. The thought pierced her like a knife, seemed so unfair when she finally felt closer to him than she had in so many years.

"That same semester was when I started drinking. And the rest, as they say," Sameer finished, "is history."

Lena felt tears blur her eyes. Tears for her little boy and the memory that had appeared so clearly in her head that she could hear it. She scooted up carefully on the bed so that she was cradling his head in her arms. She rubbed the back of his head gently, making slow circles on his dense, unwashed hair, utterly thankful that he let her. She pressed her lips to his forehead. "That time, when you said you hated me?" she asked. Oh how it all made sense now.

Sameer started to cry, huge sobs that turned his words back into mumbles like the delirium was coming for him again. "I wanted to come and live with you again. I wish I'd never moved in with him."

"I wish I'd never let you."

Chapter 36

Lena's phone started blaring as she walked back toward the waiting area; it was Anita. "I'm sorry I had to leave. I got a phone call that she was missing, I just . . ."

Lena's friend was blubbering and sounded like she was in a mess. It was becoming the day for it. "What's happened? Is Kookie okay?" It seemed to be the wrong question, as Anita let out a loud wail on the other end of the line.

"I found her in the temple, peeling vegetables for the *langar*." That didn't seem so bad, but Anita was making it sound like the end of the world. "She had no memory I had left her at my neighbor Deepa's house," Anita went on. "She wandered out of Deepa's home and into the temple down the lane, and she thought I had been sitting there eating the free meal all along. I'm telling you, Lena, I think it's too much now, she needs to be in the hospital."

"Okay, Anita," Lena soothed her, finding an odd and comforting familiarity in dealing with her often-fretful friend. "Look, don't feel you have to come back—"

"I want to!" Anita snapped in a shaky voice, as if coming back to the hospital to be with Lena were the only thing keeping her together. Lena could picture her, more skittish than ever, a bunched fist that now hid her diamond nose pin pressed to her flat red nose to keep the tears at bay.

Anita's worry poured over her like a waterfall, turning her insides rigid. Lena briefly closed her eyes. Then she lied and told Anita that everything was A-okay, and insisted that her friend stay with Kookie.

Goldie wasn't there when Lena arrived again in the now all-too-familiar waiting area. Sameer's confession, if that was what you could call it—and it seemed to Lena the most terrible crime to refer to it that way—had exhausted him, and he had passed out on his mother's graying hair, which had fallen loose while she lay in the bed next to him.

A part of Lena had just wanted to stay there beside him, although she had known that reality waited for her beyond the walls and the large glass window of Sameer's hospital room. Besides, the guard had kind of forced the issue by coming to stand and glower at Lena through the glass door. So, she had slowly and awkwardly extricated herself and her trapped hair from the bed beside Sameer, not even causing her son to stir in his exhausted slumber, before returning to the waiting room.

Pinky stood up from her plastic chair as soon as she saw Lena, handing her a flimsy polystyrene cup full of lukewarm liquid that resembled something out of a dishpan, rather than the scalding-hot, strong cup of tea Lena usually favored.

"How is he doing?" Pinky asked, placing a hand on her friend's arm.

How is he doing? It should have been a much simpler question than it was. Lena wanted to be honest with her, but she wasn't ready to be honest yet. More than that, she now felt entrusted with the terrible burden that Sameer had shared with her. Oh, her broken, fragile, lost boy. Her heart ached for him. Even though she had more than half a century behind her, Lena knew that she didn't have any idea how to process what she had just heard, or whether it would ever be right to share this new burden with her friends.

"He's sleeping now," Lena answered evasively. "He's . . . you know."

Pinky nodded as if she understood. Which was ironic, because Lena wasn't sure she understood anything at all.

"Where is Goldie?" she asked. She shouldn't care—she really shouldn't care—but for everything she had just learned, he was still Sameer's father, and it just felt like she should be talking to him right then. Not about . . . that. She knew that for Sameer's sake she could not say anything. All the same, she should tell Goldie about how their son was doing.

Pinky's face took on a sour, disapproving look that Lena knew well. Pinky had a range of sour, disapproving looks, and this was the one reserved for men who had stepped out of line. "He said he needed to get some air," she said flatly.

Lena's face closed down. There was no space in her brain for fruit-less anger. She glanced up at the TV, which was full of flaming images. "Any news?"

Pinky took a steadying sip of her tea, then turned a stoic face to her. "No news from our husbands," she said finally. "Although they won't even be halfway there yet."

"And the reports?"

The plastic cup quivered in Pinky's hand, and Lena found herself removing the cup from her friend's tightly clenched fist. "It's so bad, Lena," she said, her voice trembling. "Our children . . ."

Lena brought her friend into an embrace. She could almost smell her fear and, beneath it, the familiar exotic perfume Pinky always wore.

Sameer's brush with death, her uncertainty about where Maya was—all of it wore heavily upon Lena's ideas of mortality. Even with everything life had ever thrown at Lena Jaitly, she had never been one to feel vulnerable, to feel like she would splinter into a thousand pieces.

Making her way out into the hall, Lena looked out the windows and saw a rather tired-looking attempt at a sensory space, a combination of hardy plants, decorative stone, and paving slabs. It was not, Lena was fairly sure, supposed to be a smoking area. However, there was Goldie, puffing away and talking on his mobile phone. A part of her wanted to leave him there and just go back to the waiting room, yet the same compulsion that had given her the need to talk to him after leaving Sameer drove her forward again right then.

She found a way out into the sensory garden at the far end of the corridor and was screened in her approach to Goldie.

"Ay, Carole, I've got to go back in a minute, I'm on a time crunch here, don't want to miss any news. I've got to stay here at the hospital and do my bit, you know. I'll be back soon to give you what I didn't give you last night." There was a pause as a presumably lurid reply came from the other end of the phone. Goldie gave a dirty laugh and took a short drag on his cigarette before throwing the end down and crushing it out as he exhaled. "You bet, Daddy's going to make you very happy, eh?"

"Daddy?" Lena screamed, her face contorted with anger. "Daddy?"

Goldie turned around and let the cell phone fall slightly away from his ear. A great blast of wind found its way down past the hospital buildings and into the sensory garden, rustling long-leaved plants so violently that they made a noise like waves crashing on a beach.

"Who's that on the phone?" Lena demanded, advancing on him. "Because if it isn't your son, Sameer, or your daughter, Maya, then . . ."

Lena didn't finish the thought, but she trembled as she turned fierce eyes on her ex-husband. A voice spoke unheard words through the small speaker on the cell phone in his hand. Goldie brought the phone back up to his ear.

"It's all right, Carole," he said. "It's just—"

"The mother of his children!" Lena bellowed, her voice defeating the wind to echo slightly off the walls and windows around them.

Speaking into the phone again, Goldie frowned at Lena. "Sorry, darl—"

He was cut off again as one of Lena's hands slapped the cell phone from his hand. It went spinning quite some distance to land with an audible crunch on the gravel behind Goldie.

"Eh!" Goldie cried. "What are you doing, you crazy woman?" Despite his words and a furious expression, Goldie took a step backward as Lena continued to advance on him.

"How many years, Goldie?" Lena seethed. "How many years were we together?"

"Too many, you fat, crazy, old bitch."

"All those years, and I still don't get you," Lena continued, ignoring the insults. "I still can't work out if you really are that selfish and . . . and . . . heartless. Or if you're just, I don't know . . . made wrong."

Lena stopped advancing on Goldie, who had been backed right up against a bush. His expression was somewhere between shock and hatred.

"Your son has lost an arm today and will have to go back to prison for another decade or more like that. How will he manage is what I'm thinking about. Your pregnant daughter is in a town that is on fire, and we don't know whether she's alive or dead right now . . . and you. You're talking dirty to your latest case of chlamydia."

Goldie bristled at Lena's comment. "Carole and I have been together for—"

"That's not the point, Goldie," Lena said, shaking her head and sounding a little tired.

Goldie took a step forward, bringing himself up to his full height. He wasn't the tallest of men, yet, even in his late fifties, he could appear imposing when he wanted to.

"I think you're just jealous. It's pathetic how you're still not over me, Lena. I left you, and you can't take it." Goldie sneered, in control of the conversation again. "All you ended up with was that stupid farmer."

"He's been more of a father than you ever have," Lena said.

"Are you kidding me?" Goldie shot back. "I brought that boy up after we split, while all you had to deal with was Maya, who was already grown. You would have been a useless mother on your own."

But she hadn't been on her own, had she? There had been Maya, and surprisingly soon after Goldie had gone and left behind what, at the time, seemed like a shell of a woman, there had been Manuel. No, the soft-spoken farmer hadn't brought up either of her children, but what he had understood was that parenthood didn't end when a child turned sixteen or eighteen, or even twenty-one. Parenthood went on indefinitely and always began with the little things, the everyday things . . . being there at just the right time.

Sameer had never accepted Manuel, never treated him as much more than an intruder in his mother's life, yet Manuel had been there just a few years ago when Sameer had called the house drunk and without his wallet—and, let's face it, likely without any money in the missing wallet, anyway. Manuel had been the one to drive out to the middle of nowhere at three in the morning, finding him by the side of the road just off the 580. Shoeless.

And Manuel had provided a lift back home.

Sameer had called their house, not Goldie's, asking for Manuel when Lena answered the phone. Manuel, who would be there, no judgment, no questions asked. Like a father would.

Then there had been Maya's leaky pipe in her first little apartment, before the high-flying job and that absurdly extravagant place with the tiny kitchen that she lived in now. No money for a handyman to fix it, but that was okay, because Manuel would drop everything and run around with a wrench and some tape.

Lena looked at Goldie, who was still living off the paternal glory of one decision a teenage boy had made half a lifetime ago. A decision that may have ruined his life.

"He looked up to you, Goldie," Lena said, her words now having lost their heat. It was an accusation, but it came out almost like a sob. "He looked up to you, and he wanted to be like you. Why didn't you do better by him?"

Lena felt exhausted suddenly and looked around to see a small stone bench nearby. Goldie didn't say anything as she moved over to take a seat. Instead, he walked past her to retrieve his mobile phone.

"Screen's broken," he grumbled quietly as he returned to stand in front of her.

"I'll pay for a new one," she said tiredly.

"Don't want you to," Goldie replied, his tone that of a petulant child. The bluster seemed to have gone from his own indignation and anger, even as the wind continued to whip through the space around them. Perhaps her words had somehow hit home.

Probably not, though; the man was never going to change.

"You should go," Lena said. "He's out of danger now and I can stay. I'll call"—she noted the broken phone—"your office with any news about Sameer or Maya."

Goldie nodded and slowly began to step away. Lena remembered that from when they were married, the way he would always be eager to leave but didn't want it to seem so.

No, the man would never change.

She watched Goldie head back out into the corridor, caught the sullen look he threw at her as he passed by the windows. Her cell phone rang shrilly, bringing her out of her thoughts. Manuel's name was showing on the screen, and she fumbled to answer it quickly.

"Yes?" she snapped.

"It's Manuel," her husband shouted. Although Lena had heard the two words clearly enough, she could tell that it was noisy where he was, and wind crackled loudly like rustling paper into the microphone.

"What's happening? Where are you?"

"We're southwest of the town a few miles," Manuel answered. "It was as far as we could get. No traffic into the airport and . . ." He paused.

"What? Tell me, damn you. What's it like there?" Lena shouted, fear making her voice hollow.

"It's bad. Flames the size of skyscrapers, sprinting up the mountain-side," Manuel answered with a great release of breath that sounded back down the line to her. "I've never seen smoke like it, Lena. Visibility is so bad motorists have had to flip on their headlights. It was too much to stay in the air, and the pilot put us down in a parking lot. We're seeing if we can find a vehicle to go farther."

Lena trembled, panic threatening to overwhelm her again. "Oh, my baby . . . If she's in that."

"We'll find a way in, my love, I promise."

"Be careful!" Lena blurted out. She wanted him and Harry to go and find the children and bring them out, yet the thought of sending these two older men into the inferno he was describing wrenched at her heart.

"We'll find a way," Manuel said again. He meant it, she could tell, even if he didn't believe it.

Chapter 37

Every instinct within Veer was screaming at him to head back the other way. Every instinct except one. In a way that one instinct was the most primal of them all; more than the survival of the self, it was survival of his family. Of love. Of his unborn child. With a renewed sense of urgency, he pushed forward.

A road that had earlier in the morning been so familiar to Veer—a road he had driven or walked along countless times in the last half a year—had become unrecognizable in the smoke and artificial darkness, a thick fog that stung his eyes and scratched at his throat. Veer's chest burned as he ran, he was coughing and choking, yet still he stumbled along, feet working on instinct alone—that familiar rhythm of being placed down one after the other like a sure-footed horse. Sweat ran down his dirty, soot-stained face in jagged rivulets, and he could taste the ash when the sweat found his lips.

He didn't know where on the road he was, so he just kept moving, eyes peering through the stinging smoke to try and make out every car that passed him by—or, that he passed, as the traffic was now moving at a crawl.

Almost every driver gestured for him to turn around, and more than one stopped to offer him a space. He kept going, though, one foot in front of the other into the continuous blasting heat, into the smoke and the orange-glowing firework sparks that whipped past in the wind like swarms of angry fireflies. He was more scared than he could ever have imagined for the safety of his fiancée and unborn child, yet there was a simplicity to the moment that had stripped everything else away, lifting other weights from his shoulders as if every one of them had been only an illusion.

He was no longer Veer the trust-fund playboy with his father's credit card, nor the musician always a lucky break away from making a name for himself in his own right. He wasn't even the poor guitar teacher who needed something a bit steadier. He was merely a man with only one place to be . . . with his family.

Then, the thick black smoke clearing momentarily, Veer got a brief view of what lay ahead of him. About fifty yards away, a police officer stood in the middle of the road, attempting to control the traffic flow between the main road that he was on and a side road.

"Move! Move, now!" shouted the police officer over his loudspeaker.

Beyond the police officer, almost everything was aflame, or so it appeared, and Veer wondered how the cars coming down the main road had not already all burst into flames. As he watched, a tree somewhere just beyond the intersection fell, sending a great spout of flame skyward, as if the fire itself were celebrating.

The flame died down but was immediately followed by a whirling stream of sparks coming his way, and Veer doubled over, his hands splaying up protectively as they stung his skin. As he straightened, he had to beat away a particularly large one that had landed on his shirt and was burning a hole through it.

Up ahead, the smoke was beginning to obscure the police officer again. Not wanting to risk being turned back, Veer started to his right and ran into the trees.

∾

"Can't she just hold it in?" Derek asked from the front of the car.

Despite the situation, Sarah belted her husband's arm. "No, she cannot 'just hold it in,'" she chastised him. "It's not a goddamn turd!"

Doubled over in discomfort, Maya still couldn't help but raise an eyebrow in the back of the vehicle. She had never heard her usually God-fearing neighbor take the Lord's name in vain before. Nor, for that matter, had she heard her refer to human waste in any way, shape, or form—and certainly not as a *turd*.

"I do apologize for my language, honey," Sarah said, turning around to Maya and recovering her poise a little. "My scared ol' potty mouth isn't the first thing your little one is going to want to be hearing."

The whole thing was surreal, and the fire was getting closer by the minute. Maya briefly mused that she didn't want her final moments to be like something out of a fiasco of a sitcom, but then another contraction came, more painful and sudden than those before it, and she thought of nothing else.

She cried out in pain, and Sarah gave her a concerned look. The car began to move along the road again, at least three or four car lengths this time.

"Not far now, honey," Sarah said. "I can . . . just about see the junction now, I think."

Maya met the other woman's eyes before she turned back again, aware of the wild look in her own. "I've never had a baby before," she panted.

"I know, I know, honey," Sarah said, reaching over and patting her hand.

But the older woman had cut Maya off.

"I mean, I've never had a baby before . . . but it feels like it wants to come soon."

Another concerned look; Sarah had no poker face. "If you want, I could come in the back with you?" She turned to Derek. "Can we get the seats down?"

Derek shook his head. "Not with the bags back there, too."

Sarah turned back to Maya. "It'll be a bit cramped if I'm in the back with you, but if you want to lean against the door, we could give it a go."

That sounded like a horrible idea to Maya; perhaps she wasn't quite there yet. "No, we'll . . . um, not yet." Sweat ran down her face, blurring her vision and dripping its salty taste into her mouth. She didn't know how much the sweat was because of the discomfort of the contractions and how much of it was because of the flaming vortex swirling a hundred feet away, radiating heat through the window and the metal door.

The contraction ebbed. The pain receded.

They moved forward another car length, and even though it came at a right angle to them, the fire seemed to be matching the pace as Maya looked out the car window. Were they farther from the junction than the fire was from them?

Would they be okay? Maybe. Then she remembered the cars behind them—there were at least four or five that she could make out. Even if their car made it through before the fire reached the road, she could not believe that all would make it. What would they do? Would they jump out and try and outrun the fire? Maybe the three of them should have done that ten minutes ago. Then again, just one abandoned car could block the narrow lane for everyone.

"What do we do?" Maya grunted.

"Huh?" Sarah said.

"What do we do if the fire gets here before we get onto Pearson Road?"

Sarah looked at Derek; Derek didn't reply.

"Veer . . ." Maya began to blab. "We . . . why did we fight, Sarah?"

"Now, now . . ." Sarah began, but it was too late; the floodgates had opened.

"We're going to die here," Maya went on, an edge of hysteria creeping into her voice. "And I won't see my mom." She looked down at her belly. "She won't see her grandchild. And now Sameer's in prison.

I visited him only once. I . . ." Her eyes went wide, regret pulling deep grooves into her face. "And Manuel . . . The last time . . . I called him 'Mexican' in a way that was a slur. I never meant to hurt him, and oh my, the look on his face."

Maya went silent for a moment. Then, more quietly, she said, "Veer's dead already, I know it. He's dead, and we're going to die here and . . ."

"Hey!" Sarah said sharply. Then, more gently, but with just the same firmness. "He's coming. Your husband is coming."

~

It was treacherous going in the near darkness. Out in the woods, the trees were thick, and they were tall, obscuring the sky. Even worse, terror was dulling his vision in a way the darkness couldn't.

Focus on Maya. Focus on the baby. Eyes in front, Veer.

Veer tripped three times in the first ten yards or so, and quickly started to think that he had made a mistake, that staying on the road would have been quicker and that he could have outrun the cop if he needed to. He could feel and sense small animals passing him in the darkness—does and coyotes, skunks and squirrels, foxes and rabbits—late runners fleeing the oncoming death, like the other Paradise residents leaving their homes at the mercy of the fire.

Veer stopped short suddenly, squinting at a shape moving quickly through the trees not far from him. Was that . . . ? It was a mountain lion running for her life. Just as he was.

Another thirty yards farther on, and Veer began to get the sense that the fire had morphed into an angry beast, like something out of legend. Enormous, jagged, and merciless, this flaming, multiheaded monster was rapidly destroying whatever forest Paradise had left.

Still, fear pushed him forward. He was coughing and his chest burned. His breathing roared in his head, as if he were next to a gigantic tandoor, a blower stoking a hellish fire.

All around him, the rolling and crackling sounded like a million fireplace fires released from their controlled confines and free to rampage in the wild. Accompanying that sound was the terrific snap and crash of enormous pines, as the fire leaped uphill, roasting everything in its path. He watched in horror, through a gap in the trees, as a deer, hopping and darting frantically to put as much space between itself and the fire, was overtaken at a full run.

Just keep going, he willed himself. *You have to reach the road. Reach the road first, and . . .*

His brain was struggling to maintain coherence, even to finish his thoughts anymore. Adrenaline had given and given to him today, but it seemed that the reserves were finally running dry. His eyes closed for a moment, and it felt so good to do so. If for no other reason than to be rid of the blasted sting of the smoke in them for a few moments. Without even realizing he was doing it, Veer stopped and rested his head against a trunk, his knees starting to sag, pulling him inexorably toward the ground.

There was a scream inside his head: *But what about Maya? And your baby?*

Veer lurched up and stood there in the lavender light, backlit by the crackling bonfire of a tree forty feet to the east. It had the effect of jerking him back into a fuller sort of consciousness. He took a deep breath and began to jog even faster. He had to get out of here alive. He owed it to his unborn child.

~

"It's right there, Derek," Sarah screamed. "It's right by my door!"

Maya had never seen or smelled a fire so close before. The heat of it was now palpable in the car, there was no mistaking it. She could smell the smoke and taste its bitterness at the back of her throat, scratching at her esophagus.

"I can see it, Sarah!" Derek snapped, as if Sarah was somehow overreacting. There was an element of *What the hell do you want me to do about it?* In the way he spoke.

The fire was like liquid, dripping from trees and flowing along the ground, making it seem like a living thing, a monster coming for them, intent on devouring them, intent on ensuring that her child would never know life. She hated it almost as much as she feared it.

"We need to get out," Sarah said.

For a moment, Maya thought she was just stating the obvious, at least until Derek screamed at her. "You do that, and we die!"

Sarah's hand, she noticed, was on the handle, and Derek pressed a button that must have been the central locking. They were now the third car in the line, merging with the vehicles still moving west along Pearson Road in an almost civil manner, perhaps thanks to a police car whose lights flashed somewhere ahead and to the left on the main road.

"Look," he said, "you see those cars still coming from the east, from where the fire is? There's no bushes, no trees on the road, so the fire can't burn here. It may be hot as hell in this car, but it's a lot better than being out there right next to the fire."

Derek cleared his throat, and the edge in his voice dropped away just a little bit. "We stay in the car," he said, "and we'll be out of here soon."

I wish you sounded more like you believed that, Derek. Maya was hungry and weak. Her face and neck were soaked with sweat. She pressed her nails into her skin so hard she was afraid she would start bleeding.

"Oh my god," Sarah said, bringing one hand to her mouth and pointing with the other out onto Pearson Road. A car had stopped just to the right of the junction and had caught on fire. A family of four jumped out of it and ran toward the police car's blue flashing lights as the fire raged in the trees and bushes right beside them. Within moments the car was a ball of fire, every inch of it wreathed in flames.

Sarah turned to Derek as the cars close to the burning wreck tried to move around it, giving it the widest berth that was possible considering the flames that licked at them from the side of the road. "You were saying?"

Derek looked like he was seething, but he didn't reply. There was something reassuring for Maya in that, as she tried to find a comfortable position in the back of the couple's car. Their town was on fire, but how could it be that bad if there was still time for some point-scoring and bickering? As she moved her back against the door that faced the approaching fire, she could feel an intense heat through it.

"Veer," she said, his name becoming a mantra that she yelled as the pain intensified.

And, as if by magic, he appeared. He was outside, beyond the opposite window where wind, soot, and burning sparks whisked past like a tornado.

The shock made Maya cry out. "Veer!"

"I know, honey," Sarah said soothingly. "He'll be here."

"He is here," Maya said, watching her fiancé appear stumbling from among the trees to the car's left. With a great effort, she pulled herself up, thumping the window in case he missed them, but suddenly Veer disappeared. In fact, everything disappeared, as there was a blinding flash.

Chapter 38

Veer instinctively dropped to his knees as he felt a blast of hot air—hotter even than the air blowing almost constantly from the east. Looking over to the main road, his eyesight spotty from the bright flash that had accompanied the blast, he saw a car aflame, the remnants of a fireball folding and rolling skyward to join the black and orange of this particular Thursday in Paradise, California. Presumably, the vehicle's fuel tank had blown, and what was left of the car was engulfed in flames. Veer hoped that no one had been in it.

Not far from the flaming car, a police officer had been knocked to the ground, but was shuffling to his feet again, and moved to keep directing traffic away from the fire racing toward them.

Veer turned back to the blue SUV that he had spotted as he came out of the trees. He had almost missed it until he heard someone thumping against the rear passenger window and turned to see Maya's beautiful, sweaty face pressed against it.

For just the briefest moment, all of his fears had left him. Now, he ran up to the window and pressed his face against it. "I'm sorry," he mouthed, scrabbling for the handle. He pulled it, but the door didn't open. "I've been so stupid; I love you," he continued to yell as he tugged frantically at the handle again and again. Maya mouthed the words back.

"Open the goddamn door, Derek!" Veer heard Sarah scream, even through the closed windows, and there was a click as the door opened.

"Your child's coming" were Maya's first words to him as she scrambled backward to make space for him, her back against the opposite door, her feet against his leg.

"My . . . what?"

"I didn't think we had enough problems," Maya quipped with a brittle laugh, although he could see the fear etched into her expression. Her mouth twisted like she was fighting to remain brave, to stop from shouting and screaming uncontrollably. Finally she mumbled, her eyes glistening with tears, "I thought I'd never see you."

Veer felt his love for her pouring out, and across the back seat of the car, waves of feeling that he wished could wrap around her like a fireproof blanket so that, whatever happened in the next few minutes, she and their child could at least be safe.

They pulled out onto the main road, and he could see that the whole landscape outside the little SUV blazed orange. Veer's face heated up when he turned to look at it. But, at least now they were moving again. The fire had overtaken them to the north, he could tell. They had not outrun this monster yet.

Below him, Maya lay as prone as it was possible to be in the cramped back seat, and Veer found himself glad she couldn't see what he was seeing. His fiancée was having their child, and this wasn't how it was supposed to be. He took in the fear mixed with the sweat and rigid pain on Maya's delicate features, her lip quivering slightly, watery eyes just a little too wide.

They continued along Pearson for some time. The traffic was moving slowly, although at least it was moving. Every time they passed a junction, things slowed as cars merged from the side roads—more aggressively where there weren't police officers guiding them in, causing temporary jams and lots of horn thumping, as people drove for their lives. And, all the while, everything was fire and smoke and darkness overhead.

Maya let out a pained gasp, and Veer found her hand. She squeezed back, and her fingers locked into the grooves between his knuckles.

"How's it going back there?" Sarah called from the front passenger seat. Veer looked down at Maya—her eyes now closed against the pain, front teeth biting into her bottom lip—and felt helpless. "Do you want me to come back there?"

"No!" Maya screamed, her eyes flicking open again. When she next spoke, she did so through the pain of another contraction. "That's . . . okay . . . Sarah." She half grimaced a smile up at Veer through the contraction. "My fiancé's got this."

Veer smiled at her gratefully. *Thank you,* he mouthed.

I trust you, she mouthed back.

The SUV was now climbing the hill that would then lead into Pearson Road's commercial stretch, which ran straight and more or less flat for over half a mile. They passed another burning car—the third—with no sign of any occupants.

As they hit the crest of the hill, Veer glanced past Derek and Sarah and through the windshield, seeing for the first time in quite a while an area that wasn't all on fire. It was even a little light up ahead of them, although this only meant that an eerie twilight hung over the elementary school, the liquor store, the RV yard, and the area's other businesses, as opposed to the total darkness they had just emerged from.

"The road is getting wider ahead," Derek said, "and things are moving faster. I think we might be past the worst of it."

That was when one of the poles that held up the overhead lines—the only thing close to the road that was on fire along this little stretch—collapsed into the road less than a hundred yards in front of them.

In the front of the car, Sarah turned to Derek. "You had to say it, didn't you?"

~

"No, no, no!" Veer cried out, slamming a fist onto the headrest of one of the rear seats. Everything was grinding to a halt.

"What?" Maya shouted from where she lay on the SUV's rear seat. "What's going on?" It was horrible lying where she couldn't see what was happening.

"There's a little blockage up ahead," Sarah said in a placating tone that made Maya feel about three years old. "I'm sure it will all get sorted in a minute."

Veer went very still. "Electrical poles," he told her.

"Is it a problem?" she asked. Her voice was hoarse, even between the contractions. "A big one?"

Veer looked beyond the windshield at the parking lots of the roadside businesses—a boarded-up liquor store, a mom-and-pop hardware store, Koontz coffee shop—trying to figure out if there was a good way to drive around it. Probably not.

"I think so," he replied slowly. "There's no police or fire crews to help." He peered hard out past the windshield. "Some people are getting out of their cars, looking at it. One of the poles has come straight down on the front of a truck."

"Then you need to go and help them."

Veer's eyes shot back down to the woman he loved, sweating and moaning with pain, and feared for their unborn child's life. "No," he said immediately. Then: "I ran across the whole town to be here with you. I'm not—"

"Can you be more useful here than out there?" Maya asked, her breath coming in short gasps.

Veer looked back at her for another moment, and she could see him wanting to disagree with her logic—with any logic—that would keep him from her while their world burned. But he couldn't.

"Go and fix things," Maya shouted at him, breathing through flared nostrils. "Fix things, and come back to us."

Sarah got out of the front passenger door to take Veer's place as he exited, then clasped one of his hands between hers. "We've got this," Maya heard her say, and then the older woman appeared, her face worried. Sarah's presence in the back of the SUV was comforting, although it made Maya want her mom all the more.

~

Veer felt strange to be out of the car again. The gale-force winds blew unleashed across the open space, carrying an almost overwhelming scent of woodsmoke that reminded Veer of campfires and marshmallows and anything but this day of wild flames and horror.

More people were getting out of their cars as he ran down to where the fallen pole blocked the road, although only one other person followed to help. The others seemed mostly paralyzed by shock and indecision, and a couple of people started to run away from the road as if figuring they could survive the fire on foot. He didn't like their chances.

Veer looked back just before he reached the blockage and saw that the whole tree line was on fire less than two hundred yards behind him, sending down flaming embers like the molten rain from an erupting volcano. If the fiery downpour continued, surely the whole area would become a death trap before long.

As he turned back again, Veer noticed that the liquor store—separated from the pole and damaged truck by a small parking lot—was already pouring smoke from its far side. There was a loud pop somewhere nearby, and he jumped, glancing briefly back to see a jet of flame had erupted into the air no more than fifty yards away.

"We're all going to die!" a man cried out next to him, his eyes bulging with panic. It was the other person who had followed him down from the line of cars—a bespectacled, balding forty-something with pointed ears shaped like a fox's, who visibly trembled as he looked at the broad pole that had embedded itself in the hood of the bright-red truck. "The fire's coming for us."

Two men were already working on trying to move the pole, but they could barely even shift the thing an inch, as after every push, it rolled straight back into the deep groove that it had made for itself in the hood of the vehicle. The two of them stepped away from the pole, panting and sweating; the man closest to Veer was shaking from the effort. He was a mountain of a man, fit and muscled and in his twenties, with a thick beard and a lumberjack shirt.

Veer didn't know what he and Terrified Glasses Guy could add that Mountain Man wasn't bringing already. But then, just as he finished that thought, Veer had another one.

He tapped Mountain Man on the shoulder and spoke as he turned. "Hi, I'm Veer," he said, "and I have an idea."

∼

It turned out that no one trying to move the pole was the owner of the stricken red truck. The owner must have fled on foot, although at least they had been considerate enough to leave the keys in the ignition. Sitting in the driver's side with little more than a thick wooden pole visible through the windshield, Veer tried to start the truck. Not surprisingly, considering the pole in the hood, the thing didn't even turn over.

"It won't start," he called out as loudly as he could. "Let's go with plan B."

The sudden gunning of an engine behind Veer made him turn around to witness an ancient-looking and low-slung gray Chevy station wagon pull out from the line behind them, and head straight for the curb. "Fuck!" he shouted in the pickup truck's cab, gripping the steering wheel tight in frustration.

Veer could see what the driver of the station wagon was trying to do. They were attempting to see if it was possible to drive around the blockage through parking lots and commercial premises, but the maneuver began with an unorthodox entry into the liquor store's parking lot. If they didn't make it, they were about to screw his plan forever for moving that pole.

Even in the minute or two since he had come to help, the fire had started to find its way around to the sides of the commercial area and, with an ever-greater rain of fiery detritus falling from the sky, more things were beginning to catch on fire. If the people in that station wagon trapped them all because of their selfishness . . .

The curb was kinder to the old gray Chevy than Veer had expected, and the station wagon bounced up over it and entered the liquor-store parking lot.

"Yes!" he celebrated, turning back to look through the windshield at the four figures waiting, ready to push and put his plan into action. But then everything went white.

∼

Maya was just peeking up and past Derek's shoulder when the liquor store exploded about a hundred yards away. The ball of flame whooshed out from the store, and the sound of it hitting them a fraction of a second later was felt through the SUV floor as much as actually heard.

Glass flew in a discernible spray across the street, the wash of the explosion engulfing the station wagon and reaching out onto the street as if to grab at the red pickup.

"Where's Veer?" Maya cried from the back seat.

"He just went into the pickup," Derek answered shakily. "He'll be all right."

~

Tinnitus sliced painfully through the center of Veer's skull, and for several seconds, he had no idea what had happened. By instinct, he reached for the handle of the driver's door and fell from the truck, landing on the asphalt and finding himself almost face to face with a live, sparking wire.

He could see the thing dancing angrily at him—shifting about because of the wind, or perhaps some other force—but he couldn't hear anything aside from the slowly dying note in his ears.

Veer got to his knees, then pulled himself up the truck's side, which now had very little glass in its windows. He could feel that his face was cut, but the thought of it was distant and inconsequential. Mountain Man was on his feet nearby, pulling off his now-smoldering lumberjack shirt. Finally, Veer looked toward the ruined liquor store—the explosion's source—and the station wagon, which had become a blasted wreck. Only the driver was stumbling out of it, and no one else inside the vehicle was moving.

He should help them, that was what his instincts told him to do. But there was no time, Veer realized, with a sickening feeling in his stomach. Helping them delayed moving the truck, which put more people in danger in that line of vehicles that extended past the top of the hill behind him and out of sight.

"Are we ready?" he called out as he climbed back into the cab. The other helpers—Mountain Man, Terrified Glasses, and two others were back on their feet now, tearing their eyes from the nearby burning wreck.

Once settled in the cab again, Veer turned around in the seat as he attempted to visualize the path he was going to steer to move the pole far enough out of the way. But then he stopped.

"Hello there," Veer said to the two husky puppies huddled together in an open duffel bag in the rear of the cab. Who the hell would leave these teeny puppies in the path of the fire?

"Tell us when!" Mountain Man shouted impatiently from in front of the truck. The shout prompted Veer back into action.

He turned back and tried to take a steadying breath. It didn't work very well, and he looked at his hands, which were trembling slightly as they gripped the steering wheel. They would have only one shot at this. If the truck didn't roll far enough or if he didn't steer it the right way . . .

Just do it, he thought to himself.

Veer reached out and pulled the hand brake. "Go!" he shouted.

The road's camber took over, and the truck wheeled even faster; with relief and hope flooding his chest, Veer could see that the pole was pivoting as he had hoped it would. "Hard now!" he screamed. "And keep on the pole!" Which was the last thing he had the chance to say before the right-rear tire of the truck thumped into the curb with a stomach-wrenching jolt, twisting his world at an angle until the left-rear tire did the same thing.

At the last moment, the pole twisted sharply, no longer going along with the plan. It rose out of the deep groove it had made in the hood of the car and—almost a miracle—came to a rest near the front edge, mere centimeters from toppling off and causing serious injury to those who had been pushing it.

In the driver's seat, Veer found himself panting, and he wiped a bead of sweat away as it trickled onto his nose, smearing a semiclean line across the back of his ash-stained hand.

With a farewell wave to his four helpers as they hurried on their way, Veer slid clumsily back out of the cab. He felt drained, the moment's adrenaline seeping away from him.

But they weren't out yet. Already the queue of cars was moving, and he had a fiancée who was trying to give birth to their child in the back of an SUV nearby. Yet, as Veer took his first step back up the road, something stopped him.

~

Maya watched Veer get back into the front of the McKessons' SUV as swiftly as he could while carrying a large duffel bag.

Sarah was crouched over Maya, who could feel the baby's head beginning to crown. As part of the exhalation and cry as she pushed, Maya called out, "What's . . . in the . . . *ba-a-a-ag?*"

"Um . . ." Veer paused for several seconds, then added, "Puppies." The man had never sounded more guilty.

"Puppies?" the two women exclaimed together from the back of the vehicle, although Maya's quavering question turned into a wail as she pushed hard once again.

"They were in the back of that truck," Veer said, indicating the red vehicle as they approached and passed it. "What was I going to do, leave them to die?"

Maya shrieked out a chuckle—a panting, wheezing sound that was so unlike her usual laugh. "That's my Veer," she said a little deliriously. "Always has to do the right thing."

Veer smiled and pushed a hand between the front seats, finding one of hers. Sarah looked at the hand as if about to complain that such an unsanitary thing was going anywhere near the birth, but she kept her disapproval to herself. "I do," Veer agreed, "eventually."

Soon, they were heading southwest away from the town on Skyway Road, and that was where their son was born, with almost the whole of the sky behind him still obscured by the dark mass of the smoke that rose higher and more imposing than the greatest and meanest of thunderheads.

Maya had sat up a little and held her child, fighting against the urge to sleep when they came through a roadblock that was stopping traffic toward the town. Derek pulled over into a field that had been made into a temporary lot for those fleeing the town, and there, right by the entrance to the field, Maya saw two older men she recognized.

Chapter 39

Lena sat on one side of Anita, Pinky on the other, the three women on a long bench-back sofa that was about as inviting as cement, all in the waiting room at Zuckerberg San Francisco General Hospital. It had been two days since Lena's two friends had stayed with her, supporting her as she waited for news of her son in the hospital, and of her daughter in the burning town of Paradise. Today, Lena was there to support Anita, although it was a tough day for all three women.

Tear tracks ran down each of their faces as a doctor emerged from a nearby room. In her thirties, she was a geriatric-care specialist and had dark shadows under her eyes. She snapped off a pair of green plastic gloves while she talked to them.

"Now will be the time to say your goodbyes," the doctor said softly. She tilted her head and gave them a weary smile, then turned to move up the corridor. As Lena watched her go, it looked as if the doctor's mind was already on the next patient.

The three women stood up. Lena blew her nose noisily into a crumpled tissue and put a hand on Anita's thin shoulder, squeezing it gently. For just a moment, Anita closed her eyes and laid her head against Lena's.

Swallowing rapidly, Anita glanced toward her two friends, one on either side, and asked, "Should we do this together?"

"Are you sure you don't want some time with her alone?" Pinky asked, dabbing at her wet eyes with a white-linen, monogrammed handkerchief.

The flesh on Anita's face sagged. Her left eye twitched maddeningly as she shook her head.

Lena gave a slow, approving nod. "I think she would like to see the three of us together."

They joined hands, but as they took their first step, Anita faltered. "I'm not ready," she said in a small voice and rubbed a hand over her forehead.

"It'll be okay, Anita," Pinky said soothingly. "We're here with you."

"She was so good for so long," Lena pointed out, trying to raise her friend's spirits. "That was a blessing, at least."

"Hmm," Anita replied, aggressively wiping away a tear from her twitching eye. "She was always at her best around you lot, somehow. It was the usual everyday things, the routine that got so difficult for her to remember. All the same, she went downhill so fast these last few weeks." She took a steadying breath. "Okay, let's not keep her waiting."

Lena took Anita by the arm and led the way, opening the door to reveal a small ward room with just a single bed in it. Before they entered the room, Lena could smell the sickly scent of medicine and death. Oh, how she hated hospitals.

The woman lying in bed with a mountain of pillows behind her back turned a face of blank incomprehension toward them.

Lena's chest tightened, and a heaviness descended over her. Kookie's bright eyes were sunken and dimmed; her fine black hair had become wispy and completely white. Bits of pink scalp showed through. How could her appearance have changed so quickly, like a body letting go of life?

Anita approached the bed with a smile that looked as if it had been pinned onto her face.

"Who are you?" Kookie snorted, frowning heavily at Anita.

"Mom, I'm your daughter, Anita."

Anita ducked her head. As she rubbed away the tears that had gathered at the corners of her eyes, Lena and Pinky closed in on her. Lena moved her big strong fingers over the curve of her friend's back in gentle, even strokes. Pinky draped a palm over Anita's shoulder.

"It's too sudden." Anita sniffed, sitting on the side of Kookie's bed and cradling one of her hands. "I'm not ready for you to go."

"Go?" Kookie asked, her words a whisper of air. "Where am I going?"

Behind Anita, Pinky laughed, but the sound quickly became a sob. There was something oddly right about that, Lena thought. Happiness and sadness, laughter, and anger; Kookie had often invoked such feelings within her daughter only moments apart from each other, Anita frequently said. And, after all, that was life . . . wasn't it?

∼

The three women stood outside the door again about five minutes later. Anita hugged Lena and Pinky in turn before heading back into her mother's room.

"I'll be along again soon," Anita promised. "You just try to keep me away." She smiled weakly.

Lena gave Anita a quick, tight hug. "There will be plenty of time," she replied, her face bright with reassurance. "Your place is here with your mother."

Lena and Pinky made their way only a few yards up the corridor, took a left turn, and went straight into the first room they came to. Maya was lying on the hospital bed with Veer on the chair beside her cradling their baby, still unable to stop looking at his tiny face. Manuel and Harry sat on the far side of the room and looked up from a conversation as their wives entered.

Lena noticed how much better Maya was looking for the days of rest since the fire (or as much rest as one could get in a hospital with a newborn baby). Her hair was blow-dried in her signature waves, and she had put some gloss on her lips.

"Come on," Lena said loudly, "let's have another cuddle with my grandchild." She turned to Pinky and gave an excited shrug. "I can't get enough of saying the words *my grandchild*."

"My grandchild," Pinky corrected her with a grin.

Veer raised an eyebrow in the direction of his fiancée as he put the baby in Maya's arms. "This should be fun for the next few years."

"The next few decades, I expect," Maya retorted. "Anyway," she continued, "Veer Jr. is sleeping, so no one will be cuddling their grandchild right now."

Pinky turned to Lena. "Oh dear, she's so bossy already, isn't she?"

"And she has a right to be," Harry put in from across the room. "I've never seen anything like the sight of that town burning, and we only saw it from several miles away." Manuel nodded his agreement next to Harry. "I can't imagine what it must have been like for these children," Harry continued, "just to get out of there, let alone giving birth while you are at it."

"Yes, yes, they are both amazing," Lena agreed, "but there is no chance that my grandchild is going to be called Veer Jr." She looked around at the Kapoors in the room. "No offense . . ."

"And only a small one taken," Veer answered.

"It's a . . . placeholder," Maya said. "Coming up with baby names is hard."

"Manuel's a good, strong name," Manuel offered with a mischievous smile, and next to him, Harry gave a small grin of amusement.

Lena noted how much more at ease the two men were in each other's company after their helicopter trip together. When she had mentioned it to Pinky, her friend had agreed with her. Manuel shrugged at a withering look from Lena. "Just saying."

Maya looked at her baby, who had tapped his tiny hand against her breast, as though claiming her. Lena knew Maya's look, that natural concern for something so tiny and wrinkled and vulnerable. So innocent. Yet born in fire.

"Do you think they will let me see Sameer yet?" Maya asked, still looking at the infant in her arms, as if she were asking her son for permission.

"It depends on how long they keep him here." It was Manuel who answered her. "I expect they will move him to a secure hospital, once the doctors let them."

"I think you should wait," Lena said, and Maya looked up. When their eyes met, Lena gave her a hard, bright smile. She knew her daughter understood there was more to explain, things that could not be said right there and then.

"Until he's stronger, eh?" Maya said, and Lena nodded back gratefully.

"I wasn't even sure that you should know about what happened to your brother," Pinky said. "With all you have been through, it seemed . . . too much. But then, keeping secrets bottled up, that always seems to do more harm than good."

Pinky could not know how right she was, Lena thought. Although not a uniquely Indian curse, she felt it was one they dealt with as a people perhaps more than others.

Maya didn't respond, instead clenching and unclenching one corner of the baby blanket she was supposed to be pulling over the baby's feet. "What news from the other room?" she asked, and the air in the room seemed at once to grow both thicker and cooler.

Pinky shook her head. "Anita is with Kookie now, and she's . . . more or less herself, I think. But the doctors have not given her long, and they have said she will worsen again soon."

"Perhaps there is some mercy to it," Harry said, stroking his chin reflectively. "My mother went in the same way, though much more drawn out. Better that there is more of the person still there, if you ask me."

"Easy in hindsight," Pinky said, raising her hands in a sort of hopeless gesture. "But I'm not sure anyone could tell Anita that right now."

Lena moved over, next to Maya, and looked around the room at the others gathered with them. "Can I just have a few moments alone with my daughter?" she asked them. "Would that be okay?"

They all obliged, Pinky suggesting a round of hot drinks in the cafeteria, although there were some questioning looks as they filed out of the room. She turned back to Maya, who was frowning and looked worried. "What's the matter?" Maya asked.

Lena settled into the seat that Veer had vacated. "I . . . um . . . I don't want to say too much now," she began. "I'm sure it will all come out in time, but I found out that Sameer had a hard time of things when he lived with your father. Harder than we knew." Lena held out a placating hand, seeing a thought flash across her daughter's features and fury rise in her cheeks. "Not so much anything Goldie did to him, but . . ." She trailed away, not knowing how to go on. "But it got me to thinking that, as much as I couldn't be there for Sameer, perhaps I overcompensated with you, and you weren't even a child anymore. I put two lots of a mother's stress and expectation on you. I was harder on you because I never had a chance to be hard on him."

Maya's lip quivered, her eyes going glassy as she looked down at the child in her arms again.

"Be nicer to this one than I was to you, eh?" Lena added, but Maya shook her head.

"I get it all now," Maya sobbed. "It's like they come out, and a whole side of you comes into being at the same time. One that says, 'Life will be better for you than it was for me. You will not make the same mistakes.'"

Lena gave a deep laugh, twice as deep because of the relief it carried within it. "Yes," she managed. "It goes something like that."

Maya's index finger stroked the fine downy hair that covered the baby's head. "We're all doing the best we can," she murmured.

Epilogue

Ten Years Later . . .

"Why must you be gardening on such an important morning?" Lena hissed at Manuel as he struggled to keep up with her. They had parked the old Chevy that Manuel would endlessly fix and respray rather than replace out on the street close to Anita's house. Lena had leaped out of the passenger seat the very moment that they had come to a stop, clawing irritably at the seat belt like the next victim in a horror movie mauling unexpected cobwebs. "Look how late we are—there is no room on Anita's driveway."

Early fall leaves danced in a cool breeze across Anita's brick-paved driveway, which turned in a full circle before the garage and was obscenely large for the medium-size suburban home that it served. Two rows of cars had taken up all the available space, however.

Manuel looked suitably chastened as he followed his wife to where the steps began up toward Anita's house. The front garden was a wide, sloping lawn that stopped abruptly at the foot of a natural rockery, the home of blue-headed lizards. Beds of abundant pansies and sunflowers, the dearly departed Kookie's pleasures, were laced about the house.

Manuel's hair was no longer the salt-and-pepper it had once been, now instead a uniform silver, as was the stubbly beard he always sported, the one that seemed to sprout again around fifteen minutes after shaving, like the hairs had merely ducked back into their holes to avoid the razor. He stooped just a little as he walked—perhaps the result of too many years spent bending over the vegetable patch—yet there was still a spring in his step.

Lena, for her part, looked the same as she ever did. She noted a Second-Chance Curry van in the driveway's front row of vehicles as they continued on up the steps. "At least they were here on time," she said with a nod. "I should have—"

"No, you shouldn't," Manuel interrupted firmly, but not unkindly. "This is the perfect test for them, to let them spread their wings without you—"

Lena gave her husband a sharp look as they turned at the top of the steps and approached the front door. Probably wisely, he didn't finish the thought, although his firm jaw set slightly, and he did carry on speaking.

"A shot across the bows, that's what the doctor said," Manuel told her, adding a wry smile. "You're not the spring chicken you were when we met, even if you are just as beautiful. You need to take it easy."

"Meh, meh, meh," Lena said, doing a rather childish impression of her doctor, even as she grinned back. "That's all I heard him say. I'm as strong as an ox."

Manuel's eyes narrowed, but he didn't say anything more. Marriage was a decades-long war full of tactical retreats and only the very occasional carefully picked battle.

Lena knocked on the oakwood front door and a flushed-looking Anita answered with the sound of bells drifting out from somewhere inside. "Oh no, we've missed the start," Lena said, looking crestfallen. "I'm so, so sorry Anita."

She threw a brief glare at her husband and looked back again, adding through gritted teeth, "Manuel's turnips," as if it constituted some sort of an explanation.

Anita broke into a broad grin. "No, no, it's Sur. He got hold of the puja bell, and now the dogs are chasing him around my living room."

"Ha!" Lena barked out one of her monstrous laughs, her demeanor relaxing instantly. "The joys of being the hostess." Just as she crossed the threshold, there was a distant but loud enough crash that Anita winced, smiling weakly back at Lena, a thumb and forefinger coming up briefly to rub unconsciously against the little diamond stud in her nose, as if the ornament were a small and expensive stress ball.

"Sur, get those dogs outside!" came a familiar shout—Maya. "It's your fault for encouraging him!" The last part could equally have been for Veer or Harry. Or both.

"And my people have not been in your way?" Lena called back over her shoulder.

"They have been very professional," Anita answered quickly. "I'm just hoping that wasn't the sound of all that lovely food landing on my Oushak carpet."

Those gathered in Anita's south-facing lounge all stopped what they were doing and glanced up as Lena entered, looking not unlike the assembled suspects in a murder-mystery movie, especially as one or two of them wore guilty faces as they caught sight of Anita. At the back was Pinky, straight backed and playing the part of the dowager heiress in a simple beige-and-white silk *salwar-kameez* with exquisite embroidery. With a red pashmina shawl that matched the soles of her $1,000 pumps draped over one shoulder, she glowed like a pearl. She appeared to be trying to distance herself from the chaos in the center of the room.

Harry Kapoor stood in a dark-green *jodhpuri* suit with elegant golden stitching along the front, looking down on a felled table and its contents as if playing the role of cleanup supervisor, while below him Veer and Maya knelt down by the silver cake stand and breakfast cookies that had been the victims, a guilty look on Maya's face, a mildly amused one on Veer's. To their right, Anita's husband, Chintu, held out a hand as if trying to tell them to leave things for him to take care of.

In the background, Lena's ten-year-old grandson, Sur, was now being chased around the garden by two huskies as he continued gleefully jingling the brass bell clutched in his hand, apparently unconcerned by the pandemonium he had caused. Lena's lips upturned at the sight of him.

"I'm so sorry, Anita," Maya said, finally finding her voice. She wore a red-and-gold *salwar-kameez* and, with the passing years, was beginning to fill out just a little, her mother's genes finally beginning to win the battle because she nowadays managed to use her beloved exercise bike only occasionally. "Him and those dogs." She looked over at Veer, her ever-youthful husband, as if he were to blame for the three of them. In many ways, he was.

He might now head a record company and have an extremely important and responsible job, but Veer was still doing what he loved, and that kept him young and just a little bit foolish. *Long may it continue,* Lena thought generously. Not so much a kid in a candy store as a kid running his own candy store. "Sur's a bad influence on Paradise and Pearson, what can I say?" Veer answered, amusement playing at the edge of his voice.

"*Tsh,*" Anita replied, evidently relieved that the Oushak carpet was going to survive. "I think there's a few cholesterol counts among the older ones in this room that won't miss the cookies." Her face fell, like she thought she had said the wrong thing.

"Absolutely," Lena said quickly, lightly slapping Anita's back. "And Tara will be serving us *gulab jamun* trifle later, so we have to save our sweet tooth for that."

"Well, from now on, let's make sure Paradise and Pearson stay out in the garden," Pinky asserted firmly from her position safely on the other side of the room. She clucked sympathetically at Anita. "Your lovely carpet won't survive that so well, I think."

"And maybe Sur can stay out there, too," Maya muttered.

Lena frowned at her daughter. "Don't be mean to my grandson." She looked out for a moment at the dark-haired boy, trying not to dwell on the fact that he was leading the two husky dogs through one of the well-manicured flower beds in Anita's garden. He wore thick glasses with perfectly round lenses that made his brown eyes appear unnaturally large, and had just gotten to that age where all his limbs suddenly became gangly and awkward. Yet he would one day become a stunningly beautiful young man—everyone thought so. He had the parents for it.

Then she turned to her right, to the opposite side of the lounge from where Pinky was. There, a door led out toward the kitchen and, in the corner of the room, a table that had thankfully survived the dogs was laid with ceremonial items. Lena could see ahead to the altar nook that housed statues of Hindu gods and goddesses. Smoke from a dozen lit incense sticks curled and rose to the ceiling. It was the corner where Kookie Aunty had always sat when she visited. On the wall just beyond the table, a garland of marigold flowers adorned a portrait-size framed photograph of her, the honored guest at her own ten-year puja.

"We will light the ghee lamp and begin the puja in a moment, shall we?" Anita said.

Lena pointed toward the kitchen. "Do you mind if I just . . . ?"

Anita gave her a knowing smile. "No. Carry on. There's no hurry."

Lena moved swiftly, before Manuel could tell her to mind her own business, and went out to Anita's good-size kitchen, where three people were hard at work preparing and reheating far more food than those present could possibly consume. One—Anita's daughter, Selena—was dressed in a white-and-cornflower-blue sari that plainly fitted the occasion, while the other two were in chefs' clothing. All of them had their backs to Lena, and she came up behind the senior chef, who was stirring a large vat on the stove with his only arm; his other side had the sleeve tied off.

Lena was rarely so stealthy, but the three were absorbed in what they were doing. "I hope you are not making a mess of things," she barked loudly, making all three of them jump.

"Mom!" Sameer chided as he turned around laughing. "Get out and leave us to it! You are one of the guests today."

"A cook is never not a cook," Lena retorted loftily, like she was reading the words from a tiny piece of paper that had come out of a fortune cookie, rather than making them up on the spot.

Sameer looked over to the other figure in chef's clothing, who dwarfed Lena's son. His bulk seemed to fill half the kitchen, and beneath the chef's hat, sweat glistened at the base of a hairless skull. "Hear that, Gus? We're being judged."

Gus was the about the same age as Sameer, although he never admitted his real age to anybody. He was Sameer's latest apprentice, and Lena's son had passed on only positive comments to his mother about the ex-convict, who, with the promise of a job waiting for him on the outside, had secured parole on his first attempt only about two months before. "No pressure, then," Gus replied, although he didn't look up from what he was doing.

In some ways, Lena reflected as she picked up a cubed *gulab jamun* soaked in *elaichi* espresso from the tray, this was not just a puja for Kookie, but for so much that had happened in that year before she had died. Mistakes and loss, relationships torn apart and put back together more solidly for it. And even a gift or two. *If we do not pause to remember and reflect on the events of our lives, they become lost in the mists that time places in between.*

"When you cook, you are being judged on every bite," Lena said, popping the dessert into her mouth. "You outdid yourself, Gus," she said as a pinch of sweet and spice hit her tongue.

Lena turned to leave them to it but stopped and spoke to her son again. "You're going into the prison for another session on Monday, is that right?"

"Uh-huh," Sameer replied absently, his attention already back on the pot in front of him.

"It's so good that now we can get them into cooking even before they are out of prison," Lena said proudly.

"Gus, you okay to watch it just for a moment?" Sameer said as he fiddled around in his breast pocket with the fingers of his only hand, a slightly guilty look on his face. "We've got a few minutes; I might just pop out . . ."

Lena frowned at her son as a packet of cigarettes came out of the breast pocket. It was her job to, even if he was nearly forty now. "Those things nearly finished off your father, you know," she said sternly.

Sameer smiled ruefully. "Many things nearly finished off Dad, but somehow he's still with us."

"What is it they say?" Lena said, her voice stiff like cardboard. "Only the good ones die young."

Sameer's brow creased. Although Lena had given up trying to be in the same room as Goldie for even a moment longer than necessary many years ago, her children maintained a relationship with their father, especially following his heart attack. He lived on his own now, age and ill-health finally having rid him of all but a little of that Sharma charm.

Sameer held up the cigarettes as he backed out of the opposite door. "Well, these are my one vice. I'm allowed one, at least."

Lena turned and headed back into the living room, where Sur was being smartened up—leaves removed, glasses cleaned, hair combed—as he complained and cringed away like the comb was red hot while two large huskies looked at them with giant eyes, noses pressed to the glass from beyond the great big sliding doors. Barefoot, and with a white stole covering her head, Anita came forward to light the ceremonial lamp. Lena took her place next to Manuel and looked up at the picture that hung on the wall, seeming to gaze down upon them as they all gathered there.

Lena fancied she saw Kookie wink at her with a small wave. Yes, she would have approved of them—a motley, mixed, and sometimes mixed-up crew though they might be. That was all you really wanted as you got older. All that really mattered was just to see everyone together and happy.

Acknowledgments

It takes village upon village to birth a book.

My thanks go first and foremost to my agent, Jessica Faust, who took a chance on me when I doubted my own talent (still do); who continues to guide, shepherd, and brainstorm with me; and who knows much better than I what works and what doesn't. I am in awe of your experience and your critical eye, and I will be in your debt for as long as I have books in me.

Thank you to my editor Chris Werner for your encouragement, for fighting so hard for this story, and for your vision for my novel. Chris, your guidance feels like a gift I have been given, and I'm immensely grateful for that. Also at Lake Union: my editor Jenna Free, for pushing me to dig deeper and for being a patient in-house critic. Jenna, I hope you know that you added considerable value to this novel.

The tireless team at Lake Union—Jen Bentham, Hannah Buehler, Kellie Osborne, and Jill Schoenhaut—for never missing a beat in these uncertain times; for painstakingly going over the mistakes, errors, and inconsistencies in the manuscript; and for suggesting changes as needed. You made the book sparkle.

To my friends and the earliest readers of my work, Teresa Burns Gunther, Nikhil Shah, and countless others—too many to name, but to whom I owe a thousand thanks for sustaining me in countless and profound ways over the years, reading my blog posts and providing me feedback, showing up at my book readings, and cheering me on.

To my mom, Inderjit Kaur Ahuja, for the gift of life, and of storytelling. You are the angel on my shoulder.

To my dad, Joginder Singh Ahuja: you are my rock and spiritual hero.

To my niece, Harnoor Walia, for making sure everyone falls in love with my stories, and for being my youth ambassador.

Finally, to my three lifelines, Tony, Amaraj, and Ghena, for believing in me, for letting me talk about my characters for hours upon hours, and for understanding all the times I needed to withdraw into my fictional world. Your support and encouragement make everything I do possible.

I love hearing from readers, so if you'd like to get in touch, find me at www.anoopjudge.com or visit me on Facebook (anoopjudgeauthor), Instagram (@judgeanoop), and Twitter (@judgeanoop).

Glossary of Indian Terms

Ammi ji: mother; *ji* is gender neutral, and when used at the end of a sentence, it is used as a term of respect.

Angarkha: an upper-body garment usually with an asymmetrical opening in the chest area reaching down to the knees, knotted or secured traditionally by strings. Worn by men.

Beti: daughter, though it is widely used by older people to refer to almost all females who are their daughters' age.

Beta: son. Masculine form of *beti*.

Bhagwan: God.

Bhangra: a type of popular dance music combining Punjabi folk traditions with Western pop music, fusing traditional drum-based music with elements of reggae, hip-hop, rock, and dance.

Bindi: an ornamental dot or beauty mark worn in the middle of the forehead, especially by Hindu women.

Chamak-dhamak: glitter.

Dal makhani: one of the most popular lentil recipes from the North Indian Punjabi cuisine, made with whole black lentils, to which butter (*makhan*) is added. *Dal makhani* is literally *buttery lentils.*

Dhol: a large barrel-shaped or cylindrical wooden drum, typically two headed, used in South Asia.

Diya: a small oil lamp, usually made from clay.

Elaichi: cardamom.

Garam masala: a blend of ground spices, originating from South Asia, used to season many Indian and Pakistani dishes.

Gulab jamun: an Indian sweet consisting of a ball of a deep-fried mixture of flour, milk, and cream, boiled in a sugar syrup.

Haldi: turmeric.

Jodhpuri: a formal evening suit; western suit-like attire, with a coat and trousers.

Karahi chicken curry: *Karahi* means *wok* and is used in the Indian subcontinent to make various dishes.

Kurti: (or *kurta*) a snug-fit top that is more like a tunic, with the length anywhere beyond the waistline to the hemline ending just above the knee.

Mandap: a temporary structure with pillars. It is often adorned with floral decorations and bells. It serves as an altar for Hindu weddings.

Navratan dal: a mix of nine lentils and legumes.

Pakoras: a fried snack made with gram flour, spices, and any main ingredient like onion, spinach, or other veggies.

Pheras: the seven rounds that a couple takes around the sacred fire; the true essence of a Vedic wedding.

Qayamat: judgment day.

Sagan: a prewedding ceremony hosted by the groom's family in which the bride's family gives gifts to the groom's family.

Salwar-kameez: a traditional combination dress worn by women, and in some regions by men, in South Asia. *Salwars* are trousers that are typically wide at the waist but narrow to a cuff at the bottom. The *kameez* is a long shirt or tunic.

Sangeet: literally translates to *music*; a prewedding event, filled with dance, music, and vibrant colors.

Sari: a garment worn mostly by Hindu women, consisting of a long piece of cotton or silk wrapped around the body with one end draped over the head or over one shoulder.

Thaal: platter.

Tikka: a mark made on the forehead by Hindu Indians.

About the Author

Photo © 2020 Anvaji

Anoop Judge is the author of *The Rummy Club*, which won the 2015 Beverly Hills Book Award, and is a 2019 Pushcart Prize nominee for *The Awakening of Meena Rawat*. A recovering litigator, former TV presenter, and blogger, she has had essays and short stories published in *Green Hills Literary Lantern*, *Rigorous*, and *Scarlet Leaf Review*, among others. Born and raised in New Delhi, Anoop now resides in California. She is currently pursuing an MFA in Creative Writing at Saint Mary's College and is the recipient of the 2021–2023 Advisory Board Award and Alumni Scholarship. She is married with two nearly grown and fully admirable children. For more information visit www.anoopjudge.com.